# The True Confessions
# of a London Spy

# THE TRUE CONFESSIONS
# OF A LONDON SPY

## A Secret Life of Mary Bennet Mystery

### Katherine Cowley

TULE
PUBLISHING

# Praise for *The Secret Life of Miss Mary Bennet*

"Beautifully written, masterfully plotted, meet a Mary Bennet every bit as fascinating and twice as daring as her more famous sisters."

—Gretchen Archer, USA Today bestselling author of the Davis Way Crime Capers

"Cowley's creative continuation of the story of one of literature's famous forgotten sisters into a world she could never have dreamed possible, broadens her horizons and ours. Following the pedantic Mary Bennet in her adventures after the conclusion of Pride and Prejudice was a delight that Jane Austen and mystery fans will embrace and cheer."

—Laurel Ann Nattress, editor of *Jane Austen Made Me Do It*, and Austenprose.com.

"In *The Secret Life of Miss Mary Bennet*, Katherine Cowley takes the least interesting sister from Jane Austen's *Pride and Prejudice* and turns her into the heroine of her own story. It's very fun to watch Mary transform into a competent spy, but the true delight is how Cowley masterfully keeps Mary true to her pedantic, socially awkward self from Austen's original while making her a whole person we can root for."

—Molly Greeley, author of *The Clergyman's Wife: A Pride and Prejudice Novel*

"A delightfully fresh take on Miss Mary Bennet. A story I didn't even realize I was waiting for until I read it."

—Jess Heileman, author of *A Well-Trained Lady*

"An intriguing historical mystery that fans of *Pride and Prejudice* will find compelling."

—Tina Kashian, author of the Kebab Kitchen Mysteries

# Dedication

to my husband,
Scott Cowley

# CHAPTER ONE

*"Various reports have been for some time in circulation respecting the measures which BONAPARTE has adopted... After a careful investigation, we believe it is in our power to give an authentic statement of the facts which have really occurred."*

—*The Times*, London, January 24, 1814

WHEN MISS MARY Bennet agreed to become a spy for the British government, she had not realised how many dead bodies the job would entail. True, since accidentally discovering a corpse on the beach in Worthing she had not seen any additional individuals bereft of life, but now she was headed to London for her first time in an official capacity, and she already had an appointment to call upon a corpse.

The carriage windows fogged with the warmth of their breaths. Despite pressing her feet against a hot rock, Mary's toes felt frigid. She shifted closer to Fanny, one of her fellow spies, to better share the blanket they held over themselves. The other inhabitant of the carriage, a spy named Mr. Withrow, rubbed his gloved hands together.

Snow continued to fall outside the carriage, adding to the piles already on the London streets. A man stood on a roof, pushing at the two or three feet of accumulated snow. It fell heavily onto the walk and road below, to the anger of a couple who had walked into the snow shower.

"Do you want to play another round?" Mary asked Fanny. During their journey from Worthing to London, they had come up with a number of ways to entertain themselves, but Mary's favourite was a game of associations. A player would give a word, and within three seconds the next player provided an associated word, and the game continued on and on. If a player did not believe a word had a strong enough association with the prior word, it could be challenged. To make the game more difficult, they had added themes.

"You shan't win this time," said Fanny.

"As I have won six out of eleven games, the odds are actually in my favour."

"That's what *you* think," said Fanny. "Theme and first word?"

"The theme is London," said Mary, "and the first word is snow."

"Streetsweepers," said Fanny without pause.

"Lord mayor," said Mary. He employed the streetsweepers, after all.

Fanny nodded. "Guildhall."

"Politics," said Mary.

"Sancho," said Fanny.

She must mean Ignatius Sancho, who, like Fanny, was a black Londoner. He had been an abolitionist and was the first black man in England to vote in Parliamentary elections.

"Parliament," said Mary.

"Corruption," said Fanny.

It was an overgeneralisation, but a common enough association that Mary decided not to challenge it. "Rotten boroughs."

"I challenge you," said Fanny. "While plenty of rotten boroughs send representatives to Parliament, I do not believe there are any rotten boroughs in London itself."

They turned to Mr. Withrow.

"I believe Miss Cramer is correct," he said drily.

Mary shook her head. She had been foiled by her own theme. "I concede defeat."

"I am sure you did as best you could," said Fanny with a teasing smile. "You should play with us, Mr. Withrow. Maybe you would provide some actual competition."

"Once again, I must decline."

Mary had met both Fanny Cramer and Henry Withrow at Castle Durrington in Worthing. After the death of Mary's father, she had stayed at Castle Durrington, where Lady Trafford and her nephew Mr. Withrow had trained her as a spy. At the castle, Fanny had pretended to be a maid, which was also the role she had volunteered to play in London. Fanny was perceptive, opinionated, and seemed unafraid of anything. She had always been kind to Mary and treated her as someone deserving of respect. Mr. Withrow, on the other hand, had often been dismissive of Mary. That had changed somewhat since Mary had exposed the murderer of Mr. Withrow's friend, but still, he was a disagreeable man. At the moment he appeared downright sullen.

"If you are not going to play with us, at least read a book or do something to make your journey more pleasant," said Mary.

"I would, if it were possible," he said. "One of my greatest regrets in life is that reading in a carriage leaves me indisposed."

It appeared that riding in a carriage, even without a book, left him indisposed.

"Will you at least give us a theme?" said Fanny, leaning towards the window. Outside, thick billows of smoke rose from a factory. She grimaced. "There's a carriage following us."

At this, Mr. Withrow went rigid. Mary shifted in her seat, unsure of what action to take in a situation like this. Did someone know who they were, and their purpose in London? If the carriage were attacked, Mary would be of no use, but at least Mr. Withrow knew how to fight; he had once tackled and disarmed Mary—who had been brandishing a fire poker—in a matter of seconds.

Mr. Withrow peered out his own carriage window, then tapped a pattern of knocks on the carriage wall. The driver took a quick left turn. The wheels of the carriage slid on the ice and Mary was pressed against the carriage wall. The carriage wobbled, almost tipped, but finally, the wheels found surer purchase. Withrow strained his neck as he watched out the window, shook his head in frustration, then tapped again.

"They are still following," said Fanny, her hands clenching into fists. As the carriage turned, Mary caught a glimpse of a black carriage with purple curtains behind them.

The driver took another quick turn, almost running into another carriage, and then yet another turn. Mary glimpsed a face in the other carriage's window, a face she thought she recognised.

"It appears to be Stanley," said Withrow, shaking his head. "He should know better than to trail us without informing us in advance." He tapped a different rhythm and the carriage slowed and returned to the main road.

Mr. Stanley was another spy, who, like Mr. Withrow, was from Sussex. Mary had only met Mr. Stanley once before, which did not provide the requisite time to truly judge a person's character, but he seemed a genuine, polite gentleman of respectable background.

"Has Mr. Stanley been asked to visit the body as well?" asked Mary.

"I can only assume so," said Mr. Withrow. "I do not know why Mr. Booth needs *me* to look at it. I will not have any time for work before I leave." Mr. Withrow would be returning to Sussex in only a few days.

Mary would stay in London with her sister Elizabeth for the entire duration of the Season. The Season coincided with a session of Parliament and was an opportunity for those of the upper class—from all over the country—to gather in London and engage in social events. She did not care much about the Season itself, but in theory, this would give her time to be of true assistance. Yet there was so much more she needed to learn before she would feel confident in her duties as a spy.

They turned onto another road and parked in front of a row of shops, at the end of a line of carriages.

"Quickly now," said Withrow, opening the door. "But do not draw any attention to us."

How easily he stepped into the position of leadership. His aunt, Lady Trafford, carried herself with the same sense of authority.

Mr. Stanley approached, his hand extended. "May I?"

Mary nodded and he helped her down from the carriage, and then did the same for Fanny.

"Come," said Withrow, and they followed him down the street and into an alleyway.

Mr. Stanley walked at Mary's side and spoke in a low tone. "Miss Bennet, it is a pleasure to see you again."

"The pleasure is also mine," said Mary, for it was the sort

of reply her sisters would make to such a statement.

"You look so lovely, one cannot even tell you have been travelling."

At this Mary did not know what to say. She had not often been on the receiving side of compliments, particularly compliments from gentlemen, so when she had time for private reflection, she would need to practice possible responses.

Mary lifted her skirts so they did not drag in the snow. The alley had not been cleared as well as the main road. In the alley, a woman sang as she rocked her baby, but as they approached, she stopped. Withrow paused in front of a door and said, more to himself than anyone else, "It should be this one." An hour earlier, as they had changed horses outside of London, a messenger had informed them of the body and given them a series of complicated directions which Withrow clearly remembered better than Mary did.

Withrow knocked four times, then pushed open the door. They stepped inside a candlelit room, and the woman outside resumed her song. There was a fireplace, but it had not been lit, and the flat was almost as cold as it was outside. Despite the cold, it was a very comfortable-looking parlour with quality furnishings and framed lithographs on the wall. Mary would guess that the inhabitant was solidly middle class.

A stout middle-aged man opened his hands in welcome, then greeted them each in turn. "Miss Cramer, Mr. Withrow, Mr. Stanley. And you must be Miss Bennet. I am Mr. Booth."

There was another man who remained farther back, in shadow, but he did not come forward, and as no one else questioned his presence, Mary did not, either.

She curtsied. "It is with great anticipation that I have

come to London, in the hopes that I may offer some assistance in this great work."

"Yes, yes," said Mr. Booth. "Patriotic ideals and the lot. Now who you are about to see is—"

The woman outside stopped singing. Mr. Booth stepped towards the door as he pulled a pistol from his belt. The other man, the one in the shadows, also stepped forward.

"What is—" Mary began, but Mr. Withrow held out his hand in a gesture of silence.

The moment stretched long and taut, a string about to break.

The woman resumed her song, and everyone except Mary relaxed.

"If she stops singing," said Fanny, "that means someone is approaching."

Mary nodded, once again feeling the weight of all she did not know.

Mr. Booth continued as if he had not been interrupted. "The individual you are about to see is a Mr. Oliver Rice. He was found here in his flat last night by his sister, Mrs. Alys Knowles, who came looking for him when he did not join her for dinner. He worked as a messenger, primarily for members of Parliament. Now come, I will let you discover the rest by yourself."

He led the way to a second room. Mr. Stanley turned to Mary and said, "If you do not feel comfortable viewing a body—"

"Miss Bennet will be fine," said Fanny, taking Mary's arm in her own and dragging her ahead of Mr. Withrow. "Excuse us, ladies first. Good manners dictate that women should always have the best position in investigations."

Mary tried to halt in the doorway, repulsed by the smell

of urine and barn and butcher shop, but Fanny pulled her farther in.

The body, well-lit by the light shining through the windows and several lamps, lay on the hard wooden floor, legs curled as if he had fallen. Age: late twenties. Eyes: open, bloodshot. Face: discoloured. Neck...oh the neck: large, purple bruises, and huge red and black masses under the skin, which looked as if they wanted to escape the body's confines.

"Strangled to death," said Fanny. "Not how I'd like to go, honestly. I'd prefer to look put together at my funeral."

Mr. Booth and Mr. Withrow chuckled. Mary could not understand how Fanny could jest at a moment like this.

"No rope or other tool," said Mr. Stanley. "Someone did this with their bare hands."

Mary's stomach turned.

"Notice the signs of internal bleeding on the neck," said Mr. Withrow. "Likely, his airways collapsed."

Everyone had keen observations and insightful hypotheses. Everyone except Mary. Their conversation washed over her, and both her body and voice felt paralyzed.

"The attacker did not remove any signs of Mr. Rice's struggle," said Fanny, gesturing at some books and a small table that appeared to have been knocked over. Mary had not even noticed them; she was so distracted by the body that she had forgotten to consider its surroundings. It was a small but friendly study, full of books and papers and mementos, and it would have been comfortable were it not for the dead body. "The man or woman who did this may have physical signs of struggle on their own body—scratching or bruising from where Mr. Rice fought back."

"A woman could never have done such a thing," said Stanley.

"You have much to learn about the fairer sex," said Fanny. "Mr. Rice is not a tall man. A woman with enough strength of mind could do it. In ten or fifteen seconds you can knock out a man through strangulation, though it can take a few minutes to fully kill."

Mr. Stanley raised his eyebrows. "And you would know this how, Miss Cramer?"

"I am not saying I've done it myself. But it is good to know these things."

How *had* Fanny learned all this? Lady Trafford had taught her much to prepare her to be a spy, but nothing to prepare her to analyse death.

Mr. Withrow removed his travel gloves, placed them in his cloak pocket, and pulled on leather gloves, the sort a farm worker might wear. He held an extra pair out to Mary.

She hesitated.

"Take the gloves, Miss Bennet," he said. "Consider this an opportunity to learn."

She pulled the gloves over her own, and when he crouched next to the body, she approached it and attempted to crouch in a ladylike manner. She held her breath, trying to block out the smell of rotting flesh, but it filled her nose.

"I do not know if I can do this," said Mary.

"Do not be disheartened, Miss Bennet," said Mr. Stanley. "It is commendable to have a sensitive soul."

She knew he meant to be reassuring, complimentary even, but she could not interpret it that way. *A sensitive soul.* An incapable soul would be more accurate. Mr. Withrow gave her a look of pity. He had never believed she could become a spy, and now she was proving him correct.

She forced herself to look directly at the remains of Mr. Rice. His left eye was bloodshot, and tiny red spots discoloured his face. There was dried blood in both his ears, his lip was swollen, and his entire face seemed to droop.

She reached her gloved hand towards the body, but she could not bring herself to touch the man's face or neck, so she touched his shoulder instead. Suddenly, she felt as if she might lose all the contents of her stomach. "Excuse me," she said, backing away and tearing off the work gloves. She covered her mouth with her hand and exited the dwelling. The woman with the baby looked at her reproachfully but did not stop her song.

The open air was welcome after the stuffy room of death. She breathed in and out steadily, watching her breath made visible by the extremity in temperature. Already, the sensation in her stomach lessened a little. She walked a little up the alley so as to not draw attention to the door with the body within.

Why could she not do it? Why could she not examine a body dispassionately and discover something—anything—useful? When she had found a body at the beach a few months before, the body had disturbed her, but she had not felt nauseous. Of course, that man had drowned and did not have quite the same smell, and no one had expected her to touch the body or examine it in more detail.

The baby began to cry. At least it was well-bundled and did not appear cold. The woman finished her song and, after a pause barely long enough for her to take a breath, began another lullaby.

Baby, baby, naughty baby,
Hush! you squalling thing, I say;
Peace this instant! Peace! or maybe
Bonaparte will pass this way.

Baby, baby, he's a giant,
Black and tall as Rouen's steeple,
Sups and dines and lives reliant
Every day on naughty people.

Did Mary even want to be a spy? If she could not contribute, if she could not suffer the basic vicissitudes the
occupation required, then it would not be too late to withdraw.

Baby, baby, if he hears you
As he gallops past the house,
Limb from limb at once he'll tear you
Just as pussy tears a mouse.

Mary expected the woman to begin a new song, but instead she sang a fourth verse that Mary had not heard before.

And he'll beat you, beat you, beat you,
And he'll beat you all to pap:
And he'll eat you, eat you, eat you,
Gobble you, gobble you, snap! snap! snap!

At this violent ending, the baby quieted. Despite the bar-
baric way in which Napoleon Bonaparte had ravaged the
continent, he was useful for something: he assisted British
parents in their quest to instil good behaviour in their
children.

Britain and her allies had done much to push back Bonaparte, but he and his forces were still a threat. This was one of
the reasons Mary had become a spy: to stop threats to her
homeland, both external and internal. And she had managed,

singlehandedly, to prevent a man from helping Bonaparte invade Sussex. She could not let her inadequacies and her lack of experience stop her now. She would contribute in her own way.

She returned to the carriage and collected her pad of paper and pencils before returning to Mr. Rice's flat. This time, the woman did not stop singing when Mary approached and let herself in.

Mr. Booth nodded wordlessly as she entered the room with the corpse. Fanny, Stanley, and Withrow had moved on from the body, and were examining different objects in the room. The other man stood, arms crossed, watching, and Mary wondered again at his purpose here.

"Can the body be placed as it was previously?" asked Mary. "I would like to draw the corpse within its surroundings." Her stomach still threatened to revolt, but as long as she remained at a distance and did not touch the body, she thought she could keep her breakfast.

Fanny and Mr. Withrow placed Mr. Rice back as he had been when they entered, helped by a few suggestions from Mr. Booth, and Mary began to draw. She was no great artist, but she had taken three months of drawing lessons as a result of Lady Trafford's generosity. As Mary drew, she pretended that she was capturing a landscape, rather than a still life.

"There was a nasty note from Sir Francis Burdett in Mr. Rice's pocket," said Fanny as she watched Mary draw. "He is now one of our suspects."

"Sir Francis Burdett?"

"He is a Radical in Parliament," said Stanley.

"I see," said Mary, trying to capture the angle of the books on the floor.

"Let me read it to you," said Fanny, and Mary listened as she drew.

*My dear Mr. Rice,*

*You have disappointed us one too many times. You must not let information fall into the wrong hands.*

*When you come to our next meeting, prepare to provide evidence of your sincerity to our cause. If you do not, know that things cannot remain as they are.*

*Your servant and fellow seeker of liberty,*
*Sir Francis Burdett*

"That is almost a direct threat," said Mary. She sketched Mr. Rice's wounds, trying to capture the rawness of the neck. The paper and pencil acted as a sort of barrier between her and the body, a protective distance, but it also humanised it, allowing her to truly look at Mr. Rice and see that he had been a real person, full of hopes and desires.

Mr. Stanley was flipping through the pages of some sort of register. "It appears Mr. Rice attended a meeting with Sir Francis Burdett, Lord Cochrane, and John Eastlake, sometime yesterday before he died. Perhaps he disappointed them at the meeting, and after, Sir Francis Burdett killed him. It is well known that the Radicals have been plotting to overthrow Parliament."

"That is too much conjecture," said Mr. Withrow. "This is all circumstantial evidence—nothing of substance."

"They should be investigated, though," said Fanny.

"Yes," agreed Mr. Booth. "But Mr. Withrow is correct; we must keep our minds open, or we will blind ourselves to much that is relevant to the case."

"What I want to know is why *we* are here," said Mr. Withrow. "This is a simple murder. Surely it can be investigated by the constables and their detectives."

For the first time, the silent man who had kept to the edges of the rooms stepped forward and spoke.

"I would that we could." His voice was gravelly, yet not harsh. "I am Mr. Donalds, constabulary detective. We have requested the assistance of Mr. Booth and yourselves in an effort to not...ruffle feathers. We can only do so much, without substantive evidence, to investigate members of Parliament. Too many members of Parliament have oversight over us, our actions, and our records. Further, the in-depth investigation of popular figures like Lord Cochrane and Sir Francis can lead to public outrage and inflame the masses into violence."

"In the past weeks," said Mr. Booth, "we have intercepted several letters smuggled into the country. They are a subtle attempt by friends of Bonaparte—prominent French men and women who act as his agents—to gather support for his cause.

"Bonaparte is desperate. The tides of war have finally changed, and he will do anything to avoid loss. There are people he seems to think would be sympathetic to the French cause. But for the most part, he has been trying to sow dissent, to disrupt our country and tear us apart from the inside. The Radicals' ideologies already lead them to threaten the status quo, and if he can manipulate them into action, the consequences would be dire. While none of the intercepted letters were to these Radicals, it is likely that many of the letters have reached their intended recipients without our notice."

"I hope you can see why I need your help," said Mr. Donalds. "This is a sensitive, urgent affair, and the identity of our suspects will make it harder for us to find the truth."

Mr. Stanley stood a little taller. "Do not doubt that we will do all in our power to find the truth."

Mary finished her sketch of the body, and then asked to see the note from Sir Francis, which she copied down. The way he wrote his capital W was peculiar, so she traced it onto her own page. Then she read the final week of Mr. Rice's register, taking notes on a few details.

The others seemed to be wrapping up, so Mary looked quickly through Mr. Rice's letter box. Something about it left her unsatisfied, so she first walked through the flat's kitchen and bedroom, and then returned to the front parlour.

On the wall hung a pencil drawing of Mr. Rice with his parents and his sister. She took it off the wall and looked at Mr. Rice's face when he was whole and alive. He seemed very serious, almost sombre, while his sister's smile made it look as if she was almost laughing.

Mary flipped over the drawing. On the back were the death dates of Mr. Rice's parents. Now Mr. Rice's sister, Alys Knowles, was alone.

She hung the picture back on the wall, and then straightened it.

On a table was a copy of *The Two Gentlemen of Verona*, Shakespeare's famous play about friendship and love and infidelity. On the first page Alys Knowles had written a note.

*My dearest brother,*

*Thank you again for watching little Oliver today, and with such little notice. He loves the time and attention you give him.*

*I hope you will agree to reread this book with me. Within this copy, I have marked passages that I think will uplift your spirits and inspire our conversation.*

*Forever your friend and sister,*
*Alys*

Mary flipped briefly through the pages, reading the notes in the text that Alys had written her brother, and the comments that Mr. Rice had added. As she did so, she sensed a deep, abiding friendship between them, something that had been a pillar through all of life's storms.

Oliver Rice and Alys Knowles had the sort of relationship that Mary had never had with any of her four sisters. Mrs. Knowles's loss must be very great indeed. Mary shut the book and blinked away the moisture in her eyes.

She stood. She still felt like something was missing, so she examined every piece of furniture, every cushion and pillow, and finally, the fireplace. The mortar between many of the stones was cracked. If she were to hide something, this might be where. "I already looked there," said Withrow, but she ignored him, and methodically checked every single stone in the fireplace. Finally, one of them pulled free from the structure. Behind it she discovered several letters, and a large folded sheet of paper, written in multiple handwritings.

"Good find, Miss Bennet," said Mr. Booth.

Mary could not resist smirking at Mr. Withrow. He gave her a terse nod, and she felt vindicated in her thoroughness.

First, they looked at the large sheet. A group of people had been drafting something with Mr. Rice's assistance. The original text was not written in his hand, but Mr. Rice had corrected spelling errors, and added words and phrases. "We, as workers, have come together, to expose the injustice perpetrated upon us, by both factory owners, and even the very powerful members of government. At times, the injustices are so great, that systems—even government systems—should be challenged, and at times, overturned." Specific grievances were addressed—long hours for child workers, injuries at factories, and the like—but then the writing stopped, as if it had not been finished.

"The original writers were not well educated," said Mr. Booth. "Sir Francis, Lord Cochrane, Mr. Eastlake—none of them would have needed these basic grammatical and spelling corrections. This was written by workers. But there is no indication of *who* specifically, which makes it much more difficult to prevent a possible uprising."

Mr. Withrow reread the paper. "It is in keeping with Radical ideologies, though more extreme measures than Lord Cochrane and Sir Francis typically propose. I cannot speak for Eastlake."

"What are the other papers?" asked Mr. Donalds.

Mary opened and skimmed the letters.

"They appear to be love letters," she said, blushing. "And they are not entirely appropriate."

"Who wrote them?" asked Mr. Booth.

"They are all from the same woman. An S. König."

"Does anyone know S. König?"

"Ah yes," said Mr. Stanley, a little reluctantly. "Mrs. Selena König."

"Perhaps you should have a conversation with her then," said Mr. Booth.

"I do not think that would be prudent," said Mr. Stanley. "I danced with her once at a ball, and received a note from her, which I never returned. But I believe she lives quite close to the Darcys' London home, so perhaps Miss Bennet will be able to investigate."

Mary wondered at Mr. Stanley's exact relationship with Selena König, but did not know the best way to ask, so she said nothing on the matter, instead saying, "Fanny and I will be well situated to investigate her."

Other assignments were given—while none of them

would assist Mr. Donalds in his official interviews with Sir Francis Burdett, Lord Cochrane, or Mr. Eastlake, he did request Mr. Stanley's assistance in interviewing Mrs. Knowles. Mary wished that she had been asked, but at least she had a specific assignment to investigate Mrs. König, and a more general assignment to investigate the others should the opportunity arise.

Before they left, Mary forced herself to look at the corpse one last time. He was a messenger, a revolutionary, a lover, and a beloved brother, but none of that explained his death.

"Mr. Rice. What led you to this end?"

The dead man, of course, did not respond, but that would not stop her from discovering the truth.

# CHAPTER TWO

*"On the Dover road, the snow is 10 and 12 feet deep…
between 300 and 400 men are employed to clear a pas-
sage through it."*

—*The Times*, London, January 24, 1814

"YOU ARE NERVOUS," declared Mr. Withrow as the
carriage came to a stop in front of the Darcys' townhouse, a stately, four story overlooking a park that even in the
winter appeared well-cultivated, with pathways cleared of
snow.

"I am not nervous." Mary released her skirts, which she
had been twisting around with her hands. "Why would I be
nervous to see my own family?"

"I am sure they will be happy to see you," said Fanny,
placing her hand on Mary's shoulder.

"Thank you." Mary swallowed. In truth, she *was* a little
nervous, though of course there was no reason she should be.
She had spent the past four months at Castle Durrington with
Lady Trafford and Mr. Withrow, and while it had been
liberating to venture off on her own, it would be good to see
her family.

She looked at her faint reflection in the window. What
*would* her family think when they saw her? She touched the
watch which hung on a chain around her neck. It was a gift

from Lady Trafford and came with a clip so she could attach it to the inside of her pocket or a reticule. She wished, for a moment, that she were back with Lady Trafford at Castle Durrington. She shook her head and banished the thought.

The driver opened the door, and Mr. Withrow helped Mary out of the carriage and over a pile of snow. Mary waited expectantly for Fanny to follow, but Fanny shook her head.

"I will come after with your things, as a servant should."

"But you are not—" Mary began.

"Let her play the part she has selected," said Mr. Withrow. Surprisingly, his voice had none of the sharpness he often employed when he spoke to Mary. "People will underestimate her, just as they sometimes underestimate you, and you will both be more effective for it."

Mary was confused by this admission. From Mr. Withrow, this was practically an apology. He was also right— if she treated Fanny as more than a servant, it would draw excess attention to her. Yet this complicated things. For Mary's entire life, she had known how to treat people based off of their class and its relationship to her own. Now Fanny was acting as her inferior, but in their occupation as spies, she was Mary's equal, or to be honest, her superior, because of her greater experience and knowledge.

The butler opened the door of the Darcys' house and ushered Mary and Mr. Withrow into a drawing room. Immediately, everyone stood. Mary had expected to see Elizabeth, Mr. Darcy, and his younger sister, Miss Georgiana Darcy, but she had not expected her sister Kitty and her aunt and uncle, the Gardiners.

Elizabeth approached and took Mary's hands. "It is good to see you, Mary. We hope that you enjoy your stay with us."

The warmth in Elizabeth's voice surprised Mary, as she

had never been particularly close to any of her sisters. Of course, Elizabeth was skilled at making the necessary polite greetings and could make any guest feel welcome. "Thank you for agreeing to let me join you in London. Lady Trafford thought it would be an essential part of my education."

"Education?" said Kitty with a laugh. "That is not why I am here. However, I suppose a London Season is a type of education. All the balls and the dancing and the shops…think of the fun we shall have together. Maybe we will even find you an officer."

The last officer Mary had danced with had been a murderer, which dampened the already limited appeal that officers had held for Mary.

Something on Miss Darcy's face showed a similar disinterest in officers, perhaps even a revulsion. Mr. Darcy put his hand on her shoulder, though whether to warn her or comfort her, Mary could not tell.

"While there are men aplenty in London," said Elizabeth, "they need not be the prime attraction. Nothing could make London so dreary as the singular pursuit of matrimony."

"It is well spoken," said Mr. Gardiner.

Mary was about to make a statement on the necessary suppositions that formed the basis of matrimony when Mr. Darcy stepped forward and began a conversation with Mr. Withrow.

"Come, Mary, sit with me next to the fire," said Mrs. Gardiner. "Your cheeks are red with cold."

"Thank you." Mary was indeed quite cold.

Mary sat next to her aunt, who took the teapot off its hook next to the fire and poured her a steaming cup. Mary's hands shook as she took the hot cup and raised it to her mouth, sipping carefully lest she burn her tongue.

"I did not expect to see you and my uncle on my first day in London," observed Mary.

"We have been here for several hours, to make certain we were here for your arrival."

"I apologise that you suffered the inconvenience of waiting for me—"

"Do not apologise, my dear," said Mrs. Gardiner, setting her hand on Mary's shoulder with a motherly sort of affection. "We could not miss the opportunity to see you. And we would love to host you at our home as soon as the opportunity permits. Your cousins are clamouring to see you."

"Spending time with them would be a great pleasure." She studied her aunt's friendly face and then it occurred to her that she had never drawn a single family member. "Would it be possible for me to draw you?"

"To draw me?" Mrs. Gardiner smoothed her skirts and straightened her shoulders. "Of course."

Mary called a servant, and a minute later, Fanny entered the room with Mary's drawing supplies. Fanny curtsied politely and then left.

Mary found a blank sheet of paper and began to draw Mrs. Gardiner. Her aunt had a dignified look, coupled with a softness of features, and sharp yet kind eyes. As Mary drew, she wished she knew how to capture more than just Mrs. Gardiner's physical features. How did one capture someone's essence on the page?

Miss Darcy approached. "I am so glad to have another sister in the house."

"Thank you, Miss Darcy." Mary had met her only twice before, first at Elizabeth and Mr. Darcy's wedding, and then when Elizabeth and Mr. Darcy had come to visit the family at Longbourn, and Miss Darcy had accompanied them.

"Please, you must call me Georgiana. I insist. And may I call you by your given name?"

"Of...of course," said Mary. Lady Trafford and Mr. Withrow had always remained formal with Mary, and as a result it had been months since anyone had called her anything besides Miss Bennet.

"We have only been to one ball since we arrived," said Georgiana. "But we have several more invitations, and I hope that you will join us."

Balls could provide opportunities for espionage, so she nodded. "I would find that most agreeable."

"Lizzy is a wonderful chaperone, but I think that you could chaperone me as well."

In Georgiana's mind Mary had already obtained spinster status. "I am only a few years older than you," said Mary. "I am not sure I would be suitable as a chaperone." Besides, she needed to focus on her work, not on protecting a young woman whose personal fortune would afflict her with the attention of every money-seeker in London. She moved on from drawing her aunt's nose to focus on the details of her mouth.

"Then we shall have to act as chaperones to each other!" said Georgiana.

Mrs. Gardiner smiled, and Mary lifted her pencil, unable to draw until Mrs. Gardiner resumed a more neutral expression. "I am sure Mary will enjoy spending time with you and Kitty when she is not busy dancing with young men herself."

"We shall have a lovely time," said Georgiana. "It is a pity that I cannot be fit for my new gown before the ball on Thursday, but I shall not let it dampen my spirits."

"When will the gown be ready?" asked Mary, switching to a softer pencil. When she had begun drawing, her instructor had allowed her only one pencil, but now she had five, some with harder and some with softer leads, each of which could achieve a different effect.

"It was delivered this morning, but the seamstress is ill and will not be able to check its fit, and to be honest, it needs more modifications than a simple fitting will provide." She paused, and then said, hurriedly, "But that is not nearly as important as her being ill. I hope, for her sake, that it is nothing serious."

"My maid—well, one of Lady Trafford's maids, that she has sent with me—is quite the expert seamstress," said Mary. "She should be able to finish the dress."

"Would she really?" said Georgiana. "That would be marvellous."

"Assuming she is able to access any needed supplies, I am certain it would not be a burden for her." Mary used her finger to smudge the pencil lines that made up Mrs. Gardiner's hair. It created a nice effect, but Mary was left with lead all over her finger. She held her hand slightly in the air, uncertain of how to solve this problem without ruining her dress or the upholstery.

"Lady Trafford must truly favour you," said Kitty, "to give you your very own maid."

"I suppose she does," said Mary. That must be the excuse, for no one in her family must ever learn their true relationship—that Lady Trafford had trained her as a spy. "I am very grateful for all that she has done for me."

Mrs. Gardiner passed Mary a small table linen. Mary smiled in gratitude as she wiped the lead off her finger.

"Is it strange being waited on by a black girl?" asked Kitty.

"Kitty!" said Elizabeth. "Do not be impertinent."

"I am just curious." Kitty turned back to Mary, clearly

expecting an answer.

"It is not any different," said Mary. Even though Fanny was not present, she felt guilt—and even anger—at her sister's statement. "Assuming that difference creates strangeness implies that the other is inferior to one's self."

"I am sorry," said Kitty, but she did not sound nearly as apologetic as she should. Mary would need to find her some readings which would broaden her perspective.

"It is a pity that the Bingleys will not be visiting London for the Season," said Mary. "I would have liked to see Jane."

"With her condition, it is best for her not to travel," said Elizabeth.

"Her condition?" said Mary.

"She is in the family way," said Kitty.

"Oh." Mary turned her face to the fire to hide her disappointment that no one had told her the news. "I did not know."

There was a moment's pause. Everyone, including Mr. Darcy and Mr. Withrow, had fallen silent.

"That is why Mother is travelling to Derbyshire to be with Jane," said Kitty. "She intends to be of assistance when Jane enters her confinement."

"I am sure that everyone assumed that someone else had already told you," said Elizabeth. "I myself have only known for a month."

This was not the first time they had forgotten to inform Mary of something important. Once her family had even managed to not inform her of her grandmother's death for an entire week. If Mary did not know better, she would think there was a secret competition amongst her family members to keep things from her. It would not surprise her in the least if she were the last person to find out that she herself had become engaged or died.

Mary turned her focus back to the drawing of her aunt. The conversations began to ebb and flow around her, but she did not attempt to join any, savouring instead her little island of solitude.

Mary finished the drawing and showed it to her aunt, who complimented her effusively. Mary accepted the comments graciously—it was one of her better drawings, after all. Then Georgiana approached, her hands clasped together. "Mary, I have heard you are quite skilled at the pianoforte. Will you please play for us?"

Mary wanted to try the Darcys' pianoforte—after all, each pianoforte had a slightly different sound and feel—so she agreed. Georgiana stood by her, turning the pages for her.

"Georgiana," said Mary quietly, for she did not want everyone to hear, "I heard someone, I cannot remember who, mention that they know a family who may live close to you, here in London. I believe they were named the Königs."

"Oh yes, they live next door. A delightful family, really. Their daughter, Henrietta, is such a friend." Mr. Stanley had been correct. Mary could only assume that Georgiana did not know of Mrs. König's infidelities, or she would find the acquaintance less than desirable.

"I would love to meet Henrietta and her mother." Then, realising that this might seem strange, she added, "I have yet to meet anyone in London who I did not already know."

"We should call on them," said Georgiana. "I have not seen Henrietta since before Christmas."

"Perhaps you could write them a note," recommended Mary.

"What an excellent proposition," said Georgiana. "I shall do so today."

Mr. Darcy called for Georgiana, who crossed the room to join him, Elizabeth, and Mr. Withrow in a conversation Mary could not quite hear. Yet even without hearing the words, Mary noted that something about Mr. Darcy's mannerisms were different, here in his own home. It was as if they were a bit softer, as if he could finally drop the reserve—the distance—that he held around everyone else.

Kitty approached and slid next to Mary on the bench, which restricted Mary's arm movement, making it harder to reach the high notes.

"However did you convince them to let you join them in London?" Kitty spoke quietly, as if in intrigue.

"I simply presented my case, and they offered the invitation I desired."

"I tried to solicit an invitation for months. But then, once they had invited you, they had to invite me as well."

Kitty had always been more sociable than Mary, always more the centre of attention, always more apt to receive invitations.

"I am certain they would have invited you regardless," said Mary, and then, in a moment of inspiration, she knew the comforting sort of thing their oldest sister Jane would say in a moment like this. "Surely they were still finalising their plans and could not offer an invitation until they had done so."

Kitty shrugged, and the movement caused Mary's fingers to stumble on the keys. Quickly she put the melody back to right. "It is good to see you, Kitty. I am glad you are here."

"I am sorry no one told you about Jane."

They sat awkwardly for a moment at the pianoforte, Mary playing and Kitty keeping her silence, and then Mr. Withrow approached, leaning against the side of the pianoforte closer to

Kitty.

"Miss Catherine," said Mr. Withrow, "how has your stay in London been so far?"

Kitty's face lit up. "London is pure diversion."

"Surely London has been rather dull, with such copious amounts of snow." He looked at Kitty with the sort of attention that always led people to answer his queries. Mr. Withrow could be quite charming, when he wanted to be. Mary focused on the keys, wishing they had chosen to hold their conversation elsewhere, as they were distracting her from her music.

"You will not think it dull when I tell you what I did two days ago."

"What *did* you do, Miss Bennet?"

Both Mr. Withrow and Kitty leaned a little closer to each other. Mary rolled her eyes, amused by their overt expressions of interest.

"I went ice skating at Hyde Park." She proceeded to describe—with animated gestures—how wonderful it had been and the fancy ice manoeuvres she had seen performed. Kitty's arms kept jostling Mary's, and Mary made more and more mistakes in the piece.

Mary shifted and stepped on Kitty's foot—accidentally, of course—and then Kitty gave her a little more room.

Finally, Mary finished the song. Between travel, the dead body, and her family, she needed time for repose and relaxation. She stood and asked, loudly enough for all to hear, if she might excuse herself, both to rest, and in order to see to her things in her room.

"Of course," said Mr. Darcy.

She said her farewells to each family member. The Gardiners embraced Mary and made her promise that she would soon call upon them.

Mr. Withrow stood in Mary's path, forcing a farewell between them, which Mary, in all honesty, did not see as necessary. "I hope you have a pleasant—and productive—stay in London," he said.

"I am sure it will be quite eventful." Mary fully intended to defy his low expectations of her and prove her merits as a spy. "I hope you have a pleasant visit with your sister, and please express my best wishes of health and happiness to your aunt."

"Of course."

At the doorway, she stood and looked at her family once more. Even though she had never been to the Darcys' London home before, the people made it feel familiar. It was good to be back with her family. She knew how she would be treated, and she knew how they expected her to act. It was like putting on an old glove; even if worn and not the best colour, at least it fit comfortably.

# CHAPTER THREE

*"BRUTAL CRUELTY.—A [nurse at the Westminster Infirmary] by the name of Seymour, was…charged on suspicion of having caused the death of A. Perrot, a lad about 16 years old, entrusted to her care… [After the feverish boy insulted her,] she forcibly dragged the unfortunate boy from his bed, and with dreadful imprecations, threw him on the floor, where she violated every act of humanity, by beating him most violently."*

—*The Kentish Gazette*, Kent, Surrey, and Sussex, England, January 25, 1814

A S FANNY LACED up Mary's dress, there was a light knock at the door. Once she was decent, Mary said, "Come in."

A servant opened the door a few inches. "I am sorry to intrude, Miss Bennet, but may I borrow Fanny? I have been made to understand that it's an urgent matter."

"Of course," said Mary.

Fanny left, and Mary arranged her own hair. In a few minutes, she and the rest of her family would dine with the Königs. After Mary and Georgiana's conversation, Georgiana had indeed written a note to Henrietta König, which had led to an invitation for the whole family. It would provide an opportunity to observe Mrs. König and form a judgment about her character.

Fanny returned to the room, a letter in her hand. She broke the elaborate paper locking mechanism and said, "It's from Mr. Booth." They both read the note.

*Detective Donalds interviewed the three men discussed. All appeared shocked at the news of Mr. Rice's demise. They claim that Rice never came to the meeting, and they all have alibis for the day, though Sir Francis relies entirely on the witness of his servants.*

*Donalds and Stanley interviewed Mr. Rice's sister. She was distraught. Lately, in addition to passing messages for the Radicals, Rice has assisted other members of Parliament, both Whigs and Tories. He was a particular friend to Sir Francis. He had never mentioned any romantic interests to his sister.*

*Mrs. König has not been informed of Rice's death. Find some way to inform her, observe her reaction, and see if there is anything you can learn.*

"It appears that we have the perfect opportunity," said Fanny. "We will tell Mrs. König tonight."

"I cannot very well inform her of Mr. Rice's death without raising suspicions," said Mary.

"True," said Fanny, "but if an urgent letter arrives, you will be there to observe when she opens it. I will prepare a brief note, and a disguise, so I can deliver it."

Mary agreed to the plan, though she wished that they had more time before executing it, and she wished they could guarantee that Mrs. König would open the letter while Mary was present. She pushed away her worries. She could be like her eldest sister Jane, always calm and sure in the face of challenges, and like her sister Kitty, excited for any new opportunity.

It was not long before Mary was seated at the Königs' table, enjoying rich sausages that gave off a pleasant aroma, roasted pork with cabbage, and spätzle, a German type of dumpling. The silverware was ornate, with fanciful patterns on the handles in a rococo style. The Königs' house was very similar to the Darcys' in size and in its quality of furnishings, though it had much brighter wallpaper.

Mr. König did not speak much during the meal, but in between bites he offered pleased looks to everyone. When he directed one of these towards Elizabeth, she asked, "Are you enjoying your meal, Mr. König?"

"Very much so."

"At least someone is," said Mrs. König. She was dressed in a fashionable evening gown, with heavy jewellery on her neck and wrists. "Mr. König insists on spending all our money on a German cook, when we have other servants who are quite capable in the kitchen."

Elizabeth gave Darcy a knowing look, and Mary wondered if this was a common complaint from Mrs. König. In her mind, Mary attempted to construct a picture of the Königs' relationship.

"I should be able to eat what satisfies me in my own home." Mr. König was a tall man, a bit large, with a slight German accent.

"Of course you should," said Mrs. König. "Though there are many other places one could choose to eat, with as good, or better fare. Why, there are even several French restaurants in London, where a fine woman can eat in a public room, observed by all around her."

"That seems almost scandalous," said Kitty.

"That is half the pleasure." Mrs. König had a glint in her

eye, a thrill-seeking that she shared with Mary's youngest sister, Lydia. Both seemed drawn to scandal. Lydia had run off with Mr. Wickham, and as evidenced by the letters in Mr. Rice's flat, Mrs. König had found herself a lover. This behaviour was so outside the realm of Mary's inclinations and experience that she could not understand how a woman could do something so unvirtuous, so unfaithful to the commitments she had made under the eyes of God and the laws of man.

One of the servants standing next to the wall whispered something to another servant, but neither Mrs. nor Mr. König corrected—or even seemed to notice—this undisciplined behaviour.

Mrs. König turned to Darcy and gave him a warm, sultry smile. "Mr. Darcy, I am certain you have a refined palate. What do *you* think of our meal?" Her tone made Mary wonder if Mrs. König was talking about more than the food.

"I fear I lack such judgment," said Mr. Darcy stiffly. "My wife is much more willing to venture an opinion on new foods."

Mrs. König smiled at Mr. Darcy but did not ask for Elizabeth's opinion. Elizabeth offered it anyway, giving a diplomatic response in a clear attempt to appease both Mr. and Mrs. König.

After dinner, the men and women retired to separate rooms. Elizabeth played the pianoforte—it seemed to Mary that she was trying to avoid further conversation with Mrs. König—and Kitty sat with Henrietta and Georgiana near the fire. Henrietta was only thirteen, and she seemed to adore Georgiana. Mary took the opportunity to engage Mrs. König in conversation.

"You have a fine home," said Mary.

Mrs. König shrugged.

Mary considered how to proceed. If Lady Trafford were here, she would make the suspect comfortable, to make it more likely that they would provide useful answers to her questions. Perhaps she would try to sympathise with their underlying emotions.

Mary took a guess as to Mrs. König's dissatisfaction and said, "It must feel confining to be in such a snow-filled London winter."

"I have been longing to go out, and Mr. König refuses to go into the office."

"What does he do?"

"He is a partner at a bank," said Mrs. König dismissively. Then quickly, as if she did not want Mary to think less of her, she added, "I myself am the seventh daughter of an earl."

Likely, Mrs. König had married for security and wealth. Titled families did not always have money to spare for all of their children, particularly for a seventh daughter.

Mrs. König glanced pointedly at Elizabeth. "Your sister has done quite well, hasn't she? She even seems to be fond of Mr. Darcy."

"How long have *you* been married?"

"Fourteen years."

Mary took a risk, expressing a sentiment not truly her own. "That seems enough time for fondness to…lessen."

"Why Miss Bennet, I did not take you as quite so worldly." She smiled. "When I was seventeen, I had the opportunity to visit the continent, but I did not take it. I should have. Maybe I would have stayed in Paris or Brussels or Zürich. Of course, I would not trade anything for my dear Henrietta, so I suppose that life works out as it should."

Mary was shocked by the openness of Mrs. König's response. These were the sort of details one told an intimate friend. "I do not know that I would want to live in Paris right now," said Mary. "What with Bonaparte and his army."

"I do not care the least about politics. It has never concerned me at all." She looked around the room. "Oh, I fear that Henrietta must be boring poor Miss Darcy and your sister. I should attend to them, but we must continue our conversation soon."

"Yes, we should," Mary said, and she followed Mrs. König to stand near the others.

Mary had never been so effective at prying someone's story from them, but this had required hardly any prying at all. Yes, Mary had tried to establish rapport, show sympathy, and ask good questions, but Mary had no delusions as to her skills with people. Mrs. König had opened like a nut that had already been broken. She likely shared these intimacies with anyone, which suggested she must hold deeper secrets beneath the surface.

She wondered when Fanny would deliver the letter. She should have brought her drawing supplies to occupy herself. That would provide an excuse to look at everyone without anyone wondering about the cause of her interest.

After about thirty minutes, the men rejoined their party. Elizabeth stood up from the pianoforte and met Mr. Darcy halfway across the room. Soon, Mrs. König had gathered her guests in a large group conversation.

"This is looking to be the worst Season there has ever been," lamented Mrs. König. "With the snow, some of the best balls and dinner parties have been cancelled."

"I prefer it when London is quieter," observed Mr. König.

She spared her husband a glance before continuing as if he had not spoken. "It is a pity you have chosen this year for

Miss Darcy to come out in society. If you need the assistance, I can help you obtain invitations to some of the remaining events, some of which are rather exclusive."

"That is very generous of you," said Elizabeth. "Yet I am sure that we will be able to obtain whatever invitations we need."

Mary could not tell whether or not Elizabeth meant her comment as a slight, but Mrs. König did not visibly react.

"In two days, we are going to the ball hosted by the Morrises," said Kitty. "Will you be there?"

"I would not miss it for the world," said Mrs. König.

"I wish I was old enough for a ball," said Henrietta.

"In a few years, you shall be the talk of the town," said Mrs. König.

"We shall have a pleasant time here, Henrietta," said her father. "If you like, I will play cards with you all night."

At that moment, the butler entered the room, his face red with cold.

"What is the matter?" asked Mr. König.

"An urgent letter for the mistress," said the butler. "The lass who delivered it insisted that it could not be delayed and must be read immediately."

Mary schooled her features so as not to betray her knowledge of the contents.

"What urgency could there be at this time of day?" said Mrs. König, snatching the letter from his hand. "It is probably another friend who has decided to quit London because it is too dreary this year. Maybe I should quit London myself." She laughed at her own statement as she opened the letter.

Her eyes raced down the page as her body became almost unnaturally still. Seemingly unaware of her actions, she crumpled the paper into a ball.

"Why is everyone so quiet?" she said sharply. "What were we speaking of?"

"We were speaking of the ball," said Elizabeth. Mary did not know that she would have been brave enough to respond so quickly, given the rancour in Mrs. König's voice.

"Yes, the ball," said Mrs. König. "Mr. König makes a point of never attending balls."

"A man should have what gives him satisfaction inside his own home," said Mr. König. "He should need no more or no less than that."

"It simply shows that if one attempts to join good society too late in life, he will never be comfortable there, for he will always know that he does not belong." Mrs. König glared at her husband. "Is that not right, Mr. König?"

Mr. König's face turned a deep red. Kitty rubbed her hands on her dress and looked at the floor, and Mr. Darcy appeared almost angry at Mrs. König's treatment of her husband.

Mary swallowed. She and Fanny had brought on this family conflict. Mrs. König was insulting her husband, very cruelly, very publicly. It did not seem like a normal expression of grief, though people grieved in all manner of ways. However, Mrs. König did appear genuinely shocked at the news of Mr. Rice's death.

If this was a Shakespearean play, it would be a tragedy, and this moment would lead to worse events, and possibly more death. Of course, this scene could just as likely appear in a Shakespearean comedy, except Mr. Rice would not actually be dead, and would have disguised himself as either Mr. König—which would be a nice dramatic touch—or a new acquaintance, like Kitty. There would be a series of escapades, Mrs. König would manage to prove her love to either her lover or her husband, and eventually harmony would be restored.

"I am sorry to disappoint you, my dear," said Mr. König.

"Now *that* is something you are good at," said Mrs. König, choosing the tragic Shakespearean path.

"Mother," said Henrietta, "Please do not—"

"Be quiet, Henrietta. I did not ask for you to speak."

Henrietta looked as if she had been slapped. After a quiet sniffle, she fled the room.

Georgiana moved as if to follow her, but Mr. Darcy put his hand on her arm.

Mrs. König closed her eyes, and her jaw moved back and forth. "Henrietta, I am sorry," she called after her daughter. But Henrietta did not return.

"What is the news you have received?" asked Mr. König, attempting to take his wife's hand.

"It is nothing of import," she said, wrenching her hand away. She smoothed the wrinkles of the note, careful not to reveal any of its contents to the group. "I have a terrible headache," she said, "and I must retire for the evening." Without any personal farewells, she too left the room. At least she had not taken the Shakespearean method of hiding behind a curtain with a dagger.

"I see that I am left to make my wife's apologies for her," said Mr. König. "She is a troubled woman, and I had hoped—" He stopped, and ran his fingers through his greying hair. He had clearly been hurt by his wife's words, and yet still he was trying to help her save face. Why was he still loyal to her, despite how she treated him? "I regret cutting this evening short. As always, I have appreciated your family's company, and I particularly enjoyed meeting the two young Miss Bennets."

"I hope that whatever the news is that has plagued Mrs. König, she will hear better news soon," said Georgiana. "I hate to see your family in such pain."

"Thank you, Miss Darcy," he said solemnly.

"We will trouble you no longer," said Mr. Darcy. "Thank you for being such a gracious host."

They left quickly then, donning their cloaks and hats and gloves in preparation for the brief moment it took to walk from one house to another. Taking a carriage such a short distance would be preposterous, but this evening, the walk felt uncomfortably long.

"What an unfortunate spectacle," said Mr. Darcy, once they were inside.

"It is fortunate, at least," said Elizabeth, "that it occurred with a small number of guests rather than a large number."

"I wonder what the note contained," said Kitty.

"I have never seen Mrs. König act like that before," said Georgiana. "It must have been dreadful indeed."

Mrs. König's grief seemed deep indeed. Mary recited,

"Ah! Wherefore should my weeping maid suppress
Those gentle signs of undissembled woe?
When from soft love proceeds the deep distress,
Ah, why forbid the willing tears to flow."

Everyone stared at Mary.

"It is part of a poem by William Cowper. I thought it appropriate for the situation."

"Thank you, Mary," said Elizabeth, and then immediately changed the subject, as she often did when Mary spoke. And Mary, as always, pretended not to notice.

Later that evening, Mary described Mrs. König's reaction in detail to Fanny, recounting every word, every shift in tone, every facial expression. They stayed up late, debating the implications by the light of a single candle. In the end, Mary concluded that Mrs. König showed too much genuine shock to be the murderer, while Fanny would not eliminate that possibility, drawing attention to Mrs. König's almost violent anger, which she was unafraid to inflict on those closest to her.

# CHAPTER FOUR

*"CRIME.—The body of a Mr. Oliver Rice was found in his London home on Sunday, having been strangled to death. As of yet, no progress has been made towards discovering the identity of the murderer."*

—*The Morning Post*, London, January 27, 1814

KITTY SPUN AROUND the library with her arms outstretched, wailing, "Where on earth are the novels?" She collapsed into a chair in a rather overdone display of despair.

Mary set down a book on recent maritime exploits, which provided useful information about Lord Cochrane. Lord Cochrane, Mr. Eastlake, Sir Francis Burdett—any of these suspects might be at attendance at tonight's ball, and Mary thought it would be useful to learn more about them in advance.

Mary considered lecturing Kitty on the virtues of patience and a proper perspective when it came to finding things, but something held her back. It did not help anyone to place too much emphasis on correction. "I can show you how to use the catalogue." She paused. "But first, can I draw you?"

"Draw me?"

Mary lifted her pad of paper and her pencil, which were next to her chair. "Yes. I read a book that said I should practice drawing things in motion. Do not worry—it will not take long. I am supposed to draw quickly, capturing just the essence of the movement, without any details."

"I suppose I could pose for you," said Kitty a little reluctantly. "What do you want me to do?"

"Spin around as you were before." Kitty began to spin. "A little more enthusiastically—yes, like that. Pause there, no a moment back, yes, perfect."

"This is rather uncomfortable," said Kitty, grimacing.

Mary drew a few brief vertical lines, curved like Kitty's dress, then Kitty's arms, outstretched. Mary added just two lines for each of Kitty's hands, and then created a sweeping line to capture the angle of Kitty's head.

"Done." She needed more practice, but she could see the virtues in this sort of exercise.

Kitty approached and lifted the paper. "I do not think anyone would recognise me. But I like it." She handed back the page and crossed her arms. "Now show me the novels."

A few minutes later, Kitty had all the reading material she could possibly desire.

"You should read this book when I am done," said Kitty, "and then we can act it out together. It was excessively diverting last time."

A few months before, Mary had written to Kitty, needing her help. She had not told Kitty she was a spy, nor provided any details about her investigation, but she had used a fake name from a novel they had both read. Kitty had enthusiastically found all the information Mary needed, and seemed to believe it was a sort of game in which they acted out the parts of the novel. It was better that she believed that than knew the truth.

"If you find a novel with enough intrigue, that would not offend my sensibilities, it would be a pleasure."

"I will see if this one is adequate." Kitty lounged in a rather unladylike position on a chair and began to read.

Mary turned back to the book on maritime exploits. Lord Cochrane had joined the Royal Navy at the age of seventeen and had achieved much success in the twenty-one years since. When he had commanded the *Speedy*, a ship of eighty men, he had captured over fifty vessels, most of them French or Spanish. Then, with a crew of 215 on the *Pallas*, he had performed even more spectacular feats. He had fought hard for their country, and in doing so had also earned a considerable amount of prize money. From the capture of one particularly desirable ship, Cochrane had earned £40,000, a truly incredible fortune.

According to the book, Lord Cochrane was much admired by the general public and those who sailed with him. An oblique reference indicated that Cochrane had come into conflict with some of his superior officers; he had been court-martialled in 1801 for the loss of the *Speedy* to the French. Beyond that, the book gave no further clues to Lord Cochrane's character.

Mary set the book aside and perused the shelves for others which might be of use. Kitty looked up occasionally—the novel must not be gripping yet—but Mary ignored her looks. Her whole life, she had always spent large amounts of time in the library, reading things Kitty had no interest in. Even if Kitty showed interest in the books Mary was reading, she would not guess Mary's true purpose.

Finally, Mary found a book which contained a brief mention of Sir Francis Burdett. It read:

*In March 1810, Burdett protested the imprisonment of John Gale Jones, who had sought to destroy our military, thus leaving us defenceless against the onslaught of the French. Yet Burdett did not limit his protests to speeches at Westminster; at his request, a fellow conspirator, Cobbett, published his inflammatory words against the government. After a warrant was issued for Burdett's arrest, a mob stood in front of Burdett's house, guarding him and tormenting innocent passers-by. Other mobs ransacked and looted the houses of Lord Castlereagh, Spencer Perceval, and other key figures of the government. The Foot Guards, Light Dragoons, and Horse Guards were ordered to stand by, but fortunately Burdett was taken and imprisoned in the Tower of London without further confrontation. Had he not been, a horrific revolution, similar to what happened in France, could easily have resulted.*

*Burdett was released several months later, in June. There was talk of possible insurrection against the government to celebrate his release, but fortunately, this did not come to pass.*

Sir Francis seemed quite the subversive character. Indeed, a full-scale insurrection would cripple their country as much as an invasion by Bonaparte.

Mary found no references in the library to John Eastlake. She did, however, find a copy of Sir Francis Burdett's tract, *Magna Carta and the Bill of Rights*. It had been catalogued improperly, without his last name, or she would have found it hours before. It was not very long so she set herself the task of reading it before the ball.

THE DARCYS' WEALTH meant that everyone at the ball willingly paid them their attention. It did not surprise Mary that more notice was paid to Georgiana than to herself; Georgiana had a handsome appearance and was the heir to a large fortune which had been allocated to her by her parents. Kitty also drew people to her; she was in her natural element at balls and managed to reserve her first two sets of dances within two minutes of their entrance. Mary did not mind if the focus was on other members of her family, for she met all the same people.

Before long, one gentleman had reserved Georgiana's second set of dances and Mr. Darcy had introduced her to two others who reserved the first and the fourth dance.

After Georgiana was escorted to the floor for the first dance, Elizabeth asked her husband, "Did you plan out Georgiana's entire evening?"

"Not her entire evening. But there are several gentlemen she should meet who are very suitable."

"Some things are best left to chance," said Elizabeth, smiling at him.

Darcy's lips quirked into a smile. "Was it only by chance that I was drawn to you?" he said quietly. "I do not believe it was."

Mary wondered how exactly they had ended up married. Mary had only heard bits and pieces of it and suspected the only person who knew the whole of it was Jane.

"What about you, Miss Bennet?" said Darcy. "Do you wish to dance?"

"I would be satisfied either with or without dancing, but I do not plan to actively seek out dance partners." She did not need Darcy arranging a dance for her, which might prevent an opportunity to meet Sir Francis Burdett, Lord Cochrane, or

John Eastlake. Unfortunately, she did not even know what they looked like, but Mr. Darcy likely knew them. "Would you indulge me for a moment? Lady Trafford instructed me that it was essential to learn people's names and who they are. She recommended doing so, if possible, before introductions are even made."

"That is perceptive," said Mr. Darcy. "It makes it easier to foster preferred interactions and avoid less agreeable ones."

Darcy supplied the names of those he recognised. While none were on her list, Mary tried to remember as many as she could; it might be useful to know them later. Darcy proved adept at describing salient points of character or profession, which made it easier for her to fix them in her mind. Elizabeth was able to name a number of people Darcy could not, and she seemed to find this an amusing sort of game. The people were a more diverse group than at country balls Mary had attended: several from East India, a black politician and his family, and an heiress from Siam.

"That man, with the dark hair, is Mr. Eastlake," said Darcy. "I do not recommend making his acquaintance."

"Why not?" asked Mary. Could it be *John* Eastlake from her list? If so, she did need to make his acquaintance.

"It is a personal matter," said Darcy. "The details do not need to be repeated."

"Sometimes a little context can prevent a multitude of error," said Elizabeth.

"Very well," said Darcy, giving Elizabeth a knowing look. "We had a disagreement over a contract and how it should be executed. I find him rather hypocritical for one who is so high-minded."

"I see," said Mary, noting the information. Yet the apparent tension between Darcy and Eastlake would entirely prevent her from receiving an introduction.

Though Darcy and Elizabeth continued to name guests they recognised, they seemed to have lost some of their enthusiasm for the task.

"That man, to the right of the woman in the purple dress," Darcy remarked a short while later, "is Sir Francis Burdett. He is very opinionated about certain topics, and he is a Radical in Parliament, but a decent fellow." Darcy had pointed out several Whigs and Tories in Parliament, but this was the first Radical.

"Sir Francis Burdett?" Mary said, trying hard not to betray her excitement in her voice. "I read one of his essays. I did not agree with him on several points, and I would like to ask him a few questions."

"This sort of conversation will provide Mary more pleasure than dancing," said Elizabeth with a wry smile.

"Very well," said Darcy. He led Mary around the room—Elizabeth paused to talk to a female acquaintance—all the while keeping his eyes on Georgiana as she danced with her partner. He seemed to possess almost an excessive amount of brotherly concern; he was a knight willing to go into battle for her.

Reaching their target—a slightly balding man with a large nose and kindly features—Darcy bowed slightly and said, "Sir Francis, it is a pleasure to see you again."

"Mr. Darcy, the pleasure is mine."

"This is my wife's sister, Miss Bennet."

"A pleasure."

Mary smiled and curtsied. It was hard to believe that this polite, balding gentleman before her might be a murderer, but she knew that it was possible. Appearances could be incredibly deceiving.

"How is Parliament treating you?" asked Darcy.

"Not as well as I would like, but I have great plans for moving several issues to the general focus. How is Pemberley?"

"Very well. This heavy winter makes me want to return, but I know that it is no better at home."

"It has been a nasty winter, the worst I have seen since '95."

"I have a particular request. Miss Bennet has read some of your works and wanted to speak with you about them."

Mary gave what she hoped was a winning smile.

"Of course, it would be my pleasure."

The first dance ended, and Georgiana's second partner escorted her to a different part of the floor, more difficult to see from where they stood.

"If you do not mind," said Mr. Darcy, bowing, "I will excuse myself." After what she had read about Burdett's imprisonment in the Tower of London, Mary was surprised that Darcy would leave her alone with him. Perhaps Darcy did not know of the events, or perhaps he trusted that she would be safe at a ball. Regardless, it suited her purposes to have a more private conversation, so she did not protest.

"What did you read of mine?" asked Sir Francis.

"*Magna Carta and the Bill of Rights*."

"Oh yes, based on a speech I gave a number of years ago."

"Well," said Mary, trying to collect her thoughts by summarising, "you spend a significant portion of the essay describing what you see as attacks on the rights and liberties of the English people."

Sir Burdett nodded patiently.

"You also talk about these events as attacks on the Magna Carta and the Bill of Rights."

He nodded again.

"But as I read the Magna Carta itself, it seemed to me that it really was not offering the same freedoms as we have today." Mary realised that she had found the thrust of her critique and spoke more quickly now. "In fact, it spoke specifically about giving rights to landowners, and from my understanding of history, there were not many landowners in the year 1215, only a few barons and other members of the nobility. It is only those people, and a few members of the clergy, and widows of barons, who were mentioned in the document as receiving any protection under it. Many more people have *liberties* today, so I cannot understand how there could actually be a conspiracy against the Magna Carta."

Sir Francis Burdett looked thoughtful. "I have never had a young lady critique my work before."

Mary felt suddenly self-conscious. Her mother, her sisters, and even her father had spent their whole lives trying to prevent her from making speeches like this in front of people, and now she had critiqued an important gentleman both directly and forcefully.

Before she could apologise or flee, Sir Burdett said, "You have a solid understanding of history, and a good eye for pulling apart arguments. If you were a man, you could do well in Parliament."

His compliment surprised her, and she did not know what to say.

"In terms of your critique, you are correct in your assertion that these protections benefited a much more limited group of people than they do today. But regardless of all of its many limitations, the Magna Carta was a dramatic rethinking of the role of government: the very idea that power could be limited, that a king could, and should be held accountable to anyone else for his actions, was shattering, life-changing, revelatory. Over the centuries that have passed since then, we have progressively gained more liberties, both by limiting the powers of the monarchy and by expanding who these liberties cover, and expanding the liberties themselves, such as in the Bill of Rights and through many small acts of Parliament."

"Is it really fair to say that there exists an actual *conspiracy* against our liberties?"

"Do I think there is a group of men, sitting around a table, plotting to take away our liberties? I sincerely hope not. But people always reach for more power or money, and the easiest way to gain power or money is by taking it from someone else."

Mary thought on this. Before she could respond, Sir Burdett continued, "There are always justifications used when rights are removed—'this is only for a short time,' 'this is necessary for our security, et cetera, et cetera.' And then you have the abuses I detailed in the text: the suspension of habeas corpus so anyone can be imprisoned without stated cause and without trial, as well as excessive bail, buying government seats, corruption in all levels of government, those who are guilty of crimes receiving no consequences because of their money and position... Each of these injustices chip away at our liberties."

"I agree that each of these things can be considered unjust," admitted Mary. The presence of injustice, however, did not mean that someone like Burdett should be given an opportunity to overthrow their system of government.

"That is why I spend my days attempting to improve the system. I would like to send you several of my more recent writings. I think you will find them enlightening."

"I would appreciate it," said Mary. He must believe she

was interested in his cause, but if it would allow her to gather more information, she would not correct him. She did not think it would be useful to press him on Mr. Rice's death; he had already been interrogated by the police detective. Yet she would venture one potentially risky question.

"I read that you were imprisoned in the Tower of London for your efforts. Does that not discourage you?"

"My imprisonment was unjust. All I did was protest another losing his own liberties. Yet my punishment has not deterred me—I am willing to suffer a little, and to make choices others are unwilling to make, in order to relieve the much greater sufferings of others."

This could be an innocent comment, or Mr. Rice's murder could be considered one of the choices others were unwilling to make.

"Do others in Parliament want the same changes?"

"There are a number of us, yes. Many of the Whigs want certain changes as well, and a number of Tories. Yet someday there will be more of us."

"Is there anyone else here tonight?"

"Why yes, in fact. I saw Mr. Eastlake earlier." If the Eastlake here was a Radical, he must in fact be her suspect, John Eastlake. "Johnstone is here as well. Andrew Cochrane-Johnstone," he added, by way of explanation. "He was governor of Dominica for a time."

"Cochrane-Johnstone? Is he any relation to Lord Cochrane?"

"Yes, he is Lord Cochrane's uncle, in fact. Lord Cochrane is a good friend of mine. He is not here tonight, but perhaps I can introduce you another time."

"I would much appreciate that," said Mary.

She considered asking him more, but she remembered

something Lady Trafford had taught her, about allowing people graceful exits. "Thank you for your time, Sir Francis, and for answering my questions."

"I always enjoy conversing with inquisitive young people, especially those who keep an open mind."

Sir Francis bowed and Mary curtsied, and then Mary made a slow circuit about the room. Mrs. König was dancing with an unmarried man. If Mrs. Bennet was here, Mary reflected, she would say that was not very fair of her to monopolise an unmarried man, as there were more unmarried women present than men.

Mary walked past Mr. Eastlake and paused nearby, as if looking at the scenery. He was complaining loudly about the price of coal and bread being out of reach for the average man. These were the sort of people who had started the French Revolution, who would overthrow an entire government for the price of bread.

After several minutes, with no way to obtain an introduction, Mary moved on.

Feeling something brush her arm, Mary turned, but no one was there. A minute later it happened again, and this time she spotted Mr. Stanley. He pretended to not see her noticing him and left the room. A minute later, Mary discreetly followed him.

She found Stanley in a small drawing room, standing to one side of a potted tree. Placing herself on the other side, she spoke in a quiet voice. "We cannot be seen talking to each other. We are not supposed to know each other."

"True, but we do need to coordinate our efforts."

Mary held her hand over her mouth, as if coughing into it. "I spoke with Sir Francis. I also spotted Mr. Eastlake, but I cannot obtain an introduction."

"I will make sure to engage with him. What does he look like?"

Mary gave him a brief description. "Is there any way in which I can be of assistance to you?"

"No, I am simply grateful I had the opportunity to speak with you."

Mary turned her head to see him, and he gave her a dashing smile. She quickly turned her head away. Gentlemen did not give Mary dashing smiles unless they wanted her to do something for them, typically something unpleasant.

"I wish I could dance with you," he said.

This was a more pleasant request than she had expected.

"I would say yes," said Mary, "except I suspect Mr. Booth would frown upon it."

"Someday we will find a way."

She felt suddenly flustered, and she did not know why, so she did the only logical thing and prepared to flee. "I must be getting back to the Darcys, before they come looking for me."

Her heart pounded, and she had a sudden urge to look at him again, but she could do nothing that might lead people to assume a connection between them, so she walked stoically away.

As she entered the ballroom, the second dance ended, and the family gathered on the side of the room: Kitty and Georgiana, Elizabeth and Darcy, and Mary.

"I have been having a delightful time on the floor," said Georgiana, "But I am so grateful to have a break for this next dance. I refused to let anyone dance with me for this one."

"However did you manage that?" asked Mary. "I thought that if you refused someone, you could not dance at all for the rest of the night."

"I have not refused anyone," said Georgiana, smiling. "I

simply am scheduling people to dance with me later in the evening in order to give myself a respite."

"I need no respite," said Kitty. "This is much better than the balls in Meryton. If only Lydia were here! She will be so envious of me when I write. Maybe she will even send a reply." Prior to Lydia's marriage to Mr. Wickham, Lydia and Kitty had been inseparable. Since her marriage, Lydia had only once written a response to Mary's letters—apparently, she was too busy—but it was surprising that she did not write more to Kitty.

Kitty's partner for the third dance came and led her, beaming, to the floor.

"Oh, to be young and at a ball." Elizabeth looked fondly at her husband. "Do you remember the first time we danced, at Mr. Bingley's ball?"

"How could I possibly forget?"

Elizabeth smiled. "I was rather judgmental."

"And I could not help but spar with you."

"I would enjoy dancing with you again, sparring optional. Actually, sparring required."

"People will talk," said Mr. Darcy.

When married women danced at balls, they typically danced with someone other than their spouse.

"Let them think what they will. I must have one dance with you, unless you no longer wish to dance with me."

"If it were possible, I would spend the entire ball dancing with you," said Mr. Darcy, his eyes intent on Elizabeth.

"Oh, you must dance together," said Georgiana. "How can you not?"

Mr. Darcy turned to Mary and Georgiana. "Georgiana, please stay with Mary during this dance. She is your official chaperone."

"Of course," said Georgiana, rather quickly. "I would not dream of leaving her side."

Mr. Darcy would still be in the room, so why should his sister need an additional chaperone? It seemed rather overprotective, but Mary agreed to the request.

As Darcy led Elizabeth to the dance floor, Mary saw that Mrs. König was once again dancing, this time with a Tory from Parliament who Darcy had pointed out earlier, Mr. George Sharp. Mr. Sharp wore a blue coat with very large buttons.

Mary noted that Mr. Stanley must have managed to receive an introduction, for he was speaking with Mr. Eastlake. Hopefully he learned something useful.

Georgiana bit her lip and looked around the room wistfully.

"Would you like to take a turn with me about the room?" asked Mary.

"No, I am fine here," said Georgiana, but she seemed unsure of herself.

Sir Francis Burdett approached, accompanied by a distinguished-looking gentleman with grey hair.

"Miss Bennet and Miss Darcy," said Sir Francis with a bow. "This is my good friend, Mr. Andrew Cochrane-Johnstone."

"It is a pleasure," said Georgiana, and both Mary and Georgiana curtsied.

Sir Francis gave his excuses—he had an urgent matter to attend to—leaving them alone with Mr. Johnstone.

"Is it Mr. Johnstone, or Mr. Cochrane-Johnstone?" asked Georgiana.

"Officially, Mr. Cochrane-Johnstone, though you are welcome to call me Mr. Johnstone—many do," he said. "I loved my wife dearly, and so when we wed, we both took each other's last names. My last name was Cochrane, and hers was Johnstone, and I became Mr. Cochrane-Johnstone. When I lost her, I became even more determined to always have her name be a part of mine."

It was rather unusual for a woman to not give up her surname in favour of her husband's, and for them to create a new, hyphenated surname. Mary liked it. It gave a woman a more equal stance in marriage—she was not just a man's property; they both belonged to each other.

"What became of her?" asked Georgiana.

"She died not long after the birth of our daughter, Eliza. I miss her every single day."

Georgiana took one small step closer to him, her face full of sympathy. "What was her name?"

"Her given name was Georgiana Hope Johnstone."

"Georgiana is *my* given name."

"Is it truly, Miss Darcy?" He placed his hand over his heart. "What a lovely world of coincidences we live in."

Mary was not sure how she felt about Mr. Johnstone, or how Mr. Darcy would feel about him, but as the designated chaperone, she felt like she should at least shift the focus of the conversation.

"Sir Francis said you are related to Lord Cochrane," said Mary.

"Yes. He is my dear nephew."

"The great war hero?" asked Georgiana. "I have read of him."

"I have fought myself. Between us, we can tell many a fine story, some of which may not be suited for a young lady's ears."

"It would be best to spare us those," said Mary. "For propriety is an essential virtue, that must be maintained in order for polite society to function." She paused, and then, because she could not help herself, she said, "Though perhaps you could tell us one of your more tame ones."

Johnstone agreed. Instead of a war story, he told of his purchase of thousands of Spanish merino sheep and their shipment to a buyer in New York. While he had not accompanied the sheep himself, his agent had, and Johnstone recounted the escapades of the sheep in confinement, including sheep that escaped their pens and ran in circles about the ship's deck, and a sheep whose wool was somehow dyed blue. "There was constant noise, at every hour. No one got a bit of sleep. Unfortunately, most of the sheep perished upon arrival in New York, yet even with this loss, my true ends were served—to eliminate the possibility of Bonaparte seizing the sheep and using their wool. I will embrace any gain against Bonaparte, even if I suffer financially as a result."

His final statement leaned too heavily towards self-aggrandisement, but Mary supposed it was allowable from someone who had been a governor, and she quickly forgave him, for he then turned his attention to Georgiana, finding out details about her favourites books and music and plays. He even asked Mary several questions, though his eyes kept returning to Georgiana's face.

When Darcy and Elizabeth returned from their dance, Mary introduced them to their new acquaintance. "This is Mr. Johnstone. He is a friend of Sir Francis."

"Mr. Darcy, it is a pleasure," said Johnstone. "I know your cousin, Colonel Fitzwilliam."

When Georgiana's next partner, a Mr. Davies, arrived to lead her to the dance floor, Mr. Johnstone continued conversing with Darcy and Elizabeth. Not once did his eyes seek out

Georgiana on the dance floor, and to Mary this seemed quite intentional.

As Georgiana returned, Darcy led the conversation to a close. It surprised Mary that she could notice these sorts of cues now, when she never had noticed them before Lady Trafford's training.

Mr. Johnstone said, "I would love to continue our conversation another time."

Mary felt this was an appropriate moment to push for her own purposes. "And I would very much like to meet your nephew, Lord Cochrane. An insider's view on the success of the *Speedy* would be extremely useful for the studies I am making on recent maritime conflicts."

"Then perhaps we could have a dinner," said Johnstone. "All of you, and I could invite my nephew and several others known for engaging conversation."

"I would very much like that!" exclaimed Georgiana. "Please, brother, can we go?"

Mr. Darcy agreed, and seemed pleased by his sister's smile.

"Excellent, I will be in touch." Johnstone bowed to each of them in turn. "Mr. Darcy, Mrs. Darcy, Miss Darcy, Miss Bennet, it has been a pleasure."

Georgiana tugged on Mary's arm. "Now I want to take a turn about the room, before the next dance."

Once they were out of hearing, Georgiana said, "What do you think of Mr. Johnstone?"

"His daughter is likely older than you are, and it would not surprise me if he is on the wrong side of five and forty."

"That is of no import. I think his grey hair is very dignified."

"He *was* the governor of Dominica."

"What a responsibility! He seems very kind, and attentive. And it is terribly sad how he lost his wife. He must be so lonely."

"I am sure he has plenty of friends to keep him company."

"I do not know what my brother thinks of him, and I *need* his approval if I want to be truly interested in someone."

"I would not worry too much. Dinner will be a perfect opportunity for your brother—and you—to learn his character before any of us come to conclusions."

"You are very wise," said Georgiana. "I am so glad you came to London, Mary."

"I am glad, too." This sudden friendship with Georgiana surprised her—it surprised her that she could consider anyone her friend, after only knowing them for a few days—but it also gave her pleasure.

"Also, thank you so much for asking your maid to fix my dress. Miss Cramer was brilliant—the dress is ten times better now, and I have received so many compliments." The dress did indeed look stunning, with the almost puffy gathered collar Fanny had added, as well as a short, filmy train which made it appear that the dress might lift Georgiana off the ground.

As they returned to Mr. Darcy and Elizabeth, Mary's steps felt lighter.

The rest of the ball passed in a blur: eating dinner, playing the pianoforte while attempting to listen to one of Sir Francis's conversations, advising Kitty that she should not drink too much wine or be quite so free with her affections, and watching Georgiana's constant excitement. It also took a fair amount of effort to keep track of Mrs. König's dance partners: Tories and Whigs, soldiers and landed gentry. Mary had never seen a married woman dance every single dance before.

Mrs. König danced the final dance with Mr. Sharp, the Tory with the large buttons who she had danced with earlier in the evening. Halfway through the dance, Mrs. König appeared quite distressed, so Mary made her way towards their place in the line, arriving nearby just as Mrs. König and Mr. Sharp stepped away from the other couples and off the dance floor.

Mr. Sharp looked around, as if to make sure no one was listening, and Mary kept her eyes fixed on the dance.

"The fellow—what was his name?" asked Mr. Sharp.

"Rice. Oliver Rice."

Mary's interest in the conversation shifted from mild to extreme. She angled herself so she could see them from the edge of her vision.

"I will send you a letter about the matter soon, with whatever information I discover." He paused. "You will likely receive it on Saturday."

"Thank you, Mr. Sharp. You do not know what this means to me," said Mrs. König.

Mr. Sharp lifted her hand and kissed it. "Anything for you, Selena." His tone was not nearly as warm as the words themselves—in fact, it was almost cold.

Mary wanted to observe Mrs. König's reaction, but suddenly, Elizabeth took Mary's arm and led her away. "I was looking for you, Mary. I am afraid that it is time to leave. How was your experience at your first London ball?"

"It was quite invigorating," said Mary. "I conversed with a number of interesting people, and I had the opportunity to observe and reflect on a wide range of human behaviour." More reflection was still needed, particularly on Mrs. König. "How was your experience?"

"Chaperoning three unmarried young ladies is quite the task. I can see why our mother never managed to give us any direction at all; though, on further reflection, I think it likely that she did not even try." Elizabeth gave an amused smile. "At least I did not have to worry about you."

"I am glad to not cause you trouble."

"You are no trouble at all, Mary."

As they joined the others, Mary felt herself bumped, and found a paper in her hand. She caught a glimpse of Mr. Stanley. It must have been him—but why? He must have discovered something of import; that could be the only reason for him giving her a secretive note. She kept the note hidden from her family but could not stop thinking about it the entire way home.

# CHAPTER FIVE

*"Mr. Editor,—Being situated in the centre of the poor Irish in St. Giles's, in the capacity of a schoolmaster, I have been an eye witness of the extreme poverty and misery which many of my fellow countrymen endure for want of employment. Upwards of 6000 labourers are destitute of work, and their numerous families in a starving condition. Out of 70 children at my school this morning, 60 of them had received no food till I gave them some bread at noon."*

—From a letter to the editor in *The Times*, London,
January 28, 1814

ONCE DRESSED FOR bed, Mary and Fanny examined Mr. Stanley's note. He had used a closure method for the letter that Lady Trafford would approve of: it looked like an ordinary letter, closed only by a seal, but had a paper dagger trap inside, which would reveal if anyone opened it before her. He had written the letter with a quick but legible hand.

*MB—*

*I met Mr. Eastlake and convinced him that I am sympathetic to his cause. Nothing of note, except he did mention that there are several private meetings, soon to occur, with several key Radical members of Parliament.*

*Did not disclose when or where those will be.*

*I long for the day when you agree to dance with me at a ball.*

—*WS*

Mary tried to stifle a great yawn but failed. She found herself flattered but a little bewildered by his attention. Why did he once again mention dancing with her? He had already made that polite gesture at the ball.

"Mr. Stanley fancies you," said Fanny.

"Fancies me?" said Mary, climbing into her bed. "You are mistaken."

"I have seen the way he looks as you, as if you are the centre of the room."

"No one ever fancies me. I am not my sisters, with beauty and cleverness, and the knowledge of how to flirt." Her eyes threatened to close, and she blinked rapidly, trying to stay awake. "I am just Mary Bennet."

Fanny gave a smug smile. "When his attentions continue, it will prove me right. Trust me, I know these things."

And indeed, the next morning, during a brief meeting at Mr. Booth's office, Mr. Stanley seemed to seek Mary's approval as much as he sought Mr. Booth's.

"I managed an appointment with Admiral Markham," said Mr. Stanley, "and while there, we spoke, in part, of Lord Cochrane. Lord Cochrane has many enemies—he has irritated many in both the Navy and in Parliament, because of his inability to follow social protocol and his defiance of authority. Most of his enemies are his superiors—Lord Ellenborough in Parliament, and Lord St. Vincent in the Navy. He has even managed to anger the writer and philanthropist Hannah More. She has publicly declared that she believes him to be a greater threat to our country than Bonaparte."

He looked triumphantly at Mary. Hannah More was one of Mary's favourite authors, and her religious texts always inspired her.

Stanley continued, "I am attempting to set up meetings with Lord Ellenborough and Lord St. Vincent to see if I can gather any information which might be relevant to the case."

"You had better provide a good justification for meeting with them," said Mr. Booth.

"A legitimate business deal that I am considering," said Mr. Stanley smoothly, and then he smiled at Mary, whose cheeks suddenly felt warm.

Fanny elbowed Mary and gave her a knowing smirk.

"Any other progress you have made?" asked Mr. Booth.

He described, in detail, his conversation with Mr. Eastlake, and Mr. Booth encouraged him to build a friendship with Eastlake and, if possible, attend the Radical meetings.

"Consider it done," said Mr. Stanley.

Mr. Booth turned to Mary. "Your report, Miss Bennet?"

She described her conversation with Sir Francis and the dinner invitation which would likely include Lord Cochrane. Then she failed to hold back a yawn.

"Any updates on Mrs. König?"

"Mrs. König danced every dance, and twice with Mr. Sharp, who is a Tory."

"Yes, I am familiar with him," said Mr. Booth.

"She must have requested that he find information for her on Mr. Rice's death, for he said that he would discover what he could and write her a letter, that might be delivered as soon as tomorrow."

Mr. Stanley smiled and nodded, she assumed in approval.

"Mr. Sharp. That is very interesting indeed," said Mr. Booth, putting his hand on his chin. "More and more members of Parliament are taking interest in this case—they have already crippled Mr. Donalds's ability to carry out any further public investigation. And now we must add Mr. Sharp to the list.

"Miss Cramer and Miss Bennet, I need you to find a way to read Mrs. König's letters, including the one that Mr. Sharp sends."

Fanny cleared her throat. "Last night, while Miss Bennet was at the ball, I visited the Königs' servants. One of them, George, has the exclusive task of collecting the family's letters from the post office. George keeps careful track of the letters and delivers Mrs. König's to her directly. She always opens her letters immediately, and about half of her letters she burns promptly after reading."

"Then she has likely burned any prior sensitive material," said Mr. Booth. "How does George feel about Mrs. König?"

"George is very loyal, but he seems willing to talk about the Königs as long as it stays in abstractions rather than particulars."

"Could you convince George to let you look at the letters before he delivers them to Mrs. König?"

"Certainly not." Fanny seemed unafraid of the possibility of Mr. Booth's disapproval. "We are friendly, but not that friendly. Maybe with another week of developing a relationship, but I do not want to damage the rapport I have built by asking him before then."

"I need you—either of you, both of you—to intercept the letter from Mr. Sharp before Mrs. König receives it."

"Could we coordinate with the post office and have them give it to us?" asked Mary.

"No," said Mr. Booth. "I am trying not to violate habeas corpus, and seizing mail in an official manner without stated cause would do so. Besides, the post office is a government organisation, and we are investigating three members of Parliament, and now Mrs. König is dragging in another. I do not need Parliament getting wind of our role in the investigation. We need to maintain our independence if we are to discover the truth." He tapped his fingers on the table. "Find another way to read the letter before she burns it."

Mary swallowed. It seemed an impossible task, and he had given them no suggestion as to how they were to accomplish it. Perhaps that meant he trusted their abilities. Or at least he trusted Fanny's.

Mr. Booth stood, looked at each of them in turn, and then spoke. "I had hoped that we would already know the culprit by now, but nothing is clear. I still fear that there is a connection to Bonaparte. I need each of you to keep pressing forward on this case with due diligence. Now off you go—get to work."

Mr. Booth left to a back room. They stood, and Mary donned her cloak.

"Miss Bennet," said Mr. Stanley. "Before you go, I have a gift for you."

Fanny nudged Mary towards him.

"A gift?"

"Yes. I very much enjoyed the song you played on the pianoforte, and I thought you might like *A Selection of Irish Melodies*. It is the fifth volume, published last year. Do you have it already?"

"No, I do not own it, and I am not familiar with it." Honestly, her performance on the pianoforte had not been her best, but she was glad that Mr. Stanley had appreciated it.

He held out an elegantly bound book. "Then please, take this as a gift from me."

"Thank you," said Mary.

She took the book and flipped through the pages. It was quite a selection of music, with poems set to traditional Irish melodies, and titles like "The Last Rose of Summer." A gift like this was no small gesture, and she felt a strange tingling in her chest that anyone would do something like this for her. He must be interested in her, or he would not do such a thing for fear that it would be misinterpreted.

"Thank you," she said again, unsure of how to better express her gratitude. "Thank you very much. I look forward to learning these pieces."

"I hope that I will soon have the honour of listening to you play them."

She nodded, and he bowed and opened the door.

Mr. Booth's secretary, Mrs. Granger, held out her hand to stop Mary and Fanny. "One person or group at a time, that way we do not attract undue attention. And Miss Bennet, if you are ever in a spot of trouble, you can often find me here. Or if you ever need a ready-made disguise, I am the person to talk to." She peeked out the door. "It has been long enough. Off you go."

As they exited, Fanny said, "What did I tell you?"

"About what?" said Mary, stepping over some slush. The temperature had warmed a little, and the massive amounts of snow and ice were melting, making everything soggy.

"About Mr. Stanley, of course."

"That one should never, ever, in any time or place, argue or disagree with Miss Fanny Cramer."

"It's true," said Fanny. "There's no denying it."

Fanny laughed, and then Mary realised it would be awkward if she did not laugh as well, so she joined her. She was not used to laughing with people—she did not laugh much at all—but she found she rather liked it.

"Mr. Stanley is quite charming, but it is only fair to warn you that you are not the first woman to receive his attentions. That said, I do not doubt the sincerity of his interest."

"I have limited experience with men, so thank you." While Mary had felt interest towards several gentlemen, the most recent case being Mr. Collins, Mr. Stanley was the very first man to ever show interest in her. Suddenly, her steps felt lighter, the sun brighter, and the day warmer.

"Would you mind terribly if we stopped at a nearby dressmaking shop? It will not take long."

"Not at all," said Mary.

Fanny led the way through the streets, confident and purposeful. Beggars stepped out of her path and did not accost her, and she kicked her foot at a small boy who got too close.

"He would rob you, and you would not even know it," said Fanny.

They approached a sinister-looking walled complex, with guards out front, and only tiny windows. The road in front of it was quite clear; no people lingered.

"What is that?" asked Mary.

"A workhouse."

"A workhouse?"

"Yes, for the extremely old or infirm or exceptionally poor. They provide forced labour in exchange for the basic necessities of existence."

"Why are there so many guards?"

"It is a reminder that you never want to get so poor or so desperate that you need true assistance, because once you enter, you will never leave."

Mary swallowed. "You cannot leave?"

"I have heard of one person leaving before, but generally no."

"Then it is a prison!"

"We must punish the poor for their poverty. How else can we keep them in their place?" Her tone was icy, and unlike the melting icicles on the rooftops, showed no hint of thaw. Fanny looked for a long moment at the workhouse, her eyes pained. Then she turned away. "Come, there is nothing we can do to help them. Let us be on our way."

Mary could not believe that there truly could be nothing to do to help these people. Her books had always advocated private charitable donations as *the* solution to society's ills. Yet clearly it was not enough. The Radicals often shouldered these sorts of issues, and they believed that societal and governmental changes were needed to fix deeper underlying problems. Perhaps, at least on some subjects, their views had merit.

A few blocks later, they approached a dressmaker's shop. The shop was small and a little worn, the paint peeling on the sign. As they stepped inside, a bell rang, signalling their entrance.

The shopkeeper stopped her work of adding ornamentation to a dress. After a dismissive look at Mary, she said, "If it isn't Fanny Cramer. You still better than us, or are you beggin' for your job back?"

"I am doing quite well, thank you for asking, Mrs. Yates."

"Then why're you 'ere?"

"If you give my parents a twenty-minute break, then I will tell you how to improve that dress." Fanny gestured at the dress in the woman's hands.

Mrs. Yates's face twitched, but after a moment she relented. "Fine. Go at it, then."

Fanny gestured to Mary, and then led the way behind the counter and through a door in the back room. There were large windows, presumably for light, yet they were coated with dirt and grime. A dozen people, men and women and a few older children, were hunched over tables, sewing.

All looked up at their entrance, and a man and a woman stood. "Fanny!" they said together, and soon they embraced. Like Fanny, both of her parents were black. Fanny had once told Mary that her mother was from London, and her father was originally from Virginia. He had earned his freedom and a ticket to London by fighting with the British against the Americans during their war for independence.

Fanny paused and turned.

"This is Miss Mary Bennet. These are my parents, Zebedee and Luisa Cramer."

They shook her hand in turn, with genuine warmth.

"It is a pleasure to meet you," said Mary.

"It is a pleasure to meet you, Miss Bennet," said Mrs. Cramer. "Our Fanny likes you very much."

"Thank you." Suddenly, Mary realised she had spent every single day in London with family members, and Fanny had not had the opportunity to even see her parents. It was quite unjust, and now Mary was intruding on the small amount of time they had to spend together. "I would love to socialise with you, but I know the time is short, so I will give you your privacy."

"Thank you," said Mr. Cramer, and the family moved to the corner of the room for what seemed a joyful conversation.

Mary sat down in Mrs. Cramer's spot on the bench. She looked at the piece Mrs. Cramer was sewing, and then watched a small girl sew neat little stitches on a sleeve. Needlework was not one of Mary's better accomplishments.

After a few minutes she grew bored, but she could not distract those sewing from their work, or they could get in trouble for it, and she did not want to interrupt Fanny, nor did she want to return to the main part of the shop with its unfriendly owner, so she sat, attempting to be a paragon of patience. Then she realised she had the new music book with her, so she spent the rest of the time looking at the pieces, imagining the melodies in her mind.

The door to the room slammed open. "Your time is done up," said Mrs. Yates stiffly.

Fanny said her farewells to her parents and gave the shop-keeper advice on the dress. As they left the shop, Fanny gave the front window a disdainful look.

"My parents used to work for better places, but first the place me ma was at failed, and then the place where me da was at failed…" She paused, cleared her throat, and spoke slower and more clearly, shifting back to the manner of speech she normally used with Mary. "Now, both my mother and father work here. Mrs. Yates is a nasty woman. She thinks all blacks should've left for Sierra Leone. But your education probably did not teach you about that, did it?"

Mary shook her head.

Fanny sighed. "In the 1780s, as slavery became less common in Britain, a number of poor blacks lived on the streets, without sustenance or employment. Some Tories and others decided London would be a better place with fewer blacks in it. They also did not like the marriages happening between blacks and whites, as if that were a problem. They decided to start a settlement in Sierra Leone, and they paid blacks—and their white spouses—if they would go to it. Many people took up the opportunity—they thought it would be better if they had a place of their own. But many others saw through the scheme, people like Equiano and Cugoana, and so most blacks decided to stay.

"Many people died on the voyage, and the settlement did not have the proper resources, so many more died once they arrived."

"That is terrible!"

"It really is. Unfortunately, Mrs. Yates is not the only person who thinks we all should have been forced to leave."

"That must be infuriating, interacting with people like her."

"It is. I hate the snide remarks, the denigrating comments. Yet in general, London's not a bad place to be. There are black politicians, artists, heiresses, shop owners. People with dark skin are treated much better here than in the United States and other places that still have a slave trade." She paused. "I will prove Mrs. Yates wrong. I *will* get my own shop. I've saved about a third of the money I need to start."

"Your own shop." Mary could picture it. "Then your parents can work with you."

"That is the plan," said Fanny. "I will treat everyone with the dignity they deserve."

"I think anyone would love to work for you. And I am sorry that you had not seen your parents before now. I should have—"

"If I need something," snapped Fanny, "I have no qualms with asking for it. The Darcys' servants receive one day off every fortnight, on a rotational basis. I had planned to do the same, if it is acceptable to you."

"I am not your employer," said Mary. "You can do what you like, when you like."

"True, but we must do everything we can to keep up appearances."

So much of being a spy depended on appearances, and at many times, false appearances, which sometimes still made Mary uneasy. If everything were a lie, then how could one possibly find the truth?

# CHAPTER SIX

*"The Allies have not manifested that consistency of conduct, that magnanimity of design, that justice and purity of character, to which they have all along made such loud pretensions; there has been much trick, contrivance, shuffling, and evasion."*

—*The Statesman*, London, January 28, 1814

BEFORE MARY HAD even finished removing her cloak and gloves, Mr. Darcy asked if they could have a private conversation. His brow was creased, his tone serious. She swallowed. He spoke like her deceased father, Mr. Bennet, when he had intended to give correction.

Fanny took Mary's music book and said, "I will put this in your room." Silently, she mouthed, "Good luck."

Mary sat down in the front drawing room. She straightened her hair, smoothed her dress, then clasped her hands together, trying to keep them still.

Mr. Darcy regarded her, his lips pressed together. He was likely attempting to choose his words rather than intimidate her, but it intimidated her all the same.

"Miss Bennet," he said. "Mary. I was very concerned when all of us awoke this morning and you were gone, without a trace. London is not Meryton or Worthing. It is not safe or appropriate for a young lady to wander about the city on her own."

"I apologise, Mr. Darcy. I—I went to a music shop and bought a book of Irish melodies. I did not mean to concern you, and I was not alone. I brought my maid, Fanny, with me, and she was with me the entire time." She hoped he did not ask where she had bought the music, for she did not know the name or location of a single music shop or bookseller in London.

"When Elizabeth and I agreed that you could join us in London for the Season, I accepted responsibility for your well-being, and I take that responsibility seriously."

Mr. Darcy was looking at her in the same protective way he looked at Georgiana, and suddenly, Mary realised her full lack of power as a woman. In a moment, Mr. Darcy could restrict her movements and make her entirely ineffective as a spy. Yet she could not lose the ability to do her work. She could not—she would not. She had found something that was hers, something with meaning and significance, that made a difference in the world. She would not give it up now. She searched her mind desperately for something she could say or do to protect her time and independence, and she remembered something Lady Trafford had taught her: a well-crafted apology could be an effective weapon.

"I have betrayed your trust, Mr. Darcy, and I am ashamed of myself. I am used to independence—too much independence, perhaps—and I did not think of the consequences of my morning walk on you and other members of the family. I hope that you will allow me to continue my stay here, so that I may have a full educational experience in London."

"I have no intention of sending you away, Mary. I just need you to be careful."

"I understand," she said, lowering her head in what she

hoped was a contrite manner. "If I let others know that I am leaving the house, would it still be possible for me to take walks and go to shops with my maid, Fanny? She is from London, and I would trust her with my life."

"She does seem to be the responsible sort, and you are a trustworthy person, so I give my permission. But only during the day—never at night—and only in respectable areas of town. And you need to tell someone where you are going."

"I understand," said Mary.

"I am sorry to restrict you in any way, but I would never forgive myself if anything happened to you."

"Thank you for your concern for my well-being," said Mary. While he had given her permission to leave the house with Fanny, she still felt restricted. She needed something more, perhaps another reason for leaving the house so she would not need to constantly justify her behaviour. But she was not her sister Elizabeth—she could not immediately bring to mind the best thing to say in a given situation—and so she said nothing more.

When Mary returned to her room, she heard raised voices within. She stood next to the door, which was cracked open.

"I have done nothing wrong," said Fanny.

"You are taking advantage of Miss Bennet's good nature and being negligent in your duties." The voice belonged to a maid named Hannah. She had been assigned to be Mary's maid, because Mary had forgotten to inform Elizabeth that she was bringing her own maid. Apparently, Hannah had been quite disappointed to lose such a desirable position in the household and had taken an instant dislike to Fanny.

"The fact that Miss Bennet desires my companionship does not mean that I have neglected my other duties. I take very good care of her, her room, and her things."

"But you are too good to help the rest of the staff, aren't you?"

"That is not what I have been hired to do," said Fanny. "And I would not dare to disrupt a perfectly running household with what you clearly see as my imperfect approaches."

"What were you *actually* doing last night at the Königs? Don't tell me it was just a chat."

Mary did not want Hannah to come too close to guessing the truth, so she pushed open the door.

"Is there anything we can do for you, Hannah?"

Hannah's face blanched and she shifted uncomfortably. Quickly, though, her face returned to its normal colour. "Sorry to disturb you, Miss Bennet. You are looking very well today. Very well indeed. Please let me know if there is anything that you need assistance with, Miss Bennet. Anything at all."

"Thank you, Hannah. If I need your assistance, I will let you know." When Hannah did not immediately leave, Mary was forced to add, "Fanny is quite good at anticipating my needs."

"Yes, Miss Bennet, I understand," said Hannah. She lowered her head and left the room.

They waited several long moments, then Fanny peered out the door. "She's gone."

"Good."

"Insufferable woman." Fanny shut the door fast. "Of course, she is right about me being negligent as a maid—I have not dusted this entire week." She shrugged. "What did Mr. Darcy want from you?"

"He was worried that we had gone out this morning without leaving word. I think he will watch me more carefully now."

"We are besieged on all sides."

Fanny looked in the mirror and touched up her hair. "I think I shall infuriate Hannah even more by going next door to the Königs. As a side benefit, I can find out when George is planning to get the mail."

"Excellent," said Mary. "Wait one moment—I will write a note for you to deliver to Henrietta, so we have a justifiable reason, in case someone more important than Hannah asks."

Fanny returned a few minutes later. George had already retrieved the mail for the day, but Mary was not worried; Mr. Sharp had not yet had time to gather the information he had promised and had told Mrs. König to expect a letter on Saturday—tomorrow.

Which gave Mary plenty of time to enjoy her new book of Irish melodies.

As she walked downstairs with the book, she thought of the smile on Mr. Stanley's face as he had given it to her. It was an extremely generous gift. She realised that she had stopped in the middle of the room and was gazing at nothing in particular, so she quickly sat down at the pianoforte and schooled her features. She could not risk Kitty catching her with such an expression on her face, or Kitty would accuse her of being a lovesick dairymaid and torment her until she discovered the truth.

Mary sat but did not place her fingers on the keys. Instead, she examined every page of the book, noting key signatures and accidentals, complicated chords, and easy melodies. One of the tunes had an entire page of sixteenth notes and looked quite the challenge. Once she had previewed the entire book, she chose two of the easiest songs and two of the most difficult ones. And then she practised, alternating between them.

After a while, she lifted her now-sore fingers from the keys. She breathed in and out, deeply. Her entire body felt at peace. She looked at the clock on the wall and realised that two full hours had passed without her even realising it. She always loved when that happened, when she managed to completely lose herself in her music.

She left the book at the pianoforte and found Fanny so they could make a more detailed plan for intercepting Mrs. König's mail.

THE NEXT MORNING, George left the Königs about thirty minutes later than he normally did to retrieve the mail.

"Time to don our cloaks," said Fanny, who had been watching the front walk through the window. "It will not take him long, so we must be on our way."

After putting on not only her cloak, but also her gloves and her bonnet, Mary found Mr. Darcy reading in the library. "I wanted to let you know that I plan to take a short walk outside with Fanny. Just in the square."

"Good," said Mr. Darcy, a look of surprise on his face. "Very good. I hope you find it refreshing."

Mary and Fanny left the house. While their pretence had been to walk, they did not walk—they stood, on the corner, out of sight of both the Darcys' and the Königs' windows, yet so they could see when George returned.

Mary shifted her feet back and forth in the cold. Fanny picked up some cleaner-looking snow off a rail with her gloves and patted it into a ball. She set it on the ground and then started making another ball of snow.

"What are you doing?" asked Mary.

"Have you never played in the snow?"

"It does not snow very often, so no."

"All the more reason to play in it." Fanny made another ball of snow and threw it at Mary. It hit her chin, splattering cold, wet snow all over her face.

Mary wiped it off with her sleeve. "What was that for?"

"This is how you play in snow."

"That is terrible."

"You are no fun, Miss Bennet."

Mary crossed her arms. "That is people's general consensus." Being fun was overrated.

"You just need to relax a little, that's all." She squinted. "Oh, that's George. Come, pretend to walk." Together, they meandered down the path.

After a few minutes, the servant who must be George approached. He was a comfortable-looking man, with a neat beard. His face lit up when he saw Fanny, but then he deferentially nodded his head to Mary.

"George, fancy seeing you here. I was taking a walk with Miss Bennet."

"I am sure you runnin' into me was completely coincidental." He winked at Fanny.

"Certainly," said Fanny. "May I have a moment, Miss Bennet?"

"Of course," said Mary, and she turned partially away, as if to give them privacy, though she could still see them from the edge of her vision.

"You have snow in your hair," said Fanny, and she reached up and brushed George's hair, and then her hand brushed his cheek.

Mary pretended not to see such forward behaviour, though of course it was all an act. Gentry had stricter standards about physical interaction between men and women than other classes of society, but still, it was strange to watch. Mary could not imagine touching any man's face. Not Mr. Stanley, not Mr. Withrow—not any of the men she knew.

"Your cheeks look so cold," said Fanny. "They are bright red." As she pulled back, she bumped into his arm, causing him to drop his parcel of letters on the ground.

"I am so sorry," said Fanny. "This is all my fault. Please let me help you." Fanny managed to gather all of the letters without any of George's help. She gave George back the satchel and then slipped a letter into Mary's hand.

Mary promptly hid the letter under her cloak. "I will be back in a moment, Fanny. I forgot something inside. Please wait for me?"

"Of course," said Fanny, who immediately turned back to George. "I hope you will entertain me."

"It would be my pleasure," said George.

Mary walked deliberately back to the house, amazed at Fanny's execution of that manoeuvre. George had not noticed anything awry. Now it was Mary's turn to attempt the impossible.

Once inside, Mary did not remove any of her winter things, instead rushing straight upstairs and into her room. She barred her door with a chair and rushed to her desk.

The last name of Sharp was written on the outside. Unfortunately, Mr. Sharp had used a rather secure method of closing it, with both a seal and the edge sewn together with thread. Fortunately, he had not affixed the seal on top of the thread, or it might be impossible to open without leaving evidence. Mary had only minimal practise opening letters without detection, but her knowledge would need to suffice.

She slid the tip of a small knife against the thread then

sliced, sliced, sliced the pieces. She pulled out as much of the thread fragments as she could, her fingers trembling. She wished she could work faster, for she could not leave Fanny outside forever. Despite Fanny's skills, she would not be able to occupy George indefinitely.

Mary laid the knife on its side, placing it under the edge of the seal. She worked at it slowly, attempting to pry the seal off the bottom sheet without doing too much damage to it. Finally, she unlodged the entire lower side of the seal. She checked the top of the seal: it was undamaged. This was good, as she had no way to recreate Mr. Sharp's seal, and Mrs. König would certainly notice if it was missing or changed.

She pulled open the letter. As she did so, the paper ripped in two places, both spots where the thread had tied the letter closed. Mary sniffed. They were small rips, hopefully ones that Mrs. König would think she herself had made while opening the letter.

Mary turned to the words, which were written in a large, flowery hand.

*My dearest Selena,*

*Thank you for the dances yesterday evening, though I fear you forcing me to dance with you twice may raise suspicions. Are you not afraid that your husband will hear of it?*

*After more thought, I think I remember the messenger you mentioned, Mr. Rice. If I recall, he seemed an amiable chap, with grand aspirations. Unfortunately, I have not yet had time to learn anything of note, but I **will** attempt to find out who Mr. Rice delivered messages to, who he might have been in contact with before he died, and whether or not he had any family who might* *be open to you contacting them.*

*Meanwhile, you should look again at the notes, and see if anything gives a clue as to the identity of the writer—perhaps the murderer himself sent this to you to unnerve you. It is quite horrifying that Mr. Rice was strangled to death in such a gruesome manner. They should not have told you that.*

*I will put pressure on some of my fellow members of Parliament who have connections to the peacekeeping forces, in the hopes that we will bring this matter to light. I do wonder why this matters so much to you personally.*

*In the future, rather than writing letters through the post office, we should return to our previous, more secure method of communication.*

*At your service,*
*George Sharp*

Mary read the letter a second time, trying to fix the words in her mind. She did not have time to copy it, so she folded the letter quickly. If she were sealing her own letter, she would rotate a stick of wax over a flame until the wax began to melt, then she would drip the wax onto the letter and press down on it with a seal. But she did not have Mr. Sharp's seal, nor could she duplicate it, which meant she needed to reheat the wax which had been pressed by Mr. Sharp's seal. She needed to use enough heat that she could re-secure the seal to the rest of the letter, but not too much heat or she would damage the imprint.

She held the letter over the candle, positioning the bottom of the wax over the flame. Once she thought it sufficiently heated, she removed it from the flame and pressed around the seal with her fingers. Then she took a thread, almost the exact same colour as the original, and sewed the edges of the letter together again. She snipped the excess thread and smiled. The letter was not as securely affixed as freshly melted wax and a firmly pressed seal, but it was likely not noticeable, except—

Except for the fact that she had singed the paper with the flame.

There was a small brown spot near the seal. She wanted to curse, and the feeling surprised her, and left her ashamed.

When sealing a letter, one never held the paper near the flame, just the wax stick. There was never a reason that the paper could be singed in the process. Yet there was absolutely nothing she could do except pray that Mrs. König did not notice, or that she was too distracted by the contents of the letter to give it much heed.

Mary blew on the wax to cool it further, then slid the letter back into her cloak and hurried down the stairs. She had almost reached the front door when she was waylaid by her sister Elizabeth.

"Mr. Darcy told me that you were out with Fanny for a walk," said Elizabeth. "You never seemed to enjoy walking in Meryton."

"Lady Trafford taught me to appreciate it." She looked at the door. Elizabeth seemed prone to conversation, but Mary could not keep Fanny waiting. "Just one moment, I will be right back. I think I lost something outside."

Ignoring the surprised look on Elizabeth's face, she hurried out the door, shutting it firmly behind her. Instead of standing down the path, now Fanny and George stood just a few feet from the door.

"I apologise for taking so long," said Mary, aware of

George's inquisitive eyes on her.

"You never need to apologise to me." Fanny placed her hands in a reassuring manner on Mary's hands, and as she pulled them away, took the letter from her. "Thank you for your lively conversation George, I—" And then, Fanny was slipping on the ice.

George caught Fanny and helped her upright. "Thank you," said Fanny. She used her hands to smooth her skirt.

The letter was gone, and despite watching the entire time, Mary had not even seen the moment of transfer. Yet she must have gotten it back into George's satchel.

"You must be careful, Miss Fanny, I would not want to see you hurt."

"I would have been, if you had not moved with such speed."

"Thank you for your service to Fanny," said Mary. "I find myself indebted to you."

"I do what I can," he said. "Now I must return to Mrs. König, for she will be missing me." He nodded his head, first to Mary, then to Fanny.

Mary and Fanny walked down the street, away from George, until they looked back and saw that he had entered the König's residence. Then they turned back and entered the Darcy's home.

Inside, Elizabeth was waiting for them, an amused sort of smile on her face.

"Did you find what you were looking for?" asked Elizabeth.

"Oh? I mean, yes, yes I did."

Fanny helped Mary remove her gloves and cloak.

"Were you looking for Fanny?" asked Elizabeth.

"No," said Mary, and then more quickly, "No, I knew

right where Fanny was. It was my handkerchief."

Fanny left to put Mary's things away.

"I am glad you were able to find it in the snow," said Elizabeth. "Perhaps next time we can walk together. I do very much enjoy walking."

"Yes, Elizabeth, that would be very agreeable." She wished the conversation would be over, wished that her older sister would stop examining her with penetrating, perceptive eyes.

"Why do you always call me Elizabeth, never Lizzy? Everyone else calls me both."

Mary felt like one of her father's mounted butterflies, caught and pinned in place, only to be examined with a magnifying glass. "I do not know." She had not realised that she did that. "Perhaps, after further reflection, I will have an answer for you."

"No need to trouble yourself, Mary. It is not an important matter, simply something that occurred to me in passing."

They stood there in silence. With no way of knowing what Elizabeth was thinking, Mary felt more uncomfortable by the second.

Finally, Mary said, "I think I will read in my room."

"Very well," said Elizabeth. "I will join Georgiana in the drawing room. She is practising the pianoforte. If you would like to join us and read there, we would be delighted."

They went their separate ways.

Mary walked up the stairs at a deliberately normal pace. She had not realised how much work it would take to avoid the suspicion of family members.

In the room, Fanny was putting away the letter locking supplies, some where they belonged in Mary's desk, and the others in a secretive storage compartment which they had placed behind the bed frame. Mary went to work immediately, transcribing as much of Mr. Sharp's letter as she could remember, before the words fled from her mind like birds, startled from their perch in a tree. Then she went back and made corrections. When she was satisfied, she gave the transcription to Fanny.

"It is quite horrifying that Mr. Rice was strangled to death in such a gruesome manner," Fanny read aloud. "They should not have told you that." Fanny rubbed her hand across her forehead. "In the note I wrote to Mrs. König, informing her of the death, I did not tell her that Mr. Rice had been strangled."

Mary shook her head. "I see only three possibilities. One, as you conjectured previously, Mrs. König could be the murderer. Two, she has been in direct correspondence with the murderer. Three, she has been in correspondence with someone close to Mr. Booth, or a constable or peacekeeper."

"Or she could have found out from Mr. Rice's sister," said Fanny. "I wonder if she knows her. Another alternative is that she was an accomplice or bystander." She looked again at the transcription. "The phrasing is peculiar: they should not have told you that. It does not make it seem likely that she is the murderer. We also must consider why she would involve Mr. Sharp in this matter, and what she hopes to gain by it. If she is the murderer, she may hope that her current actions throw suspicion on someone else."

Mary looked again at the letter—her remembered copy of it, anyway. "I wrote 'note' here, but the original may have said 'notes.' I wish I had been able to copy it down properly."

"I think you did well," said Fanny.

"You as well."

"It was a good two-person operation."

They prepared a note for Mr. Booth. The entire first page was a diversion in case someone else opened the letter: Mary's supposed thoughts on an imaginary society for morals, which Mary pretended to be a part of.

Fanny left to send the letter, and Mary went down the stairs to join Elizabeth and Georgiana. She paused outside the drawing room, listening to their voices. They sounded happy, and completely comfortable with each other.

While Georgiana had treated Mary like a friend, it was her natural inclination to do so with everyone. Yet Georgiana and Elizabeth shared a much deeper friendship, a true connection, full of sisterly affection.

Mary's reflections were interrupted by hearing Elizabeth say her name.

"Do you think Mary has been behaving strangely lately? I mean, different than usual."

"She has been acting a little odd," said Georgiana. "At the ball, the way she watched people... It was as if she were looking for something, or someone."

Mary swallowed. Not only had she raised Mr. Darcy's and Hannah's suspicions, she had also raised Georgiana's and Elizabeth's. Fanny was right. They truly were besieged on all sides.

# CHAPTER SEVEN

*"WHY ARE WE AT WAR WITH FRANCE? This is a question which few people will be at the trouble of asking... We shall very soon, however, find, that a party existed in this country, who were enemies to the rights of the people."*

—*Cobbett's Weekly Political Register*, London, January 28, 1814

THE BUTLER USHERED them into Mr. Johnstone's stately house. After removing their many layers of coats and gloves, bonnets and hats, they were led into the drawing room, where they were greeted by Mr. Johnstone. The weather had again taken a sharp cold turn, and after the chill in the carriage Mary was grateful for the large fire.

"Thank you again for accepting my invitation," Johnstone said, opening his hands towards all of them. "It is a great pleasure to have you in my home."

"It was a great pleasure to make your acquaintance at the ball," said Georgiana eagerly. Mr. Darcy studied her, and Mary wondered if Darcy could tell how much Georgiana was interested in Johnstone.

"We were glad to make your acquaintance," said Elizabeth. "And grateful for your invitation." She nudged her husband.

"Thank you for allowing us to join you today," said Mr. Darcy, whose thoughts still appeared to be on Georgiana.

"This is my daughter, Miss Eliza Johnstone," Mr. Johnstone said, introducing her to each of them.

Miss Johnstone looked to be about Mary's own age.

"You are all exactly as my father described," said Miss Johnstone. "How perfectly charming!" She began a discussion with Georgiana. Mr. Johnstone asked Darcy and Elizabeth a question, and Kitty joined Georgiana and Miss Johnstone. Mary felt torn between the two conversations, but ultimately followed Kitty's lead.

"It must have been difficult," said Georgiana, "having no siblings to grow up with. My brother was always there for me, and it made such a difference in my life."

"My father always made certain I was surrounded by friends and family," said Miss Johnstone, "and I have a number of cousins."

"Will any of them be joining us tonight?" Mary asked, hoping that Lord Cochrane's attendance had indeed been secured.

There was, just then, a sound in the hallway. "I would not be surprised if one of my cousins just arrived," was the reply.

A moment later the butler opened the door and in walked a gentleman, holding up the hand of a woman who, if Mary was not mistaken, would be contributing to the world's population in a few months. She did not yet look ready for her lying-in, so it was not unusual for her to still be out in public. She had delicate features, an almost mischievous smile, and her eyes sparkled in the candlelight.

The man was tall, the sort of person who commanded attention. His hair was slightly curly and at first it looked a sandy colour, but as he stepped into the light it appeared more auburn. He had a distinctive nose and blue eyes.

Mr. Johnstone embraced the guest. "I see you have brought Kate," he said quietly, a slight question in his voice. He turned to the group. "This is my nephew, Lord Cochrane. And his wife, Mrs. Cochrane."

Mary noted that Johnstone did not call Lord Cochrane's wife Lady Cochrane. In every case she was aware of, when a woman married someone with a title, she gained a title as well. From her reading Mary knew Lord Cochrane to be thirty-eight years old, but his wife was likely not much older than Mary.

Johnstone introduced each of them in turn, and Lord Cochrane greeted them in a rich, lowland Scottish accent.

"I did not realise you were married," said Mary. Elizabeth gave her a harsh look, but Mary thought it was a warranted observation as nothing she had read on Lord Cochrane suggested that he was anything but a bachelor.

"We eloped to Scotland several years ago," said Lord Cochrane. "It is not exactly public knowledge."

That might explain why Johnstone did not call his nephew's wife Lady Cochrane.

Lord Cochrane's wife seemed to take no offence. She tipped her head to Mary and said, "Maybe someday *you* will meet someone, fall instantly in love, and elope with him."

Elizabeth covered her mouth with her hand and appeared to be stifling a laugh.

"I very much doubt that will ever happen to me." Mary had no interest in ever allowing her emotions to overpower her sense. Unlike her youngest sister Lydia, she was not a wild and impulsive sort of person, and she cared too much about her family and their expectations.

"Any news from Spain?" Mr. Johnstone asked his nephew

in what appeared to be an attempt to change the subject.

Lord Cochrane shook his head. "No news."

"Hopefully that is good."

"One never knows, with this war." Lord Cochrane turned to their party to explain. "My brother is an army officer, serving in Spain. I fear it is not a safe place at the moment." The war against Bonaparte had British troops spread across the entire continent. If you had a family member at war, any letter could contain the very worst news.

Another guest entered, a handsome man, with brown hair and a moustache, probably in his early thirties. To Mary, he looked like a Frenchman. He carried with him a roll of papers.

"And this," said Johnstone, "is my dear friend, the Baron de Berenger. Among his many other talents, de Berenger is a great architect. He is helping me with some plans, which he appears to have brought with him tonight."

Johnstone introduced de Berenger to each of them in turn. De Berenger, who did indeed have a French accent, interrupted Johnstone when he attempted to introduce him to Lord Cochrane.

"I believe we have already met," said de Berenger.

"I do not recollect meeting," said Lord Cochrane.

"It was briefly, a month or two ago. You asked if I might do a drawing for you."

"I do not remember," said Lord Cochrane, truly puzzled. "But it is a pleasure to make your acquaintance again."

A servant announced that dinner was ready, so they formed a procession and entered the dining room.

Lord Cochrane was seated only two persons away from Mary, so she thought she should address the subject that had provided her excuse for wanting to meet him.

"Lord Cochrane," said Mary, "I have read a great deal about your naval successes. While the reports include many details about your victories in terms of dates and enemy losses, they do not address how you consistently gained an advantage over your enemies when you often had inferior numbers and smaller ships. And so I must ask, what tactics did you employ?"

Lord Cochrane thought for a moment, no longer interested in his food. "In part, I was born with an inherent drive. I will push, I will attempt, I will fight, no matter the potential risk, no matter the potential cost." His words were surprisingly soft-spoken as he delivered this grand statement.

"But you implemented specific tactics as well," said Johnstone, "that the Navy would be wise to more broadly emulate."

"I suppose you are right, but some of them would not be as effective on a broader scale."

"What sorts of things?" asked Mary, genuinely interested.

"We would sail at night or attack early in the morning, before the enemy was prepared. Sometimes I would use false signals or put up fake flags."

"How would fake flags work?"

"Simple," said Lord Cochrane. "You raise the flag of your enemy's ally, or a neutral party. Once I spotted a Spanish brig with eight cannons, and a French ship with ten. I put up a Danish flag and pretended to escort a nearby group of Danish ships. I sailed close to the enemy ships and they hailed me, asking what I needed. Faster than you can say Bonaparte we pulled down the Danish flag, hoisted our own colours, and fired. We managed to capture both ships."

"That is incredible," said Kitty, speaking before Mary could.

"I have seen women perform similar tactics at a ball," said Elizabeth, drawing smiles and laughter. "It is quite effective."

"I can only imagine," said Mr. Johnstone.

"Oh, tell them about the *El Gamo*," said Mrs. Cochrane to her husband, with a sort of reverence.

*El* meant *the* in Spanish, which meant Mrs. Cochrane had repeated the word *the* twice in a row. Elizabeth gave Mary a look, and Mary stopped herself from correcting the woman's grammar.

"*El Gamo*," said Lord Cochrane quietly. "A grand warship it was, with thirty-two guns. They could have blown us to smithereens with only two or three broadsides."

He was silent, as if he was imagining the ship before him. Everyone waited in expectation, not wanting to interrupt his story.

"We were doomed. *El Gamo* had twice as many guns as the *Speedy*, and I knew in an instant theirs had better range. They had over three hundred men, compared to our meagre fifty. Most officers would have retreated in haste, and perhaps we should have. But I could not bring myself to do it. Instead, I kept my course.

"They hoisted their flags. As a matter of reply, I raised an American flag. They had been about to fire, but now, in their confusion, they did not. We sailed closer, positioning ourselves so that their first broadside could not harm us. Realising we were not Americans, they fired. It went above our heads. We raised our British flags with pride. I had instructed my men to raise the guns, pointing them up, towards *El Gamo*'s decks. We shot our cannons, and with our first broadside managed to kill the Spanish captain.

"We went back and forth, shooting at each other, trying to keep out of reach so they could not board and slaughter us with their superior numbers. But our sails were ruined, and I knew we could not last, so I yelled to my men, 'We must take the frigate, or we ourselves be taken!'

"We left only one man at the helm of the *Speedy*, and two boys. The rest of us, to the man, boarded *El Gamo* and fought for our lives. I looked up, saw the giant Spanish flag billowing above us, and knew we had no hope. So I said to one of my trusted men, 'Haul down the flag, if it's the last thing you do!'

"Somehow, he made it to their flag and took it down. The Spanish saw that the flag had been lowered and assumed that one of their officers had already surrendered. They put down their weapons and we took the ship."

There was silence and awe in the room as they took in the story. Johnstone, who had surely heard the story many times, was leaning towards his nephew with rapt attention. Even Darcy seemed captivated by the tale. Everyone seemed to have forgotten their food.

"What happened to the Spanish sailors?" asked Georgiana, breathless.

"We took them captive," said Lord Cochrane. "Two hundred sixty-three unwounded prisoners. Our victory, however, did not come without a cost. Three of my men were killed and eight wounded, several very seriously."

"There is always a cost for any victory," mused Johnstone.

"While this war is necessary," said Darcy, "it is unfortunate that the cost has been so high."

"If only the Admiralty would listen to you," said Johnstone to Lord Cochrane. "Your gas would save many lives."

"What does your gas do?" asked Darcy.

"By burning sulphur you can create clouds of sulphur dioxide," said Lord Cochrane. "This sulphur dioxide can have severe effects on the skin and the lungs, and with enough concentration can be lethal. I drew up plans for how this could be used as a weapon, but they are still being considered."

It seemed a gruesome, inhumane way to kill people. For a moment, Mary had been so enraptured by Lord Cochrane's heroic story that she had forgotten that he was a murder suspect. He was a murder suspect who had experience at killing—a great amount of experience, by all accounts, and while it was in defence of his country, what was to say he could not turn those skills to other ends?

"The Baron de Berenger has also put his mind towards new military inventions," said Mr. Johnstone.

Lord Cochrane turned to him with interest. "What have you developed?"

"A flame-throwing device," said de Berenger. "It is quite effective."

"It would bring me great pleasure if you would allow me to test one," said Lord Cochrane.

"The trouble with new weapons," said Mary, "is that they are of the greatest advantage when your side is the only one to possess them. But inevitably, the other side gains them as well and the advantage is lost."

"That is well spoken, Miss Bennet," said Lord Cochrane. "We inventors would do well to remember that."

"Do you have any non-military inventions?" asked Mr. Darcy.

"I am working on a few things, none of which are likely to be of interest to the ladies."

"Yet you claim to have enjoyed Wollstonecraft's writing on the equality of the sexes," said Miss Johnstone, in a tone that could be interpreted as either serious or teasing, perhaps both at the same time. "None of us are simple women. Tell us, cousin, what are you working on?"

He sipped his wine. "I have a strong interest in the mechanisms of light delivery. I have patented a number of improvements on the lamps used in towns and cities, to make them more efficient, more effective, and more specific to their purpose, whether that is more light or less light or light focused in a particular direction. At the moment I am developing prototypes for my convoy lamps."

"How do you develop prototypes?" asked Mary.

"I have partnered with a factory owner who helps execute the designs."

A factory owner. The conversation continued, but Mary could not give it heed. She suddenly remembered the large paper that she had found behind a stone in Mr. Rice's fireplace. It had been written by factory workers, protesting, in part, their working conditions. Could these men have been from the factory working on Lord Cochrane's convoy lamps?

She forced her mind back to the present conversation, which had shifted to a related technology.

"The Admiralty has a system of telegraphs," said Johnstone, "developed by Lord George Murray. There are towers with shutters raised above them. The position of the shutters corresponds to certain letters within a code book. The towers are placed within visual range of each other—sometimes up to twenty miles apart—and are used to send important messages. In one test, a message was sent from Dover to London in less than two minutes. For an express rider with a constant supply of new horses, the same message takes at least six hours of hard riding to deliver." He gave de Berenger a meaningful look, as if this were a significant point in their own, separate conversation that included only them. The moment passed and Johnstone turned to Mr. Darcy, in what appeared to be an attempt to engage him more deeply in the conversation. "Do you not agree that this is incredible?"

"Yes, very," said Mr. Darcy. He did not seem apt to forge friendships quickly, or partake fully in conversation with new acquaintances.

The conversation broke into smaller groups for the rest of the meal, and after dinner the women and the men retired to separate rooms.

Mary found herself at a loss for how to start a conversation with either Mrs. Cochrane or Miss Johnstone. Lady Trafford would approach this sort of task with zeal, but it was not so easy for Mary. After a minute of deliberation, she asked a servant to fetch the drawing supplies she had left in the carriage. She returned to the women, and found Mrs. Cochrane talking to Elizabeth.

"If you meet Lord Cochrane's uncle, Mr. Basil Cochrane, please do not tell him that Lord Cochrane and I are married."

Elizabeth's eyes went to Mrs. Cochrane's round belly. "Hiding a marriage does not seem a task that can be sustained for an extended period of time."

"You may be correct," said Mrs. Cochrane. "But we must try if we want to maintain good relations. I feel like every family has something they must hide from the world. Does not yours?" She gave Elizabeth a piercing look.

Elizabeth's eyes reached Mary's, and Mary knew they were both thinking about their sister Lydia running away with Mr. Wickham prior to their eventual marriage.

"Well, if we must hide things from the world," said Elizabeth, "then let us not out of fear, but out of the thrill and delight which naturally arises from a good intrigue."

"An excellent proposition," said Mrs. Cochrane.

"Mrs.—" Mary decided to start again. "Lady Cochrane,

may I draw a portrait of you? I have had several months of drawing lessons, but I believe further practice will give me greater proficiency."

"Of course," said Mrs. Cochrane. "It would be my pleasure."

She arched her eyebrows and turned to give Mary an angled view of her face, which was much more difficult for Mary than drawing from a direct, head-on view. However, she did not ask Mrs. Cochrane to change her position; Mary would accept the challenge.

Mary sketched Mrs. Cochrane. She was a beautiful woman; some might even say more beautiful than Mary's eldest sister Jane. After a minute, Mrs. Cochrane rested her hands on her rounded figure.

"Tell me about Lord Cochrane," said Mary.

Mrs. Cochrane agreed readily, describing him in an almost worshipful manner. She gave a detailed description of their meeting, their courtship, and their elopement.

"Is Lord Cochrane almost finished refitting his ship?"

"He hopes to be finished soon, but as for the day or the month, I do not know."

"When he sails, how long will he be gone from England?"

"They are headed to North America. It could easily be six months or a year."

"Do you miss him when he is gone?"

"Of course," said Mrs. Cochrane. "But it has always been this way for us. He is engaged in a noble work, and these great men must be given the space and the time to accomplish their tasks."

"I know that he is also a member of Parliament. What does he contribute?"

Mrs. Cochrane smiled, and Mary wasn't sure whether it

would be best to capture her face with or without a smile.

"I am not sure that I am articulate enough to explain." She turned to Miss Johnstone and called her to them. "Dear Eliza, Miss Bennet has a question about my husband's politics."

Miss Johnstone, Elizabeth, Georgiana, and Kitty joined their conversation.

"Could you please move your head back to the original angle?" Mary asked.

Mrs. Cochrane obliged.

"What did you want to learn about Lord Cochrane's politics?" asked Miss Johnstone.

"Anything, really," said Mary. "I heard that he was a Radical member of Parliament. What does that really entail?"

"For Lord Cochrane, it means standing on a platform of reform. He sees social injustices and does whatever he can to fix them. He is particularly interested in the treatment of the common man, whether it be a sailor or a labourer."

"I read a little about this in passing with my tutor," said Georgiana. "Is Lord Cochrane a Leveller?"

Miss Johnstone grimaced and shook her head. "He is most certainly not. Levellers want to eliminate social classes, eliminate wealth and capital. The idea is preposterous. Lord Cochrane simply wants to set things to right. For instance, sailors and their families often go months without pay, even when they are at sea. Or there are thousands of French prisoners of war being kept in horrid conditions. It takes people like Lord Cochrane to bring their causes to light."

"Your father is also a member of Parliament," Elizabeth observed.

"Yes, and also a Radical." She looked at Georgiana and added, "While the Whigs and the Tories have many merits, I believe it is my father's care for all of humanity that would not allow him to be anything other than a Radical."

Mary wondered that Mr. Johnstone had not been part of the Radical meeting the day of Mr. Rice's death. "Are there particular causes your father is forwarding?"

"Not at the moment, though he does all he can to help his fellow members of Parliament."

Perhaps Johnstone was less active in politics, or more inclined to follow than lead.

After a few more minutes, Mary finished her sketch of Mrs. Cochrane. It was not her best work, but it was adequate, and Mrs. Cochrane praised it and asked if she could keep it.

A few minutes later, the men joined them. Darcy walked in first, in conversation with de Berenger. As everyone greeted them, Mary stepped closer to the door. Lord Cochrane and Mr. Johnstone were still in the hallway. As they approached, she heard the final few lines of their conversation.

"I have instructed Mr. Butt to sell every time the price raises by one percent, and by that I have made quite a profit," said Lord Cochrane.

"But what if you could earn even more by—"

"I appreciate your concern about my fortune, Uncle, but you will find that it is not necessary."

"Ah, but my new plan will put you in a position where you would no longer have to worry about your enemies— present ones, or past ones who will not truly die."

"I am fine, Uncle," said Lord Cochrane.

Mary backed away from the door as Lord Cochrane and Johnstone entered the room. Past enemies who would not truly die. Could Johnstone be referring to Mr. Rice? Did Johnstone know something of Lord Cochrane's involvement, or had he been involved in some way himself?

Mrs. Cochrane rose to greet her husband.

"What do you have, Mouse?" Lord Cochrane asked her.

"Miss Bennet drew a picture of me. Isn't it lovely?"

"No art can ever fully depict your beauty."

As people broke into conversations, Mary started drawing again. She tried sketching Lord Cochrane, but he seemed larger than life, and she could not capture him on the page. Instead she drew de Berenger. Kitty spoke with him, but he did not seem interested in her conversation or her gregariousness, and after a minute, Kitty went to speak with Georgiana.

De Berenger began a conversation with Johnstone, and Mary started a new sketch of him. She liked de Berenger's face and his expressions.

As the two gentlemen finished their conversation, Johnstone looked in her direction, and then, to Mary's surprise, de Berenger approached her. Even in a small group, men did not normally go out of their way to seek her company.

"Miss Bennet," he said, bowing.

"Baron de Berenger," she said, trying to stand without dropping her drawing supplies.

"Do not concern yourself with standing," he said. "I noticed you were drawing me."

"Yes," said Mary, suddenly embarrassed, for she had not asked his permission.

"May I see?"

She showed him both pictures.

"Have you been taking drawing lessons?"

"Yes, from a Mr. Linton in Sussex. I still need much more practice."

"You are making good progress."

"Do you draw your architectural plans?" she asked, thinking of the rolls of paper de Berenger had brought with him.

"Yes, let me show you." He called a servant and asked him to bring the rolls from the other room.

While they waited, Mary asked, "*Pouvons-nous parler en français?*"

"*Ah! Vous parlez français?*" He sounded surprised.

"*Oui, j'ai suivi des cours de français.*"

He agreed to practice French with her. They spoke briefly about the weather, and Mary thought if Lady Trafford were here, she would say he was bored with the conversation. From the corner of her eye, she noticed Kitty watching them, with a hungry sort of expression.

De Berenger's eyes lit up when the servant returned with the roll. He let Mary open it, and as she did so, she could not prevent an overwhelming feeling of wonder. What de Berenger had created was an architectural rendering for an outdoor pavilion, but it was not just directions for builders, with sizes and angles, it was also art, with detailed renderings of the statuary and structure of an outdoor pavilion.

"Did you draw this out of your own mind, without anything in front of you to look at?"

"Yes," he said.

She felt suddenly embarrassed at having shown him the picture of him, embarrassed at having drawn it at all. De Berenger was as good as Mr. Linton, perhaps even better.

"Do you create plans for many people?"

"Whenever I find the opportunity. I once drew a set of plans for the Prince Regent."

Mary shifted the paper and examined the page beneath it, and the one beneath that. The final page was unlike the others: it was a small, but beautifully designed, country home.

"What is this?" she asked.

"It is something I would like to build for myself."

"Where will you build it?"

He shrugged. "It is a wishful project. I do not have nearly the funds it would require, but I can dream."

"Without aspirations and dreams, civilisation would see very little progress." It was one of Mary's better sentence constructions, almost profound; she would need to write it down later.

Mary had never met someone like de Berenger before, an artist-dreamer. She looked around the room. Johnstone was intelligent but did not seem to be a dreamer. He and Georgiana were having a private conversation, and Georgiana laughed at something he said. Lord Cochrane seemed a bit of a dreamer. He sat next to his wife, holding her hand, a tender expression on his face.

De Berenger must have noticed her watching the Cochranes, for he said, "What do you think of Lord Cochrane?"

"He is not quite what I expected," observed Mary.

"I have only met him once before tonight, and it was very brief, so I do not know him well. I have heard that when he is angry, he becomes a lion." De Berenger paused. "It is said that Bonaparte calls him *Le Loup des Mers*—the Sea Wolf."

A lion or a wolf seemed not at all like the man before her, yet as she considered the intensity in Lord Cochrane's voice when he had described his military exploits, she could believe it.

De Berenger excused himself and Mary watched the room for a few minutes, not drawing, simply observing. After a while, Kitty came and sat with her. She took Mary's pad of paper and flipped through the pages.

"You are very accomplished," said Kitty.

Mary sighed. "I hope to someday be *truly* accomplished at

drawing. But I have improved a great amount over the past months, and I take great pleasure in it."

"I wish I had *any* accomplishments. You can play the pianoforte and sing and draw and speak French. And you have read so many important books that you have interesting things to say to distinguished men."

"You are very good at dancing," said Mary. "That is a fine accomplishment."

"So is every other young woman in the country." Kitty leaned back against the sofa, and her eyes wandered along the designs on the wallpaper. "I was always happy, growing up, that our parents let me and Lydia follow any trivial pursuit that came into our heads. Yet now I find that I am thoroughly unprepared for the rest of life. I have no skills that can be of use, or that can give others pleasure, or bring pleasure to myself."

"You are eighteen years old, Kitty. Your life is not yet fixed. *You* are not fixed in a particular position. I do agree that our parents ought to have done more to direct our learning and development, but you do not need to allow this to wall off your possibilities. I had no drawing ability six months ago, and while I could read French, I could not speak a single word."

Kitty looked at her hands.

"Georgiana has tutors; join her for her lessons. Or choose something you want to learn, and if one of us has skills, we will teach you, or if we do not, Elizabeth and Mr. Darcy are surely in a position to find you a tutor."

"I do not even know what I would want to learn," said Kitty quietly.

"Then try things until you find out," said Mary.

Mary had always felt out of place in her family, always felt like she had been the disadvantaged one, the one who had been left out and ignored. She had never before considered that any of her sisters might also feel familial neglect.

"I have always admired your ease with people," said Mary. "You understand people, you know how to talk to them, you are energetic and good-humoured. I know that people have called you silly, but I think you have an intelligent mind. I know you can succeed at whatever you set yourself to."

Kitty sniffled.

Mary was not one for making physical gestures of affection, comfort, or intimacy, so she hesitated for a moment, but then she reached out her hand and set it on top of Kitty's.

They sat there in companionable silence for several minutes, and then Kitty turned to face her. "Thank you, Mary."

"You are welcome, Kitty."

"I think I will take a turn about the room, and maybe get a drink. Would you like anything?"

"No, thank you."

Mary suspected that their evening engagement would not last much longer, so she thought she had better take advantage of the opportunity for a little more conversation with Lord Cochrane. Lord Cochrane's connection to a factory was suspicious, but Sir Francis had written the threatening note to Mr. Rice. She wanted to know Lord Cochrane's perspective on his friend. Leaving her drawing supplies on the chair, she approached Lord Cochrane.

"Lord Cochrane, I apologise for my intrusion, but I hope I can speak to you."

"Of course," he said.

She sat down next to Lord Cochrane and his wife.

"What would you like to speak about?"

"I met your friend Sir Francis Burdett at a ball. He was amiable and passionate about his views, but some reports of him leave me very much confused. I read that prior to his imprisonment in the Tower of London, he incited mobs, resisted arrest, and sought to rally the people against the government."

"Burdett had no interest in causing any disruption. I was much more hot-headed than he. Did you read how the entire affair started?"

"The book did not say."

"You have heard of the Walcheren Campaign?"

"No."

Lord Cochrane sighed. "It was an attempt to gain an advantage over Bonaparte but was poorly conceived and poorly managed. Large sums were spent with no real gain, and we lost 4000 men to the fever.

"A committee in the House of Commons was appointed to investigate the debacle, but they decided to exclude the public from all hearings and meetings, simply so the government could hide its own errors. Yet the people need knowledge of Parliament's doings, for they must be able to hold Parliament accountable for its actions. John Gale Jones protested against this infringement of democracy by making the knowledge public. He was then thrown into prison without trial.

"This, of course, was denying habeas corpus to Jones. Sir Francis would not have that, and he spoke against the action in front of Parliament, angering many. When his words were not heeded, he asked our friend, Cobbett, to publish them, which he did.

"This led, then, to an order for Burdett to be arrested.

"The people were angry and formed mobs, completely on

their own. We did not ask them to do this—we did not desire the destruction they caused—but they were outraged, and justifiably so.

"Burdett, meanwhile, was hiding in his house. He could not leave, for he would be arrested, and we were afraid of a siege or an attack in the night. I wanted to protect him, and I thought the best way to do so would be to get him out of the house."

Cochrane's wife leaned into him, captivated by his story.

"I brought a cask of gunpowder. I thought we might blast a hole in the wall and help Burdett escape." He chuckled. "The things I would do for a friend. But Burdett would not let me use the dynamite. He insisted that he had no desire to resist arrest.

"The next day a sergeant broke into the house, arrested Burdett, and carted him off to the Tower. He was forced to remain there until Parliament was dissolved.

"Many of us thought that Burdett's release would be a great moment. We would have gathered crowds; there would have had been cheering in the streets and people flooding to our cause. But Burdett did not want that, he did not want any risk of riot. He left the Tower by boat to avoid anyone seeing him."

This was not the account that the book had given at all, and Mary disparaged herself for consulting only one source on the matter and accepting it as truth. Lady Trafford had tried to teach her not to do that. Not that she would accept Lord Cochrane's account, either—he seemed, for instance, a little too insistent that he had done nothing to incite the mobs.

Regardless of the truth surrounding the matter, Lord Cochrane's account did give her more insight into Sir Francis, and into his own character. It was clear from Lord Cochrane's heroic military service and his words that he was very patriotic and would willingly give his life for his country. Yet he also seemed willing to take radical actions if he deemed them best for democracy and his country, even if those actions could lead to mobs and revolution, even if those actions could tear the country apart.

# CHAPTER EIGHT

*"During the whole of the afternoon of yesterday hundreds of people were assembled on Blackfriars and London Bridges, to see several adventurous men cross and recross the Thames on the ice."*

—*The Sun*, London, February 1, 1814

MARY WAS TORN between the hope that none of her family would want to spend time with her, which would make spying on Mrs. König easier, and the hope that they valued her company. Elizabeth had chosen to accompany Mary on her walk through the park this morning as Mary trailed Mrs. König, yet this was somewhat inevitable, given how much Elizabeth loved walking. Despite the complications of Elizabeth's presence and the frigid air—it was surely the coldest Mary had ever been in her life—the walk had been fruitful. After Mary had begun a conversation with Mrs. König, a boy had handed Mrs. König a ring that had supposedly fallen off her hand. As she was wearing gloves, this seemed an impossibility; Mary thought it must be some sort of message.

Unfortunately, Mrs. König had then returned to her house, with Mary none the wiser as to what the ring meant, so Mary announced that she wanted to call upon Henrietta and her mother, since Henrietta had not been at the park and they had been unable to converse. Elizabeth once again decided to join her, but so did Georgiana and Kitty. Of course, their joining likely reflected more on Henrietta's popularity than Mary's own.

"You have become quite socially active," observed Elizabeth.

"It is not a burden to fulfil my duties to society," said Mary, "and I think Henrietta is benefited by our positive influence and examples."

Mary hoped that this explanation satisfied. She had unintentionally raised Elizabeth's suspicions at the ball, and she did not want to do so again. If Elizabeth noticed changes in Mary's character or approach to life it could raise questions. However, over the past months, Mary *had* changed in some ways as a person, hopefully for the better, and she could not entirely go back to who she had been. Nor did she want to.

Henrietta was positively delighted at their presence, but Mrs. König did not seem as pleased.

"To see you twice in one morning is quite the unexpected pleasure," said Mrs. König, almost sardonically. Her hands were behind her back, and Mary could not see if she still wore the ring she had been given at the park.

Mary searched for some sort of comment to allay Mrs. König's suspicions, but before she could say anything, Elizabeth spoke.

"Too often one's neighbours receive fewer calls than those friends who live farther away. It would be a pity if we neglected those closest to us." Elizabeth paused. "Besides, surely we cannot be the worst guests you have received."

Mrs. König softened. "Surely not."

From Elizabeth, the comment sounded clever and perceptive, and it achieved the desired effect. Yet when Mary made the same sorts of overarching comments, which attempted to point her listeners to greater meaning, they fell flat, and her listeners often brushed them aside. Perhaps it was Elizabeth's delivery that made it so effective, or the fact that she added a joke at the end, yet it felt a little unfair.

As they entered the drawing room, Mary glimpsed Mrs. König's hands. She wore three or four rings on her fingers, but Mary could not see them in enough detail to ascertain if any of them were the ring from the park. Mary tried to sit close to Mrs. König, in the hopes of spotting the large, dark ring.

"Please, would one of you play?" asked Mrs. König. "I need something diverting." Mrs. König looked pointedly at Elizabeth, who agreed to play.

Elizabeth turned to Mary. "Would you mind if I played a piece from your book of Irish melodies?"

"Of course not," said Mary. "Go ahead." She had left the book of Irish melodies on the Darcys' pianoforte, which meant anyone was welcome to play it.

Apparently, Elizabeth already had one of the easier pieces memorised, a lilting melody. Kitty leaned in, intent on the music, and Mrs. König seemed to relax. Elizabeth had an agreeable expression on her face, and her body shifted a little with the music. She made several technical errors that Mary had never made while playing this particular song, and yet somehow, this did not detract from the performance.

It had always troubled Mary that people complained, at times, when she played the pianoforte, yet they never did for Elizabeth. Was it possible that Mary could be better than Elizabeth on a technical level, and yet somehow worse overall?

Mary turned away from the instrument, looking towards the window. In some ways, Elizabeth and Mary were very similar—they both loved to read, they both played the pianoforte, they both sought to understand the world and make it better, and they both tried to contribute clever, wise statements to group conversations. Yet their similarities were what made them so very different: their similarities created contrast between them, and not just contrast, but a great, impassable gulf.

Elizabeth was who Mary had always wanted to be. And yet, Mary would never measure up to Elizabeth.

Mary's back and neck felt tight, her jaw tense. She had not yet managed to memorise a single song from the book of Irish melodies.

She looked back at Elizabeth, who still played intently. She had always admired Elizabeth, but Elizabeth rarely deigned to notice her. Of course, it was not just Elizabeth who had never really noticed or understood Mary—none of her sisters did.

Elizabeth looked up from the keys, saw Mary, and smiled.

The smile took her by surprise, as did the smile she gave in return. Suddenly, the words of the Greek playwright Menander came to mind: "The envious man is an enemy to himself, for his mind is always spontaneously occupied with its own unhappy thoughts."

Mary could admire Elizabeth. She could aspire to some of Elizabeth's attributes, and she could use her knowledge of how Elizabeth acted in particular situations to help her take the best possible actions as a spy. But she would not let herself be consumed by envy. She could set it aside, and not let it be a focus of her attention. It was better to become one's fullest self than to attempt to become someone else.

A weight seemed to lift from Mary's shoulder, an old, familiar weight, that she had carried for many years. When she breathed in, she felt freer, lighter than before.

Elizabeth finished the song, and then gestured to the pianoforte, inviting someone else to take their turn.

Henrietta nervously approached, and Mrs. König encouraged her, helping her arrange the music. As she did so, Mary was finally able to see Mrs. König's hands in detail. She wore four rings, but none of them appeared to be the ring she had been given in the park.

The ring was no longer on her hand.

Mary wished Fanny was here—she would know precisely what to do—but it was Fanny's day off. She was visiting her family and investigating another lead assigned to her by Mr. Booth.

Cold air seemed to be coming in through the shut window, and Mary rubbed her arms. The fire was insufficient for a day as cold as this. She tried to think of where she herself would place a ring. She looked at the ring on her own finger, the mourning ring she wore in remembrance of her father. The only place she removed it was in her room.

Once Henrietta finished her song, Mary clapped vigorously. Then as Georgiana stepped to the pianoforte to play, Mary excused herself to use the washing room.

"I can find my own way there," she informed a servant who attempted to assist her. Mary headed towards the washing room, then looked around to make sure no one watched. The Königs ran a haphazard household, but Mary still needed to be careful.

She found what appeared to be Mrs. König's room and looked everywhere for the ring—drawers, the clothes press, next to the mirror. She began to fear that Mrs König had not placed the ring in her room. There were numerous other places in the house she could keep it, if she had kept it at all.

She frantically searched the rest of the room, sure she would be discovered at any moment.

In one of the last drawers, Mary found a black, velvet-covered case. It was unlocked. She opened it and discovered a mourning rings graveyard.

There were over three dozen mourning rings in the case. Many of the rings were small and simple—those generally would represent the deaths of friends and more distant family members. But at least a dozen were large or ornate. How many people, who must be very close to her, had Mrs. König lost?

One of the rings was not made of metal, but of hair. The colour matched Mrs. König's. Many women saved their hair and used it as thread for embroidery or for other handiworks, but Mary had never seen a ring made entirely of hair. Perhaps it was made in memory of someone who Mrs. König would not receive an official mourning ring for, but wanted to remember.

There were three rings that looked similar to the one she had seen in the park. Swallowing her guilt at interfering with Mrs. König's commemoration of the dead, Mary removed each of the three from the case and examined them. There was nothing remarkable about them, no reason a boy would hand her one of these rings in a snowy park.

Mary thought she heard a sound and her eyes darted to the door. There was no manner in which she could quickly hide the evidence of her actions. She waited, expecting someone to open the door, but no one did.

After a moment, she returned to the rings, puzzling over them. She almost decided to put them back in the case when she thought, again, of the mourning ring for her father. Its bezel could rotate, depending on which side she wanted to face out: the side that had a painting of a broken column and a willow tree, or the side that included a lock of her father's hair.

She examined the bezels of the three mourning rings and discovered that one had a tiny latch. Her fingers trembled, which made it difficult to open, but she finally succeeded. Inside was a small piece of paper with a few words written on it.

*11:00 a.m. tomorrow. The fair near London Bridge. Do not be late.*

Fairs were mostly saved for the warmer months and were normally more for the entertainment of the lower classes. She wondered what fair would be happening in London this week.

She placed the note in the ring, the ring in the velvet case, the case in the drawer, and then hurried out of the room.

In the hall, she collided with Kitty.

Once they had both ascertained that they had done no permanent damage to each other, Kitty said, "I was looking for you."

Mary swallowed, then said the first excuse that came to mind. "I got turned about after using the washing room."

"You have no idea how many times I have done that," said Kitty, smiling. She proceeded to tell a story about how she got turned about at a private ball, and somehow ended up in a nursery of screaming children.

Mary smiled and nodded, grateful that Kitty did not notice anything amiss, and they returned to the parlour. Unfortunately, as soon as Mary sat, she realised that she actually did need to use the washing room. However, she had just returned from what was supposedly a very long trip to the washing room, so she had better wait until they returned home. She crossed her legs, willing the conversation to be quick and her control over herself to be strong.

"Are you unwell, Miss Bennet?" asked Henrietta.

"No, I am quite well," said Mary. "I just felt a slight draft in the room."

MARY STOOD ON the bank near the Thames River, trying not to slip on the ice, as she waited and watched for Mrs. König. She and Fanny had left the house together, with the excuse that they were working on a charity project, but Fanny was shadowing Sir Francis for Mr. Booth. Now Mary was on her own, feeling a little more nervous about following Mrs. König than she had been yesterday. Of course, yesterday had been at a small, safe park next to the Darcys' home, and today was in a crowd in the middle of London. Mr. Booth had offered to send someone else—it could be problematic if she were seen, alone at a fair, by someone who recognised her—but Mary had wanted to go. She still felt that she needed to prove herself.

The Thames was completely frozen over, and out on the ice, ice that had been a flowing river the last time she had seen it, were hundreds and hundreds of people, holding a fair.

Mary spotted a hooded woman exiting a carriage and pulled her own hood tighter around her face. As the woman paid the carriage driver, Mary glimpsed her face. It was Mrs. König.

Mrs. König proceeded to walk down a path—well-packed in the snow—towards the river. Mary followed, almost slipping at one point but catching herself. She maintained some distance from Mrs. König, keeping her within view, and simultaneously taking in the impromptu festival. They were between Blackfriars Bridge and London Bridge, with its grand old fragile arches. When she looked behind her, she could see the dome of St. Paul's Cathedral.

She tread carefully on the ice and paid a few small coins for entrance to the fair. People called out to her, selling knickknacks and scarves and piping hot tea. There were children running and playing, and women dressed in gaudy, cheap fabric, not well-covered for the cold, and with their faces painted in bright, unseemly colours. These women did not call out to Mary or Mrs. König, but they kept trying to strike up conversation with the men. A few convinced men to follow them into some very dingy tents.

Who was Mrs. König trying to meet? What was her purpose in coming here? There were others in finely dressed clothing on the ice, so Mrs. König did not stand out. But why come in secret, without her servants' knowledge, and without bringing Henrietta? Surely the girl would enjoy this sort of spectacle.

Mrs. König paused to examine some scarves, and so Mary paused as well to avoid catching up with her.

"Roasted bull! Get your roasted bull!" a man called out. And indeed, on the ice, a man and a woman were roasting an entire bull. Their children were adding more sticks to the fire. It seemed rather hazardous to light a fire on ice, but no one seemed concerned by it, and the river must be frozen thick enough that it did not melt the ice significantly. The aroma of the roasted meat cut through the air, heavenly, warm, and rich.

"How much, for a very small piece?" Mary asked.

"Four pence."

Mary fished the coins out of her pocket and passed them to a man.

"Thank you, m'lady." He cut off a piece of meat that was much larger than Mary had expected, wrapped it partially in a piece of brown paper, and passed it to Mary. "Me family 'as been roasting meat on the ice for centuries."

Mary glanced towards Mrs. König. She was still examining the scarves. "The Thames cannot possibly freeze over very often."

"True, but when it does, this 'ere is our spot." He pointed at one of the lads. "I was me son's age last time it 'appened."

"And what do you do during the years when you are not roasting meat on the river?"

"I'm a sailor, I am. That there, is me boat."

The boat in question appeared to be frozen into place.

Mary took a bite of the meat. It was almost hot enough to burn her tongue, and the flavour seemed to fill not just her mouth, but her entire body.

"*Mmmm*," she said. "It is very good."

"You wants some more?"

"Thank you, but this is plenty."

Mrs. König had moved on, so she followed.

A group of musicians had started up and people danced a sort of peasants' dance. Mary walked around them, not heeding calls for her to join the dance. So far her neighbour had not done anything that merited secrecy. As Mary walked past the scarf vendor, she gave the woman a look, but she seemed to be just a normal woman, with nothing particular about her.

Mrs. König stopped again at another vendor, so Mary stopped as well. The people next to her had managed to get an entire printing press out here on the Thames. A boy wearing fingerless gloves used leather balls to ink the metal text, and then a man pulled the wood frame with the paper down on top of it, then raised it. Another boy pulled out the newly printed sheet of paper and hung it on a rope to dry while the others repeated the process.

Mary ate her last bite of meat and leaned in to look at the hanging paper. It had dozens of copies of the same image and text which needed to be cut out. Each one included an etching of the tents on the frozen Thames with a view of London in the background. The view was not quite accurate, as the buildings were rather compressed together, but it was an adequate design. In a florid font, the words read, "This View of London Printed on the Ice of the River Thames. February 5, 1814."

"Three pence for your own special souvenir to remember this day of your life forever," said a well-dressed man. "And for an extra two pence, we'll print your name, 'ere in this spot, to prove to everyone that you yourself were 'ere."

"If I paid you for it, would you be willing to print someone else's name on it?"

"Of course."

"Then it does not actually prove that I was here, only that someone asked for a name to be printed."

"I suppose you're right, miss, but you can only get these souvenirs 'ere, on the ice, for as many days as the river stays frozen."

Ahead, Mrs. König appeared to be pacing back and forth across the ice to stay warm. Mary removed her watch from her pocket. It was past eleven, and whoever was supposed to be meeting Mrs. König was late.

"I suppose I will purchase a souvenir," said Mary. It was a completely unnecessary, superfluous expense, but she found herself wanting one. At least she could justify it—if Mrs. König looked in her direction, all she would see was another person visiting the frost fair and partaking in frivolities.

"What name would you like on it, miss?"

"No name, just the flier." She passed him the coins and he gave her the paper, which she slipped into her cloak pocket.

She walked on, closing a bit of the distance between her and Mrs. König. Many of the vendors were selling alcohol, and the yeasty smell of beer filled the air. She was continuously offered it, and continuously turned it down. Another vendor offered "sugar candy," which appeared to be brandy. The crowds had already become quite unruly for this early in the day—she would hate to be here for the festival in the evening.

A girl darted out from between two tents, directly in front of Mary. She looked perhaps thirteen or fourteen. Her clothes looked like those of a maid—high-quality, but not originally made for her—and she had a smudge of dirt on her cheek.

She knelt in front of a man also attending the ice fair and pled, "Help me!" but he pushed her aside.

Mary reached her hand out, as if by instinct. "I can help you." Offering charity to those in distress was an essential part of being a good Christian woman.

"Thank you! Thank you!" The girl stood and clung to Mary's arm. She had brownish-blond hair and fierce eyes.

"What do you need help with?"

Before the girl could respond, a man with a gaunt face and even gaunter clothes sprung out from between the two tents. The man was a bit taller than Mary and looked to be about her own age, or perhaps five or ten years older. Mary had no doubt in her mind that he was after the girl, so she pulled her close and stood tall, though her heart raced with fear.

The man lunged at both women, attempting to grab the girl from Mary.

Mary tightened her grip on the girl and raised her voice loudly so those around could hear, and spoke with authority and indignation, as Lady Trafford would. "Do you dare touch me, a lady? This young woman is under my protection, and it would serve you well to be on your way. Immediately."

The man paused for a moment, and several of the vendors approached. They were burly men, probably sailors like the man who had sold her the roasted bull.

"Unhand me, right now," declared Mary.

"You 'eard the lady. Be off with you!" one of the men said, threatening the attacker with his fist.

The attacker's eyes darted to all the big men and he stepped back, letting go of Mary and the girl. He scowled at them and then ran off.

"Thank you for your assistance," Mary said to the men, as prim as she could, and then she curtsied as best as she could with a girl clinging to her side. Then she thought of what Lady Trafford might do and turned to the man who had spoken for her.

"And what might you be selling today?"

"Bowlas."

They appeared to be sugared apples, wrapped in bread to form a sort of tart. "I will take three."

The price was a bit higher than she had expected, but he had helped her, so she paid without complaint.

She gave two of the tarts to the girl, keeping one for herself.

"Eat," said Mary. "This will help you feel better." She did

not know if it actually would, but it felt like the right thing to say, and the girl followed her directions.

Mary tugged the girl's arm. "Now come with me." She could no longer see Mrs. König, and needed to find her. "What is your name?"

"Minerva Randall."

"Do you know that man, who was chasing you?"

"A little. Fred's upset with the colonel, but Fredzie doesn't even know him."

Minerva's story did not make any sense. "Who is the colonel?"

"I don't have parents. The colonel and his sister took me in."

"And who is Fred?"

"The man who was chasing me."

"I see." Mary took a bite of her own tart—it was very good—and tugged on the girl a bit to change directions. They had reached the end of this path, and she needed to find Mrs. König. She did not regret helping the girl, but she could not lose sight of the reason she was here.

"Has Fred chased you before?"

"No, but he has cornered me. A couple of times."

"Have you mentioned him to the colonel and his sister?"

The girl shook her head.

"I think you should. You should go straight back to them and tell them all about it."

"I suppose you're right."

"Do you need help getting home?"

"No. I live just on the other side of London Bridge." She pointed at an ornate white building with multiple levels and tall windows. "At the Custom House. We're the caretakers."

That was a relief. She could not possibly help the girl

home now. What if Mrs. König had already left, and Mary never found out why she had come to the frost fair today?

"Thank you again for your help, ma'am. What's your name?"

She considered giving a false name, but she wanted the girl to be able to contact her if she needed help again. "Miss Mary Bennet." She gave the Darcys' name and address.

"Thank you, Miss Bennet."

"Be safe, Miss Randall."

The girl scampered off, and Mary could not help but watch her. An orphan with no parents. At least she had a family who had taken her in, people who cared for her.

Mary forced her attention back to the frost fair. There was nothing more she could do for the girl now.

She walked up and down the paths of the ice fair, hardly paying attention to the stalls, simply trying to catch sight of Mrs. König and her green cloak. If she had ignored the girl's pleas, she would not have lost her neighbour. But she had not ignored them, for doing so would have been unacceptable.

Out of breath, Mary rounded another corner. She slipped and landed on the ice, flat on her back. Several people offered her help, but she waved them off and got to her feet. Her body ached and she had ice and snow fragments all over her cloak; snow had gotten up her skirts and somehow, down her back. She sniffed. At least she had not suffered any major injury.

She blinked her eyes. There was an elephant in the distance. Maybe she had hit her head when she fell. But numerous people were pointing at it and shouting in awe, so it must be real. Someone was leading an elephant—an elephant—across the frozen Thames. It was close to Blackfriars Bridge, and everyone turned towards it, but Mary did not have time for elephants, even though she had only seen pictures of them in books.

She glimpsed someone whose face she recognised. She had a memory for faces, but still, it took her a moment to place him as a man from the ball. She did not know him and could not remember who he had spoken to or danced with at the ball. He had curly hair, but honestly, there had been a number of men with curly hair. He stood, talking to the man with the gaunt face who had just attacked the girl, Minerva Randall. Several coins passed from the man's hand to the attacker's. He must be acting the part of a beggar now, pleading for assistance, pretending to be good and innocent and oppressed in spirits and means.

Finally, Mary saw the edge of Mrs. König's green cloak and headed in that direction only to find the confounded woman with none other than the Tory, Mr. George Sharp. As Mary discreetly approached, Mr. Sharp wrapped his arm around Mrs. König's waist. In full view of everyone at the fair, with no thought even to hide her sins from the world, Mrs. König kissed Mr. Sharp on the neck, and then the chin, and then the lips. Mr. Sharp pulled Mrs. König into a tent.

Mary stood frozen in indecision, but after a minute willed herself forward. She leaned close to the tent, listening. The tent walls were thin, and she could make out the noises from within with clarity. Mrs. König and Mr. Sharp were certainly not speaking of Mr. Rice's death; the sounds they were making led Mary's ears to feel so unclean that when she returned to the Darcys', she would need to scrub them with soap and water. She turned away, her cheeks chapped with cold. Clearly this was a romantic liaison, nothing more. She was ready to return home, but before she left, she might as well examine the elephant.

# CHAPTER NINE

*"All the accounts agree, that BONAPARTE has completely failed in his endeavours to raise the people in a mass against their invaders."*

—*The Times*, London, February 9, 1814

MARY SAT UPRIGHT in her bed, sorting the correspondence she had received—some of which she had to keep hidden in the space behind the bed, lest someone in the household find it. She reread the most recent letter from Mr. Booth, which had been disguised as a letter from a woman leading various charitable efforts.

Mr. Booth had discovered the factory that created prototypes for Lord Cochrane: Mr. King's Manufactory. He and Mr. Stanley had investigated, and both agreed that it had the best working conditions of any factory they had ever visited—higher pay, shorter hours, and proper light and ventilation. They had concluded that these factory workers must not have been those who had written the manifesto with Mr. Rice's help. It was a shame, for the lead had seemed so promising.

She turned to the two letters from Sir Francis Burdett.

Sir Francis had a fine hand, and his capital letters S and B had a distinctive swoop. His first letter had detailed what he saw as necessary reforms; he had even sent a copy—unbound—of one of his books. Normally it was not considered appropriate for an unmarried woman to correspond with a man, but it was acceptable for a scholarly purpose, and she had Mr. Darcy's tacit permission. Mary had written a letter in reply, thanking Sir Francis and asking additional questions, but his second letter had been short, and while not terse or negative in tone, had made it clear that he did not have the time or the interest to engage in a lengthy correspondence.

Fanny made an unladylike noise, some sort of frustrated snort. She was working on her own notes as she sat at Mary's desk.

"Whatever is wrong?" asked Mary.

Fanny turned the chair around to face Mary. She had bags under her eyes, apparently from sewing in the middle of the night by candlelight, as she had no other time to work on her own projects.

"I cannot help but feel that we have accomplished nothing. We have been investigating for two weeks and we have *nothing* to show for our time."

Mary did not think it was *that* bad. They had learned things about all of their suspects, and while they had not made profound discoveries during the week since the ice fair, the progress they had made should not be discounted.

"I think you would feel better if you slept."

"No time for that. What's that letter?" she asked, pointing. "The one with the cheap paper."

Mary picked up the letter. "It is not relevant to the case."

"Anything can be relevant," said Fanny, waiting, but Mary did not give her the letter, and after a long moment, Fanny turned back to her work.

Mary also turned away, to face the other wall. She opened the letter in question. She had not wanted Fanny to see it, in part because it was *not* relevant to the case, and also because she felt ashamed that she still had not responded to it. She had much more discretionary time than Fanny—Mary had been making good progress on the Irish melodies Mr. Stanley had given her—yet she always found herself too busy to respond to this particular letter. She had placed it and the printed souvenir with the secret letters simply because they revealed that she had been to the ice fair. She looked again at the words, penned by the girl she had assisted at the fair.

*Dear Miss Bennet,*

*Thank you for helping me ~~Wedneas~~ the other day at the fair. I did not thank you well then. But I want to thank you now. I was truly afeard that Fred would hurt me. He has hurt me before.*

*There are so many things that I don't know what to do about. You said I could write for help, and maybe you can help me.*

*I think the mistress loves me. Miss Kelly must love me or she would~~n~~ not have taken me in. But then why is she so hard on me? It is always work, work, work, when she's around. Sometimes I feel like a servant. But I don't know what else I could ever be. I am not pretty enough or smart enough or refined enough to do something better, and Miss Kelly always says I will never be able to get a husband, even though I am doing well at my lessons.*

*I lost some ribbons, and Miss Kelly is still angry about it. I would like to buy more, but I am afeard I do not know the best type. Should I buy satin ribbons? Or do you think another type would be better?*

*I should tell you more about Fred. Colonel Kelly is a good man, a fair man, and he works so hard at the Custom House and helps people, but sometimes he ~~hurts~~*

*makes choices not everyone likes. One of the trading ships was fined and then people lost their jobs including Fred, and he knows that I live with the colonel, because he knows me from before, and he makes all kinds of silly threats, and I have never taken them seriously, he's not really going to light me on fire or kill my poor little dog, but then he started chasing me, and I truly was afeard that he would hurt me.*

*I do not write as well as Miss Kelly thinks I should. I am sorry for making you read all of this. You told me to tell the colonel what happened at the ice fair, but I could not. They have too much to worry about already, and I am afeard I would get in trouble for it.*

*Do you have advice? I ~~need~~ would appreciate your thoughts.*

*Thank you for your kind help again.*

*Yours truly,*
*Minerva Randall*

Clearly, the girl needed advice and mentorship. But where would one even begin? She had already ignored the advice Mary had given her, and Mary had nothing more to say: Minerva simply needed to talk to the colonel. Perhaps if Mary wrote to her, she could reemphasise that solution, but she had found that young people, once their minds were fixed, were very difficult to persuade in any direction.

Mary stiffened at the feel of breath on her neck. She turned to find Fanny reading over her shoulder.

"I thought I said this letter was not relevant to the investigation."

"Sometimes things are related in surprising ways. In this case, though, you are probably right." She stepped back a little and crossed her arms. "You did not tell me there had been an incident at the ice fair. What happened?"

"A girl, probably fourteen or so, was being chased by a rascal. I intervened."

"I am glad you did," said Fanny, "but I still cannot believe that you just left the ice fair without discovering anything of import."

Mary sighed. "I know, I know. I should have stayed longer to see if anything useful was said after their assignation."

Mary folded up Miss Randall's letter, hoping Fanny did not ask how—or if—Mary had responded. The best way to prevent the question would be to change the subject.

"I think we should consider Mr. Johnstone as a suspect."

"He was not mentioned in Mr. Rice's logs, and there is nothing tying him to the crime."

"But he is so connected to the others. I cannot stop feeling like he is important."

Fanny shook her head.

"Maybe you should talk to some of Mrs. König's servants and see if they know of Johnstone."

"That would be a good idea, now wouldn't it?" said Fanny, gritting her teeth.

"I am not saying you should talk to George again." Fanny and George had had a bit of a falling out. "Talk to one of the others."

"All of Mrs. König's servants are irritated at me, so that is not an option."

"It is much better for them to feel irritation than suspicion," said Mary.

"I suppose you're right."

There was a knock at the door. "One moment," said Mary, and she and Fanny hastily hid all their spy materials.

"Come in," Mary called.

"Miss Bennet," said Hannah with quite a pretty curtsy, "the family has visitors and thought you might like to join them."

"Thank you, Hannah," said Mary. "May I ask who it is?"

"Your aunt and uncle, the Gardiners. And their children."

"Thank you," said Mary. "I will be down in a moment."

"Do you think that perhaps I could freshen up your hair before you descend?" said Hannah meekly. She shot a look at Fanny. "Of course, only if you don't mind, Fanny."

"Why would I mind?" said Fanny, leaving in a bit of a huff.

Mary wanted to call after her but did not feel she could with Hannah present. Fanny was more tired and strained than Mary had realised.

Hannah started working on Mary's hair, and Mary cringed. Hannah must have taken the lack of a negative response as permission, but now that she was working on it, Mary felt it would be rude to ask her to stop.

Once Mary's hair was finished, she descended the stairs to the drawing room. She stood in the entrance to the room, watching the others. Mrs. Gardiner was speaking to Elizabeth and Kitty, Georgiana was spinning in circles with one of the young cousins, and Mr. Gardiner was engaged in a lively conversation with Mr. Darcy. They had developed a deep friendship since Elizabeth and Darcy's marriage.

Mrs. Gardiner crossed the room and embraced her. "Mary, it is splendid to see you." Of her aunts and uncles, Mrs. Gardiner was always the one who made Mary feel the most welcome. She noticed Mary, even when others did not. "And you did your hair differently."

"Yes, it is…an experiment."

One of Mary's cousins, Charles, tugged on her hand, so Mary sat down to read him a book he had brought with them. It was nice—nice to spend time with family, and forget, for a moment, their stalled progress on the case. For Fanny was correct: they had not progressed as they should.

After the story, Charles played with his siblings, and Mary joined in conversation with Mrs. Gardiner and her sisters.

After a few minutes, the housekeeper announced, "Miss Johnstone has come to call."

Miss Johnstone entered and greeted everyone with warmth. She spoke for a few minutes with Mr. Gardiner and did not seem bothered at all by the fact that he was involved in trade, even though she came from an important family and her father had been the governor of Dominica. Then she methodically went through the room, conversing not only with Georgiana, but with Elizabeth and Kitty and Mr. Darcy.

Mary supposed that when someone like Mr. Johnstone decided to court a woman his daughter's age, having his daughter as a confederate was a very useful tool. By calling on the Darcys, she could help him court not just Georgiana, but the entire family. Some daughters would not be quite so willing to give up being mistress of the household. Perhaps she had her own plans to marry and gain a house of her own.

"It is unfortunate that your father could not call on us as well," Mary overheard Elizabeth tell Miss Johnstone.

"He very much regretted not being able to come today, but he is often busy with his duties to Parliament."

"Mary, are you all right?" asked Mrs. Gardiner.

Mary realised that she had not heard the last several things her aunt had said.

"Yes, I am fine. I think I need to take a turn about the room." It was not the most graceful exit, but it achieved

Mary's purpose, and after walking about for a minute, she stopped to address Miss Johnstone.

"I heard you earlier, speaking of your father," Mary said. "How do they prepare whatever business they have decided to bring forward in Parliament?" Then, as a sort of justification, she added, "Before coming to London I never knew anyone who was a member of Parliament. I am fascinated with the process."

Her father seemed to be one of Miss Johnstone's favourite subjects. She spoke eloquently on his work, yet while she was effuse in her descriptions, none of what she said was useful to Mary.

"I am interested in how specifically he interacts and prepares with others of the same political leanings," said Mary. "Surely they meet together in advance. When do they meet and where?" Mr. Stanley had still not managed to learn this information from Mr. Eastlake, and they needed to know.

"I cannot possibly keep track of his schedule," said Miss Johnstone with a smile. "He is not beholden to me, just as I am not beholden to report all my movements to him. I like the independence."

Mary did not think she could be any more direct in her questions without raising suspicions.

"Your father seems the very independent sort," said Georgiana.

"Yes," said Miss Johnstone. "He values independence both for himself and others. For him, life must be full of new experiences, new places, new people, new adventures, even new food."

"New food?" asked Georgiana.

"Yes. Have you been to the French restaurant… Oh, I cannot remember the name, it is near the Thames."

"No, we have not," said Georgiana.

"Our neighbour, Mrs. König, mentioned several French restaurants," said Kitty. "It sounded quite scandalous."

"They are not nearly as scandalous as they sound," said Miss Johnstone. "I have been there myself. They allow only a very good sort of customer there. Like going to a ball, you know some people, not all. Like an inn, you can reserve a private room to eat. Sometimes my father meets there with other members of Parliament." At this, she gave a nod of acknowledgment to Mary, who inwardly beamed—she had answered, yes, she had actually answered the question.

"More than anything else remarkable about the place, is the food. Unlike an inn, where you have two or three choices, imagine a menu where you can choose any number of items and they will be made for you immediately. Every single food is divine, because it is made by a French *chef.*"

"A chef?" said Kitty. "What does that mean?"

"Like a cook, but much better. Someone trained by the best in the world, who has the skills to serve a king or a queen. Not that they have royalty in France, anymore, but I do appreciate being fed like one."

"Oh, I hope that at some point in my life I can go to a restaurant," said Kitty.

"We should all go together," said Miss Johnstone.

Having discovered something of note, Mary was impatient throughout the rest of the visit. The only other highlight was performing two of the new Irish songs she had been given by Mr. Stanley.

She found Fanny in the bedroom, airing out Mary's dresses. At Mary's entrance, she put the dresses away.

"Fanny, I have learned something."

"I cannot believe you let Hannah do your hair."

"I did not want her to do it. And you said you did not care."

"I would've done better," said Fanny. "Well, what did you learn?"

Mary swallowed. "Miss Johnstone said that the Radicals often meet at a French restaurant."

She waited for Fanny's praise, but it did not come. After what seemed like a very long time, but was probably only fifteen seconds, Fanny said, "Do you know when their next meeting is? Or which French restaurant?"

"No, but I think we should write Mr. Booth."

"I think you should find out when and where they are meeting first. Might as well be thorough, right?"

"Yes, but I am just not sure how I would find that out," said Mary, feeling the weight of Fanny's eyes on her.

"It is simple," said Fanny. "Learn what French restaurants are in London—there cannot be many—visit them, and find out if the Radicals have a scheduled meeting for a certain time, or if there is a certain time that they normally come."

"I think that would work," said Mary. "But maybe you should do it."

"It's your lead."

"Yes, but it may not be considered proper for me to visit restaurants, by myself."

"Now you worry about upper class propriety. You didn't for the ice fair."

It was a fair point. To be honest, Mary was afraid to go to a restaurant. She was unsure how to find the possible restaurants, had never been in one, and did not have the least idea of how she could ask the right questions to learn the necessary information. But she would not let the possibility of new things deter her—with some preparation and planning, she would be capable.

"I will do it tomorrow."

"Tomorrow?" said Fanny. "I will go do it myself, right now."

"You cannot simply walk into a restaurant without a plan."

"You cannot let a lead waste away. I will go to Mr. Booth's office first, change into something more ladylike, and then I shall find the information we need in short order."

There was no persuading Fanny when she got like this, and admittedly, Fanny was likely more capable than Mary regardless of the amount of time spent in preparation.

Indeed, a few hours later, Fanny returned, triumphant.

"The restaurant is named Le Pavillon, and it is right next to the Monument. They have a meeting scheduled for Saturday the twelfth, at eight thirty in the morning, in the private dining room. I want you to secret yourself in the room ahead of time and listen to the meeting. Can you do that? If you feel uncomfortable, Mr. Booth will send Mr. Stanley."

Mary felt embarrassed by her reluctance to visit the restaurant and find out about the meeting. She would not show such reluctance again. "Yes, I can do it. With no trouble at all."

"Good," said Fanny. "A servant position has opened up at Mr. Eastlake's residence. Mr. Booth wants me to take the position, so I can better spy on Eastlake and the others."

Mary felt like a grape that had been squished on the ground. "You are going to leave?" Perhaps this was the true reason Fanny had seemed so much happier since her return from the restaurant.

"Likely only for a week or two," said Fanny. "Maybe a month."

"I see," said Mary, looking at the ground.

"Are you sure you can handle the restaurant without help?"

"Yes," said Mary firmly.

"Good," said Fanny. She patted Mary's shoulder. "I know you can do it, Miss Bennet. You are more capable than you think. And I do not want to leave—it is simply a job that needs to be done."

"Of course," said Mary.

"Please tell the Darcys and the other servants that you have allowed me several weeks off to take care of…my dying sister."

"I will do that," said Mary. "Best of luck with Mr. Eastlake."

"Best of luck to you, too."

Fanny left and immediately, Mary missed her—missed her more fiercely than she had missed her sisters when they had married and left home. Mary considered Fanny her closest friend; however, it was unlikely Fanny felt the same way. She must have many friends. And now Fanny had left, and they had argued—not exactly argued—but things had been tense between them all day. Mary had let the one non-family member who might possibly be her friend walk away, without even an apology.

# CHAPTER TEN

*"Extract of a letter from Captain Lyle:—'I have brought home with me, at this time, a female sailor, who went away with the Ocean transport, of this port. She has been five years at sea before discovered, and would not have been found out then, but having accidentally fallen overboard. When taken up, she was stripped to be put to bed, at which time her sex was discovered. She...went under the name of William Macdonald.'"*

—*The St. James's Chronicle*, London,
February 12, 1814

"LE PAVILLON, LE Pavillon, Le Pavillon, Le Pavillon," Mary repeated quietly to herself, shivering in the cold. She wished there was a quicker way to get there.

Apparently, Mr. Booth could provide a department carriage and driver, but she had not reserved one with enough advance notice, and they were all being used, so she had hired one at a carriage exchange. Unfortunately, the only one available was open air. It was warmer than the day of the ice fair, yet still a fierce wind ripped through her cloak, chilling her to the bones. She could not remember a single winter that had been like this, with such endless snow and cold. The sky was tinged a dreary grey, a combination of clouds, fog, and smoke from factories.

"We're gettin' near London Bridge, miss," said the driver.

"Yes," said Mary. "I know."

"Me grandpa lived on London Bridge, as a little boy, before they took off all the shops and 'ouses and churches." Now it was only a plain stone arched bridge, ancient in appearance.

It would be rude to not say anything, so Mary thought what her sister Elizabeth might say—something generic, that did not encourage further conversation. "I have read that it was quite the sight."

"Indeed it was, indeed it was," said the driver, as if he himself had been there.

She looked out at the Thames. It was no longer frozen, and she had read in the papers that as the ice had broken up, a number of people had drowned.

She turned her head away from the river. A large white column with a gilded structure at the top came into view above the buildings. "Is that the Monument to the Great Fire?" asked Mary.

"That it is. The fire started right near it. Burned down me great-great-great-great-grandpa's house, it did. Killed two of his brothers, too."

The driver looked back at her plaintively, and after a moment, Mary realised he was seeking sympathy, which seemed rather unnecessary as he had never known them, and they had died almost 150 years before. "I am sorry to hear that."

The driver nodded, appeased, but then he slowed, then stopped the carriage.

"Why are we stopping?" asked Mary. All the carriages in front of them had stopped and the horses were huffing out warm breaths that instantly turned into little clouds.

"It's London Bridge of course. Lot of traffic, always crowded right next to it on both sides. We'll get even with it, and then I'll turn left and we'll be where you goes soon enough."

Mary sniffed, taking in the disgusting, smoky smell that often pervaded the city. The air was much better in the countryside.

"I do need to be there sooner rather than later." She needed to arrive at the restaurant several minutes before the Radicals, or she would be unable to position herself.

"This *is* a bigger heap than normal. See ahead, how the carriages are stopped on the east side of the bridge, well past the Custom House, almost to the Tower of London. But since you wants to go to the Monument, miss, this is still the fastest way. Don't you be impatient."

Mary was never impatient; at least she tried not to be impatient publicly. A little internal impatience could not be helped.

She gritted her teeth. She had better arrive in time, and then return before the Darcys noticed her absence. Mr. Darcy had requested that she inform them if she was leaving the house, and to only do so if she were accompanied, which made things more complicated with Fanny gone. Mary had told Hannah she was feeling unwell and simply wanted to sleep for several hours, and asked her to be vigilant in not letting family or servants disturb her. In case someone did peer into her room, she had piled clothes under the blankets on the bed, with the hope that someone might mistake it for her, asleep. There were any number of ways this could go wrong; yet while she feared being caught, there was a surprising sort of thrill to breaking the rules. This explained much of her youngest sister Lydia's behaviour over the years. Not that

Mary had any intention of engaging in the full extent of Lydia's behaviours. That simply would not do.

The carriage finally reached London Bridge. After rather too much swearing for Mary's tastes, the driver managed to turn left and join the traffic exiting the bridge. The driver pointed at a church and said, "Good Old Saint Magnus. He was a martyr, you know."

They drove up the road. It turned out that the Monument was on this street, and driving up to it gave her a much clearer view. The column was a Doric one, she believed, and on top of it was the gilded statue, which appeared to be a giant urn, with jagged, metal pieces coming out of the top. They seemed to represent fire, which made sense.

"Will you climb it?" asked the driver. "It's only 300 steps or so."

Mary squinted. Even at this early hour in the morning, there were several people on a platform near the top of the column, beneath the gilded urn. Climbing it seemed the sort of activity that Elizabeth or Georgiana might relish. "Maybe another time."

The carriage driver drove only a bit past the Monument and then stopped the carriage on the side of the road. "'Ere's your restaurant, miss. Should I waits for you?" he asked hopefully.

"That will not be necessary," she said, paying her fare.

Mary stepped up to Le Pavillon but did not go to the door, instead stopping in front of a glass window. There were dozens of small tables set up inside, filled with men, women, and even a few children. At some tables they were eating, at some, looking at stiff papers that must be the menus. The tables had enough space in between them that one was not seated *with* strangers, but the tables were close enough that one might overhear conversation from a nearby table.

In the glass she could also see her own reflection. She looked a little timid, so she imagined herself as Mrs. König, entering the restaurant with confidence. She smiled at herself, feeling more capable.

Her dress was one that Fanny had made—a nice cream-coloured morning gown with intricate embroidery, much fancier than anything she normally wore. She had worn this dress only once before, when she was pretending to be someone she was not, on the day she had met Mr. Stanley and tricked him into revealing several secrets. She remembered the words Mr. Stanley had used to describe her: stunning hair, a smooth complexion, a delicate nose, piercing eyes, and a regal manner of bearing. She was surprised that she could remember Mr. Stanley's words with exactness, and a sudden warmth filled her chest.

Unfortunately, her hair did not look as it had that day. Fanny had done it up then, and was much more skilled than Hannah, not that it mattered as Mary was feigning illness, which would make it illogical to request assistance with her hair. Mary should have asked Fanny to teach her to arrange her hair, but now Fanny was gone, and she feared it would be for longer than a few weeks.

She set her musings aside and approached the door. As she reached her hand to the handle, a smartly dressed man opened it for her.

"*Bienvenue, mademoiselle.* Welcome to our humble establishment. I will be your host for the morning. May I take your cloak?"

"Yes, thank you."

He passed her cloak to another man wearing a matching outfit.

"Do you have a reservation?"

"No, and I am not interested in eating this morning. But I might like to make a reservation in the future, for myself and a group of friends. Would it be possible for you to show me the restaurant?"

"Of course." He did not seem surprised at all that a woman, without the accompaniment of a man, would be making a reservation or need a tour. Perhaps it was because it was a *French* restaurant.

"Thank you," said Mary. "I have never been to a restaurant before."

He showed her around the restaurant, pointing out the fine china, the silver forks and crystal glasses, handing her a menu and describing what the experience would entail. He was quite convincing on the merits of this sort of eating experience, and Mary found herself wishing she had come to eat.

"Do you have any private rooms?"

"We do have one."

"May I see it, please?" asked Mary, tilting her head slightly at an angle, as sophisticated women seemed to do in order to invite acquiescence.

"It would be my privilege to show you," he said. "Unfortunately, we will need to look at it quickly. We have a group using it at eight thirty."

He took her to a good-sized back room with a private fireplace, and several large windows. The long, floor-to-ceiling curtains would provide a perfect place for Mary to hide.

"It is lovely," said Mary. "Thank you. I will send a servant in the next few days to make a reservation." She paused and looked at the floor, pretending a small amount of ladylike embarrassment. "Before I leave, may I use your washroom?"

"Of course."

He led her to the other side of the restaurant, near the kitchens. He did not even wait to see if she entered the room before turning around and heading back to his post. In case he was listening, she did open the door, step inside, and shut it behind her. A few seconds later she cracked the door open and peeked down the hall. The host was gone.

She walked back down the hallway, and then quickly past the entrance. The host's attention was on the door and a guest who was entering. If she was not mistaken, it was Francis Burdett. She thought Burdett might have seen her but hoped he had not recognised her.

Mary walked purposefully through the open seating area, careful to keep her face free of nervousness. Lady Trafford had told her, several times, "If you act as if you belong in a place, people are less likely to question you." The approach seemed to be effective, for while several people glanced at her, no one's eyes lingered on her and no one questioned her. She entered the private dining room.

She heard voices in the hall—voices she recognised—as she dashed across the empty room towards the windows. Without looking back, she stepped behind one of the curtains, concealing herself in its fabric.

"I think someone has been following me," said Lord Cochrane.

Mary tried to keep herself from panting, to focus entirely on their words.

"You are imagining things," said a familiar voice that Mary could not quite place.

"I know what it is like to be followed," said Lord Cochrane. "I have been followed before."

The curtain was a divided one, multiple panels of fabric

not sewn together. Mary pulled two of the panels apart enough that she could see out of the gap with one eye. At the far end of the room stood Lord Cochrane, Sir Francis, and Mr. Eastlake.

"We are not considered suspects in the unfortunate affair," said the familiar voice again. It was Mr. Eastlake. "If we were, the police detective would have subjected us to more than just a single, cursory interview."

Sir Francis shook his head. "Lord Cochrane is right. Someone thinks we did it." The way he looked into the others' eyes made Mary wonder if he suspected one of them of the deed, if he could not quite trust their innocence. "It may not be the detective, but someone is digging."

There was a moment of pause, too long, perhaps, and one of their heads shifted in her direction, so she let the pieces of fabric fall closed in front of her.

"But why?" said Lord Cochrane. "Why would we possibly kill our best messenger? And what is leading the authorities to believe we have done it?"

"It is a frame job, I have no doubt." Mr. Eastlake's voice seemed nervous.

They were silent for a moment, and then Mary heard other voices—other Radicals entering the room, greeting each other, some boisterously, some solemnly.

She shifted uncomfortably, feeling the cold from the window. She realised that part of her was positioned in front of the window, which meant she could be seen from the outside of the building, so she stepped farther to the side, so all of her was between the curtain and the wall. It made the space more cramped and less comfortable.

For several minutes the men participated in inconsequential chitchat, which was interrupted when they made their orders to a server. The food they selected sounded delicious, and Mary realised that she had not eaten nor drunk anything before leaving the house.

"Now," said one of the men, "as for our purpose today. What are our priorities, gentlemen?"

She shifted the curtain slightly, but did not recognise the man who was speaking, nor a number of others in the room. She again let the drape fall closed.

"We need to end corporal punishment of soldiers—especially sailors—once and for all," said Lord Cochrane.

"While that is important, I think we should focus more on parliamentary reform," said Burdett.

"You have been going on about this for years," said a man with a low, quiet voice.

"But we have not met our goals," said Burdett. "We have achieved hardly anything. Look at all the rotten boroughs, with only a handful of voters, and then there are entire towns and cities with no representation whatsoever."

"We know the arguments," said the first man, the one who had opened the meeting. "But what is to be done?"

"We need to entirely overhaul the system," said Burdett. "Create boroughs from scratch and—"

"That will never pass," said Lord Cochrane. "Even if we can get a number of Tories and Whigs to side with us. Better to take smaller steps to change—eliminating corruption and bribes, and banning the purchase of votes to ensure a seat."

The man with the low voice laughed. "You are one to talk, Cochrane. You yourself purchased quite a number of votes."

Lord Cochrane sighed. "And it did not even end up being necessary—I would have won anyway. But sometimes you must play the game in order to change the game. Of course, most of us have bought votes at one time or another."

"We must be better than that," said the fourth man. "We must be impeccable and beyond reproach. If we want to save our country, if we want to make it stronger, we must set the example."

This was not at all what Mary expected. With the way everyone spoke against Radicals, she had thought they would be seeking a French Revolution or a complete redistribution of property. Instead they wanted to eliminate corruption from Parliament.

"In the long run," said Sir Francis, "I would like to see universal male suffrage."

"*Universal* male suffrage," came the voice of Mr. Johnstone, who had been remarkably silent until now. "What? Would you give any man, regardless of education or resources, a say in electing officials?"

"Yes. *Every man.* Imagine how much change we could create if the representatives were meant to represent every person living in their borough, and not just the interests of a select few."

There was silence for a moment as they reflected on his words.

"Now I do not think we should propose this now—not while everyone is so wrapped up in this war," said Sir Francis. "Maybe in a few years we can work up to this. But what can we do now? What proposals have you been working on that might be brought before Parliament, that we could convince Tories or Whigs to vote for?"

"We will earn the support of the Whigs," said the man with the low voice.

"But we do not want to ally ourselves too closely with them or the Tories. We do not want to simply become a part of their efforts."

"It is true," said Sir Francis. "But if we ever want to pass anything, we need more reformers elected, or we must craft things in such a way that they can receive more general support."

The others agreed, and they moved specifically to the proposals. They paused for a few minutes as their food was delivered. Mary now desperately wished she had eaten before leaving this morning. Sometimes she forgot to eat when she was wrapped up in her studies with a good book, but it was much easier to keep one's mind off food when one was not surrounded by its smell.

The men returned to their proposals as they ate. Not only did Mary's stomach hurt, but her legs had begun to cramp. One of the things she had never guessed about being a spy was how difficult it was to stay completely still. She had always looked down on people who were restless, always moving, but now she sympathised with them. She attempted to shift her weight without rustling the curtains as Lord Cochrane presented a proposal to protect naval officers and sailors. Hopefully after the meeting Sir Francis, Lord Cochrane, and Mr. Eastlake would speak privately again, because none of this was relevant to the case.

Many people distrusted the Radicals, and while she could see why they disliked some of their plans and policies—the thought of universal male suffrage made her cringe, for what did the shoe shiner or the labourer know about government?—they seemed a very patriotic group who were genuinely trying to do the best for their country and make reforms in order to ensure the health of Parliament and prevent its collapse. They were nothing like the men she had exposed a few months before in Worthing, who would welcome Napoleon Bonaparte to their shores.

"Now here," said Lord Cochrane, "should I propose that the naval officers—"

There was a brilliant flash of light which Mary could see even from behind the dark curtains. A fraction of a second later everything happened at once: an ear-splitting boom, a rush of smoke, the walls and floor of the building shaking as if they would fall apart, voices screaming, and the shattering of glass.

# CHAPTER ELEVEN

*"On Saturday morning…a dreadful fire broke out in the Custom House, in Lower Thames-street, which burnt with great fury, and in a few hours destroyed that old but useful pile of building… That several lives were lost, we have little doubt, but it was utterly impossible, from the confusion which prevailed, to collect any minute particulars."*

—Excerpt from an initial report by *The Times*, about the events occurring on February 12, 1814

MARY'S ARM STUNG, and something warm and sticky dripped down it. Her eyes hurt from the brightness of the light, the light and sound that had—what had happened? She was behind some sort of fabric, against a wall, she was in pain, and only when she was about to pull the fabric back did she realise where she was: spying on the Radicals in a restaurant. She stopped herself from opening the curtain, but she could not stop herself from letting out a gasp.

She did not have the words for what had happened, did not understand what could have caused the noise and the light and the shaking, and so she stood, pressing her front teeth against her lip, trying not to make any more sounds. Whatever was wrong with her arm—why did it hurt with such intensity?

Slowly she became aware that the Radicals were speaking and moving around. She had not heard them at first.

"That must have been quite a large explosion," said Lord Cochrane. "Less than a mile away, if I am not mistaken." There were footsteps near Mary—Lord Cochrane, walking towards her. Perhaps he'd heard her gasp. But the steps stopped at the window, and he did not move the curtain. He was so close that she could hear him breathing.

"Are you hurt, old chap?" said one of the men.

"Some scratches, but nothing deep. Lord Cochrane, how do you fare? You seem to be bleeding."

"I have been through much worse. This does not merit medical attention."

"Perhaps we should adjourn the conversation for another day," said Sir Francis, as if the wails and sobs coming from the rest of the restaurant were a mild inconvenience.

"Yes," said Lord Cochrane. "We should see if anyone needs assistance."

Footsteps moved this way and that, and a rustling, and Mary felt as if her perception of sound had been jumbled. Finally, there was silence.

Mary counted slowly to ten. Something wet slid down Mary's right arm.

And then, a voice, inches away from her. Lord Cochrane. "I know you are there. Did you find our conversation enlightening?"

Blood pounded in Mary's head. The Sea Wolf had caught her scent, and now would devour her.

"We have done nothing," said Lord Cochrane. "Look elsewhere for your answers."

Mary waited for Lord Cochrane to rip away the curtain, to drag her out and tie her up. But there was silence, absolute silence, and after a minute, when Mary could stand the game no longer, she pulled back the curtain.

Lord Cochrane was gone.

He had known she was there, he had spoken to her, and then he had let her go free.

She did not understand.

Did he know her identity? She did not think he had seen her at any point, but she could not be sure.

Suddenly, she noticed the state of the room. Glass littered the space, shards up to ten or twelve inches long, and many other pieces mere fragments. She stepped carefully through the debris and turned. The windows were gone. Not entirely: a few pieces of glass clung to the frames, here and there, but whatever explosion had shaken the building had destroyed not only these windows, but all the windows in the building across the street.

She peered through the almost empty frame. Above the building across the street she saw smoke, a giant, billowing cloud of it, taking over the sky, spreading out from some location—the source of wherever the explosion had occurred. The smell of the smoke made her nose itch. She shivered with cold.

Stepping away from the window, she stumbled into one of the chairs and finally looked down at her arm. This was the arm that had been nearest the window, the arm that perhaps even had been in front of it as she hid behind the curtain. A three-inch piece of glass was embedded in her upper arm. Blood stained the beautiful dress Fanny had made her, its cream turned an ugly red, especially on the sleeve, but also on the skirt and the bodice.

She turned away from her own arm, her stomach feeling queasy despite its emptiness. She swallowed back the taste of bile. She wanted to flee, the way she had fled from Mr. Rice's body, but she could not flee from herself. A military man like Lord Cochrane would know exactly what to do, but she could not bring herself to request his assistance, or all would be revealed.

Her breath felt ragged and weak, so she breathed in deeply, again and again, and suddenly she was panting. Everything was out of control and she took in more and more air, faster and faster, but it did not soothe her, it left her winded and empty. She clutched the tablecloth in her hands, forced herself to focus her eyes on a roast chicken that had been left on the table. After a minute, she managed to slow her breathing to a more normal pace.

Mary gritted her teeth, selected a napkin from the table, and forced herself to look at her arm. Without giving herself time to think, she seized the glass with the napkin and pulled it out.

Her body shuddered. The shard—which was closer to three and a half inches long—slipped out of the napkin and fell to the ground. She blinked moisture from her eyes.

Now the blood seemed to pour from her arm. She desperately grabbed another napkin and pressed it to it, but the fabric did not stop the flow. She took an additional napkin and wrapped it tightly around her arm. It took several minutes of fumbling, but somehow she managed to tie it using one hand.

She left the private room, slipping into the chaos of the restaurant. People were moaning and screaming and crying. There was blood everywhere, and Mary felt more sick than before. At one table, right next to the window, a woman had blood streaming from multiple cuts in her face. And—how very dreadful—there was a man with blood dripping from his eyeball.

She gathered her wits about her and walked carefully through the room, avoiding Lord Cochrane and the others. They were devoting all their efforts to helping the injured, though Johnstone was taking more of a hands-off approach. She slipped into the cloak room, donned her cloak, and left the restaurant.

Mary walked down the street, back towards the Church of Saint Magnus and the London Bridge. A scrap of paper fluttered from the sky and landed on the ground in front of her. She picked it up. The edges of the paper were charred, and she guessed that it was less than half its original size. It appeared to be the remnants of a five-pound bank note.

She walked farther, finally reaching the intersection with the bridge. From there, as she turned to face downriver, about half the distance to the Tower of London she could see a building in flames, billowing fire flying out the windows and from the roof. It was a massive building, white and stately. It must have been magnificent—

Before.

She walked the block towards it along with other fascinated onlookers, compelled to know more. She wondered if perhaps it might have been burning, a little, for hours—that would explain the smoke she had smelled earlier. A small fire, somewhere inside. She had read that explosives were often stored in government buildings, to keep them from those who should not have access to them. So perhaps the fire had crept along, until suddenly, it was too late.

"What is that building?" she asked a man standing near her. He ignored her, so she turned to someone else. "What is that building? The one that is on fire?"

"It's the old Custom House, miss."

The Custom House. Someone had talked to her about the

Custom House. Recently. Someone she knew worked there. Or lived there. But who, and why would one live at a Custom House?

Nothing made sense. Her arm and her head were throbbing.

People were frantically taking things out of buildings and loading them onto carts—books, chests, paintings. More than one building was on fire—perhaps the explosion had started other fires—and firefighters were using ladders to help people escape. Coral beads, cracked and scorched by flames, littered the ground.

A woman up ahead was wailing, and Mary pushed forward, a taste of foreboding in her mouth. The woman was wearing only a nightgown, with a blanket wrapped around her, and reaching towards a man being carried in a large blanket by a group of constables. The face and arms of the injured man were covered with deep angry burns, and he had other cuts and bruises.

"Let us through, let us through," said one of the constables to the woman. "Please, Miss Kelly, let us take Colonel Kelly to where he can receive treatment."

"But my brother, I cannot leave him."

"He will be fine, Miss Kelly, but we have to get him to treatment."

With the extent of the burns on his face, Mary was not sure that this was the truth.

"But Minerva, Minerva!" wailed Miss Kelly. "I tried to yell, I tried to wake her!"

Minerva.

In her mind, Mary saw the girl running through the ice fair, pleading for help.

Mary swallowed. She knew what had happened, knew

what must have happened, yet she could not believe it.

Colonel Kelly opened his mouth, and croaked out the words, "It is not your fault, my dear. You could not have got her out before the explosion."

The words hit Mary like a blast of light and sound. She could not breathe; she could not think.

"Let us through! Let us through!" the constables again repeated, and managed to carry Colonel Kelly away, his sister running after them.

The crowd surged around Mary. For a moment, she thought she saw Fred, the man who had chased Minerva, jeering in the crowd as he watched the burning of the Custom House, but when she looked again, she did not see him.

Mary's body swayed. She attempted to stand upright and strong. Minerva had written to her, asking for help, and Mary had not given any assistance or advice, had ignored the girl's concerns. Perhaps, if she had written, perhaps if she had acted, all of this could have been prevented.

"You do not look well, miss," said someone standing nearby.

"I am fine," said Mary, stepping away.

She walked away from the building, away from the fire, but the smoke followed her, as did the shouts of the crowd. Her arm stung with pain—in fact, the pain was worse now than it had been before she had removed the glass. She reached her left arm inside of her cloak and felt her right arm. Blood leaked through the makeshift bandage.

She walked several minutes and finally found a carriage for hire. She almost gave the Darcys' address, but she stopped herself in time. She could not go home like this, covered in blood, with a wound that was still bleeding, and no explanation for why she had been near the site of the explosion.

She gave the address to Mr. Booth's office. She knew that she was not supposed to ever take a carriage to her final destination, but her thoughts were muddled, and she could not think of any place close to it. The carriage driver tried to engage her in conversation but eventually gave up. It was all Mary could do not to cry.

Finally, they made it to her destination. She handed the driver her payment, and then he tried to help her out of the carriage, but she would not let him, and she stumbled, almost falling on the ground.

She pulled herself upright and tried to hold herself with dignity as she walked to the door and rapped on it with her left hand.

Mr. Booth's assistant, Mrs. Granger, opened the door. Upon seeing Mary, she gestured her in. Mary took two steps into the house and then she stumbled. Her vision narrowed, and she felt herself falling, falling, falling, until she hit sweet silence.

# CHAPTER TWELVE

*"It is to be deplored, that an orphan girl whom Miss Kelly had brought up…with another whom she was also about to provide in the same manner, perished in the flames. Miss Kelly, by her shrieks, endeavoured to awake them, for it was impossible for her to reach the chamber in which they slept…*

*"The fire, according to the report of the firemen, would have…got under [control] very soon, but the explosion of the gunpowder having struck terror into the men who worked the engines, they fled and left the flames for some time to rage uncontrolled. This powder was for the use of the volunteer corps."*

—Excerpt from a second report by *The Times*, about the events occurring on February 12, 1814

MARY WOKE WITH a buzzing in her head and a sharp pain in her arm, which was covered in bandages. Mrs. Granger's head swam in and out of her vision. Mary tried to speak, but Mrs. Granger said, "Shh, quiet now. First, you must drink some broth."

The woman brought the broth to Mary's lips. Mary blinked back guilt and tears—for at least a moment, she could hold them at bay—and drank.

"Do you have bread?" Mary had not eaten at all today,

and now she felt empty, inside and out, and needed something, anything, to fill that emptiness.

"Here you are, Miss Bennet."

Mary's fingers fumbled the first time she picked up the bread and she dropped it. The second time, she was able to get it to her mouth, chew, and swallow.

"It is all my fault," said Mary miserably.

"What is all your fault?" asked Mrs. Granger kindly.

"A girl is dead, and—"

"Actually, you should wait to speak about it until I get Mr. Booth."

"But I am not dressed," said Mary. Someone, likely Mrs. Granger, had taken off her dress, and she was only wearing her chemise. Her dress—the beautiful, cream-coloured dress Fanny had so carefully made her—was ripped and bloody, sitting in the corner of the room.

"You are sufficiently covered," said Mrs. Granger, leaving the room.

Mary frantically tugged on the blanket with her left hand until she managed to pull it up to her chin. It was not as good as being dressed properly, but it would have to do, for Mr. Booth entered the room.

"Miss Bennet," said Mr. Booth, inclining his head slightly. "How are you feeling?"

"I am fine, thank you," said Mary, eager to conceal her true physical and emotional state. Mrs. Granger had already seen her in weakness, but she did not want Mr. Booth, her supervisor, to see her as less than capable.

"You had something that you wanted to tell me?"

It was not that she wanted to tell him, but she must own her actions and her faults.

She described the incident at the ice fair, Minerva's letter, and her own inaction. Then she described the brief conversation between Colonel Kelly and his sister, and how she might have seen Fred in the crowd.

"And so you see," said Mary, "that I feel responsible for Minerva's death."

"An idiotic assumption," said Mr. Booth. "The potential for prevention, even if action should have been taken and could have changed the course of events, does not place the blame for a crime on anyone but the person who directly carried out the crime."

Mary felt the sting of his words—the *idiotic* assumption. Yet his claim that she was stupid for taking blame for Minerva's death did not, in any way, relieve the sense of her own culpability.

"Colonel Kelly," said Mr. Booth, as if tasting the name. "Wait one moment." He left and returned with Mr. Rice's log, the one he had taken from Mr. Rice's flat, the day they viewed his body. He studied the entries. "Mr. Rice delivered a message to Colonel Kelly a week before his death. But it does not say who the message was from, or what it contained. I must speak to Mr. Donalds immediately. Good day, Miss Bennet, Mrs. Granger." And with that, he was gone.

Mary felt lost. Her eyes darted around the room, again landing on the ruined dress. The memory of blood unsettled the little food in Mary's stomach, and she wanted to go home.

Home.

"I must get back, or they will notice I am gone."

"You slipped out of the house?" asked Mrs. Granger.

"Yes. I told the maid I was feeling ill and to not let anyone bother me while I rested. Please, help me get ready."

Mrs. Granger gave her a sympathetic look. "It is four in the afternoon. They are bound to have noticed by now."

Four in the afternoon. She had left a little before eight in the morning. She had planned to be back, at the very latest, by eleven. She had been gone for over eight hours.

Mary pulled the blanket up over her head. What would she do? How could she possibly go back now? Her stomach now filled with dread at the thought of disappointing Elizabeth and Mr. Darcy, and the small bit of bread she had eaten felt like a stone.

"Did I really faint for that long? I have never fainted before."

"It was not a typical lady's faint for nerves," said Mrs. Granger. "If your dress is any indication, you lost a lot of blood."

Mary wanted to sink deeper into the bed and never get up. She had failed—failed Minerva, failed to return home, failed to care for herself, and now Mrs. Granger and Mr. Booth must sort out everything on their own, knowing full well that she could not contribute.

Mrs. Granger tapped her chin. "It would be much easier if Miss Cramer were not at Mr. Eastlake's. Oh well. I suppose we shall need Mrs. Hunnicutt."

"Who is Mrs. Hunnicutt?" asked Mary.

"Why, the woman who saved you today, of course."

MRS. GRANGER HAD transformed herself into Mrs. Hunnicutt so completely that if Mary did not know it was her, she would not have guessed. In part it was the clothing, over-the-top opulence on a cheap design, expressing someone of lower birth who had come into money and was trying too hard. In part it was her mannerisms, her way of speaking, the lower-class accent that came through, even though Mrs. Hun-nicutt—or the character of Mrs. Hunnicutt—seemed to be fighting it.

"Now you leave all the talking to me, dearie," Mrs. Hunnicutt said, placing her hand on Mary's knee as the carriage slowed to a stop in front of the Darcy residence.

Even though they were alone in the carriage, Mrs. Granger had spent the whole time acting as if she really were Mrs. Hunnicutt, carrying on a rambling, one-sided conversation, as if Mary truly were a new acquaintance. She was a large woman and insisted on lifting Mary out of the carriage herself, without the help of the coachman. "You poor child—no, no, no, I will do this—you mustn't exert yourself."

Once out of the carriage, Mrs. Hunnicutt wrapped her arm around Mary and led her up to the Darcys' residence. The butler opened the door before they even reached it, and then called out excitedly, "She is here! Mr. Darcy! She has been found!"

Mary wished she could disappear, wished she could whisk herself up the stairs and into her room and barricade herself against the response that she was about to experience.

Suddenly, Mary was swarmed with people—her sisters, Mr. Darcy, Georgiana, her aunt, Mrs. Gardiner, and a flurry of servants, all concerned, all worried, all asking questions and attempting to ascertain her safety and comfort. She was led into the drawing room, a chair was placed next to the fire and she on it, and she was plied with blankets and pillows and tea and worry.

"My dear Miss Bennet, I am so glad to see you back, home and safe," said Mrs. Hunnicutt.

"To whom do I owe this great debt?" said Mr. Darcy.

"Oh, I am Mrs. Hunnicutt. Mrs. Amelia Hunnicutt. Let

me tell you what has occurred. Your dear Miss Bennet has a heart of gold, a heart of gold I tell you, and was so worried about her maid, who had left to care for her dying sister, so in her worry, Miss Bennet decided to bring a nice little gift to her maid, and not being a resident of London, she got a little lost. It is natural to get a little turned about in London, why I, I who come here every single winter, and make countless calls on all my many friends and acquaintances, always get lost in certain neighbourhoods, especially when I call on my aunt Tilda. Aunt Tilda is such a funny woman, and she—" Here, Mrs. Hunnicutt paused, and a look of self-realisation passed on her face, "Actually my dear aunt Tilda has nothing to do with today's conversation. Your dear little Miss Bennet ended up near the Thames River, close to the Custom House, which exploded this morning—genuinely exploded, and I did not like the look of it, and I am sure you heard the news on it?" Mrs. Hunnicutt waited expectantly, looking at Mr. Darcy and Elizabeth.

"Yes, we heard the explosion from here," said Elizabeth.

"I expected as such," said Mrs. Hunnicutt. "I was very close, and while I was shielded by the carriage, it hurt my ears, and damaged my coachman's livery. Can you believe it, it damaged his livery! Now your poor Miss Bennet, she was not as fortunate as I to be protected by a solid, well-made carriage like mine, and she was struck by a piece of glass in her arm. Isn't that quite the most terrible thing? And then your poor Miss Bennet" (here she gave Mary a look of such sympathy and pity) "fainted on the ground, and I saw it through my window and knew with certainty that it was my call and duty to help her. A poor, unprotected single woman, on the ground in London. It was the only thing I could do if I wanted to live with myself and my conscience. I stepped out of the carriage, and I myself lifted Mary and carried her into my carriage. I am quite a strong woman you see, both in body and in mental fortitude. Now that I had Miss Bennet in the carriage, I could see that she was not only a woman of character, but also a woman of family." Mrs. Hunnicutt looked around the room, her eyes lingering on some of the nicer fixtures. "This actually exceeds my expectations—I can tell you are certainly a family of *real* quality, simply by the décor... I thought it best to have my own doctor stitch her up. Once she awoke, she told me her story and I straightway brought her here."

"We are very much indebted to you, Mrs. Hunnicutt," said Mr. Darcy.

"It is no trouble at all, no trouble," said Mrs. Hunnicutt, and she launched into another monologue, this time about the guiding philosophies she used for her life. Elizabeth and Mrs. Gardiner sometimes managed to get a phrase into the conversation, but Mrs. Hunnicutt would not let anyone else use their voice for long.

"I think," said Georgiana in a small opening, "that Mary is tired, and it would be best if we allowed her to rest."

Mary gave Georgiana a thankful smile. It was too much, being surrounded by everyone, being such a focus of attention.

Mrs. Hunnicutt bade her farewells and rejoiced in their new acquaintance—at which Mr. Darcy appeared rather uncomfortable—and then Mrs. Hunnicutt turned to Mary and took her hand. "I hope you will call on me, dearie, after you have recovered," said Mrs. Hunnicutt, and Mary saw a glint of Mrs. Granger in her eyes.

"I will," said Mary. "Thank you for what you have done for me."

Then Mrs. Hunnicutt was gone, and everyone helped Mary to her room, showing a little too much care and consideration, until Mary was in her bed and the only people left were Elizabeth, Mr. Darcy, and a maid, a maid who was not Hannah.

Elizabeth sent the maid away, and Mary felt suddenly afraid. The concern on their faces had been displaced by looks of disapproval.

"Where is Hannah?" asked Mary.

"You may have lied to her, but she still shares part of the blame for enabling your behaviour," said Elizabeth.

"Have you dismissed her?" asked Mary. Where could someone like Hannah go, if dismissed from a household like this? No one else of worth would hire her.

"No, she has not been dismissed," said Elizabeth, "but she has been moved to the kitchens."

Hannah must be devastated. She had finally reached her goal of becoming a lady's maid, and now she was forced down to the kitchen, where she would never interact with the household. It was yet another thing to add to Mary's guilt; it was not nearly at the level of consequence as Minerva's death, but nevertheless, still a dreadful thing for Hannah.

"I am terribly sorry," said Mary.

"Expressing sorrow is not enough if it does not change your behaviour," said Mr. Darcy. "We had no idea where you had gone. No one had seen you leave. Your uncle and my men have spent hours outside searching for you, and many of them are searching for you still, as we have not yet managed to contact them to let them know you have been found. We thought that perhaps you had taken a fall in the park or died of exposure to the cold and the snow or been carried off by...by unsavoury men. You do realise that any of these things could have happened to you, an unmarried woman with no experience of the world on the streets of London by herself. You were foolish, Mary, foolish indeed, and lucky to be rescued by a good soul like Mrs. Hunnicutt."

Mary felt as if she had been disgraced, she felt as her sister Lydia should have felt after running away with Wickham. Lydia had never shown any contrition or remorse, but Mary could not let things like this go. She knew how to hold onto every single one of her faults in her mind, she knew how to wallow in every single one of her character flaws, and she *would* wallow, wallow in all the things that had led to this moment.

"You have let down not just me, but the entire family," said Mr. Darcy. "For your own good, I am tempted to send you home."

"I do not have a home," said Mary quietly. With her father's death, she had lost Longbourn. Mr. Darcy could send her to live with her aunt Mrs. Phillips in Meryton, with no pianoforte and very little library to speak of, or to live with her oldest sister Jane, but either way, she would lose her position as a spy.

"We do want you to stay with us," said Elizabeth kindly, "but if you cannot adapt to living in London, it may not be an option."

"I understand," said Mary.

A piece of paper whipped against the window, and was held there, for a moment. It was partially burnt and looked to be another scrap of one of the documents from the Custom House, blown all this way.

Mr. Darcy left the room, but Elizabeth lingered, looking at Mary as if she were trying to understand what to do with a stray dog. No one in Mary's family had ever looked at her with intent, with focus; they ignored her, changed the subject when she spoke, and saw her as an inconvenience. Now, though, she had the full attention of her sister, but it was not the sort of attention she had ever wanted.

"I thought you had more sense, Mary," said Elizabeth.

Mary thought of Minerva, a fourteen-year-old girl. Dead. Her body must have been blown to tatters. Little fragments of it were probably floating around the city, like the scraps of paper blown by the wind. Mary deserved the censure of Mr. Darcy and Elizabeth, she deserved the pain in her arm, and she deserved to have lost the respect of Mr. Booth. A girl was dead. If she had acted, she might have discovered the connection between Mr. Rice and Colonel Kelly, and what that had to do with the man paying Fred at the ice fair, and how it all related to the Custom House. If she had acted, she might have prevented Minerva's death.

"One can know a great many things and still not have any sense," said Mary.

Elizabeth left.

Mary tried to sleep but could not. She was hungry and thirsty but could not bear to ask a servant for assistance. Her family had never treated her with much respect, but now, she had lost the little respect she had.

# CHAPTER THIRTEEN

*"If virtue…cannot always make a man happy in sickness or adversity, vice cannot make him so in health and prosperity."*

—*The Examiner*, London, February 13, 1814

MARY SPENT THE next day in her bed. A maid she did not know brought her food and sat with her at times. She would ask what Mary needed, but Mary had nothing to reply.

She did not attend church with her family. At one point she stood next to her window and watched as a piece of paper, probably another remnant of the Custom House, twirled around in the wind, like a dancer suspended in thin air. Then the paper lost the wind and drifted down to the ground. It landed in a patch of snow on the cobblestone road, and, after a moment, was trampled by a horse.

Mary sank down in the bed and did not move for a long time.

THE NEXT DAY, Georgiana and Kitty came to talk to Mary and enliven her spirits, as Georgiana put it. Mary attempted to converse with them, but for the better part of the visit she simply listened. She appreciated their kindness, but she deserved her suffering, she deserved the pain and hopelessness she felt.

Later, Elizabeth brought up a pile of books she thought Mary might enjoy. Mary left them untouched on the table. Instead, she removed Minerva's letter and forced herself to read the words of that lost and lonely child. When she could take it no longer, she shoved the letter under her pillow and slept on top of it.

MARY DISCOVERED, FROM a newspaper, that it was not just Minerva who had died in the Custom House, but another orphan girl as well. The newspaper did not even list either of their names. Mary knew nothing about the second girl except that she was also an orphan, and that she had died with Minerva.

Elizabeth and Mr. Darcy brought a doctor to examine Mary. He noted that her arm was healing well and commended the person who had done the stitching; besides that, there was nothing wrong with her: simply a malady of the mind, or perhaps a weakness of her nerves. He prescribed a tonic.

Later, a bouquet of flowers arrived, a gift from Mrs. Hunnicutt.

"Wherever did she get flowers in February?" exclaimed Kitty, who had helped bring the flowers up to Mary's room.

"There are hot houses that can provide them all year round, but it is not a small expense," said Georgiana.

Once they were gone, Mary read the note from Mrs. Hunnicutt. The first three pages were from the character of Mrs. Hunnicutt and expressed her concern as well as her reflections on a variety of subjects, as well as an invitation to visit her once she had recovered. Near the end was a line more in keeping with her true person: Mrs. Granger and Mr. Booth requested an update and wanted her back to work.

Mary swallowed. She did not even know the status of the case. There was some connection between the Custom House and Mr. Rice, but Mr. Booth was pursuing it, and Mary did not know what she could do. She had fewer skills and less experience than Mr. Booth, Mrs. Granger, Fanny, Stanley—than all of the other spies. Asking for her help was a polite gesture, nothing more.

At the end of the note she found a few sentences added by Mr. Stanley.

*My dear Miss Bennet,*

*It is my fervent hope that you recover quickly. If there is anything you need, give me word. I hope to see you again soon.*

*Your faithful servant,*
*Mr. William Stanley*

If Fanny had been here, Mary might have tried to read into Mr. Stanley's note and detect whatever sentiments he might feel towards her, but she did not have the energy or the desire to do so on her own.

As the day progressed, Mary found herself clenching her jaw tightly, so much that by the time the maid brought her dinner, it hurt to open her mouth to chew. She forced herself to eat but tasted nothing. It was as if she had lost the ability to feel or experience anything but pain and despair.

THE NEXT MORNING Kitty came in at a wretchedly early hour. She opened the curtains to a dreary, grey sky.

"What is wrong, Mary?" asked Kitty. "Has anyone actually asked you that?"

No one had.

But Mary could not tell Kitty what was wrong, for doing so would require explaining her work as a spy. Of course, she was not a very good spy, so what did it really matter?

Eventually, Kitty must have decided that Mary was not going to answer the question for she said, "Would you like me to read to you?"

"Not particularly," said Mary.

"That is not a very firm 'no,' so I am going to ignore your wishes and read to you anyway."

Kitty sat down and opened her book, a novel titled *The Italian* by Ann Radcliffe.

She read page after page, a story of lovers from different families who were opposed to each other, with all sorts of concealment and mystery and intrigue. Mary found herself surprisingly engaged in the story.

After a while, Kitty set down the book. "I think I am losing my voice." She checked the time on Mary's watch, which rested on a table. "I have read for over two hours, but it was worth it—it is a very good book."

At first, Mary had not paid much attention, but now she was fully invested in the characters. Strangely, she felt a little less sorry for herself.

Kitty leaned downed over the bed, and, in a moment that seemed to surprise them both, kissed Mary's forehead.

Mary gave her a quizzical look.

"Do you remember when we were very young, and Mother used to do that? Kiss us when we were feeling sad?"

Mary shook her head.

"Maybe I am just imagining it," said Kitty. "Or wishing that is what she had done."

They sat in silence. Their mother had not been the most affectionate person, especially not to Mary. She always gave plenty of attention to Jane, beautiful Jane. She also gave grudging attention to Elizabeth, and indulged Lydia and Kitty, which had not left much for Mary.

"I know what you are thinking," said Kitty. "You are thinking that you are the only one in our family who has been ignored and left out. You are not. You do not get to wear that as a badge of honour." Kitty crossed her arms, and her jaw seemed to quiver. "I was yelled at every time I coughed. I have been belittled and put down as silly and inconsequential countless times, by both of our parents, not just in our home, but also in public. It hurts.

"Our family might seem nice from the outside looking in, but we are a mess. The best embroidery is also beautiful on the back, neat and orderly, but the back of our embroidery is knots and tangles, threads hanging this way and that. The most we can hope is that nothing shows through to the front and that no one flips it over and sees what a mess we are." Kitty's voice had raised slightly, and now she spoke in a feverish pitch.

"I am sorry," said Mary. "Sorry I did nothing to help you."

"Good Heaven!" said Kitty. "I did not come in here to complain about my life. I know that we were often cruel to you, and I am deeply sorry for all the times I hurt you."

Mary blinked to keep her eyes clear. She would not cry, not in front of her sister. "Maybe we can all begin again, somehow."

"I would like that." Kitty pursed her lips. "I do not know what happened to you on Saturday morning, not really, but I know whatever it is must be dreadful. But please, Mary, do not be our mother. Do not give in to your nerves or your afflictions or whatever it may be—do not shut yourself off and let yourself waste away in your room, courting pity. It is no way to live."

Kitty left, and once again, Mary was very much alone. She thought of what Kitty had said, and of the many times when their mother had hidden in her room, wailing and lamenting about her nerves. Mary was not so different, really; she always hid from her family, always sequestered herself when things became uncomfortable or she felt particularly unwelcome. What she was doing now was simply acting in the same manner but to a greater degree.

Mary stared for a while at the wall. She needed to move forward, she needed to rise from her bed and attempt some sort of action, even if it felt like she could not. The resolution was enough for her to stand, but then once again she was overtaken by fear: fear of failure, fear of hurting others, fear of seeing her true self with all its many flaws.

Her eyes caught on the table. Kitty had left the book. Mary reached for it and sat back in her bed, her back growing a little straighter as she read page after page, feeling a little more hopeful all the while.

# Chapter Fourteen

*"The force which Bonaparte has under him, is only about 120,000 men. He has lost almost all his artillery."*

—*The Aberdeen Journal*, Aberdeen, Scotland, February 16, 1814

T HE DOOR OPENED with a creak, and Mary set down her novel. It was a rather inconvenient moment to be interrupted, full of tension and intrigue, and Mary made sure to show her annoyance on her face. Kitty and a maid stepped in first, followed by—Mary blinked several times, sure her eyes were deceiving her, but they were not, for Mr. Withrow stood in her room. But he had left London weeks ago to return to Lady Trafford in Worthing.

"What are you doing here?" asked Mary. Normally, a man would never go near a woman's bedroom, but if a woman were ill and there was proper supervision, then it was permissible. Mary supposed that staying in bed for four days qualified her as ill.

Mr. Withrow glanced at Kitty. "Lady Trafford received Miss Catherine's letter. She would have liked to have come herself, but she is feeling a bit under the weather. I had already planned to come to London this week; I simply came a few days early."

Mary turned to Kitty. "Why did you write to Lady Trafford?" Lady Trafford had a relationship with Mary, not Kitty.

"You were not yourself and I was worried about you," said Kitty sullenly.

Mr. Withrow must have come directly upon their receipt of Kitty's letter, for him to already be in London.

"It was a worthy action, Miss Catherine," said Mr. Withrow, inclining his head to her. He turned back to Mary and said firmly, "The day is wasting on—it is a quarter past three. I expect you to be dressed and ready for a walk in the park in ten minutes."

"But—"

"I leave no room for argument, for it is a beautiful day," said Mr. Withrow, closing the door behind him.

He had no control over her—she could very well choose to stay in bed for the rest of the day, but he would probably come back and bother her more, so she might as well. Mary sat up with a sigh. "Will you help me get dressed?" she said, not sure if she was asking Kitty or the maid. Both decided to help her.

"It is very kind of Mr. Withrow to come," said Kitty.

"He will do anything his aunt directs him to do," said Mary.

Mary's body felt achy, and she felt a little lightheaded, but she drank some tea and felt a bit better. She glanced in the mirror and discovered that her face looked rather ghastly and drawn, but fortunately, there was no one she needed to impress so it did not matter. She pulled her hair out of its braid and wrapped it simply on top of her head.

She descended the stairs. She felt rather shaky, and Kitty helped her at several points. When she reached the drawing room, where Mr. Withrow was waiting, she discovered that the entire family had decided to join them for the walk. It was a boisterous affair, and Mary almost retreated to her room, but Mr. Withrow gave her a look, as if he knew what she was thinking.

The walks were cleared of snow, yet contrary to Mr. Withrow's assertion, it was *not* a beautiful day. Mary was not sure there had been a truly beautiful day her entire time in London.

At first, Mr. Withrow spoke with Mr. Darcy, while Kitty and Georgiana walked together and Elizabeth walked with Mary.

"I want you to know," said Elizabeth, "that Mr. Darcy is sorry for what he said the other day. He did not intend to be so harsh with you."

"Oh," said Mary. She wondered that Mr. Darcy could not tell her that himself, or that Elizabeth did not apologise for her own words.

Elizabeth attempted to make further conversation, but Mary responded half-heartedly.

After a few minutes, Mr. Withrow moved to walk with Mary. Elizabeth smiled and then joined the others, which gave them a little privacy, as much as one could have while taking a walk such as this. Mr. Withrow slowed his pace, so that he and Mary fell behind.

"I met with Mr. Booth a few minutes ago," Mr. Withrow said without prelude. "He told me the full story."

"So you know that I did nothing, when I might have been able to stop a tragedy."

"I doubt anything you could have done would have prevented it. Still, you will likely have continued regrets. We all have these sorts of regrets, some warranted, some unwarranted. Leave a space in your life for those regrets, and as long as that space does not expand, you can use it to your benefit. It

will keep you sharp, and it will help you realise the consequences of what happens when we fail. You will be motivated
to look more broadly, to pursue any details that could lead to
the case."

Mr. Withrow knew how to be charming when he wanted
to be, but he never turned that charm on Mary. Yet in this
case, she liked that he was blunt—she did not want to be
coddled. She preferred the truth over a comforting lie.

"Thank you, Mr. Withrow."

"Now on to other matters. Mr. Booth asked me to tell
you that he has investigated the link between Mr. Rice and
Colonel Kelly. Mr. Rice delivered an aggressively worded
letter to Colonel Kelly, detailing complaints about the
management of customs and its negative impact on various
factory owners. The letter was anonymous, which Colonel
Kelly did not realise until after Rice had left, so he was not
able to ask Rice who sent it. Unfortunately, the message
burned with the Custom House."

"So we are at an impasse?"

"For now. In your most recent letter to Lady Trafford,
you mentioned your suspicions of Mr. Johnstone. I did a little
investigating, and I think you may be correct in questioning
his character. A few years ago, Lord St. Vincent wrote, and I
believe these were his exact words, 'The Cochranes are not to
be trusted out of sight, they are all mad, romantic, money-
getting and not truth-telling—and there is not a single
exception in any part of the family.' And a relative once said
that Johnstone specifically has often shown a lack of principles
and engaged in a relentless pursuit of gain."

"Do you think that I am correct in wanting to investigate
Mr. Johnstone?"

"You may be correct, or you may not. There is nothing

substantial which ties him to the case, but he may be worth pursuing all the same."

They walked in silence for a few minutes. Elizabeth glanced back at them, and then Kitty did, and then Georgiana. She wondered what they made of her walking with Mr. Withrow after nearly four days spent in her room.

"How do you recommend I investigate Mr. Johnstone?" asked Mary. "Or the other suspects? I am at a bit of a loss at what *I* can do."

"Look for the money," said Mr. Withrow. "Everything is always about the money." He had expressed this sentiment to her before, and while the way he presented it seemed less abrasive now, it still felt cynical to her.

"Is money the reason you are in London today?"

"Of course. I have a matter to discuss with one of my bankers."

"And how do you propose I learn about the suspects' financial situations?"

"I have not the least idea," said Mr. Withrow. "Luckily it is your case, not mine."

Mary thought she might have caught a hint of smile on his face, but then it was gone.

They caught up with the others. Mr. Withrow declared that he was going to stop by his favourite London bookseller, and asked if anyone wanted to join him. "If it is permissible, Mrs. Darcy, Lady Trafford would like to purchase a book for Miss Bennet. She would not like Miss Bennet to neglect her studies."

Elizabeth gave her assent, and everyone decided to accompany Mr. Withrow. Mr. Darcy joined Mr. Withrow in his carriage while the women took one of the Darcys' carriages.

"You must have spent a substantial amount of time with Mr. Withrow at Castle Durrington," said Georgiana, leaning a little towards Mary.

"Not as much as one might expect," said Mary, confused by the question.

"Do you enjoy his company?" asked Kitty with a smile.

"He finds me an annoyance," said Mary. "On my part, I find his company no better or worse than that of the average person. It is easy to tolerate people when I put my mind to it."

"I am sure he does not find you an annoyance!" said Georgiana. "What a terrible thing to believe."

"I know it to be true," said Mary. "I overheard him, once, talking to Lady Trafford."

"How terrible," said Georgiana.

"It did upset me at the time," said Mary, "but I am not bothered by it now. Honesty is a virtue, and besides, he would never have said it to me directly."

"I still cannot imagine Mr. Withrow saying such a thing," said Georgiana.

"You are like our sister Jane: you see too much good in people," said Elizabeth. "Everyone is a mixture of good and ill, and a certain awareness of those ills is helpful as we navigate society. Some ills are forgivable, while others indicate deeper character flaws."

"I take it you have forgiven Mr. Withrow for what he said?" asked Kitty.

"No," said Mary. "I simply realised what he thought of me was unimportant."

They arrived at the bookseller after a short time.

"They do not have any novels at all," declared Kitty. "What kind of bookseller is this?"

"They do have novels," said Mr. Withrow. "They are in the back, on that shelf in the corner."

"Thank you," said Kitty.

"Did Lady Trafford give any recommendations for the sort of book I should purchase?" said Mary. Often Lady Trafford had specific things she wanted Mary to learn.

"Lady Trafford did not express any preference, so I am sure that anything that interests you will satisfy her."

"Very well," said Mary.

She browsed for a while, revelling in the possibilities. There were so many subjects she wanted to learn more about: the history of Ancient Greece, the tragedies of Shakespeare, and the science of paper production. She found a book on French grammar which seemed like it would be particularly useful in continuing her studies. She had not spent very much time practising French since her arrival in London, though she had spoken several times with Georgiana.

She carried the French grammar with her as she continued to browse. She came across a section of books on the various governorships of Britain over its territories. Perhaps they had one that would be useful to her in the case. She searched through the titles and found *A Brief History of Dominica*. The book was anything but brief, and as she opened to its table of contents, she saw that it devoted an entire chapter to Mr. Johnstone's time as governor.

"We best be going," said Elizabeth, suddenly at her side, "so we can allow Mr. Withrow the rest of his day."

"Of course," said Mary, startled. "Just give me one moment. I need to make a decision between these two." The French grammar covered many of the more intricate details of the subject, yet the book on Dominica might be useful for the case, which was a more pressing need. However, while it might provide helpful information to understand Mr. Johnstone, it also might contain nothing useful.

"I will buy the second one," said Elizabeth.

"You…you do not need to do that." Her sister buying her a book seemed much more unusual than Lady Trafford doing so. Not that Elizabeth could not afford it—she and Mr. Darcy had ten thousand pounds a year, after all—but whether she was proposing this out of kindness or charity, Mary was not used to being the recipient of such attention.

"I am purchasing Kitty a book as well." Elizabeth took the French grammar and brought it to the counter.

Mary decided it was not such a terrible thing for her sister to buy her a book; one should never complain about more books.

"Dominica," said Mr. Withrow. He flipped through the book, pausing briefly on the chapter about Johnstone. "Hopefully it is an enlightening choice."

He purchased the book. When he returned it to her, there was a folded paper inside. Mary had not seen the shopkeeper put it in, so Mr. Withrow must have inserted it. She had best open it when she had more privacy.

Mary entered the carriage first. Kitty was about to enter, but then turned to Mr. Withrow.

"Thank you for coming to London, and for helping my sister," said Kitty.

"It is no trouble at all, Miss Bennet," said Mr. Withrow with a charming smile and bow. "You seemed to have helped Mary greatly on your own. You are a good sister."

"And you are a good man," said Kitty, flirtingly. Kitty could flirt with any man, but she deemed some as more worth her attention.

Mary turned away, not feeling any need to watch this sort

of interaction. After a minute it was over, and Kitty was seated next to Mary in the carriage, humming in a pleased manner to herself.

They returned to the house, with Mary, Kitty, Elizabeth, Georgiana, and Mr. Darcy all squeezed into the same carriage, as Mr. Withrow had to be on his way.

"That was refreshing," said Kitty when they reached the house.

"Yes, but I am tired now," said Mary. "I will retire to my room." After so many days in her room, the walk and the shop had exhausted her.

"Will you be joining us for dinner?" asked Elizabeth, a note of worry in her voice.

"I believe so."

Once in her room, she immediately climbed into her bed and pulled the covers up over her head. She had pretended she was fine for a few hours, but now the knowledge of Minerva's death overwhelmed her again, and once again she felt barren and empty inside.

What must the others think of her, emerging after days of isolation? They did not know what had happened. They must think her weak and pathetic, to hide in her room after an arm injury and a lecture about her inadequacies.

Her body began to shake, and suddenly she could not breathe. She gasped, sucking in huge breaths of air again and again, faster. She wanted to disappear, wanted to run away. Maybe she should leave; she could stay with Jane and their mother at Jane's estate, and everyone here would be happier with her gone.

Her breaths became ragged. Her heart pounded. She pulled at her hair with her fingers.

No—she must not think this way, must not believe that.

She tried to slow her breathing, she clutched her blanket in her fingers, she tried not to drown in her worry, and eventually, her heart did not pound so, and the air came in and out and actually filled her.

She removed Minerva's letter from underneath her pillow. She had read it so many times over the past few days, that she had memorised every line, every spelling error, every confusing explanation. She smoothed out the wrinkles and then placed the letter back with her store of secret possessions behind the bed. Then she sat at the desk and opened the book on Dominica.

The paper inside was indeed a letter from Mr. Withrow.

*Dear Miss Bennet—*

*Mr. Booth would like you to attend Admiral Loackin's ball on Friday night in order to further investigate the suspects, and, if you believe it relevant, others like Johnstone.*

*If your family is attending the ball, go as yourself. If not, go as someone else. Fanny will help you make arrangements.*

*Sincerely,*
*Mr. Withrow*

The letter was terse, and the use of "sincerely" rather than a more standard "sincerely yours" read as impersonal, but Mary preferred it that way. She wondered how she would arrange things with Fanny, as Fanny was still at the Eastlake household, but after a few minutes of thought, no solution presented itself to her, so she opened the book, turned to the chapter on Mr. Johnstone's time as governor of Dominica, and read. In addition to information about major events, laws, rulings, and trade, it also included copious descriptions of Mr. Johnstone's misconduct.

Mary turned page after page, both horrified and drawn in, the same way the large crowd had been drawn in by the Custom House fire, unable to look away. During his time as governor he fell into trouble for embezzlement. He had kept a harem—for this word, Mary had to voyage to Mr. Darcy's library to consult a dictionary, upon which, despite neither book going into particulars, she was horrified.

The book briefly mentioned Johnstone's second marriage, to a Caribbean heiress, Amelia Constance Gertrude Etienette de Clugny. Napoleon Bonaparte had forced them to divorce not long after. Mary wondered what the story behind that was; perhaps Johnstone had only been after her money.

Then there was the matter of the soldiers. As governor, Johnstone oversaw the military. The 8th West India Regiment, which consisted of free black men from Dominica, had been forced by Johnstone to serve on his own estate, building walls, performing household tasks, and clearing brush with cane bills, the local tools of slaves. They often went unpaid and did not receive the requisite clothes for their positions, as he kept the funds for his own personal use.

Eventually, the 8th regiment revolted, killing officers and taking control of Fort Shirley. Johnstone brought in other regiments and a man-of-war ship and quashed the rebellion. Yet even after the men surrendered, many of them were slaughtered. Those who attempted to escape by sea were blown apart by the man-of-war ship.

To Mary's astonishment, the regiment was seen as at fault—despite all the abuses they had suffered, their actions were considered mutiny, and as a result, dozens were hanged. Johnstone was eventually court-martialled for his behaviour, but in his trial was cleared of all charges, despite many, including King George III, who believed in the evidence of his guilt.

Mary finished reading the chapter and set down the book. Amongst her feelings of outrage and horror, it took several minutes to form coherent thoughts. It seemed incredible to her that her younger sister Lydia could almost ruin herself and her entire family forever by running off with Mr. Wickham. It had been a dreadful, sinful thing to do, and the consequences for the entire family would have been devastating, had it not been for the timely intervention of her uncle, Mr. Gardiner. But someone who was rich, well-connected, and a man, could keep a harem and enslave and massacre his own soldiers, yet still be welcomed among acceptable society, and even more, could be a member of Parliament. It made her feel sick.

While none of this related directly to the case, Johnstone was the sort of man who would kill another should it be beneficial to himself. If he had anything to do with Mr. Rice's death, Mary *would* find out.

At dinner it occurred to her that Georgiana would not benefit from Mr. Johnstone's interest in her. It did not take much to realise what Johnstone saw in her. Georgiana was pretty, young, and charming, and she was also rich. Mary did not know what Georgiana's dowry was worth, but it would surely be substantial.

Mary watched Georgiana. She was so innocent and naive; she would be unlikely to suspect any man of ill. No wonder Mr. Darcy was so protective of her.

She imagined telling Georgiana about Johnstone's true character. It would devastate her. Mary turned and studied Mr. Darcy. If she told him, he would take matters into his own hands—he would ensure that Georgiana never saw Mr.

Johnstone again. That would be the much easier option, and she almost settled on it, but something gave her pause. If she was Georgiana, she would want to know *why* she should not be interested in a certain man; in fact, she would want the ability to make the decision herself. Even if the outcome would be the same—the removal of Mr. Johnstone from Georgiana's life—the method could make a world of difference.

Yet there was no reason to tell Georgiana yet. For now, Georgiana provided the best continued access for spying on Mr. Johnstone. Perhaps she could even arrange such an opportunity now.

"I feel like I have been neglecting my duties as a sister and as a member of respectable society," said Mary. "It is a moral obligation to participate in sociality with others, and I should not shirk this obligation any longer."

"That is…commendable," said Elizabeth.

"I was grateful for Miss Eliza Johnstone's recent visit. Did you repay it while I was ill?" They could have done all manner of things during her days in bed, and she would not have noticed.

"No, we have not," said Georgiana. "However, I have written several notes to her, and have received several in reply. She has a very beautiful hand and puts her words down on the page in such a charming manner. I think calling on her is an excellent idea. Are you sure you feel ready for such an effort, Mary?"

"A small exertion, perhaps tomorrow morning, would do me good."

"That is an excellent plan," said Elizabeth. "We also plan to attend a ball on Friday night, but if you are not feeling well enough, we could stay with you here."

"A ball?" said Mary, thinking of Mr. Booth's instructions. "Who is throwing it?"

"Lord Johnathan, of Bristol," said Kitty. "It is going to be quite the elaborate affair."

So it was not the same ball as the one Mr. Booth needed her to attend. In Meryton, there could only be one ball in the region on a single night, but London was large enough that multiple people could hold balls and there was plenty of fashionable society to spread between them.

The best way to avoid suspicion would be to leave open the possibility of attending the ball with the Darcys, and then feign illness on that day so she could attend the other.

"I hope I feel well enough to attend," said Mary. "Associating with others in public settings can do a great amount of good, especially when accompanied by the awareness that the travails and tribulations of others may be greater than one's own."

When Mary returned to her room after dinner, she discovered Fanny. Today her room was simply full of surprises.

"Fanny," she said hesitantly, remembering the way in which they had parted.

"Miss Bennet!" said Fanny, and she hugged Mary with so much intensity that Mary could hardly breathe. The rare hugs given by Mary's family were always soft and restrained.

After recovering her breath, Mary smiled. "It is good to see you. I am so glad you have returned." She had worried that there would be a rift between them, but Fanny had put it behind her, so she would attempt to do so as well.

"I heard you were not doing well," said Fanny.

The reminder of her inadequacies hung heavily on Mary. She looked at the ground, and, without making a conscious decision to do so, wrung her hands.

"Mr. Booth told me the outlines, but I would love to hear it from you."

"Very well," said Mary, smoothing her skirt, and she began her story, slowly at first, and then speeding up as she added details.

"You have a strong constitution, so your fainting must have been due to losing a fair amount of blood, and not eating anything that morning."

"I am glad you do not believe that I am the fainting type," said Mary.

"Oh, anyone can be the fainting type, with enough practice. I do not doubt that if you put your mind and energies to it, you could become quite the fainting expert."

It took Mary a moment to realise that Fanny spoke in jest, but once she realised it, she smiled.

Yet just as quickly, Mary's smile slipped away. "I ruined the dress you made me. The beautiful cream one. It got ripped by the glass and covered in my blood."

Fanny's face fell, and Mary worried that Fanny would not forgive her. But then Fanny smiled. "I shall have to make you another. I have a new design in mind that will be even better for your figure."

Next, Mary showed Fanny the book and what she had learned about Mr. Johnstone. She expected Fanny to be shocked, but she simply said, "I have known plenty of men like him. These things never surprise me."

"I do think it adds weight to my suspicion of him."

"Perhaps," said Fanny. "However, there is nothing that ties him to Mr. Rice—he is not mentioned once in Mr. Rice's logbook. Now wait—hear me out. Yes, we can consider him, as we consider all possibilities, but we need concrete evidence in order to move this case forward."

"You are right," said Mary, properly chastised. The fact that Mr. Johnstone was a despicable human being who was partially responsible for a massacre did not guarantee that he was also Mr. Rice's murderer. But at least, as Fanny had admitted, he was worth pursuing.

"Why did you leave the Eastlakes?" asked Mary. She hoped Fanny had not abandoned her work to simply cheer Mary's spirits and offer advice, useful as that advice was.

"Mr. Eastlake is travelling abroad for two weeks, and there was no way for me to join him, as he is bringing only one valet. I had already learned everything I could from his house—I have looked in every drawer, at every paper and book—so I proposed to Mr. Booth that I return here."

Mary did not like to think that the case was unsolvable; to think that they could spend all this time and energy, and still not discover the culprit. "I take it you do not believe Mr. Eastlake is responsible?"

Fanny leaned in, as if about to reveal a secret. Actually, it probably was a secret. "Mr. Eastlake is giving money to some of the labour societies that are fomenting rebellion. I believe he may even be purchasing arms for them to rise up, and an armed mob can cause the deaths of many innocent people."

"Is there any connection between these labour societies and Mr. Rice?"

"It is well known that many members of labour societies are factory workers. I put together a list of all the labour societies and their local groups that are connected with Eastlake. Mr. Stanley, some other operatives, and I will infiltrate the various groups, learn of their members, and see if we can find factory workers who might have been connected to Rice. Yet even if we do not find a connection, our time will not be wasted, for we will be able to learn of and prevent rebellions."

"That is excellent," said Mary, trying to keep jealousy out of her voice. "It sounds like your time at Mr. Eastlake's was quite productive."

"I also discovered that Mr. Eastlake has a longstanding feud over politics with Mrs. König's friend, Mr. Sharp."

Mr. Sharp was the Tory from the ball and the ice fair, who Mrs. König had asked to help her find information about Mr. Rice's death.

"Maybe Mr. Sharp can help us," said Mary. "He may have discovered something useful for Mrs. König."

"It is possible," agreed Fanny. "Did you find out if the Darcys will be attending Admiral Loackin's ball on Friday?"

"They are going to a different ball that night. But I do not know how I will possibly get to the ball. I would need a chaperone, unless I pose as a widow, but then I would need to know people—"

Fanny laughed. "I will arrange things, do not fret. You can go as a young unmarried woman, and I can arrange for you the perfect chaperone, a woman who will gladly bring you with her to the ball and will not question your identity or care if your behaviour that night seems…irregular."

"Thank you," said Mary. "And—and thank you for everything. I apologise for my behaviour to you before you left for Mr. Eastlake's."

"It is forgiven," said Fanny. "I apologise as well. Though of course, it was more *your* fault."

"I know, and I—"

"I was joking, Miss Bennet."

"Oh, I see." Mary smiled. "I am trying to improve my skills at recognising jokes, but I am not improving as quickly as I would like."

"We will get you there, do not worry."

⚜

IN THE MORNING as they prepared to call on Miss Johnstone, Georgiana kept looking in mirrors and adjusting her hair. Georgiana must like Mr. Johnstone even more than Mary had supposed. At the last moment, Elizabeth decided not to join them, citing household matters to attend to, so it was only Georgiana, Kitty, and Mary.

"I am so grateful you called on me," said Miss Johnstone as they entered her parlour. "I apologise that my father is not here. He is taking a new office this morning, right next to the stock exchange, and I would be surprised if he returns before dinner."

Georgiana recovered quickly from her disappointment, and she and Kitty engaged in lively conversation with Miss Johnstone. Mary, on the other hand, was glad that the master of the house was gone, for it would make her investigations easier.

During a lull in the conversation, Mary made her request. "I have been reading about architectural styles, and the ways in which the placement of furniture and art can enhance one's experience of place. We only saw a few rooms during our last visit, and I was hoping you could show us more."

"Oh, I would love to see the house!" said Georgiana. "Please, will you give us a tour?"

"Of course," said Miss Johnstone, taking Georgiana's arm in her own.

They stopped first in front of a painting of Miss John-stone and her father in Dominica. Miss Johnstone looked young, maybe six or seven. She had only been a child when

191

they lived there. How much of her father's behaviour had she known, and how much had she learned since?

As they passed from room to room, Mary kept a sharp eye out for Mr. Johnstone's papers and anything else that might contain information. Finding possibilities was much easier than she thought it would be. In the library, letters and papers covered Mr. Johnstone's desk, for anyone to see. Perhaps he had looked at them recently, or perhaps he did not allow his servants to organise his things. Mary followed the others out of the room, and then, when they were looking at a painting in the next room, she rushed back to the desk.

She picked up letters, scanning them for anything that might be of interest. He had a number of correspondents, including several creditors requesting he pay them interest on his debts. There was also a letter from a John Dundas Cochrane. Mary read the letter, then found another letter from him. The letters made it sound as if he was Johnstone's son.

That could not be. Eliza Johnstone was an only child.

Or at least, that is what Mary had supposed.

She thought back to the dinner with Mr. Johnstone. Someone, perhaps Georgiana, had said something to the effect of "It must have been difficult being an only child," and Eliza Johnstone had agreed. But Mary thought she remembered Eliza pausing briefly first.

But if Eliza had a brother, then why was his last name not Johnstone? Perhaps he had a different mother. But Eliza's mother, Georgiana Johnstone, was Johnstone's first wife, and the phrasing in the letters made it seem as if John Cochrane was older than Eliza.

That did not make any sense, unless—unless John Cochrane was an illegitimate son, Mr. Johnstone's love child.

If Mary's intuition was correct, then Johnstone had no qualms with having an illegitimate son, and even giving him his surname, which, at the time, would have been Cochrane. Of course, if he had an illegitimate daughter, he might have been less likely to pass on his name.

Mary pushed these thoughts aside: her concern was not Johnstone's infidelities. She needed to find information that might help her in the case. Mr. Withrow had recommended she consider his finances, and so she turned to the ledger.

Johnstone had a number of debts, and he had speculated in all manner of ventures—some successful, some not. He had invested heavily in the stock exchange, in both Omnium and Consols, two types of governments stocks that paid reliable dividends, and generally rose in value over time. Over the past weeks he had purchased and sold, purchased and sold, but in general, he had purchased much more than he had sold, and if Mary's calculations were correct, he currently had at least 120,000 pounds invested in Omnium, and 100,000 pounds in Consols.

220,000 pounds. The number was astounding. Mr. Darcy had ten thousand pounds a year, but this derived not just from interest from his investments, but also from profits from his estate. To invest so many thousands of pounds in the stock exchange in a short amount of time seemed highly unusual, especially for someone who, despite his assets, had a number of outstanding debts. Add to that what Eliza had said earlier—he was taking a new office, directly next to the stock exchange.

Mr. Withrow's advice had led her in the right direction. He had also been the person who originally taught her to read a ledger, and she now looked back on their sessions in Lady Trafford's library with a surprising fondness.

Mary heard voices, so she hastily returned the ledger to its original position and stepped away from the desk.

"We thought we had lost you," said Miss Johnstone, and Mary thought she detected a hint of suspicion in her voice.

"I apologise," said Mary, frantically searching for an excuse. She turned and gestured at a framed drawing on the wall, which appeared to be of some sort of palm plant or part of a tree with palms. "Palms are not native to Britain, and I have never had the chance to see one, but I have read extensively on them." Feeling trapped by her explanation, Mary hurried on with it. "Did you know that in some cultures, palms are considered signs of fragility? However, in other cultures they are signs of grandeur and respect." She actually had no idea what palms symbolised, but it sounded reasonable.

"I did not know that," said Miss Johnstone. "Thank you for enlightening me." She pursed her lips together and then spoke again. "Honestly, that is not even one of the baron's best drawings. We have much better."

"The baron?" asked Kitty.

"Yes, the Baron de Berenger," said Miss Johnstone. "We have seen a lot of him of late." She did not seem entirely pleased by this. "Now let us finish the tour, shall we?"

She paid much more attention to Mary's whereabouts for the rest of the tour, and Mary had no chance to investigate further.

At one point, Kitty pulled Mary aside and whispered, "Why do you have to be so embarrassing in public?"

"I am sorry," said Mary, taken aback.

Kitty's words stung, and it took Mary great effort to be in control of herself and her words for the rest of the visit. She reminded herself that despite what she had said, Kitty did care about her. She had after all, written to Lady Trafford and then read to Mary for hours.

As the visit drew to a close, Mary said, "May I ask where your cousin, Lord Cochrane lives? I thought we might call on Lady Cochrane, before she enters her confinement."

"Oh it would be better to not... No... Well, my cousin and his wife are moving into a new house today. It would be better if you waited at least a week before you call on her." Miss Johnstone wrote down Lord Cochrane's new address and gave it to Mary.

As they left, Mary thought that it seemed highly unusual that Lord Cochrane was taking a new house on the same day that his uncle was taking a new office. But what did either event have to do with the death of Mr. Rice?

# CHAPTER FIFTEEN

*"War is proverbially subject to misadventure; and nothing but steadiness and strength of mind can save us from losing in one weak moment of alarm the fruits of six triumphant campaigns."*

—*The Times*, London, February 18, 1814

F ANNY PULLED THE fabric off the mirror with a flourish. "What do you think?"

Mary squinted at herself in the mirror; she almost did not recognise herself. She wore the bright yellow canary ball gown Fanny had made her months ago. She had tried it on, first to see the dress, and then for a fitting, but had forgotten how exquisite the gown was. Fanny had done Mary's hair elaborately, and she had put creams and rouges and other things on Mary's face, both to cover up the flaws of Mary's skin, and to highlight certain features and make her eyes appear bigger and brighter.

"I managed to alter the appearance of your facial structure," said Fanny smugly. "Even your family would not recognise you."

Mary leaned towards the mirror. "I look beautiful." It was not an adjective that anyone had ever used to describe her, nor one that she had ever used to describe herself. She had never minded being plain, but this look might give her an advantage tonight.

Mr. Darcy, Elizabeth, Georgiana, and Kitty had already left for their ball tonight, which was all the better. She was leaving after them, and she would return before them: no one would realise she was gone. They thought she had stayed home with a headache.

Fanny checked the sleeve of the dress to make sure it fully covered Mary's wound. Earlier in the day, Fanny had removed the stitches, and while she did not believe the injury would leave a scar, right now it still looked raw.

"Now walk around the room," said Fanny. "You are Miss Levena Kendall."

And indeed, Mary was not herself, not with this dress, this hair, this face.

Miss Levena Kendall. This was her first Season. She was from a small town named Saltdean, a few miles east of Brighton, and she was staying in London with a decrepit old aunt. Her mother was dead, and her father abroad. She would receive 10,000 pounds from her father upon her marriage to an eligible man.

"You still look like Mary," said Fanny critically.

Mary held her head up higher. She was her sister Kitty, able to fit herself into any group. She was Lydia, fearless when it came to talking to men. She was Elizabeth, witty and insightful, and Jane, refined and beautiful. She was Lady Trafford, completely set on her goal. She was even Mr. Withrow, cynical, good at asking questions and discovering answers.

"Very good," said Fanny. "Keep that."

Mary paused in front of the mirror. She was now so much of other people that there was nothing left of herself. Nothing at all.

She studied the reflection of her eyes. They were still rec-
ognisable. And in them, she saw inquisitiveness, a quest for
knowledge and truth. And a thirst to prove herself. Mary
Bennet was also an essential part of Miss Levena Kendall.

Fanny helped her don a heavy cloak that was not her own,
and a second layer of warm gloves. Then they slipped out of
the bedroom and into the hallway. Fanny led her down the
servant staircase, into the kitchen, and through a door leading
to the currently barren summer garden behind the townhome.

"I do not know when I will be back," said Mary. "Watch
for my signal."

"And wait for my reply," said Fanny. "I will be ready to
let you in." She patted Mary's arm. "You will do well. I know
it."

"Thank you," said Mary. "I hope you are able to make
substantive progress on your dress."

She smiled. "I am so close to finishing it."

Fanny shut and locked the door, and Mary walked
through the dark, past everyone's frosty garden walls, until she
reached another alley which she turned and followed until she
reached the road, where a carriage belonging to Mr. Booth
waited for her, ready to take her to meet the chaperone Fanny
had arranged for the evening, Mrs. Lawrence.

❦

MRS. LAWRENCE WAS a broad-shouldered woman with pretty
features and the faint smell of mint. She greeted Mary as if
they had known each other their entire lives.

"My darling Miss Kendall," she said, and kissed Mary on
the cheek.

"Mrs. Lawrence," said Mary, channelling Lydia's pure

energy. "I have heard such great things about you."

"Thank you, my dear. I know you just arrived, but let us enter my carriage. I do like to spend as much time at balls as possible, and we can speak on the way."

And on the way they did talk. She was one of the most effusive, ebullient women Mary had ever met. She asked constant questions about Mary's—or really, Miss Kendall's—fortune, about her father, and about her supposed great aunt.

Mary must have answered Mrs. Lawrence's questions to her satisfaction, for Mrs. Lawrence said, "I do love taking less fortunate young ladies, like yourself, under my wing. How else would you be presented to society?"

She went on to describe some of the other young ladies she had assisted, and the matches they had made.

They arrived at the ball as the second set of dances began, and Mary was immediately surprised by the attention she received during the initial flurry of introductions. When Fanny had first encouraged Mary to wear this canary ball gown, to Lady Trafford's ball in December, she had said that people would treat her differently based on what she wore. It took less than five minutes for Mary to conclude that Fanny had been completely correct. Men's eyes even turned to follow her as she walked.

"Is there anyone else you would like to meet?" asked Mrs. Lawrence.

"Well, everyone, of course," said Mary, "but let me see if there is anyone in particular who strikes my fancy."

The room was so full that it made it difficult to be certain, but she did not see Mr. Johnstone or any of the other suspects. However, she did spot Mr. Sharp.

"Do you know that man?" asked Mary. "I heard tell that his name was Mr. Sharp, and I saw him in a shop once, buying a silver embossed toothpick holder."

"Unfortunately, I do not know him, but I am certain that if you put your mind to it, you can meet whoever you like." She hooked her arm through Mary's. "Meanwhile, I do have a few people in mind for you."

Mrs. Lawrence introduced Mary to a group of both women and men, one of whom included Mr. Stanley, and then Mrs. Lawrence withdrew.

"What a delightful dress you have, Miss Kendall," said one of the women, a Miss Forster. She looked like she might be in her upper twenties. Her skin was remarkably tan, given that it was February, or perhaps it was her natural colouring. Miss Forster's dress was elaborate, with filmy layers of lace and cotton. Her eyes studied Mary's dress, up and down, and it took all of Mary's control not to flinch under such scrutiny. "Such detailed workmanship and a lovely design. I *must* have the name of your seamstress."

Mary was not sure giving Fanny's name was wise. If Miss Forster tracked Fanny down, it might lead her to Mary's actual identity. Yet she could not just say another seamstress's name and give credit for Fanny's work to someone else.

"Thank you, I do not recall—"

"I understand that you want exclusive access to such talent, but think what it might mean for an artist to have my patronage."

"Surely you can remember something," said Mr. Stanley. He did not seem to think it would be problematic if Fanny's identity were known.

Mary pretended to be thinking. In fact, she was thinking. Surely it could do no harm, and Miss Forster would probably not be able to find Fanny regardless.

"I believe," said Mary slowly, "that the designer is a Miss

Cramer. Yes, Miss...Fanny Cramer. But she is not affiliated with any shop—she sews the occasional dress on the side, and I am not certain of the best way to contact her."

Miss Forster gave Mary one of the most genuine smiles she had ever seen. "I will make sure that I repay the favour, my dear. It is much appreciated."

The others in the circle nodded their approval.

"Miss Kendall, would you be willing to dance with me later this evening?" asked Mr. Stanley. "Perhaps the third set of dances."

"It would be my pleasure," said Mary. She could not very well turn him down or she would not be able to dance at all.

"Oh, that is not fair, Stanley, to snatch her up," said one of the other gentlemen, a Mr. Walmsley. "I cannot possibly wait to dance with Miss Kendall until the fourth set, it would be agony." He looked to the dance floor. "They are just finishing the first dance of the second set. Miss Kendall, would you do me the honour of dancing with me right now?" He gave a deferential nod to Miss Forster. "If, of course, I am allowed to steal her."

"I am sure Miss Kendall craves the dance floor."

"Of course," said Mary. "What would a ball be without dancing?"

As Mr. Walmsley led her to the floor, she remembered all the people she was supposed to be, and how she should act and hold herself. She had practised dancing with Fanny over the past several days, refreshing herself on all she had been taught by the dance masters her mother had employed.

She felt especially light on her feet as Mr. Walmsley led her across the room.

"Miss Forster is a good friend to have. She is an heiress with forty thousand pounds."

"Is that all that makes someone a good friend?" asked Mary. "Their financial worth?"

"You are right, Miss Kendall. Money is a poor judge of actual character. But Miss Forster has both money and character. She is a bit eccentric—she *personally* owns four businesses, two of which she started—yet she is fiercely loyal, and she does much for those she takes under her wing."

"I like how she seems so confident in herself and what she wants. I admire that."

"Do you know what you want?" said Mr. Walmsley. There was something inviting about his smile, and his hand lingered on hers for a moment, even as they moved apart with the movement of the dance. Fanny would say he liked her, which meant she needed to say something appropriate in response.

"I will let you know when I decide," she said, trying to sound more coy than she felt. That was something Elizabeth or Lydia might say, something that would intrigue him without overcommitting herself.

Mary found she was enjoying herself, dancing with a man she did not know in a persona that was not her own. There was something freeing about a different identity: it was like slipping on a new glove and finding that it fit her hand perfectly.

Suddenly, she was wrenched from her complacency. Across the room, she saw Georgiana. Georgiana Darcy, dancing with Mr. Johnstone. She felt as if there was a gaping pit in her stomach. Georgiana was supposed to be at a different ball.

"Miss Kendall, is something wrong?"

"I am quite fine. Do you ever have dreadful thoughts attack unawares? Do memories of unpleasant things besiege you?"

"No, I cannot say that I do," said Mr. Walmsley. "How could a woman such as yourself have memories of unpleasant things?"

Her neighbour, Mrs. König, was dancing nearby, and her stomach gave a lurch at her knowledge of Mrs. König's actions with Mr. Sharp in the tent. Then she noticed Mr. Darcy at the edge of the dance floor, watching his sister. He seemed to sense Mary, and his eyes caught hers for a moment. She tore her own eyes away, looking straight into Mr. Walmsley's, and she leaned on the story she and Fanny had crafted. "My mother is long dead, my father, long away, and the mistresses of my finishing schools were not always kind."

"That sounds dreadful. Yet you seem to have turned out quite well despite all of it."

"Thank you," said Mary. "I do what I can."

They lapsed into silence, and Mary attempted to lose herself in the dance. She let herself smile at Mr. Walmsley's glances and attempted to feel as if she had not a care in the world. She felt her muscles loosen and her back grow less rigid, and she was surprised by the way in which her pretence impacted her reality.

She did not know how this had happened—the Darcys were meant to be at a different ball tonight. They had mentioned nothing about accepting a different invitation instead. Yet they were here.

Mr. Darcy had seen her, and since she had already been seen, there was no point in fleeing. It would be a test of Fanny's transformation of her, but she would stay, and she would stay in the persona of Miss Kendall at all times, and she would attempt to learn something useful over the course of the evening.

The dance finished and her partner gave her his thanks and a gentlemanly bow. "May I escort you anywhere, Miss Kendall?"

Mr. Stanley stood near her sister Elizabeth, so it would be best not to walk in that direction. It was risky to be at the same ball as her family while in disguise, but she might be able to succeed, as long as she avoided any close encounters with them, which might lead them to recognise her mannerisms or her voice. Her eyes jumped rapidly across the room. She had no notion of where Mrs. Lawrence had gone, but Miss Forster stood near Mr. Sharp. It would be a few minutes before the next dance began, plenty of time to have a brief conversation before she joined Mr. Stanley on the floor.

"I have a question for Miss Forster, if you do not mind walking me in that direction."

"Not at all."

Mary attempted to maintain a regal carriage as she walked with him. She was still not used to everyone's eyes being on her in this way. It was not that everyone was staring at her, it was simply a contrast to normal, when everyone's eyes seemed to slide over without registering her presence.

Mr. Walmsley led her to Miss Forster, and then left to find a drink.

"It looked like you had a fine time," said Miss Forster, pausing her conversation with her friends. "Did you enjoy it?"

"Very much," said Mary, self-conscious at all the women watching her, but determined to press forward. "Mr. Walmsley was a very fine dancer."

"He is quite pleasant company," said Miss Forster. "A little young for me, but just right for you."

"Will you be dancing yourself this evening?" asked Mary, unsure of how to lead the conversation the direction she needed it to go.

"Yes, I am dancing this next set. My partner should be here any moment."

This seemed as good an opportunity as any. "Before you dance, I have a brief favour to ask of you."

"Using my token of appreciation already?" said Miss Forster. "Very well. What is it that you want?"

"Do you know Mr. Sharp?"

"Yes, I do."

"Could you introduce me to him? I have a question for him, of a personal nature," said Mary. She thought of what Fanny might say in this situation and lowered her voice as if sharing a secret. This, of course, made all of Miss Forster's friends move in or tilt their heads slightly. Fortunately, it did not matter if they heard these words. "I believe he is friends with my father."

"It must be an important matter. I can certainly help you."

Miss Forster bid a temporary farewell to her friends and led Mary to Mr. Sharp. As they approached, a man speaking to Mr. Sharp hurried off. Mary did not quite manage to see his face, only his back.

"Miss Forster," said Mr. Sharp, bowing respectfully. "To what do I owe this pleasure?"

"This is my friend, Miss Kendall. She has a matter of a personal nature she would like to discuss with you."

"Miss Kendall, it is a pleasure, but I do not know what we could possibly discuss, as we are not previously acquainted."

"I am certain you will be able to help me," said Mary. "Perhaps we could speak a bit more privately."

"Very well," said Mr. Sharp, and he bowed to Miss Forster.

"Thank you," said Miss Forster. "I want you to know that you have my personal appreciation for this matter."

Miss Forster gave Mary a little squeeze on her arm and smiled. It was so strange to have a woman like Miss Forster, of elevated wealth and status, extending herself to help Mary. She would puzzle on it later.

"This way, Miss Kendall," said Mr. Sharp, and he led her to a more secluded spot in another room. Mary heard the music begin—the third set of dances was about to start, and Mr. Stanley would be looking for her. She had not thought through the timing on this very well, but the purpose of tonight was to investigate, not to dance with Mr. Stanley, so he would simply need to wait for her. Surely he would understand.

Mr. Sharp crossed his arms and considered her with a look none too gentle. "Now Miss Kendall, on what matter did you need to speak with me?"

"Well, it is a personal matter," said Mary.

"You have already informed me of such."

She needed to do better than this if she wanted to obtain relevant information. She wanted to cower and flee, she wanted to return home and hide in her bedroom where she was safe and nothing could hurt her and there was no risk of her hurting anyone else. But that would not do. She was a spy for the British government, selected because of her abilities to solve problems when others could not. She would not give up now. She squared her shoulders and spoke with the confidence and authority of her mentor, Lady Trafford.

"I am friends with Mrs. Knowles, formerly known as Alys Rice. I believe you have met her brother, Mr. Rice. Mr. Rice was recently killed, and Mrs. Knowles said that the authorities believe, without a doubt, that he was murdered." She had gotten better at thinking of Mr. Rice without picturing his body, mangled on the floor, but the image came to her now, and she felt bile in her throat.

Mr. Sharp gave a short nod. His eyes were fixed on her face.

"Unfortunately, the detective assigned to the case does not seem to have any interest in investigating. Mrs. Knowles is devastated, and I believe the only thing that will give her peace is seeing her brother's murderer brought to justice."

"There are murders in London every day that go unsolved," said Mr. Sharp. "The dregs of society have no limits to what they are willing to do for a shilling or a scrap of bread."

"True," said Mary, "but this does not appear to be one of those crimes." She paused for a minute, thinking of how she might convince Mr. Sharp to disclose whatever he might have learned. "Mrs. Knowles is worried that someone might come after her. I told her I would make a few discreet inquiries."

She saw Mr. Stanley out of the corner of her eye, approaching. He could not interrupt this conversation. She raised her hand slightly, very flat, in his direction, and fortunately, he understood her meaning and stopped. He turned the other direction but did not leave. How peculiar to have a gentleman wait for her.

"What makes you think I would be able to help you?" asked Mr. Sharp.

She said the first thing that came to mind. "Mrs. Knowles said that one of her brother's friends, a Mrs. König, came and talked to her about her brother. She mentioned your name and that you were trying to help her." It was likely untrue, but it made for a passable story.

"I see," said Mr. Sharp. He was very still for a moment,

but then he said smoothly. "You are right, I have done a little searching for Mrs. König. Unfortunately, it was insufficient to relieve her mind on this matter, and Mrs. Knowles will likely find it insufficient as well. But I will tell you, nonetheless.

"You may know that I am a member of Parliament. I asked some well-placed questions and discovered that there were a few pieces of evidence which created a connection between the crime and several Radicals, those rabble rousers who intend to destroy our society and undo all our accomplishments for hundreds of years."

"If they are Radicals, are not some of them also members of Parliament? Do you know them personally?"

"Parliament is very large, but I do know some of them." His face looked like he had bit into a lemon. "I do not doubt that one of them could have done such a deed. A few of them certainly have Napoleonic sympathies. For example, a Mr. Eastlake. And last week one of my men intercepted a letter to Mr. Johnstone. It was unsigned, but from France, and it offered him safe harbour should he ever find a need to leave England. What do you think of that, Miss Kendall?"

"It does not seem very patriotic," said Mary. "But that does not directly tie him to the crime."

"True," said Mr. Sharp. "I am afraid that those placed in charge of the case have bungled it entirely. I *know* there must be evidence that ties Johnstone, or one of the others, to the crime. I know it." His eyes were tight and his fists clenched. He seemed to take it personally that the perpetrator had not been found.

He shook his head and his whole body seemed to relax. "I have spoken a few choice words in different ears. If someone finds evidence, I will hear of it, but at this point I am losing hope that more will be found. It is quite the tragedy. Tell

Mrs. Knowles that she has my full sympathy and support, and that she can contact me directly next time if she has questions or concerns that I might be able to answer."

"Thank you." Mary sensed that he had no more to say. Yet at least he had given her something new: the letter Mr. Johnstone had received from France was not incriminating, but it was suspicious. Maybe, though, she could ask one more question. "Do you think that Mr. Rice's death could be connected to the explosion at the Custom House?"

"The fire at the Custom House? I had not considered— no—well, actually—no, that would not make sense." His eyes darted randomly around the room, but then they fixed again on her face. "I do not see any connection. I am sorry I cannot be of more help to you."

"I truly appreciate you taking the time to talk to me."

"It is no trouble at all."

She curtsied and then turned to leave, but he put his hand around her upper arm, pulling her back. His hand squeezed the very place of her injury, with its newly removed stitches. She turned to face him.

"Who are you really working for?" asked Mr. Sharp, his voice a low whisper.

Mary's heart pounded in her chest. "I do not know what you mean."

He looked intensely in her eyes for a moment. She held his stare. Whatever he saw must have satisfied him, for he released her arm and walked away.

Mary's skin felt raw. Why had Mr. Sharp asked who she was working for? What had he suspected?

Mr. Stanley approached and bowed. "Miss Kendall, would you care to join me for the dance?"

"Yes, I would," said Mary. Dancing would provide a

pleasant alternative to these thoughts. "I apologise for making you wait. I was working on…important matters."

"No apologies are necessary, Miss Kendall. I would wait forever for you."

No one had ever said something quite so charming to Mary, and certainly not an eligible man like Mr. Stanley. She felt more calm as he led her to the dance floor, and was able to set aside some of the anxiety created by her conversation with Mr. Sharp.

They entered the dance floor, finding a spot for themselves amongst the other couples. They ended up closer to Georgiana than Mary would have liked: only a few couples away. Georgiana was dancing with Johnstone *again*. He was a despicable human being on every count, and did not deserve to dance with her.

Mary attempted to focus on her own partner instead. Mr. Stanley looked at her with—well, Mary was not sure what it was. Admiration, perhaps. It was nice dancing with him; he moved with ease and confidence. Yet Mary could not shake her unease.

"I thought that there were two large balls tonight," said Mary. "One hosted by Admiral Loackin and another by Lord Johnathan, of Bristol."

"His name is Lord Johnathan Loackin, though most people call him either Admiral Loackin or Lord Johnathan. It has caused quite a bit of confusion in the past."

She wished she had spent a little more time learning about the ball the Darcys were attending, because then she would have known this. It would have been much easier to not don a disguise, nor spend the whole time hoping they did not recognise her. Even as herself, surely she would have still found a way to converse with Mr. Sharp.

For the next part of the dance, the women came together in a circle, joining hands and spinning in a circle. Mary took Georgiana's hand with reluctance. They were spinning and they were kicking and then Georgiana smiled at her. Mary could not bring herself to reciprocate.

The circle finally ended. Mary found herself bowing to Mr. Johnstone. His eyes examined her figure in a way that seemed almost lecherous. Then he was gone, dancing with Georgiana, and Mary was dancing with Mr. Stanley.

"It is such a pleasure to see you dressed as yourself," said Mr. Stanley.

"What do you mean?"

"Just that it is a pity that…the others…have you constantly dress and act a part. You are very good at what you do, but surely you could do it without the constant pretence."

If he meant to compliment her, he was going about it the wrong way. Did he truly think that her everyday self was a pretence and that this—costume—this facade was her preferred state? He did not understand her at all.

"This is not my true self," said Mary quietly.

Mr. Stanley did not seem to hear her. She took little pleasure in the rest of the dance.

As the couples began to separate, Mr. Johnstone bowed to Georgiana. With all the other noise, Mary could not be certain of what he said, but she thought it was something like, "Miss Darcy, may I speak with your brother and request a private audience with you later this evening?" Georgiana's lips formed a clear "Yes," and her warm blush said the same.

"Miss Kendall, Miss Kendall." Mary turned to Mr. Stanley. He smiled at her. He might have misunderstood her, but he was a kind man and a good man, and she was grateful for his attentions.

"Thank you for the dance, Mr. Stanley."

"Thank you," he replied. "It is unusual to have such a charming partner."

"I do not know that I would consider myself charming," said Mary.

"You do not see your full worth," he said, and then bowed his farewell.

Mary spotted Mrs. Lawrence and thought it best if she returned to her chaperone's side. Mrs. Lawrence was speaking to an older gentleman but paused as Mary approached.

Mary curtsied. "How is your evening, Mrs. Lawrence?"

"Oh, this ball is grand, simply grand. But do not worry about me, child—go off and enjoy yourself!" She shooed Mary away.

As Mary walked away, the gentleman asked, "Now who is that poor young lady that you will ruin tonight?"

"I do not ruin young ladies. And Miss Kendall is not poor." Mrs. Lawrence dropped her voice, but only a minute amount. "When she marries, she will inherit 10,000 pounds."

"Then you should keep good watch over her."

"But then how will she have any fun? I remember when I was a girl, attending balls for the first time. She can only live this moment of her life once, and she *will* have the best time she can."

Mrs. Lawrence was truly a terrible chaperone, but it suited Mary's purposes well.

She considered what she should do next. Mr. Stanley was speaking to Sir Francis. Johnstone was speaking with a familiar-looking man with curly hair. Surely she had seen him before. Of course, many of the individuals at this ball were the same as those who had attended the previous ball; she could very well have seen him there.

Mary's eyes wandered to the other side of the room. Georgina was speaking to Miss Johnstone. She seemed to be in her element, comfortable and happy. She kept looking in Mr. Johnstone's direction.

What had Mr. Johnstone meant when he asked Georgiana if he could speak to her privately later? The only times that had ever happened to Mary's sisters, they had received offers of marriage.

A dread filled Mary. If Mr. Johnstone proposed to Georgiana, she was certain Georgiana would accept. Yet it would not be a good marriage, not a happy one, not once Georgiana discovered—and experienced—his true character.

Yet what could Mary do to stop it? She could not very well interfere, not as Miss Levena Kendall. If Georgiana did become engaged to Mr. Johnstone tonight, Mary could discreetly inform Mr. Darcy or Georgiana of his true character and Georgiana could break off the engagement. Yet doing so would bring shame to Georgiana and potentially place her in disrepute. Georgiana did not need that. Mary needed to stop the engagement before it occurred.

She was Mary Bennet, spy, and her canary dress meant that she could do anything. Besides—Miss Levena Kendall's personality was as of yet only partially formed. Mary could make her more brash than originally planned.

Mary marched straight up to Georgiana and Miss Johnstone. Georgiana had not recognised her during the dance, and hopefully would not recognise her now. Mary attempted to sound as silly and giddy as possible. "Miss Johnstone! It is such a pleasure to see you again."

Miss Johnstone's brow wrinkled in confusion. "I do not believe we have met."

"We met last summer. Do not tell me you have forgotten.

We were introduced by your brother. How does he fare?"

Miss Johnstone went a little red in the face. "I think you have mistaken me for someone else."

"I would never do that. You are Miss Eliza Johnstone, and your *brother*"—Mary paused here and raised her eyebrows—"is Mr. John Cochrane. I have always thought you look so very similar to him."

Miss Johnstone opened her mouth as if she intended to say something to Mary, but no words came out. After a moment she turned to Georgiana, "Begging your pardon, Miss Darcy, but I am afraid we will need to continue our conversation in a few minutes." Miss Johnstone fled into the crowd.

Georgiana began to follow her and then stopped. She turned slowly to face Mary, who attempted to maintain the poise and confidence of Levena Kendall.

"I feel very forward speaking to you without an introduction," began Georgiana, "but I cannot help wondering at your words. What is your name?"

"Miss Kendall," said Mary, raising her head dramatically towards the ceiling.

"Miss Kendall, I am Miss Darcy. I thought that Miss Johnstone was an only child."

Mary leaned in conspiratorially. "Well she is Mr. Johnstone's only *legitimate* child."

Georgiana went very pale. Mary felt guilt for her pain, but she would do it again in an instant.

"Is there anything else I should know about the Johnstone's that they have not told me?"

"There are plenty of rumours about Eliza's father, but I should not repeat them. However, I will say that I have heard, from a very authoritative source, that he did not resign as governor of Dominica. He was forced out for his deeds." She could provide more details, but Georgiana was trembling. Surely Mary had said enough to prevent Georgiana from entering into a hasty engagement.

Suddenly Mr. Darcy was at Georgiana's side. "Georgiana, what is wrong? What has happened?"

"Nothing is wrong, nothing at all," insisted Georgiana. "I have just been having a very informative conversation with a new acquaintance, Miss Kendall."

Mr. Darcy turned to her, and Mary felt an icy chill. For some reason, she was much more afraid of Mr. Darcy discovering her than Georgiana. Maybe it was the way he looked at her with his discerning, critical eyes, as if he had already seen beneath her mask.

She wanted to flee, but that would only raise his suspicions further. Her only defence was to act as differently from her true self as possible.

"Miss Darcy," she said, with a giddiness that even her sister Lydia might envy. "Who is your handsome friend? You must introduce me and tell me whether or not he is single."

Georgiana blinked several times. "This is my brother, Mr. Darcy."

"Oh, *you* are Mr. Darcy. Then you are not single." Mary gave a sad sigh. "One cannot have everything. I have heard that your wife is quite outspoken, and I would love to meet her. I am certain she has all sorts of saucy stories she could tell me."

Mr. Darcy's expression grew rigid and cold. "I am afraid that is not possible. Now if you will excuse us, my sister and I have other matters to attend to." He stared at her discerningly, and she attempted a flirtatious, carefree smile.

Georgiana tugged on his arm, like she was a little girl,

hopeful for attention. "I would like to go home now."

"Of course, my dear. Find Elizabeth and Kitty, and tell them that we are leaving."

Georgiana walked away, and Mary thought this was an opportune time to make her own exit. She curtsied. "A pleasure to meet you, Mr. Darcy. I hope I come across you again."

She began to walk away.

"Mary Bennet," said Mr. Darcy.

She did not stop, she would not stop, and she could only hope that she had not given any discernible sign of recognition when he said her name. She kept walking and he did not come after her, which was only a small consolation.

Mr. Darcy had recognised her.

If she fled now, it would only confirm to him that she was, indeed, Mary Bennet. Besides, they were leaving now. She looked around the room but did not see Mrs. Lawrence. Even if she were to find Mrs. Lawrence and convince her that they needed to leave, she could not guarantee that she could arrive home before the others.

She could only hope that Mr. Darcy had been making a wild guess and did not truly believe that she was herself, and hope that if he did believe it, that Fanny could somehow prevent a catastrophe.

As Mr. Darcy left with Elizabeth, Georgiana, and Kitty, he looked in her direction. Mary pretended not to notice.

She mingled with various groups, but this was made more difficult by the fact that Miss Kendall did not have any previous relationships, and by the fact that she had lost all desire for pretence.

Then she saw someone she had not expected to see: the Baron de Berenger, the French architect she had met at

Johnstone's. It was not fair to assume that anyone French was in league with Napoleon Bonaparte—there were tens of thousands of Frenchmen and women living in England who felt no loyalty to him—but Johnstone *had* recently received a letter inviting him to France should the need arise, and he was clearly also in league with de Berenger.

Mary followed a little distance behind de Berenger. He bowed to several ladies, requesting their hands for later dances in the evening, but as he made his way through the space, he seemed to walk with purpose. And indeed, he came to a true stop when he reached Johnstone. Mary positioned herself near them but turned so she was not facing them.

"Not here, not now," said Mr. Johnstone, without greeting de Berenger at all. "I have too much on my mind at the moment."

"What happened?" asked de Berenger with genuine concern.

"The woman I am courting disappeared without even a farewell."

"I hope you are able to resolve the issue quickly," said de Berenger. It was as if they were speaking of a business transaction, rather than a relationship. "I do need the final details—we are almost out of time."

Johnstone nodded. "Very well. Be at your flat on Sunday at one p.m. I will give you directions then."

De Berenger passed within inches of Mary. He turned to look at her for a moment and gave her a charming smile but did not stop.

Before Mary could consider her next move, a piercing scream filled the ballroom. Everyone silenced and turned as one to the source of the sound.

Mary pushed her way through the crowd, forcing her way

forward. While most people either stood still or were attempting to get closer to see what had happened, one person was darting away: the curly haired man Mary had seen speaking to Mr. Johnstone earlier in the evening.

Finally, Mary made her way to the front of the crowd.

Mrs. König lay on the floor. Her left arm was red and looked as if it was already bruising. It was also bleeding from a thin cut.

Mrs. König was crying as she spoke, "I am so sorry. I am so very clumsy—this is no one's fault—I simply fell and hit the table."

The table next to Mrs. König had a smooth surface and rounded edges. Tripping and hitting the table would be unlikely to cause that sort of bruise, and the smooth surface would certainly not give her a thin cut. Mrs. König must be lying.

Someone must have hurt her.

Suddenly, Mary realised where she had seen the curly haired man before tonight. He had been at the ice fair and had given money to the gaunt young man who had attacked the now-dead girl, Miss Minerva Randall.

# CHAPTER SIXTEEN

*"PRICE OF STOCKS THIS DAY AT TWELVE O'CLOCK:*
*Omnium: 26 ¼ "*

—*The Evening Star*, London, February 19, 1814

MARY COULD NOT discover the identity of the curly haired man.

He had fled the ball after Mrs. König's fall, and no one she spoke to could give her his identity, or at least, no one chose to. Certainly, Mrs. König could have if she had felt so inclined, but although Mary acted the part of a sympathetic bystander, Mrs. König refused to speak a word when it came to anything or anyone connected to her fall. "There was no one near me—I am simply clumsy. I do not know who you could possibly be speaking of."

The one person Mary did not ask for the curly haired man's identity was Johnstone, but he and his daughter had left shortly after the incident.

Finally, Mary found Mrs. Lawrence, who had grown sad with a little too much wine. "Did you, at least, have a good ball, Miss Kendall?"

"It was wonderful," said Mary, "and I am so very grateful to you for bringing me here tonight and for all you have done for me."

"I am glad you found pleasure." She almost sobbed. "How I wish I had not lost all of my youth!"

Mary did not know how to comfort her.

Mrs. Lawrence fell asleep in the carriage, and Mary asked her carriage driver to drop her off two blocks from the Darcy's. It was eerie walking through the streets at this time of night. They were mostly empty, yet Mary could not shake the feeling that she was being watched, maybe even followed. Even at this time of night, some of the lamps were still lit, and they played tricks with the fog, which curled and wrapped around her.

Mary made her way to the back of the townhouse and tapped three times on a metal box affixed outside the wall of the kitchen garden. She waited for Fanny's signal—three flashes of light from within the kitchen window—but no signal came.

She tried again, but once again, there was no result. She wondered if she should tap louder, but she could not risk waking the family or other servants.

After counting to two hundred, she tried again. What if something had happened to Fanny? What if Mary's absence had been discovered, and Fanny had taken the blame?

Mary could not stand out here all night, yet she could also not simply barge into the house. She shivered and rubbed her hands against her arms. A ball gown with a cloak provided inadequate protection in the face of a cold February night.

A few minutes later, Mary tried again. Again, there was no signal—but wait. Three flashes of a candle in the kitchen window. Mary stepped forward to the kitchen door. It opened and she slipped into the house.

Fanny placed her finger to her lips to signal silence, which was rather unnecessary, as Mary had not intended to make a sound. They crept through the house and into Mary's room, shutting it fast. Fanny slumped on the floor, her back against the door. The light of the candle she held flickered on her face, which was creased with worry.

"What happened?" asked Mary.

Fanny shut her eyes, and for a minute did not speak. "Georgiana saved you."

"What do you mean?"

"The Darcys came home from the ball early, very early. Mr. Darcy wanted to see if you were feeling any better from earlier in the evening. I said that you were a little better, but had fallen asleep, but he would not let it alone. He was insistent on seeing you himself."

"I was at the same ball as the Darcys," said Mary. "I thought it would be a different one, but it was the same, and he recognised me."

"I tried to delay Mr. Darcy, I tried to distract him, and I did, for a minute, but then he entered your room, with me and Elizabeth and Kitty behind him. I was sure all was lost, but then a sleepy, grumpy voice came from your bed, and an arm reached out of the covers, and Mr. Darcy was convinced and left. Once the others were well and gone, I discovered Georgiana in the covers, pretending to be you."

The meaning of this had not managed to penetrate Mary's mind when Fanny continued. "She must have crept into your room while I was delaying Mr. Darcy, but I do not know why."

Mary gave Fanny a whispered accounting of all that had happened at the ball, including her conversation with Georgiana. "It did not seem like she recognised me, but perhaps she did."

Either way, Georgiana had taken a risk by pretending to be Mary.

⚭

BREAKFAST WAS HELD late, which suited Mary, as she had the disadvantage of even less sleep than the others.

"How was your night, Mary?" asked Elizabeth.

"I enjoyed reading from *Fordyce's Sermons*. I have neglected them for too long. Then, as planned, I retired early. I feel very much refreshed from a long night of sleep."

"It sounds like it was a good decision for you to not attend the ball," said Mr. Darcy. He did not seem like he was still suspicious of her, but she could not be certain.

"I generally attempt to participate in social obligations, but they should not be undertaken at a detriment to one's own health."

Kitty yawned, and Mary very consciously looked away. She managed to prevent a yawn by swallowing a large sip of too hot tea that almost burned her tongue and throat.

"I am glad you feel well," said Kitty, "but I have a terrible headache."

"Was it a nice ball? Were there many people there?"

"Everyone was there!" said Kitty. "I danced with four different men, though I had to leave the fourth dance early. I wish we could have stayed long enough for me to at least finish the dance."

"If we had stayed longer, you might have an even worse headache," said Elizabeth.

"Dancing is worth any price." Kitty smiled and twirled her spoon. "Georgiana danced twice with Mr. Johnstone."

"Yes, I did, and I will never dance with him again," said Georgiana firmly. Elizabeth and Mr. Darcy looked at her in surprise. "While he is charming, has a good fortune, and is a member of Parliament, he does not have what it takes to interest me. I would prefer if we do not speak of him again."

"What would it take for a man to gain your affections?" asked Elizabeth.

"A sound character and wise judgment," said Georgiana, her head held high. "Someone who is good to all people in all places, is willing to admit mistakes, and is honest and forthright." Her lower lip quivered.

"It is often difficult to discern all of those qualities with a new acquaintance," said Elizabeth, patting Georgiana's hand.

"Now that is the unfortunate truth," said Georgiana. "Mary, would you be willing to take a walk with me after breakfast? Perhaps a short stroll through the park. I would like your advice on interpreting Fordyce."

It was a convenient excuse that would almost guarantee that neither Elizabeth nor Kitty would join them. Georgiana must want to talk about what had happened. Mary swallowed. Better to be done with it and have the inevitable conversation. "A morning walk in the snow can be very invigorating, and I have several of Fordyce's sermons memorised."

The first few minutes of the walk were taken in silence, which Mary desperately wanted Georgiana to break. She did not know how much Georgiana knew and did not want to bring up her escapades, yet surely this was what Georgiana wanted to discuss.

Yet Georgiana would not talk. She walked briskly forward, her face set as if in stone. It seemed they could pass the whole walk in less-than-companionable silence.

"Why did you help me?" asked Mary finally.

Georgiana slowed. She brushed a snowflake off her forehead and said, "After...the incident with your arm, my brother and your sister decided they would send you home if something similar were to happen again." She spoke more quickly now. "I know what it is like to be in trouble for something you have done, and to have the perceptions of the people you care about changed forever. I love my brother with all my heart, and I am so grateful that he saved me from…a situation, when I was younger, but I would not wish his disapproval on anyone. He looks at you with sadness and censure, like you are a puppy with a broken leg who brought its pain on itself."

Mary did not know what Georgiana had done at some point in her past to earn her brother's disapproval. No one had ever spoken of the matter to her. Yet the weight in Georgiana's words meant it must have been something shameful or rebellious.

"Thank you, Georgiana, I owe you a great debt." If not for Georgiana's actions, she *would* have been discovered. She would have been sent to live with her mother and Jane, leaving the case unfinished, and probably ending her career as a spy. They would not let her visit London or Lady Trafford after something like that. All she had worked for, all that she was trying to prove about herself, could have been taken away in a moment.

"I would never have guessed it was you at the ball last night. You looked vaguely familiar, but I could not place you at all, at least not until my brother insisted on checking on you in your room as soon as we arrived home. He did not even take off his cloak before he started up the stairs, and I saw the fear on your maid's face, and I knew I had to do something."

"I feel that I owe you some explanation of my behaviour," said Mary. She could not tell Georgiana the truth, but perhaps she could give her a partial truth, something that would provide some level of justification for her actions.

"Please, do not," said Georgiana. "I have enough weight of my own to carry in silence. I have no interest in carrying your secrets as well. I will speak of your…acting a part to no one."

"I appreciate it." If Mary was in the same situation, she would want to know, she would want to unravel every detail until all was explained. Yet Georgiana did not. She was an intelligent, curious person, but greater than her curiosity was her goodness and her respect for the boundaries of others.

"When I was in your bedroom last night, I took the liberty of borrowing your book on Dominica."

"Oh? I had not noticed it was gone."

Suddenly, Georgiana sobbed. Her body shook, and she reached out her arm and leaned against a passing tree, closing her eyes as if that could shut out the world.

After a moment of hesitation—Mary did not typically engage in acts of physical comfort—Mary placed her hand on Georgiana's shoulder.

Georgiana tried to speak, but every few words she stopped to gasp for air. "Why is it—only horrible men—who make me fall in love with them?" Her whole body seemed to shake. "Why do they see me—as easy prey—and why"—Georgiana let go of the tree and covered her face with her hands—"why do I always fall for their traps?"

Suddenly, Mary understood. The thing that had happened in the past, the trouble from which Darcy had saved Georgiana, also had to do with a man. How utterly terrible to have her hopes, her dreams, her love dashed twice, and she not even twenty.

Mary wrapped her arms around Georgiana, holding her as

they stood in snow. For a time, Georgiana's sobs continued unabated, but then they slowed. Georgiana removed her hands from her face, and Mary stepped quickly away, in what she was afraid was a rather awkward manner. She did not have enough experience providing physical comfort to know the best way to stop providing physical comfort.

"What do I do, Mary? What do I do?"

This might be a time to quote Fordyce's sermons, and several passages did come to mind, but Mary stopped herself. That was not what Georgiana wanted, and probably not what she needed. "I do not know, and I do not know why Johnstone and others targeted you. What I do know is that you are a good person, a kind person, intelligent and talented. You are the sort of person who lights up a room, the sort of person I have always been rather jealous of. It may not have happened yet, but you will find someone who is right for you, someone who loves you truly, someone who is good both inside and out."

"I am starting to doubt that such a man exists."

"He is out there. You will find him some day."

"I can only hope," said Georgiana. "You had quite the handsome partner last night."

"Oh, Mr. Stanley. Yes, I would say that he is handsome. And he is very complimentary."

"He only had eyes for you. Is he…a good man, by our requirements?"

"I would say so," said Mary. "But I am not certain that he understands me, not truly."

"Maybe he will learn to," said Georgiana with a smile.

Mary nodded. It was a pleasant thought. If Mr. Stanley could learn to understand and accept her true nature, then he would make an ideal match.

Georgiana took Mary's arm in hers and they walked down a lane that would take them back towards the house. "Thank you for giving me the information to come to a conclusion on my own, without telling my brother."

"I would hope that someone would do the same for me," said Mary.

When they entered the house, Mary remembered Kitty's headache. Sometimes, when her sisters were ill, she had read to them from an uplifting, religious text, but today she offered to read Kitty a novel, an offer which Kitty readily accepted.

AFTER CHURCH ON Sunday, Mary claimed that she wanted to do her Christian duty and accompany Fanny to see her ill but recovering sister. They took one of Mr. Darcy's carriages and asked the driver to drop them off at a church near the Baron de Berenger's residence.

After the ball, they had sent a message to Mr. Booth asking if he could find de Berenger's address. Apparently, it had been quite easy for him to do so: de Berenger had been brought to court for debts several years before and found guilty. Now, as part of his continuing obligations to the King's Bench, he had to register his address with the government, and he was not allowed to travel outside of London without notifying them.

They were short on time, so they walked quickly through the brisk air. De Berenger's flat shared a front door with a number of other flats, and probably shared a landlord and housekeeper. They tried the door but it was locked. They debated knocking, but if someone came to the door, they did not know a way to enter de Berenger's flat, undetected, before the meeting with Johnstone. The time was fast approaching, so Fanny secreted herself in a bush next to the front door, and Mary stood across the street, a little way down, watching. If only church had not gone long; if only Kitty had not insisted on speaking with three people after the meeting; if only the roads had been better and the horses quicker, then Fanny and Mary would have arrived earlier and been better able to position themselves.

At promptly one p.m., according to Mary's watch, a carriage stopped in front of de Berenger's residence. Mr. Johnstone exited the carriage and knocked at the door, which was opened immediately by de Berenger. He must have been waiting, just inside. Johnstone handed de Berenger a letter, returned to the carriage, and drove away.

It was quite unusual. Normally, there was no reason to deliver a letter oneself: in some ways, that defeated the point of writing a letter rather than having a conversation. It did not make sense, unless it contained a message that could not be allowed to pass through anyone else's hands, that could not risk being read by anyone other than the writer and the recipient.

After a moment, Fanny walked across the street to join Mary. "We need to get inside de Berenger's house, immediately."

"Why?" asked Mary.

"Mr. Johnstone just told him, 'These are your final instructions. Memorise the letter and then burn it. There must be no evidence.'"

"That is a problem."

"De Berenger will remember you, will he not?"

"He should," said Mary. "We spoke for quite some time."

"We must call on him, now."

"A woman—or even two women—cannot simply call upon a single man," said Mary. It would be scandalous.

"Who is going to know?" asked Fanny. "We cannot very well retrieve Mr. Darcy and bring him along."

"You are right, of course. You are always right."

"Quite true." Fanny tucked her arm in Mary's and practically dragged her across the road. "Time is wasting. No time to plan."

Mary knocked on the door, and after a minute, a disgruntled housekeeper answered. "What is it that you want?"

"I am here to call on the Baron de Berenger," said Mary.

The housekeeper looked her up and down, and then did the same to Fanny. "You seem the respectable sort. Very well. Wait here."

She walked down the hall and knocked on the first door. "De Berenger! Visitors for you."

He came to the door, seeming a little nonplussed. "Miss Bennet. To what do I owe this unexpected visit?"

"Baron de Berenger. My pleasure. I had heard you lived here, and I happened to be nearby, for a charity I assist with. We were feeling quite parched, and I was wondering if you could help us?"

"Parched."

"Yes, we would love some tea. It is very cold, and I am also having trouble with the subjunctive form in French. Unfortunately, my French instructor is in Sussex, but I thought that you might be able to help me."

He paused, considering. "Certainly, you are welcome to come in for a few minutes." They followed him down the hall. "I am afraid I only have one type of tea. May I ask the name of your friend?"

"This is my maid and companion, Miss Fanny Cramer."

"A pleasure to meet you, Miss Cramer," he said with a bow, all politeness. He lifted her hand and kissed it.

"The pleasure is all mine," said Fanny smoothly. "Miss Bennet says that you are quite the artist."

"Art is one of my primary pursuits," said de Berenger, leading them into his apartment. He seemed quite charmed by Fanny and showed her several of his pieces before gesturing for them to sit down on a large sofa. It was a fine-looking chair, obviously a high-quality product, but it looked worn, the upholstery a little frayed. He must have acquired it secondhand. Mary sat down and determined that the chair must have been quite comfortable, when it was younger.

"Are you still practising your drawing?" asked de Berenger.

"I have unfortunately neglected it this past week." Mary had not picked up a drawing pencil or pad of paper since the explosion at the Custom House. "Yet I have plans to be more diligent in continuing to develop my skills."

"You should," said de Berenger. "Your sketches of people show promise."

"Thank you." Mary attempted to discreetly survey the room, looking for any trace of the letter he had received from Cochrane Johnstone. De Berenger's eyes glanced at his table and then quickly away. It was definitely something he did not want her to see, and he had inadvertently revealed its exact location.

"You said that you needed help with your French," he said as he poured water for them from a pot that had been resting near the fire.

"Yes, I am having great trouble with the subjunctive form of verbs."

"The subjunctive form?" He passed her a cup, and said, "I

apologise, the water is only lukewarm." He did not offer to heat the water further.

"I do not mind," she said.

Mary sipped her drink and forced herself to swallow. There were few things worse in life than tepid tea. De Berenger obviously did not want them here, though he was too polite to say so. Of course, she had forced him to invite her inside.

She thought for a moment, and then asked something that had been unclear in her new French grammar book. "*Nous n'utilisons pas souvent le subjonctif en anglais, alors j'ai des problems pour savoir quand il faut l'utiliser en francais.*" We do not often use the subjunctive form in English, so I am having trouble knowing when to use it in French. "*Comment puis-je savoir quand je dois utiliser le subjonctif?*" How do I know when to use the subjunctive?

"*Ah, oui, cela peut être compliqué!*" he said, agreeing that it could be complicated. "*Ce qui m'aide, c'est de penser au subjonctif comme un temps d'attitude, au lieu d'un temps temporel.*" It helps me to think of subjunctive as an attitude tense, rather than a temporal tense. "*Si on veut exprimer un doute, un sentiment, un jugement, ou une possibilité, il faut employer le subjonctif.*" If we want to express a doubt, a feeling, a judgment, or a possibility, we must use the subjunctive. He paused, considering for a moment, and then went on to give an example of how the subjunctive form could express a sort of doubt or surprise, and how, with the substitution of a single word, the entire attitude of the speaker could change.

Mary nodded, wishing she had brought something to take notes. It was a much clearer explanation of when to use the subjunctive than that provided in the grammar book, and for a moment she forgot that learning French was not her true purpose here.

"Is that a sufficient answer? While French is my native tongue, I am not a teacher, and am not accustomed to explaining how the language works."

"That is very helpful and will be sufficient until I receive a letter from my French instructor."

"Very well, then I am afraid that I have several important matters to attend to—"

"Oh!" Mary exclaimed as she stood up. He seemed ready to invite her to leave and she refused to do so until she had a chance to see the letter. "Is that a picture of the Thames in the summer?"

"Yes," he said hesitantly.

She walked across the room to examine the picture, which hung on the wall near the window, only a few feet from the desk with the letter. "I have only ever seen the Thames in the winter. A few weeks ago it was completely frozen into ice. There was even an ice fair—did you know?" She did not wait for him to respond, instead trying to say something, anything, that might continue the conversation. "But I cannot imagine it in the summer. Is it loud?"

"Loud?"

"Yes, loud. Writers always describe the rushing of rivers and I wondered if the Thames was loud."

"No more so in the summer than in the winter."

"I see," she said. "It is quite—" And at that moment, she fumbled with her teacup, causing it to spill all over the wooden floor (which was intentional) and all over her dress (which was certainly not intentional).

"I apologise," she said, putting her hand over her mouth in feigned shock. "I can be ever so clumsy, at the most dreadful times."

Fanny looked around frantically. "Oh, Miss Bennet! I wish I was more prepared and had brought something I could use to clean this."

"It is not a problem," said de Berenger, though his face said otherwise. "I will fetch the housekeeper."

She could not believe that her diversion had actually worked. As de Berenger left the room, Fanny went to the door to watch for his return, and Mary picked up the letter.

"My Dear Captain Random de Berenger," it said in an elegant hand.

"Hurry!" whispered Fanny.

Mary nodded and continued to read.

"Everything must be set. There is no turning back now—we are all in this together, and we must either succeed—or fail—together. You know what an important part you have to play, and you will be compensated well for it. But in order for the plan to work, you must ensure that—"

"They're coming!" whispered Fanny.

Mary's eyes raced over the letter, catching only words and phrases.

*when you reach Dover*
*telegraph*
*fastest carriages*
*coins*
*in the morning*
*Mr. Butt*
*opening of the stock exchange*
*Hallway*
*tomorrow*

"Mary!" hissed Fanny, stepping farther back towards the middle of the room.

She hastily set the letter back on the desk, trying to position it exactly as it had been, then walked the few steps back to the spill. She tried to read more of Johnstone's letter, but his handwriting was too small to read from this distance.

She rubbed at the tea stain on her dress with her hand. This only forced more of the tea into the dress, but at least it made it appear like she had been doing something other than reading de Berenger's private correspondence.

On seeing the spill, the housekeeper grunted her disapproval. She passed Mary a cloth. "I will do the floor, but you'd best clean up yourself, miss."

Mary attempted to dry herself, but the cloth did not do much good, as the tea had already soaked through her dress and petticoats and onto her legs. At least the tea had only been lukewarm and not scalding.

As de Berenger passed the desk, he picked up the letter and placed it in his pocket. Mary feared that he would say something, that perhaps he had noticed that the letter was not at the exact angle that he had set it, but he did not.

He checked his pocket watch. "I am afraid, Miss Bennet, that I must cut our visit short, due to a prearranged meeting that I cannot withdraw from." More likely, it was because he needed to act on the note. *Tomorrow* it had said. *Opening of the stock exchange. When you reach Dover.*

"I completely understand," said Mary. "Thank you for indulging me and my desire to master the French language."

As the housekeeper cleaned the remainder of the floor, de Berenger led her to the door. "Please pay my compliments to Mr. and Mrs. Darcy, and give my special regards to the young Miss Darcy."

"Of course."

"Thank you so much for letting us visit you," said Fanny. "I hope you did not find our visit too forward."

"Not at all," he said, bowing to her.

They left the house and hurried down the road, in the direction of the church where they would meet the carriage.

"What was in the letter?" asked Fanny.

Mary described it, as best as she was able.

"You didn't even need my assistance," said Fanny. "I could not have said what you did and made it sound rational, but you sold it well."

"Thank you," she paused. "I wish I could have read more. He will surely burn it soon."

"I think it is enough for us to piece together. There is a plot related to the stock exchange. There is a mysterious hallway, a trip to Dover, and those involved include John-stone, de Berenger, and someone named Mr. Butt."

The name sounded familiar—someone had mentioned it once before, but Mary could not recall who. Most likely, Johnstone.

"We must assume that the plan will happen tomorrow," said Fanny.

"We need to be there, at the stock exchange. And perhaps trail Johnstone and de Berenger. What excuse will I have to be gone for the entire day?"

Fanny smiled. "I think Mrs. Granger—or should I say, Mrs. Hunnicutt—will be able to help us with that. I will send her a note and request that she liberate you from the house first thing in the morning."

"If we are headed to the stock exchange, it might be useful to ask if Mr. Stanley can join us, since he will be able to enter the stock exchange and it is possible that we will not be allowed in."

"Interested in seeing Mr. Stanley, are you?"

"No," said Mary, confused. Then she realised that Fanny

was teasing her. "Maybe a little," she admitted. "He also happens to be assigned to the case, so it would be logical to ask him."

"I will request his assistance in the note as well."

Mary shivered. "Oh!"

"What is it?"

"The tea is freezing on my dress."

Fanny laughed. "It made it seem very credible. No one would ever intentionally pour tea on herself."

"Well, I shall pretend it was planned then."

After changing out of her cold, tea-covered dress, Mary spent the afternoon helping Fanny with the new dress she had been making. Fanny had made the evening gown for herself, and she requested Mary's help with the fitting. She directed Mary on where to pinch fabric and place pins so she could make the final adjustments. As they did so, Mary gained an even better appreciation for Fanny's skill.

Later that evening, Fanny went back to de Berenger's on her own, with the pretence that they had left something there earlier. When she returned, she described what happened. The housekeeper insisted that de Berenger was there, yet Fanny did not believe her, as there was not a single lit candle or lamp in de Berenger's flat. Fanny managed to open a window from the outside and climb in. No one had been present, and she did not find any plans or any other evidence.

Perhaps he had left for Dover. Dover was a city on the beach, located at the spot with one of the shortest distances to cross the English Channel and reach France.

Which raised the question: why would de Berenger travel to Dover, breaking the rules of the King's Bench in the process, and what did that have to do with the stock exchange?

# Chapter Seventeen

*"I consider the balance of power to be, in effect, restored to Europe; and that the Allies may now make peace even with BONAPARTE, nay, that they are bound to do so, if they have proposed a basis consistent with their professions, and he has accepted that basis."*

—*The Morning Post*, London, February 21, 1814

E ARLY IN THE morning, before breakfast and long before normal calling hours, Mrs. Granger called on the house as Mrs. Hunnicutt. She expressed longwinded joy at Mary's recovery, spoke incessantly on a wide range of topics, and then requested that Mary act as her companion for the day, listing a wide range of planned activities.

"I would gladly accompany you," said Mary, keeping her voice flat and free of the anticipation for what she would actually be doing, "if the others can spare me for the day."

Elizabeth and Mr. Darcy readily gave their assent. As Mary prepared to leave with Mrs. Hunnicutt, Elizabeth pulled her aside. "It is no small thing which Mrs. Hunnicutt proposes. Are you certain you feel well enough for this venture?"

"I feel it my obligation to her to accompany her," said Mary with what she thought was the appropriate solemnity. "It is my duty to show my gratitude for her charitable actions, and I do feel fit for the task."

Elizabeth placed her hand on Mary's shoulder. "Take care of yourself, Mary."

When Mary entered the carriage, Fanny was already there; during the long conversation, she had exited out through the kitchen.

After a few blocks, the carriage stopped. "That bag is filled with clothes and other supplies, should you need them," said Mrs. Granger. "I am headed back to the office for a few minutes, but then I have the rest of the day off, and Mr. Booth will not be there either. There is a society he learned about, from Fanny's perusal of Mr. Eastlake's papers, and Mr. Booth is hoping to stop a potential riot. However, Mr. Stanley will be at the stock exchange all day, unless you request his presence elsewhere."

They said farewell to Mrs. Granger. As they drove to de Berenger's, Fanny opened the bag, and put a peasant smock and peasant cloak on Mary. They also found a loaf of bread Mrs. Granger had left for them, and ripped off pieces. After the Custom House incident, Mary should have remembered to eat before leaving for a day of spy work, but she had completely forgotten, so she was grateful for Mrs. Granger's preparations.

When they arrived at de Berenger's, Fanny exited the carriage. The night before, Fanny had left one of the curtains open enough that she was able to peek into the flat and confirm that he was still gone.

There was still quite some time before the opening of the stock exchange, so they drove to Johnstone's house. The driver worked for the department and knew how to avoid attracting attention, and so he parked three houses down.

It was a foggy morning, which made it more difficult to see as Mary and Fanny peered through the window. Mary's pulse raced, her mind running through the words she had seen on the letter. *Telegraph. Coins. Dover. Mr. Butt. Opening of the stock exchange.*

Not five minutes later a carriage arrived—and if she was not mistaken, it was Johnstone's carriage, the very same one she had seen him in the day before, at de Berenger's. Out stepped not Johnstone, but his nephew, Lord Cochrane. Mary had not seen his name in the letter, but it could have been in one of the many portions she had not read.

Once Lord Cochrane entered the house Mary checked her watch. It was 8:28.

Then they waited for what seemed like a long while. Perhaps Lord Cochrane was here for breakfast.

She shifted back and forth in her seat in the carriage. Her neck was becoming uncomfortable.

"Watching patiently is one of the most important parts of being a spy," said Fanny.

"And one of the most agonising."

Fanny smiled.

Nearly an hour after Lord Cochrane had entered, he exited the house, followed by Mr. Johnstone and a man Mary did not recognise. They entered Johnstone's waiting carriage, which made its way down the road.

"Follow at a distance," Fanny instructed the driver.

"Of course, Miss Cramer," said the driver.

The carriage in front of them drove at a brisk pace. As they approached a busier part of town, Fanny instructed the driver to keep as close to Mr. Johnstone's carriage as he could without raising suspicion. The roads were busy with carriages and horses and pedestrians, which made it easier to blend in.

The carriage did not seem to be headed to the stock exchange. It turned onto Snow Hill and slowed. They must be nearing their destination. Fanny shoved a basket of poppets into Mary's hand. "You're the one dressed up; you'd better follow them if they get out." Mary nodded. She could pretend to sell the poppets, or, if someone showed interest, there would be no harm in actually selling them.

Johnstone's carriage came to a halt in front of #1 Cock-lane, Mr. King's Manufactory. This was Lord Cochrane's factory connection.

Mary and Fanny's carriage stopped directly behind theirs, and Mary stepped out quickly.

"Are you certain you do not want to come with us to the stock exchange today?" came the voice of Mr. Johnstone through the open carriage door. "I have a feeling it might be a good day."

"There is no way to know that in advance," said Lord Cochrane as he stepped out of the carriage. "But even if it was possible, Mr. Butt has specific instructions on selling my Omnium and Consols. I do not need to be there—you always sell when mine increases by .25, do you not, Mr. Butt?"

"Or course," said a man in the carriage who must be Mr. Butt, "but sometimes you like more direct involvement."

"It is more stimulating, but I trust you to take care of my interests. And this morning I need to visit the factory."

Lord Cochrane closed the carriage door.

"Poppets! Poppets for sale," said Mary, extending her basket.

"No, thank you," he said, stepping past her without even looking at her.

As Lord Cochrane entered the factory, Mr. Johnstone opened the carriage window and leaned out. "Pity it has been so foggy."

"We will be fine," said Mr. Butt. "The plan did not *re-*

*quire* the telegraph towers."

Johnstone gave orders for the carriage driver, and Mary hurried back into her own carriage.

"Well?" asked Fanny.

"I do not think Lord Cochrane is involved, but the others are headed to the stock exchange. I think we should follow them." Part of her wanted to stay and follow Lord Cochrane into the factory. Yet Mr. Booth and Mr. Stanley had investigated this factory already, and she needed to trust their observations and conclusions, and focus on what seemed a larger risk.

They had not driven far before Mary noticed a commotion on the street, in every direction, people openly shouting, weeping for joy, celebrating. The driver rapped on the window, and she cracked it open.

"You'll want to 'ear this!" he said.

She opened the window the rest of the way, and the shouts filled her ears as they continued to drive down the road.

"News, news from Dover!"

"'E's dead, at last 'e's dead."

"My sons will come home, at last my sons will come home!"

"Bonaparte is dead! Let everyone know Bonaparte is dead!"

"His body was ripped apart they say—split between the Cossacks."

"Can it be?" asked Fanny, her hand to her chest. Tears ran down Fanny's face.

It took a moment for Mary to process the news, and then she collapsed back on her seat. Napoleon Bonaparte dead—dead at last. He had loomed like a mythical evil in the background for most of her life.

Mary felt moisture in her own eyes, which surprised her. But it was not a negative thing, to cry with relief at their victory. The series of wars with France that had begun before Mary's birth could actually, at long last, be over.

The carriage came to a halt. They had reached the stock exchange. Mary tried to focus her mind on what was happening around them. She opened the door, and she and Fanny stepped out, watching as Johnstone and Butt left their carriage.

A young lad approached them. "Bonaparte is dead!" he declared. "Bonaparte is dead!"

"Tell us, tell us all the news," said Mr. Butt.

As the boy recounted Bonaparte's death, Mr. Johnstone shook. He put his hand on Mr. Butt to steady himself, and he too began to cry.

"My nephew—at last he will be out of danger, at last he will return home." This must be Lord Cochrane's brother who they had worried over, who was posted in Spain. Suddenly, he let go of Mr. Butt and stood tall. "Incredible. When did this news come? Who brought it?"

"It was a soldier, it was. Officer du Bourg. I seen 'im meself. He's an *aide de camp* to Lord Cathcart, and 'e landed on the beach in the night. Some riders made it 'ere first, yelling from their horses, and now he's 'ere, to bring word to the authorities."

"Remarkable," said Mr. Butt.

"I am almost in no mood at all to engage in business, with such good news," said Mr. Johnstone, giving the boy a shilling. But despite his words, he followed Mr. Butt into the stock exchange.

Mary almost forgot her task for the day, what with her

THE TRUE CONFESSIONS OF A LONDON SPY

sudden desire to return home and bring the news of Bonaparte's death to her sisters, Georgiana, and Mr. Darcy. But
they would hear, soon enough, and besides, she needed to stay
here. Despite the news, despite the victory, despite this being
a day for national celebration, Johnstone and Butt might still
move forward with their plan.

Mary started to follow the men, but Fanny pulled her
back into the carriage. "We will likely fare better dressed as
ladies. The guards will not let us near the stock exchange
building if we are not."

Fanny pulled a loose gown on top of her own, and Mary
removed the peasant cloak and set aside the poppets. Fanny
set a fancy hat on Mary's head, then asked the driver to find a
place nearby where they could call on him if needed.

They walked briskly towards the stock exchange, trying to
catch Mr. Butt and Johnstone, but they were nowhere to be
seen.

"They must be inside already," said Fanny. "Unless"—she
broke off, thinking—"Eliza Johnstone said that her father had
acquired a new office next to the stock exchange, did she
not?"

"Yes," said Mary.

"I will check this office building," said Fanny. "Get a
sense for the stock exchange, and try to get a message to
Stanley." With that, Fanny was gone.

Mary walked around the perimeter of the stock exchange
building, trying to observe every detail, to notice any suspicious person or someone who might be concealing a weapon.
Of course, it was challenging to notice things out of the
ordinary when everyone was acting out of the ordinary due to
the great victory over Bonaparte. People were shouting,
crying, selling souvenirs—how they had already managed to

make souvenirs, Mary had no idea. She listened in on a few conversations, but no one seemed to have any more details of the battle or the defeat. She supposed she would have to wait for the full story in the papers over the coming weeks.

As Mary completed the circumference, she approached the doors. Despite the fact that she was dressed as a gentlewoman, the guards looked at her grimly. The stock exchange was not considered a place for women. She noted a richly dressed older woman writing a note and giving it to a messenger boy, who ran it inside the building.

Mary decided to do the same and called a messenger boy who stood, waiting, with pencil and paper in hand.

Mary wrote a quick note.

*B. and J. seemed anxious to arrive early today. Nothing of note outside, besides news of victory. Please report anything unusual.*

She paid the messenger boy and gave him directions on Mr. Stanley's appearance. It was quite a nuisance that she would not be permitted inside herself. It would make her work much easier if business was not considered exclusive to the male domain.

The messenger boy returned with Stanley's reply. She paid him more and opened the note.

*The day started with Omnium staying steady from Saturday at 27 ½, the same price it left off. After news of the Dover messenger, the price of Omnium immediately rose to 28, and has since raised to 28 ½, and shows signs of continuing to increase. I have taken the opportunity to purchase stock myself.*

Mary shook her head. Stanley was supposed to observe the stock market, not speculate in it, but she supposed buying and selling a little made it seem more natural for him to be inside the building.

*B. and J. have not done anything unusual. They have multiple agents selling their stocks, which is normal on a busy day like this.*

With good news, stock prices typically rose, and if you were able to buy when the price was low and sell when the price was high, you could make a good profit.

Fanny returned in a huff. "Was the word in the note you read from Johnstone 'Hallway,' or might it have been 'Holloway'?"

"I thought it was Hallway, but I could have read it wrong. It definitely was capitalised, and it would be an unusual word to put at the start of a sentence."

"There is a Mr. Holloway who took an office next to Johnstone's new office. He is a wine merchant, very wealthy by the looks of things. He had an argument with his stock agent. Holloway insisted that his agent sell *every single pound* of stock that he owns this morning. The stock agent wanted to sell in moderation, a little at a time with proper bookkeeping, to avoid the risk of accidentally selling more than Holloway owns. Holloway was angry and threatened to fire the agent and have him banned from the stock exchange if he didn't at least try to sell more, faster."

Mary looked again at Mr. Stanley's note. Mr. Holloway, Mr. Johnstone, and Mr. Butt would all make enormous profits today, Mr. Johnstone especially, with over 220,000 pounds of Omnium and Consols.

Even though Lord Cochrane was not present at the stock exchange, he would make enormous profits as well, as Mr. Butt always sold his stocks if there was an increase of at least half a point.

Something about this seemed suspicious to Mary. They had not, according to Mr. Stanley, engaged in any suspicious behaviour at the stock exchange. They seemed to be present solely to trade. Yet they had told Lord Cochrane that it would be a good day. How could they have possibly known that the morning would bring with it incredible, international news, at the same hour as the stock exchange's opening?

De Berenger was also involved in the plan. He was unlikely to own stock in Omnium; he owed debts and was under restrictions from the King's Bench because of those debts. Besides, he had been missing since yesterday afternoon, and might even be miles away.

Mary looked again at Stanley's note. *The Dover messenger.* The messenger bearing the news of Bonaparte's death had come from Dover, and in the note Johnstone had personally delivered to de Berenger, it had mentioned Dover.

She shook her head, trying to clear her thoughts. The conclusion she was reaching seemed preposterous, yet the more she thought on it, the more possible it seemed.

"You've figured something out, haven't you?" said Fanny.

"Maybe," said Mary. "We need to find someone who personally talked to the messenger who brought word of Napoleon's death. What was his name—"

"Officer du Bourg."

"Yes."

"Consider it done," said Fanny. She pulled Mary with her, back to the crowd of people celebrating in the street. She spoke to a few people, and then continued up the street, speaking confidently to everyone in a way Mary could not have, until they found the very same boy who had told the news to Mr. Johnstone and Mr. Butt.

"You saw the messenger from Dover?" asked Fanny.

"Yes, ma'am, with me own two eyes."

"What did you say the officer's name was?" asked Mary.

"Officer du Bourg."

"And what was the news that he brought?"

"That Bonaparte is dead. The Cossacks tore 'im to pieces."

"Did du Bourg see this first-hand, or was he reporting what someone else said?"

"I…I don't know."

"You said du Bourg was from France?" asked Fanny.

"Yes, but 'e works for an English general, General Cathcart."

That was, to Mary's understanding, a fairly common thing, so there was nothing unusual in that. "How could you tell that he was French?"

"Well, he sounded French, dinnee? And one of me friends works at the carriage exchange. Du Bourg paid 'im with a gold Napoleon. I ain't seen one before."

"What did du Bourg look like?"

He gave a description, not quite as detailed as Mary would have liked.

"Who else saw the messenger?"

"A heap of people."

"Can we find them?" asked Mary.

"Maybe." He shrugged.

Mary sighed. She didn't necessarily need more witnesses, just someone who could give her a better description and perhaps confirm her suspicions. She removed her drawing pad and a pencil from her bag.

"I am going to draw a picture of a man, and you are going to tell me if it looks like Officer du Bourg."

"I've got things to do. Can't wait 'ere all day."

Fanny held out a shilling. "You have plenty of time."

He snatched the coin from her hand. "You're right, I do."

Mary drew a hasty sketch, trying to capture the overall shape of the face and fill it in with the most salient details. It was much harder to do from memory than it was with the subject in front of her, but at least she had drawn this man before.

After a few minutes, Mary turned the paper towards the boy.

"That's 'im!" he said. "That's 'im exactly, right as ninepence. Are you sure you didn't see 'im ride in?"

"I have met him before."

"You know Officer du Bourg?"

"In a way," said Mary. "In a way."

The man she had sketched on her page, the man who had ridden from Dover bearing news of Napoleon Bonaparte's death, was none other than the Baron de Berenger.

# CHAPTER EIGHTEEN

*"PRICE OF STOCKS THIS DAY AT TWELVE O'CLOCK:*
*Omnium: 31 ¾"*

—*The Evening Star*, London, February 21, 1814

B ONAPARTE WAS NOT dead.

It was as if all of Mary's breath had suddenly fled her body, as if a crippling weight she had not known she was carrying had been removed, and now it was placed again upon her back.

Napoleon Bonaparte was not dead. If Mary were a betting woman, she would bet everything on it.

"It's a ploy to drive up stock prices," said Fanny.

Mary nodded. The plot had never been to steal from the stock exchange, or cause a disaster, like the explosion at the Custom House. The purpose, instead, was to spread false news and artificially raise the value of the stock, and profit handsomely from it. As Mr. Withrow had once told her, at the root of everything was the quest for money. Yet she did not see a connection to Mr. Rice: why had they killed him? Perhaps that too would become clear.

"I will pay you to come with me," Fanny said to the boy. She turned to Mary. "I am taking the department carriage to the carriage exchange. I will gather more information and find and follow de Berenger. You stay here, speak to Mr. Stanley, and find a way to stop them from profiting off their lies."

Mary nodded, but as Fanny went off with the boy to the carriage exchange, Mary wished she could call her back. She felt her inexperience like a rock in her shoe, and she feared she would not be capable of the task.

She breathed deeply and then marched back to the entrance to the stock exchange, paid a messenger boy to contact Mr. Stanley, and waited. The fog was not as heavy as it had been, but it still partially obscured her vision, making distant buildings melt into their surroundings and the daylight itself seem dim.

Mr. Stanley exited the stock exchange with a lightness in his step. "I wish you would come inside," he said. "Omnium has reached thirty. I have never seen it rise so rapidly!"

Mary scraped the bottom of her foot against the cobblestone, unsure of the best way to disillusion Mr. Stanley of his excitement.

"Whatever is wrong, Miss Bennet?"

She scratched an itch on her neck. "Bonaparte is alive."

"Oh God."

"The messenger was fake. It was de Berenger. They are trying to drive up the prices at the exchange so they can profit."

Stanley shook his head. "They are standing in there, looking so smug. How could I have been so blind?"

"They have fooled us all. But we need to limit the consequences—we must inform people within the stock exchange. Innocent people are making wild speculations and could lose their fortunes."

"I agree," said Mr. Stanley, "but I cannot allow people to guess my role."

How did one counter unsubstantiated rumours? The rumours themselves did not have proof yet were widely believed. She and Mr. Stanley possessed nothing definitive to disprove them. Her mind raced, but could find nothing, so she used an approach that often helped her, and pictured what her sisters would do in this situation. Thoughts of Jane, Elizabeth, and Kitty did not provoke any ideas, but then she thought of Lydia.

There had been another girl around Lydia's age in Meryton, who had said something unkind about Lydia. In turn, Lydia had spread such rumours about the girl that it had brought her to tears and an apology in a public setting. Lydia had never spoken to the girl or confronted her, yet she had achieved her goal. Mary had always judged Lydia for doing such a thing, but it had been effective. Perhaps the same would work today: maybe the best way to dispel rumours was with more rumours.

"Talk to as many people as you can, and spread seeds of doubt," said Mary. "Ask them if it is true that Bonaparte is dead. Would not we have heard official word from the government by now, if it was actually the case? Surely there would be a letter from the Secretary of State to the Lord Mayor." The Secretary of State would be the ultimate authority in this matter—that office should be the one announcing that Bonaparte was dead, not a random Frenchman riding through the streets.

"As always, you have come up with an excellent plan," said Mr. Stanley. He bowed to her. "I will do what I can."

He turned and went into the stock exchange and Mary waited in the cold.

A FEW MINUTES later a messenger boy came to Mary with a note from Mr. Stanley.

*It is working. Omnium has dropped to 29, and the price of Consols has fallen as well.*

Mary gave the messenger boy an extra shilling in thanks, both for the message and its contents. Then she noticed Butt and Johnstone leaving the stock exchange building. She followed them, watching, a little ways back, as they entered the building that held their new office. It would be better to wait longer to follow them, but unlike Fanny, she did not know the location of their office, so she slipped in only a few seconds behind them.

They went down a hall, up a set of stairs, and down another hall, while Mary prayed that they would not turn around. They did not quite shut the office door, so Mary stood outside of it.

Mr. Butt said, "People are starting to doubt, and I have not yet sold everything."

"We planned for this, and it will improve again," replied Johnstone. "Simply wait to sell more until it does."

There was a sound, and Mary stood paralysed outside the door. She could not possibly flee. All the other doors in the hallway were shut and likely locked, and it was too far to the staircase before they opened the door and saw her. She turned and covered her face with the hood of the cloak as she heard the doorknob twisting. Instead of opening, the door closed the rest of the way.

Mary put her ear against the keyhole, but she could hear no more of their conversation, so she walked down the hall and the stairs, pondering their words. As she left the building, she was struck again by the sound of people, on the road, celebrating. There was a new buoyancy to the crowd that matched when they had first heard the news.

Down the road she could see a carriage heading away from the stock exchange. It carried several men in uniform with tall plumed black hats and was thronged by people. It must have passed directly in front of the stock exchange while Mary was spying on Butt and Johnstone.

Fear spread through Mary's body. She had a foreboding that this too was part of the conspiracy.

Mary approached a woman on the street who was both weeping and laughing for joy.

"Who were those people in the carriage?" she asked the woman.

"Bourbon soldiers, celebrating the defeat of Napoleon!"

She had a printed paper in her hand, with the words, in French, "*Bonaparte est mort.*" *Bonaparte is dead.*

"Can I see that?" Mary asked.

The woman pulled her hand, and the paper, back. "No," she said firmly. "It's my souvenir, get your own."

People were already headed into the stock exchange, their own billets announcing Bonaparte's death in hand. She suspected that asking Stanley to spread more rumours against the news would accomplish little now.

A rented carriage stopped only a few feet from her. Several gentlemen paid the driver and then descended so they could spend their money on stock.

Mary hailed the now-vacant carriage. She directed the driver to take her forward, after the other carriage, but it was now quite a ways up the street, and as this was a major thoroughfare they could not move very quickly. They would never overtake them at this rate.

She directed the driver to turn left onto a side street. She urged him on faster, then had him turn right, onto a street parallel to the original one. This road was a bit less congested than the original, and Mary kept urging him to go faster until, in exasperation he declared, "I'll go as fast as I can, miss, but I'll not get you killed."

After a few blocks Mary instructed the driver to turn right down an alleyway, back towards the original road.

But then, in front of them, a carriage overturned, blocking the path of their own carriage.

Mary could hear shouts of "Bonaparte is dead!" and see the carriage with the soldiers in the distance. She hastily gave the driver some coins and climbed out of the carriage.

On the main road, the carriage with the soldiers moved on, past the intersection. Mary walked briskly, but she knew it was not fast enough. She would not make it.

Throwing aside propriety, something that happened altogether too often as a spy, Mary lifted up her skirts and ran down the street. She reached the intersecting road, darted across in front of a horse, barely avoiding being trampled, and then ran up the road. The carriage was just a little farther, just a little farther.

Finally, she made it to the carriage, reached up her hand as the man in the French-looking uniform and tall military hat handed her a billet. Her eyes skimmed the words in French: "*Bonaparte est mort. Enfin la victoire. La guerre est finie! L'oppression a cessé!*"

"*Napoléon a été vaincu!* Napoleon has been defeated!" yelled the man in the carriage. He did not sound like a Frenchman when he spoke French, and in English he did not have a trace of a French accent. He sounded more like someone from the lower classes of London.

"*Étiez-vous là quand c'est arrivé?*" Mary asked him in French. "*Avez-vous vu le corps?*"

A brief look of confusion passed the man's face, but then he turned his attention to someone else.

Mary made her way through the press of people to the other side of the carriage. She reached upwards, towards the other fake Bourbon soldier, and said, "*Vous ne parlez même pas français, n'est-ce pas?*"

He did not respond.

"*Napoléon est-il vraiment mort?*" When he did not reply, Mary declared loudly, "They do not even speak French. How can they be Bourbon soldiers?"

The fake French soldier growled gutturally at her, then yelled at the driver, who struck his whip at the horses. They sprang forward, forcing the crowds of people back.

Mary stood paralyzed in the road for a moment, plagued by indecision. She had not thought through that confrontation ahead of time, but if she had, she could have foreseen the result. Accusing them in front of an audience was not the best manner to discover information.

Another carriage almost ran her over, and she tripped on the walk as she stepped out of the way, landing on her hands and knees, her nose only inches from the ground. She stood and rubbed her hands together, trying to get the dirt off without getting any more on her dress or cloak.

She tried to ignore it and stand tall, but she was crushed by indecision. What could she, Miss Mary Bennet, possibly do? Perhaps she could find a magistrate and have the men in the carriage arrested, but by the time she found a magistrate, they would be long gone. Or she could follow them, and either see where they went or try to ascertain their real identities. That would satisfy her urge for justice. But these people, if she were right about their accents, were poor Londoners, and might receive fifty or one hundred pounds, if they were very, very lucky, for their part to play in today's events, while others, Johnstone, Butt, de Berenger—might earn thousands or tens of thousands of pounds. They were the orchestrators, the planners, the ones with the vision to pull off a conspiracy against the entire British people simply for their own monetary gain. They were the people who should be brought to justice.

Perhaps she could return to the stock exchange and Mr. Stanley, but what more could she do there? She was not certain Stanley would have a solution: he had not proffered any ideas when she first informed him of the ruse. Fanny would likely have good advice, but she had followed de Berenger. Mr. Booth was attempting to quell workers' riots, who knows where, and Mrs. Granger would have left the office by now. Detective Donalds would be useful if she had specific information about the death of Mr. Rice, but there would be nothing he could quickly do against a conspiracy of this size. There was no one to give her advice, no one to help her, and she wished that she could hide in her bed beneath the blankets until all of this went away.

There was no way in which Mary could solve this problem.

Yet perhaps she could prevent Johnstone and the others from causing more harm. She thought of the fire at the Custom House, and the people it had killed, and how many others had lost their livelihoods and had their hopes and dreams shattered. She thought of Minerva pleading for help in a letter. Mary had ignored it. But she would not ignore this problem.

She needed someone to decisively say that Napoleon Bonaparte was alive, someone that everyone at the stock exchange would immediately believe. Which meant she needed to get to a building a few miles away, and quickly.

She looked down the street, and on the side road she spotted the carriage she had hired. The driver leaned against it, arms crossed, watching her with a curious expression. She waited for a gap in traffic, crossed the road, and walked in his direction.

"You gave me too much, miss," he said.

Mary shrugged.

"What was all the commotion about?"

"Someone is spreading rumours. They do not stand to be repeated." She opened the door of the carriage and then paused. "Would you be available for another ride?"

"As long as it's not too fast, miss."

"Understood," said Mary, and climbed in. "Take me to the Secretary of State building."

The man bit his lip. "I don't know it."

"It is near the Palace of Westminster."

As the driver led the carriage down the roads, Mary shivered. Despite the food she had eaten, her stomach felt empty. She rubbed at the dirt on her dress and managed to make it look a little more presentable. Fortunately, they made it to West End quickly, and she directed the driver to a tall, white-columned building.

She almost ran up the steps of the building—something about running made her want to do more of it—but she restrained herself. She needed to put on a persona, the persona she had used to fool Stanley on her first meeting. That woman would be dignified and would not run up the stairs. But she would walk quickly and with purpose, and would not let anyone, or anything, prevent her from her task.

She marched up the steps, adjusted her hat, and, trying not to let any hesitation show, pushed open the front doors.

There was a secretary at the desk—a man—and a number of other people in the front area. But only one of them was a woman.

"I need an immediate audience with Lord Wheatley," she said to the secretary. She remembered Mr. Booth mentioning his name once and hoped that he might be able to help her.

"I am not sure what you could possibly need that for."

She leaned forward towards the man and kept her voice low. "I work for the Foreign Intelligence office."

"Really?"

"Yes, I am one of their spies, under Mr. Booth." Her fingers twitched, and she wished she had some sort of document or evidence to demonstrate her claim. "There is currently a conspiracy against the government and the people, and I need to speak to Lord Wheatley immediately."

The secretary raised his eyebrows at her. "What a bizarre claim. I am sorry, but without proof or an introduction I simply cannot schedule a meeting for you."

There was no way she could find Mr. Booth, and she did not know where Mrs. Granger lived. Further, she did not have time to find someone to help her: she needed to put a halt to this conspiracy immediately.

"A large group of individuals have created an elaborate hoax which claims that Bonaparte is dead."

"We have heard several rumours of that around the office this morning, but it simply is not true."

"I *know* that it is not true. But people are believing the hoax, people are acting on it, which harms these people who believe, and ultimately damages their faith in the government."

"I seriously doubt that." The man turned down to his paper and quill. "Now will you please leave? I have work to do."

Mary did not move. She looked at the man, trying to figure out what she could use that might convince him. The flirtation of her younger sisters seemed unlikely to affect him; neither did Jane's kindness nor Elizabeth's clever speaking. Her mother would likely throw a fit, or faint, or both, but that seemed unlikely to get her into the office.

Perhaps if she had not acted so much like herself when she first entered the office she might have succeeded. She could have started with one of those other approaches or a combination of them. But it was too late to shift now.

Very well. She would resort to subterfuge.

"I apologise for taking so much of your time. Unfortunately, my driver will not be back for another twenty minutes, and it is very cold outside. Would it be possible for me to sit somewhere and drink a cup of tea before I leave?"

"Very well," said the secretary, as if against his better judgment. The secretary led her to a sitting room and gestured to a tea pot. "I am sorry I cannot assist you further. I am needed at the desk."

Mary removed her cloak and draped it over a chair. "Thank you once again." She poured herself tea as the secretary left and took one quick sip. Once she was sure he was gone, she pinched her cheeks to give them some colour, then slipped out of the room, rushing down the hallway until she found the door labelled, "Lord Wheatley."

Her heart pounded in her chest, and she could feel her pulse in her ears. She set her hand on the doorknob, fearing that what she was about to do would completely defy the bounds of social propriety. She did not know if this was the action that Mr. Booth would have her take, but she had no other ideas. Before she could talk herself out of doing it, she rapped lightly on the wood, twisted the knob, and pushed open the door.

Two men were meeting at a grand mahogany desk. The dignified man with silver hair who sat behind the desk paused and looked up, and the other man turned his chair so he could face her.

Mary gave a low curtsy, doing all she could to act refined. "I must express my deepest apologies for interrupting. I thought you were available, and I have come on urgent business for the Foreign Intelligence Office."

"I am afraid we have not met," said Lord Wheatley.

"I am Miss Mary Bennet," she said, trying to speak slowly, without the franticness she had used on the secretary. "I work directly under Mr. Booth."

She felt as if her fate was held in the balance, being weighted on a scale.

Lord Wheatley carefully rearranged the position of his papers. "Ah, Mr. Booth. He did mention that he had a new female spy, but he did not give me a name."

The other man had the beginnings of a sneer on his face, but Lord Wheatley's face was decidedly neutral. She did not know if that was a promising sign, but she carried onward, attempting to summon the weight of Mr. Withrow's way of speaking and the eloquence of Lady Trafford, aware that if they did not believe, she could be thrown onto the street, or perhaps even arrested. "There is a large hoax, a conspiracy of individuals, who are attempting to convince people that Napoleon Bonaparte is dead. Now I understand that there is no real evidence that Bonaparte has been killed by the Allied forces. But the purpose of the plot is not to ultimately convince the government or the nation as a whole that Bonaparte is dead. The purpose is to convince those at the stock exchange of the fact. This morning Omnium was at twenty-seven. By noon, it had risen to thirty. By now, it would not surprise me if it were at thirty-two or thirty-three. The organisers of this hoax are there at the stock exchange, selling tens of thousands of pounds of stock. Innocent people who have been hoodwinked by the perpetrators have invested large amounts of funds to buy stock because of their belief in Bonaparte's death, and more will continue to do so. The conspirators will achieve their entire goal *unless* the government acts now."

"Who are the conspirators?"

"Mr. Andrew Cochrane-Johnstone, Mr. Butt, the Baron de Berenger, I think a Mr. Holloway, and several others." It was a bold claim, particularly as Mr. Johnstone was a member of Parliament.

"What would you have me do?" asked Lord Wheatley, resting his fingertips against each other to form a triangle. From his tone, she could not tell whether or not he believed her. "Well?"

Mary's mind raced—she had not thought that far ahead. She cleared her throat as something came to her. "Send an official government messenger to the stock exchange and then to other key areas of business to declare that Napoleon Bonaparte is not dead, that there has been no word of it, and that the rumours were only rumours. After, send the messenger to the press to make the same announcement."

At that moment the door opened. In rushed the secretary and a guard.

The guard grabbed Mary's arms and yanked her towards

the door. Mary tried to pull herself away but could not.

"I told this woman she could not have an appointment," said the secretary, "And I deeply apologise that she has interrupted you—"

Lord Wheatley held up his hand. "Please, unhand Miss Bennet."

The guard released her, and she stumbled, but she managed not to fall.

"Why did you not receive permission to address me?"

"I attempted to, but when I was denied permission, I knew it could take me several hours to find Mr. Booth or someone else to back up my claim. I did not want to give the perpetrators of the crime several extra hours."

"And why come to this office, rather than your own?"

"Because the Secretary of State office is considered the ultimate authority by the people on these matters."

"We will, of course, verify your identity with Mr. Booth, but meanwhile, I see no harm in following your advice and sending a messenger to the stock exchange."

"If I give you the information on the perpetrators, can you ensure they are detained?"

"That will be up to the stock exchange to arrange with the local magistrates. If they can demonstrate probable culpability, then the men you speak of can be arrested."

Mary had always thought of justice as an immediate, swift thing, but it seemed that was not the case. But at least Lord Wheatley had listened to her and not allowed the guard to drag her away, and at least he took steps to swiftly resolve the immediate problem. Within ten minutes Mary found herself in a carriage next to the man Lord Wheatley had been meeting with as they headed back to the stock exchange. After a few minutes of drumming her fingers on the seat she said, "I am afraid we have not been properly introduced."

"I am Mr. Kimsley. I am guessing that you are a sister, by marriage, to Mr. Darcy."

"Yes. Do you know him?"

"A little. I can see some resemblance between you and Mrs. Darcy."

"Please do not mention my involvement in this affair to them. They do not know about my connection to the Foreign Intelligence office."

"Very well."

They were quiet the rest of the way. Mary tried to keep her hands still and her heart calm.

The carriage arrived and they walked towards the building. She held back and Mr. Kimsley gave her a nod before he entered the building.

She rubbed her forehead, but it did not relieve the tension. She wanted to be inside, to witness the events as they happened rather than hearing an accounting afterwards. She had managed to enter Lord Wheatley's office on her own; surely, she could do this.

She walked up the steps to the stock exchange, her head and her chin held high.

The guards did not attempt to stop her, or even say a word to her, as she walked past them and opened the doors. She assumed it was a rule that no women were allowed in the building, but she had been mistaken. Of course, there were only men inside, so it was a rather established custom.

She found a small alcove set back from the mass of people from where she could observe without being observed. Of course, all attention was on Mr. Kimsley, who stood next to an official-looking man who was alternately ringing a bell and calling for silence.

All around Mary was the physical weight of commerce and wealth. Even inside the building were tall, stately pillars, and there was an intricate half-round glass window against the opposite wall, made of dozens of panes. The room was filled with hundreds of men in their fine suits and cravats, tall black hats on their heads. She felt very out of place as the only woman.

She spotted Stanley in the crowd. After more searching, she found Mr. Butt and Mr. Johnstone. She could just make out the side profile of Johnstone's head.

The room quieted and Mr. Kimsley spoke. "I am Mr. Kimsley, an officer of the Secretary of State. This morning there have been a number of reports of Napoleon Bonaparte's death, spread by official-looking individuals. Fortunately, the stock exchange sent a messenger to the office of the Secretary of State to verify the information."

She had not been sent by the stock exchange, but it was a logical explanation for why he was here. Johnstone's face was very still.

"I have come to declare that the reports were false, an elaborate conspiracy meant to fool the British people. Napoleon Bonaparte is not dead."

At this there were numerous shouts, and instant conversation across the room. Johnstone turned his head to Butt and shook it.

The bell was rung again until the conversations silenced.

"Bonaparte is still alive and leading his troops. Hopefully, in the near future, we will receive true good news. But know that this will come through official government channels.

"And for those who have participated in this conspiracy, know that justice will be exacted."

Johnstone's face was stoic, passive. Butt leaned a bit forward, and Mary could now see his face, which was a mirror to Johnstone. They would attempt to put on a mask of innocence, but if she had anything to do about it, they would be held accountable for their actions.

Johnstone and Butt left the stock exchange. Mr. Kimsley gestured to Mary, and she followed him into a room with the head of the stock exchange and Mr. Stanley, where, after the head of the stock exchange swore to not reveal her and Stanley's identities, she told them everything she knew.

# CHAPTER NINETEEN

*"Never, perhaps, was a greater agitation produced in the metropolis by any foreign news, than was yesterday occasioned by a fraud of the most impudent and nefarious description....The Stock Exchange was instantly in a bustle....Vast sums were sold in the course of the day,— not less, it is supposed...than half a million [pounds]."*

— *The Times*, London, February 22, 1814

MR. BOOTH LEANED his arms against his desk, his chin resting on his hands. He looked at each of them in turn, evaluating them. Despite what they had done, despite stopping the scandal at the stock exchange before it grew worse, Mary felt nervous under his gaze. Across the table was spread every paper, every clue related to Mr. Rice's death, including the sketch Mary had made of his dead body. The memory of the smell still made her stomach churn. A smaller pile held all the paperwork that had been compiled for the stock exchange.

"We need to find a servant willing to add to the carriage driver's testimony, someone who can verify de Berenger went to Lord Cochrane's house after his charade at the stock exchange," said Mr. Booth.

"I truly do not believe Lord Cochrane was involved," said Mary. "I think his uncle wanted him to be, but I told you what he said, outside the factory."

"Also, by the time I found him, de Berenger was still waiting outside Lord Cochrane's house," said Fanny. "When Lord Cochrane returned from the factory, he seemed very surprised to see de Berenger, and rather displeased."

"I suspect you are both correct," said Mr. Booth, "But the stock exchange and the jury need all the details, and de Berenger's visit to Lord Cochrane's provided an opportunity for him to borrow a coat and hat that would not attract attention. Now tell me again, Miss Cramer, where you saw de Berenger dispose of his costume."

She described the specific spot on the river.

"It will need to be dredged," said Mr. Stanley.

"Agreed," said Mr. Booth, making a note. He lowered his hand. "Good work, Miss Bennet; good work, Miss Cramer; good work, Mr. Stanley. Well done. It is a great thing to stop those who would steal from others, and, even worse, those who erode the faith held in government by spewing forth false reports that lead to unease and uncertainty. You are to be commended for your efforts with exposing this scandal. Everyone is happy that you nipped this problem at the bud."

Stanley smiled at Mary. He had a handsome face—he truly did—and his eyes looked at her like she was a queen. "You deserve most of the credit, Miss Bennet."

Mary frowned. She did not like that he chose to compliment her by devaluing Fanny's contributions. "That is not so, the—"

Fanny hushed her. "Mr. Booth, it seems that you have something more you want to say."

"There is no apparent connection between the stock exchange scandal and the murder of Mr. Rice. As a result, I am closing the investigation into Mr. Rice's death."

Mary felt like she was sinking, as if she were trapped in a tub of water and could not get out. They had done something that, while worthwhile, would have been figured out and stopped without their help. She had been distracted by this, and lost sight of the true goal.

"I think we are close to a breakthrough," said Fanny.

"We have had the three of you put almost a month of exclusive work into this, and a number of other agents have performed minor tasks. While we have found hints and clues, the case is messier than when we began: we have nothing that ties it all together, no promising leads waiting for us. It is better to set this aside and focus on projects with a higher probability of success."

Mary picked up the sketch she had made of Mr. Rice. His sister, Mrs. Knowles, would never be able to forget finding her brother dead on the floor. She would never have justice for him. The perpetrator was free, and who knew what further harm he or she would cause.

"It is tragic, I know," said Mr. Booth. "I will take it upon myself to break the news to Mrs. Knowles. Mr. Stanley, you have other assignments already. Miss Bennet, Miss Cramer, I will be in touch with you soon."

This seemed clearly like a dismissal, and Fanny tugged on Mary's arm. She knew she should stand. She knew she should leave, but she did not want to. She blinked rapidly, but it did not stop her eyes from stinging. She did not want to set aside the case. Logically, she knew this failure belonged to all of them, but that did not stop it from feeling like a personal failure on her part.

Fanny tugged again, and Mary finally stood. They walked together, outside into the cold. The bright, cold winter sun seemed to blind her, and she looked at the ground.

"Miss Bennet, I was hoping I could speak to you," said Mr. Stanley. "A private conversation."

Mary looked up at him. Perhaps he wanted to comfort her in their failure.

Fanny crossed her arms. "Now is not the time, Mr. Stanley. Another day, perhaps."

He bowed to both of them. "I hope, Miss Bennet, that although this case is over, I may enjoy your company further in the future."

"Of course," said Mary. "I am certain we will have opportunities to continue our acquaintance."

Stanley gave her a winning smile and walked away.

"Be careful how much you encourage him," said Fanny, "unless you are sure of what you want."

"What do you mean?" She was not encouraging Stanley in anything, simply showing the politeness of speech required of a gentlewoman.

Fanny just shook her head.

Mary and Fanny walked down the road to where they were to meet a carriage to return them to the Darcys. Mary kicked some loose pebbles with her shoe. They bounced a little down the path but did not go far.

"Mr. Booth said he wanted us to work on more productive tasks, but he has not given us anything."

"That is standard," said Fanny. "It could take days or weeks before something else needs our attention."

"But why not let us work on it, then?"

Fanny shrugged. "I find it pleasant to have a break between cases."

Mary's foot became caught on the rough edge of a cobblestone and she almost tripped. She put her hand against the cold wall to steady herself. She should not feel the way she did—she should accept Mr. Booth's judgment on the matter and let go of Mr. Rice's death. Yet the thought of doing so made her want to return to her bed and never leave it. A part of her wanted to sit down, here on the ground, and curl up with her knees pressed to her chest.

Fanny rested her hand on Mary's shoulder. "I can tell that Mr. Booth was impressed with you, and he does not impress easily."

Yet in the end, impressing Mr. Booth did not actually matter. She remembered Mr. Rice's face, the bloodshot eye and dried blood in his ears. She remembered the moment when the Custom House exploded, when suddenly the world went bright, sound thundered, glass shattered. There had been glass in someone's eye at the restaurant.

Whoever was behind Mr. Rice's murder and the explosion of the Custom House would stop at nothing to meet their aims. And so they must be stopped.

"I cannot admit defeat," said Mary. "Not this time."

She marched back to Mr. Booth's office, Fanny following. "What do you plan to do?" asked Fanny, but Mary did not respond, for she did not know.

Mr. Booth seemed surprised to see them. "Did you leave something, Miss Bennet?"

"Yes, I mean…" She took a deep breath, trying to draw in courage as well as air. "I feel like there is more that I can do to bring to light the truth."

"The case is closed."

"I only want a little more time, and if I do not make progress on it, I will give it up."

"What would you do with more time?" He shook his head. "I cannot give it to you, unless you have something more substantial that drives you, some specific, promising lead."

Mary shuffled through the papers related to the case, which were still on Mr. Booth's desk. Surely there was something in here, something they had missed, that would provide a worthwhile avenue of investigation. There were the letters she had received from Sir Francis Burdett with his looping handwriting, Mr. Rice's ledger and documents, Mrs. König's love letters, statements summarising the interviews of each of the suspects, Burdett's angry letter to Mr. Rice, Fanny's report on her time at Mr. Eastlake's, and of course, the picture Mary had sketched of Mr. Rice's body. Mary went through the papers again, aware of Mr. Booth's bemused expression and Fanny standing, fidgeting, behind her.

Her eyes wandered across the pages, barely even registering what she held in her hands, until suddenly, her eyes stopped on the looping letters of the notes Sir Francis had sent her. She found the threatening letter he had written to Mr. Rice, that had been found near the body, and she placed it next to the other letters. Now that they were side by side, the difference was startling.

"The handwriting is different," said Mary. "These are the notes Sir Francis sent me. Notice the curly part of the B, and how full this loop is, and how he angles the letter l."

Mr. Booth looked at the letters himself. "The capital Ws are the same, but the Ss and the Bs are different. Either Sir Francis had a very unsteady hand that day, or this is a clever forgery, a close enough match that we did not notice the differences on first glance, but consistently different, nonetheless. See here, the dotting of the I's is different as well."

"What if this was a misdirection, an attempt to frame Sir Francis and the others?" said Fanny. "If that is the case, the Radicals are not responsible, and we haven't found evidence because we're looking at the wrong people."

"Where do you propose we look instead?" asked Mr. Booth.

Mary tapped her fingers on the desk. This revelation put everything in a new light. The Radicals had many enemies, many Tories and Whigs who disliked and distrusted them. Sir Francis had made himself more than his fair share through his arrest and imprisonment, and despite his appeal among the common people, Lord Cochrane had many enemies in the Navy.

After the Custom House explosion, she had seen the man who had chased Minerva at the ice fair. Mr. Booth's men had made no progress at finding him. But at the ice fair he had been given money by the man with curly hair, the one who had pushed Mrs. König at the ball.

Mary explained her theory. "I think that Mrs. König knows who he is. We just need to force her to tell us."

"That is a solid lead," said Mr. Booth. "I will give you twenty-four hours."

"Twenty-four hours?" asked Fanny.

"That is not much time to follow a lead," said Mary.

"Twenty-four hours to solve the case," said Mr. Booth. "My superiors are frustrated, and Detective Donalds has closed the case, so that is as much as I can give you."

Mary sniffed. That was not very long at all.

"Miss Cramer, are you willing to work with Miss Bennet on this?"

"Yes, sir."

"Then best of luck to both of you."

They left, Mary in a bit of a daze. She had found a lead and managed to convince Mr. Booth to let her follow it, but she did not know what to do next.

"I have no idea how we are going to convince Mrs. König to tell us."

"That is easy." Fanny smiled. "We are going to blackmail her."

# CHAPTER TWENTY

*"THEATRE-ROYAL, HAYMARKET.—— The doors to be open at half past Five, and the Performance to begin at half past Six....[If] any persons indecorously [throw] any thing, of any sort, any way, during the Performance upon the Stage, [then we will give] a Reward of FIVE GUINEAS to any Peace Officer, or...to any other person, on their conviction."*

—*The Morning Post*, London, February 22, 1814

A FEW HOURS later, Mrs. König came to the park in a rush, looking wildly around her, her eyes darting this and that way as if afraid of being followed. This was not the park next to the Darcys' and the Königs' townhomes—there would be too much risk that Mary and Fanny would be noticed and recognised—but rather a park about a mile away.

Mary and Fanny waited at the large tree in the centre of the park, the place they had specified in the blackmail note. A bit of water—melting snow—dripped from one of the branches onto Mary's face. Mary was still using the pretence that she was spending the day with Mrs. Hunnicutt, and hoped that none of her family became suspicious.

Mrs. König approached with caution. First, she looked at Fanny, whom she had never met, as Fanny had only interacted with her servants, and then her eyes turned to Mary, who

THE TRUE CONFESSIONS OF A LONDON SPY

was dressed not as herself but as Levena Kendall.

"I know you," said Mrs. König quickly, and for a moment Mary feared that her disguise was insufficient. "You are the woman from the ball. The one who kept questioning me after I fell."

"Indeed I am," said Mary, attempting to adopt the persona of Levena Kendall.

"What is it you want from me?"

"If you do not help us," said Fanny, "we will tell your husband about your many infidelities. The evidence we have collected would easily warrant a divorce. You will lose everything—your marriage, your money, your place in society. Even your daughter, Henrietta."

At the mention of Henrietta, a shadow of fear crossed Mrs. König's face. "Leave my daughter out of this," she said angrily.

"Should your actions be known," said Fanny, "it could ruin Henrietta's future chances."

"We do not want to hurt you or your family," said Mary. "We just need you to talk to us, and to give us a little information."

Mrs. König's jaw worked its way back and forth. "I do not believe that you have evidence of your accusations."

"We have been watching you for some time, Selena," said Fanny. "For instance, we have witnesses that are willing to attest that on the second of this month you attended the ice fair for a...shall we say, tête-à-tête with Mr. Sharp, which involved both of you, in a tent he had rented from a prostitute."

Mrs. König's face reddened.

"There was also the incident—"

"I will tell you what you want to know," said Mrs. König,

closing her eyes as if that could shut out the censure of the world.

"Thank you," said Mary. "We do appreciate your cooperation."

"Go on then," said Mrs. König. "Tell me what you want so I can leave this wretched park."

"Tell us about Mr. Rice," said Mary.

"I suppose you already know I had a relationship with him," said Mrs. König. Mary nodded. "He understood and appreciated me, in a way that no one else did. I considered leaving my husband and daughter, but I knew it would never work."

If she had ran away with Mr. Rice, she would have lost her wealthy lifestyle and any acceptance by polite society.

She removed a pocket watch from her pocketbook and attempted to look at it discreetly—though discreet she was not—before returning it to its place.

"When was the last time you heard from him, before his death?" asked Fanny.

"I received a letter from him, a few days before. It made me angry, because he seemed to trust his sister more than he did me."

"Do you still have the letter?"

"I burned it. I burned everything from him, the moment I read it, as a sort of protection for myself. How I regret that now. I do not have anything of his that I can hold onto, and I fear my heart—the heart forgets, even while the pain remains."

"What did the note say?" said Mary.

"The normal. Words of poetry. A date and time when we could next meet, which, of course, did not occur. He seemed worried, like there was something important that he was not telling me, and then he wrote of his sister, how good and trustworthy she was."

Perhaps Mr. Rice had known something, known something dangerous, and shared something with his sister. Yet when the others had interviewed Mrs. Knowles, she had mentioned nothing of the sort.

"When did you first hear of Mr. Rice's death?" asked Mary. They knew the answer to this—or they supposed they did—but it would be useful to hear it from her.

"I received a rather shocking note, delivered by courier one evening, that contained the news. It was simple and cruel, with no useful details."

Mary swallowed her guilt. Yet Mrs. König would have learned eventually, one way or another, and it would have been a struggle for her regardless of the delivery method. And they had not been nearly as cruel as whoever had informed her of Mr. Rice's manner of death. She wondered who had done so, and how, but before she could formulate a question, Fanny spoke.

"And then you asked Mr. Sharp for help at the ball?"

"How do you know that?"

"We know many things."

"I did ask him."

"Why?" asked Fanny, her tone harsh. Mary wondered if she always took this unforgiving approach with informants.

Mrs. König worked her jaw back and forth.

"Please, Mrs. König," said Mary. "We want justice for Mr. Rice as much as you do. Your knowledge could be instrumental in discovering the truth."

Mrs. König stood a little taller. "Mr. Sharp is a member of Parliament. He knows many people, and he knows Mr. Rice. I thought he might be able to help me. He did not remember

Mr. Rice very distinctly, but he said he would see what he could discover."

"Did you mention Mr. Rice and his death to anyone else?" asked Mary.

"No, not a soul."

"When did Mr. Sharp reply to you?" asked Mary, even though she already knew the answer. "And did you learn anything else, from anyone, in between speaking to Mr. Sharp and receiving his letter?"

"The morning after the ball, when I woke, there was an unsigned letter waiting for me." So someone had written to her, before Mary and Fanny had begun watching. "I can only assume that it was from the same people who had written the original note."

"What did it say?" asked Mary, as gently as she could.

Mrs. König shut her eyes and recited from memory. "We want you to know that Mr. Rice was strangled to death. This ruined his pretty face. His eyes looked as if they would pop out of his head." She opened her eyes, and now looked as if she were about to cry. Yet she did not, instead rushing into her next statement. "It frightened me, shook me to the core. I immediately wrote to Mr. Sharp, telling him of the second note."

"And then Mr. Sharp wrote back to you." Fanny said this not as a question, but a statement.

"Yes, I received the note the next morning."

"The note about the strangulation," said Mary. "Was it written by the same hand as the first note which had informed you of Mr. Rice's death?"

"I do not pay attention to such things. But of course—no, actually, I do not believe it was."

"I assume you burned this note as well," said Fanny,

sounding a little annoyed.

Mrs. König nodded. She again removed her pocket watch, gave it a cursory glance, and then placed it back in her pocket.

Who had sent Mrs. König the second note? She had only told Mr. Sharp, but he could have talked to any number of people in an attempt to find her information. One of them could have wanted to frighten Mrs. König.

"What did Mr. Sharp say in his note?" asked Mary.

"He tried to comfort me and said that he had begun talking to members of Parliament, but there was nothing of consequence."

"Did you have any further communications with Mr. Sharp on this matter?" asked Fanny. "Obviously, there was the ice fair."

"I was hopeful that if I...acquiesced to Mr. Sharp's desires, he would be more willing to help me. Thus, the ice fair. He did tell me that some of the Radical members of Parliament were being investigated—Sir Francis Burdett, Mr. John Eastlake, and Lord Cochrane—but he was unable to find out anything more. I contacted him again, and he told me I should stop worrying about Mr. Rice and move on."

"Did you do any further investigating?" asked Mary. "Into the suspects?"

"I tried, but no one would help me." She sniffed, and then wiped her nose with a handkerchief. "I do not think anyone cares. He was not my husband, not a family member, so maybe I should just move forward. But I do not want to." She scrunched the handkerchief into a tight ball in her hand. "I was not even able to attend the funeral."

Mary thought again of the mourning ring graveyard Mrs. König kept in her room. Mary was not currently wearing the mourning ring for her father—it was not wise to wear identifiable objects when in disguise—but she still ached sometimes with the pain of her own loss. Mrs. König, despite her lack of firm morals and her propensity for poor decisions, seemed foremost to be a woman in pain. People struggling with pain often became lost—they reached for anything that might give them purpose or joy or meaning, and they clung to those things, even when they shattered. Mary had done this before, and though she had not made the same choices as Mrs. König, she understood her.

"Who knew of your relationship to Mr. Rice?" asked Fanny.

"No one. Not a single soul. I am very good at keeping my affairs secret," she said, in a manner that made it sound as if she were trying to convince herself. She again looked at her pocket watch.

"Do you have another appointment?" asked Fanny.

"Yes, and I will need to leave soon for it."

"We will not keep you for long," said Mary. "But I do have one other very important question for you. Who was the curly haired man? The one who pushed you at the ball?"

"Mr. Corbyn? Mr. Corbyn did not push me."

"But he ran from you, after you fell."

"Yes, but he was not responsible. It was Mr. Sharp."

"Mr. Sharp?"

"Yes," said Mrs. König, turning her head away.

"That is terrible," said Mary, speaking quickly, before Fanny could say something. "Mr. Sharp is your friend. Why did he push you?"

"People have been investigating, and someone had spoken to him wanting to learn more, and he was angry that Mrs. Knowles had mentioned my name. But I never spoke to Mrs. Knowles. I have yet to meet her."

Mary grimaced. She was the one who had told that lie to Mr. Sharp. She was the one who had precipitated his action. Yet she could not have known what he would do. "Why would that make him angry?"

Mrs. König shrugged. "Mr. Sharp is normally rather even-tempered, but when he becomes angry, he expresses it…more…strongly than other men."

Fanny and Mary shared a look. It was rather suspicious behaviour.

"What is Mr. Corbyn's given name?" asked Fanny. "In case we need to contact him."

Mrs. König hesitated. "Alfred. But do not mention me to him, or Mr. Sharp will hear of it. They work together." She looked again at her pocket watch. "Now I really must go. Please, I answered all your questions, leave me and my family alone."

She began to walk, but Fanny grabbed her arm, stopping her. "Where are you going?"

"It is of no import."

"It has to do with the matter of Mr. Rice's death, does it not?"

Again, she did not answer.

"I will know if you are lying," said Fanny, holding her face very close to Mrs. König's. "And you will regret it."

"Please, Mrs. König," said Mary. "We *do* want to help you. We want to help Mr. Rice."

Fanny continued to tightly grip Mrs. König's arm. Mrs. König looked ready to fight, but then she relented. "I am meeting with Mrs. Knowles. I thought that since it had made Mr. Sharp angry, I might as well do it in fact. Mrs. Knowles could know something useful."

"Does Mrs. Knowles know of your relationship with her

brother?" asked Mary.

Mrs. König shook her head.

Mary looked at Fanny, who nodded.

"What if you go," said Mary, "and do not discover anything new, but in the process, she discovers your relationship? You could inflict more injury to Mrs. Knowles, who is already in mourning. She is devastated by her brother's death—would you also taint her memory of her brother?"

She looked unsure.

"Let us go for you," said Mary. "We will go, we will find out whatever it is that she knows. And when we find out the truth, we will make sure you hear of it."

Mrs. König held still as the seconds ticked by. Neither Mary nor Fanny said anything. Either they would go instead of Mrs. König, or they would go with her: they needed to make progress on the investigation and Mrs. König had stirred the pot by contacting Mrs. Knowles. There could be no justification for Mrs. König attending the meeting alone.

Finally, Mrs. König nodded. "The meeting is at one o'clock, at the memorial to Shakespeare in Westminster Abbey."

Fanny released her arm. "How do we know this is the real location, and not a misdirection so you can go somewhere else?"

"I still have the note—I have not yet burned it." She removed it from her pocket and Fanny snatched it from her fingers. Fanny examined it, then nodded. "Thank you, Mrs. König. You have been very helpful."

Mrs. König did not respond. She hurried away through the park and then down the road.

Mary looked at her own watch. "It is already 12:35."

"Then haste is essential."

They hired a carriage and urged the driver to be quick, promising extra payment for his speed. The horses cantered across the London streets, and the driver frequently cursed at others on the road.

"That interview was quite effective," said Fanny, quietly enough that the driver should not hear. "Our approaches played well off of each other."

"What do you mean?"

Fanny smiled. "Did you think I genuinely felt hostile towards her?"

Mary nodded.

"It was an act. Some people respond when they are pressured with negative forces, and it can be especially effective when contrasted with an interviewer who acts with greater sympathy and kindness."

"Then I am glad I accidentally used the right approach." Mary felt, once again, her lack of knowledge and experience in comparison to Fanny. Yet at least now she was contributing, even if her techniques were not as deliberate as Fanny's.

"I do not know what approach we should take with Mrs. Knowles. She has not come unwillingly, so I do not think we should attempt to intimidate her." There was a large bump of the carriage, sending them both upwards so they almost hit their heads on the roof. Fanny continued as if she had not been interrupted. "We could pretend that Mrs. König was unable to come and sent us instead."

"That would be logical," said Mary. "I am still trying to understand why Mr. Sharp would become so angry with Mrs. König that he would harm her in a public setting."

"That is a good question."

"It does not make sense, unless he is protecting whoever is responsible for the crime, or he himself committed it." As she said the words aloud, it seemed possible. "You said that Mr. Sharp had a longstanding feud with Mr. Eastlake and the other Radicals. Maybe he killed Mr. Rice and then wrote the fake note from Sir Francis in an attempt to throw the blame on them."

Fanny scratched her ear. "His letters to Mr. Eastlake did indicate a strong, persistent anger. He believes that the Radicals will destroy British society if left unchecked. It would be a motivation to frame them. But we need a motive for why he would kill Mr. Rice in the first place."

"Maybe Mrs. Knowles can help us with that."

The carriage approached Westminster Abbey. It was a beautiful Gothic structure, with large towers, elegant gables, a beautiful rose window, and tipped arches around the entrance that she believed were called archivolts.

"We're late," said Fanny. She paid the driver, and they hurried up the walkway.

Even in their rush, the grandeur of the building astounded Mary. She pulled opened the grand doors and stepped inside. Instantly her eyes were drawn upwards by the ribbed vaults and the beautiful windows.

"This way," said Fanny, tugging on Mary's arm. "We need the Poets' Corner."

"I take it you have been here before," said Mary in a whisper.

"You should return when you have time to wander. My personal favourite is Queen Elizabeth's effigy."

Many appeared to be buried in the abbey—kings, queens, leaders who had been deemed important to their country and its history. There were effigies and memorials and monuments, and it felt as if not just the remains of these people, but also a part of their essence, lingered within these walls.

Fanny slowed. They must have arrived in the Poets' Corner; in white marble, on a raised platform, was a life-sized carving of William Shakespeare. He leaned on a pile of books on top of a pedestal, a scroll in his hand.

A woman sat in front of the statue in a wheeled chair, more commonly called a Bath chair, as they had been invented in Bath.

"Mrs. Knowles?" said Mary.

The woman turned her head, and her eyes moved between the two of them. "Is one of you Mrs. König?"

"Mrs. König was unable to come today," said Fanny. "She asked us to come in her stead."

"I see," said Mrs. Knowles. She rested her hand on the wheel of the chair, and Mary worried that she would leave. If they were to learn anything from her, they needed her trust. Yet Mary did not know the best way to gain her trust—she did not know much about Mrs. Knowles at all, except this was a woman who chose to meet under the statue of Shakespeare.

"What is your favourite Shakespeare play?" asked Mary.

"*Othello*," said Mrs. Knowles, without any hesitation.

Mary thought for a moment. She had memorised a few passages from *Othello*. "'Men should be what they seem. Or those that be not, would they might seem none!' Although it was spoken by a duplicitous character, I have always found it to be a worthy sentiment."

"'By heaven, I'll know thy thoughts,'" said Mrs. Knowles, skipping a little ahead in the scene, and voicing one of Othello's lines.

"My thoughts you shall have. I will not hold back, as Iago did," said Mary. She paused, considering where to begin. "The truth is that we are not friends with Mrs. König at all.

The truth is that we are part of the investigative team which has been attempting to bring justice to your brother. One of our colleagues interviewed you, and we have read your written statement."

Mrs. Knowles nodded.

"We have spent the last month attempting to discover who murdered your brother, yet the investigation was almost called off earlier today for lack of progress. I think we have been investigating the wrong people, thrown off track by false evidence that was planted at the scene."

Mrs. Knowles put her hand on her forehead and shook her head slightly in disapproval.

"We are hoping that if we can ask you a few questions we might learn something that can help us, something that the others have missed," said Fanny.

"Women are good at asking the right questions." She adjusted the chair a little to better face them. "'Ask me what question thou canst possible, and I will answer unpremeditated.' That is from *Henry VI, Part 1*."

Mary had not read or seen *Part 1*, *Part 2*, or *Part 3*, so instead she plunged in. "Did your brother ever mention a Mr. George Sharp, or a Mr. Alfred Corbyn?"

"No, I have never heard of them."

It had been too much to hope for. "Tell us about the last few weeks of your brother's life," said Mary. "Anything that comes to your mind. What was he thinking about, talking about? Was his behaviour different in any way?"

"He was busier," said Mrs. Knowles. "Certainly busier. He had started sending messages for more and more people in Parliament, and attending some of their meetings, not just of the Radicals but also of the Tories."

Mrs. Knowles went silent, but Mary knew not to interrupt, without needing Fanny to tell her not to. They had to give Mrs. Knowles time.

"At the end, though, he did not just seem busy. He seemed...worried, almost. Tired, but also restless, and perhaps a little excited, the way he was when we were children and he had almost discovered some grand connection. Of course, maybe I am overthinking things, seeing things when they were not there, because I know what happened to him."

"Did he speak about anything specific?" asked Fanny. "Any of the people he was working with, or projects he might be engaged in?"

"No. When he was with me, he was always so attentive to me and my little boy, always wanting to hear about our lives and thoughts. My boy's named Oliver, after my brother, and he wanted to hear the details of what Oliver had learned every day—if he had said a new word or smiled at something. He would ask me what I was reading, whether I had changed my mind and decided *Romeo and Juliet* deserved more attention. I suppose he would sometimes speak about his work or his goals, but never in the last few weeks before he died."

"Could you tell us about the very last time you saw your brother?" asked Mary. "When was it?"

Mrs. Knowles looked up at Shakespeare's stone head as if perhaps he knew the answer. She must have seen something there, for she nodded, and then spoke. "It was Thursday, January twentieth. He came by unannounced, during the day rather than the evening. It was...a little after two in the afternoon, and he said he was in between appointments. He smelled a little of machine oil, and when I commented on it, he said that he had met someone that morning at a factory.

"My little Oliver would not stop climbing on him and tugging at his sleeve. He gave little Oliver some sweets, and me a book that he thought I might be interested in reading, and he left a newspaper and a few pamphlets for my husband. Then he was on his way."

"When did you find his body?" asked Fanny.

"I found his body three days later, on Sunday. It was the twenty-third. He was supposed to join us for dinner, but he did not arrive. He had given me a key to his flat long before, of course, so after the maid helped me put my little Oliver to sleep, I went to his flat. I knew something was wrong as soon as I opened the door. It smelled...wrong. I went into the doorway of the room, where he lay, and for a minute I could not move or make a sound, and then I screamed, and the neighbours came and fetched the constable."

Fanny asked a follow-up question about finding the body, but Mary's mind returned to the last time Mrs. Knowles had seen her brother. The timing had been unusual, as had the smell of machinery. She remembered Mr. Rice's log clearly—nothing had been written down for the morning of the twentieth, though there had been an appointment for later that afternoon. The description of the previous interview with Mrs. Knowles had mentioned the factory smell, but it had not mentioned the gifts he had brought.

When there was a pause in Mrs. Knowles and Fanny's conversation, Mary asked, "What was the newspaper that your brother left for your husband to read?"

"*Cobbett's Weekly Register.* My brother always brought us copies of it, because he was friends with Sir Francis Burdett and the other Radicals."

"And the pamphlets?"

Mrs. Knowles tilted her head. "I do not recall."

"Did they seem out of the ordinary?"

"No, they were the sort of pamphlets my husband always reads."

"What about the book? What was it called?"

"*The State of the Poor*, by Frederic Morton Eden. The third volume."

"Only the third volume, not the first two?"

"Correct."

"That sounds like a rather opaque subject."

"It is," said Mrs. Knowles. "I have tried to read it, I really have, but I cannot force myself past the first fifty pages. I understand that he must have thought it important for me to read about the lives of the poor in Sussex and Birmingham and Bradford, but it has proved to be a challenge. Page after page of what the poor in a particular parish eat, and how many payments they received and when. It is tediously comprehensive."

"I assume your brother knew your reading tastes. Had he given you books before?"

"Yes, but they were always things I liked, plays and poetry and novels, or commentary on Shakespeare and other writers, a little history now and then."

"Would it be possible for us to examine the book, and the papers he gave your husband?"

"The pamphlets and the newspaper are long gone. My husband never keeps them for more than a week or two before he passes them on to someone else, and then they read them and pass them on. But you can look at the book, if you think it will be useful."

"It seems unusual," said Fanny, "and anything out of the ordinary is worth investigating."

"If you come with me, I can give it to you now," said Mrs. Knowles. "I do not live far."

"Thank you," said Mary. "We would appreciate it greatly."

"This way," said Mrs. Knowles. "This exit is best for my chair." She used the metal rod which extended above her legs to turn the single, front wheel of the chair, and then she pushed the two large wheels at her sides. Mary and Fanny followed her out of the Abbey and into the cold air.

"I told you that my favourite Shakespeare play is *Othello*, so you now know all there is to know about me. But now I must know yours."

"I saw *A Midsummer Night's Dream* a few years ago," said Fanny, "and I have never been able to forget it."

"The production here in London, in 1809?"

"Yes, that was it."

"I saw it as well."

Fanny and Mrs. Knowles conversed about the play, and Mrs. Knowles shared interesting facts she knew about the actors. Mary, meanwhile, thought about other future steps. If possible, they needed to find out which factory Mr. Rice had visited—it must be the same factory where the hidden manifesto had originated. They could also follow Mr. Sharp and Mr. Corbyn. Yet they no longer had the luxury of time.

"And you? What is your favourite Shakespearean play?" asked Mrs. Knowles, looking at Mary.

"I have always enjoyed *King Lear*. I like thinking about the differences between the sisters." Unlike King Lear, her own father had not possessed a large fortune to leave to one or more of the sisters.

They arrived at Mrs. Knowles's home, and Mrs. Knowles asked them to wait outside. She opened the door, and Mary glimpsed a maid playing with a boy about two years of age. Little Oliver.

Mrs. Knowles exited her house a few minutes later, a lengthy tome in hand. Mary took the book, and Mrs.

Knowles watched expectantly as she and Fanny flipped through the pages. It had been published in 1797, and it was as dry as Mrs. Knowles had described it. If you were searching for specific information, it might be useful, but it was not designed for normal reading.

Mary skipped ahead to the fifty-page mark, where Mrs. Knowles had stopped reading. She turned the pages, looking for anything out of the ordinary: a crease, writing, a piece of paper slipped between the pages. Yet the farther through the book Mary turned, the more she began to conclude that the book was just a book. Had she actually expected that Mr. Rice had left some sort of secret message inside?

"Keep looking," said Fanny quietly. "If there is a possible lead, follow it through."

Fanny was right, of course. Fanny was always right. Yet this time, Mary did not take Fanny's advice as a critique, though she likely would have before. It was simply advice, advice one would give a friend or a spy she considered a partner.

More and more pages of the book passed. Mary did not want to skip any or flip too fast, or she might miss something. Another seventy pages later, Mary's eye finally caught on something. Handwriting, written in tiny script, in between rows on a table. It said, "public dispensary," and gave an address. A few pages later, there was another handwritten note. It said, "Mr. Sharp appears to be blackmailing other Tories into stronger opposition to reform." Another page listed Mr. Sharp's involvement in not providing resources for a thousand troops on the continent, many of whom starved. Then there was a page that said, "Factory. Sharp Place. Repeated injuries." From these words was an arrow, pointing down to the word "dispensary records."

The factory in question had belonged to Mr. Sharp all along. And he had been mistreating his employees.

"You have found something?" asked Mrs. Knowles.

"I believe we have," said Mary.

"It would seem that your brother did not actually intend for you to read the book," said Fanny, "but rather, to hold it for safekeeping."

"Well, that is a relief," said Mrs. Knowles.

"Can we take this with us?" asked Mary.

"Yes," said Mrs. Knowles. "But I would like it returned. Not so I can read it, but it was the last thing he gave me." She looked at them sternly. "Find my brother's murderer, if you will."

Fanny placed her hand on top of Mrs. Knowles's. "We will do everything in our power, Mrs. Knowles, to bring your brother's killer to justice."

"I have confidence in both of you," said Mrs. Knowles. "As the Bard wrote, 'Murder cannot be hid long...at the length, truth will out.'"

# CHAPTER TWENTY-ONE

*"St. George's Fever Hospital and Dispensary—The value of the aid afforded by the joint Establishment, may be established by the number relieved, which [was] in total, in the last Year... 8846 [people], of which number 8377 received Medical Aid at the Dispensary, 334 were visited at their respective places of abode, and 135 admitted into the Fever Hospital."*

—*Saunders's News-Letter*, Dublin, Ireland,
February 22, 1814

MARY AND FANNY had meant to return to the townhouse for only a few minutes, so they could procure a few supplies, but as soon as they entered the house, and before Mary could change to a simpler dress, Mary was waylaid by Elizabeth and Darcy. She watched, wistfully, as Fanny made her way up the stairs.

"Mary," said Elizabeth. "I am glad you have returned." Her eyes took in Mary's disguise. "Did Mrs. Hunnicutt give you that dress?"

"Uh, no. Lady Trafford did. It is...too fine for my tastes, so I do not wear it often."

"I see." Elizabeth paused. "I am afraid Mrs. Hunnicutt is requiring too much of your attention."

"I find it no trouble to spend time with her, provide

friendship, and show her my appreciation and gratitude for how she has assisted me."

"Do not let her force you into too intimate of an acquaintance."

She understood her sister's concerns. Mrs. Hunnicutt was an acceptable acquaintance, but not of their social standing, and Elizabeth was attempting to protect her from society that Elizabeth likely thought Mary found unpleasant.

"I genuinely like Mrs. Hunnicutt," said Mary. "It is good to hold many people in one's circle of friendship, to provide variety and vitality in one's relationships."

"That is an admirable sentiment," said Mr. Darcy. "You see others with a generous eye."

"We were about to take tea in the parlour," said Elizabeth. "We had hoped you might join us, so we can spend time together, as a family."

This was in direct opposition to what Mary wanted and needed to do: she needed to leave again, immediately. She wished that she and Fanny had not returned, or that Fanny had come inside by herself. How would Mary extract herself now?

"It would be a pleasure to join you," said Mary. "Let me freshen myself up a little in my room, and then I will be down."

Mary went up to her room, trying to keep her pace steady so it did not appear that she was fleeing. Once inside, she shut the door firmly behind her and leaned up against it.

"I almost have everything ready," said Fanny. "How long do you need?"

Mary bit her lip. "I do not know if I can get away. My sister and Mr. Darcy expect me to join the family for tea, and they do not want me to spend too much time feeling obliged to others. I do not think I can use Mrs. Hunnicutt as an excuse again this afternoon. And then I know that my family expects the Gardiners for dinner."

"Family expectations can be both a blessing and a burden," said Fanny kindly. "It is a lot to balance, when many things are pressing for your time. If you cannot come with me—"

"I do not want you to leave me behind!" Mary stumbled onto her bed and held one of the pillows close to her chest. "That sounds very selfish, and maybe it is. But I hate feeling like I am useless, because of who I am and my background and my place in society." She pulled the pillow even tighter against herself. "I do know that you are more than capable of handling things by yourself. You have a much broader range of skills and experiences than I do, and I need to accept that my contributions are useful, even if they are not the same as everyone else's."

Fanny sat next to Mary on the bed. "I will not give you a motivational speech, Mary. We do not have the time for it, and I do not think you need it—you know you are capable, you know that you have earned your place as a spy, and you know that this work is difficult for everyone. What I will say is that we work well together, you and I. We interviewed both Mrs. König and Mrs. Knowles using two very different approaches, and I believe it was the way we played off of each other, both bringing our own insights and skills, that led to fruitful results."

"Thank you, Fanny," said Mary, setting down the pillow.

Fanny stood. "We do not have much time—the end of the day approaches quickly, and even with all we have learned, Mr. Booth may still call off the case in the morning. I am going to gather the evidence we need to prove Mr. Sharp's guilt. First, I will visit his factory, and then I will visit the dispensary. If possible, I would like you to come with me."

"I cannot sneak out of the house, not when Elizabeth and Mr. Darcy just requested that I join them for tea. But maybe I can find another way, a way that enables me to assist you without betraying their trust."

"I hope so," said Fanny. "If you are able, meet me at the dispensary."

Mary nodded. "Best of luck, Fanny."

"You, too."

Without a glance in the mirror before leaving her room, Mary made her way down to the parlour. Everyone else was already assembled—Elizabeth and Darcy, Georgiana and Kitty.

Elizabeth poured Mary tea. "How are you feeling, Mary?"

"Fine." Mary wished she had been able to leave with Fanny.

Elizabeth looked as if she wanted to inquire more, so Mary was relieved when Kitty said, "I wanted to show you something, Mary. Something I have been practising in secret. Now do not laugh—this is very difficult for me."

Kitty sat down at the pianoforte, placed her fingers on the keys, and played a very simple tune, mostly with her right hand, but occasionally hitting a note or two with her left. She made several mistakes, yet she had a strong sense of rhythm and did not pause until she reached the end of the piece.

"I did not know you were learning to play," said Elizabeth.

"Georgiana has been teaching me," Kitty explained. "I decided you were right, Mary, and that I am not too old to learn new things. I have much more to learn—obviously— but I am pleased with my progress."

When Mary had given Kitty that advice several weeks ago, she had not expected Kitty to apply herself to such a degree.

"Do you have other surprises for us?" asked Mary.

Kitty smiled secretively. "Maybe sometime soon you will find out."

"Kitty is such a good pupil," said Georgiana. "I am sure she will soon surpass us all."

"Now you have perjured yourself and must play for us," said Kitty.

"Very well," said Georgiana.

Kitty relinquished the pianoforte and Georgiana took the seat. As Georgiana played, Mary focused on her predicament. How could she get out of the house and to the public dispensary? She could not pretend to go with Mrs. Hunnicutt—Elizabeth had already prevented that possibility. She could pretend to visit the Gardiners, but they were coming for dinner and would immediately state that she had not been there. She did not know enough people in London—or at least, not enough people that the Darcys knew she knew. Maybe she should pretend to retire to her room and sneak out after all, but she was sure that they would check, and the consequences would be dire.

As the song built in intensity, so did the intensity within Mary. Her heart pounded at a rapid rate, and her forehead and palms began to feel sweaty. She wiped her hands on her dress, but it did nothing to calm her unease.

She shook her head and straightened her back. She was most certainly overthinking things. She had no problem with investigating a murderer, but she was frightened to death of making a simple request of her family.

She simply had to do it.

"I believe it is Mary's turn," said Georgiana. "Following

which we shall hear from Lizzy, and then, maybe my brother will surprise us with his skills."

"That would be a surprise to me as well," said Mr. Darcy. "Perhaps we should restrict ourselves to the talents of Mary and Elizabeth."

"Will you play one of your Irish tunes?" asked Georgiana.

Mary stood. She stepped forward but did not walk to the piano. She consciously straightened her fingers and held her head high. "Actually, I am not interested in playing the pianoforte this afternoon. You may know that I have been corresponding with several women on various charitable societies and activities. I have decided that I wanted to take a more active role, and I committed to them that I would visit a public dispensary this afternoon."

"While it is important to fulfil one's obligation to the larger public," said Mr. Darcy, "one should never neglect one's obligations to their own family."

"We just sat down for tea," said Elizabeth, "and you have been gone most of today, and all of yesterday with Mrs. Hunnicutt. Surely the dispensary can wait for another time."

How could she argue against Mr. Darcy, a gentleman of ten thousand pounds who held the respect and esteem of everyone who knew him? How could she argue with her older sister Elizabeth, who was much more clever and well-spoken than Mary?

She thought of Fanny, who might be in Mr. Sharp's factory at this very moment. She thought of her own commitment to Mrs. Knowles to find her brother's murderer. It had to be done.

"I agree that I should not have scheduled my time as I have done," said Mary. "It has, honestly, been quite exhausting, and I plan to spend more time here, with the family, in the future. However, I have committed that I would do this today, and I want to keep my commitments."

Mr. Darcy looked to Elizabeth. This would be her decision. And Elizabeth—well, Mary did not know what Elizabeth was thinking, but she feared Elizabeth would stop her.

"Please, Lizzy, please," said Mary, calling her sister by her nickname for the first time in years. "I do not normally request things of the family—I do not normally encourage others to arrange their days around my desires. But this is something I want to do, something I must do. I do not know if focusing on charity work is my life calling, but it might be, and I want to learn about dispensaries."

As Elizabeth considered, Mary hid her hands in the skirts of her dress.

"You have grown quite convincing, Mary. It sounds like an important endeavour. Would anyone else like to come with us?"

Everyone else decided to join them.

Bringing four people with her was not exactly what Mary had intended, but at least she did not need to sneak out of the house.

# CHAPTER TWENTY-TWO

*"The Public will no doubt be anxious to learn in what quarter this nefarious business originated."*

—*The Statesman*, London, February 22, 1814

NICHOL'S DISPENSARY WAS a three-story brick building with large windows and a rather imposing door. They opened it, and inside everything seemed a bit more friendly: a clean, open space with prints of landscapes on the wall. A receptionist at the front desk greeted them. "I am Miss Singh. You do not appear to need medical assistance, so how can we help you today?"

Mary glanced at her family, and then stepped forward alone to speak with the woman. In low tones, Mary said, "I was meant to meet my friend here, a Miss Cramer. She has brown skin and is wearing a blue dress."

The woman smiled kindly. "I have not seen her."

"That is fine," said Mary. She must still be at Mr. Sharp's factory. If the opportunity arose, she might be able to ask questions on her own and perhaps even investigate the dispensary's records; if not, Mary would attempt to escape from her family and assist Fanny once she arrived. "I was hoping that we might be able to take a tour of the dispensary and learn of the work of this facility and its place in the community, and what those interested in charitable activity might be able to do to assist in the work."

"Let me see if one of the doctors is available to give you a tour."

She went through a door and returned a few minutes later with a young-looking doctor. He smiled broadly and introduced himself as Dr. Robertson. "May I ask your names?"

"I am Mr. Darcy, this is my wife, Mrs. Darcy, my sister, Miss Darcy, and my sisters-in-law, Miss Bennet and Miss Catherine Bennet." Kitty gave a very dainty curtsy at the mention of her name. "The elder Miss Bennet is particularly interested in charitable activities and prompted this visit today."

"I assume you are not from London?" said Dr. Robertson. His eyes lingered on Mr. Darcy's cuff links, and he seemed impressed by everyone's general appearance. Mary had still not changed out of her nicer dress.

"No," said Mr. Darcy. "I am from Derbyshire. We are here for the Season."

"I am glad you have come to visit us. Let me tell you a little about myself. I have been a doctor for seven years. Three days a week I pay house visits and assist my private patients, and two days a week I work here.

"Now come with me," he said, gesturing for them to follow him through the door. "The work of a public dispensary is lofty, and there is much to show you."

Kitty whispered conspiratorially in Mary's ear. "I think the doctor is very handsome."

"I suppose he is," said Mary. Honestly, she did not pay much attention to physical appearance as a point in favour of someone's value. Also, she did not know what to make of Kitty confiding this thought to her. Normally, this was the sort of thing she would have told their youngest sister Lydia;

did Kitty expect Mary to respond in the same giggly manner?

Kitty again leaned close to Mary's ear. "I would wager that you find Mr. Withrow handsome."

Mary shook her head. Kitty did not understand her in the slightest. She had never thought of Mr. Withrow in this way, and never would. In fact, she hardly thought of Mr. Withrow at all, now that she was no longer at Castle Durrington. It had been kind for him to buy her a book, but he had only acted on behalf of his aunt, Lady Trafford.

The walls of the next room were lined with medicines. Men, women, and children sat in chairs, presumably waiting, while others stood at counters, describing their symptoms to the men and women behind them. One of the doctors had a man tilt his head back and open his mouth so he could look inside. Another led a woman and a baby through a door on the opposite side of the room.

Dr. Robertson led them to a corner and began his speech. "The public dispensary first began as a concept in 1696, in London, though they became much more widespread in the 1770s. At first, dispensaries were simply a place to dispense medicine, but soon they became a place to dispense medical advice and assistance. Doctors, such as myself, pay house visits to those who are of sufficient means, and in smaller communities, it is possible for doctors to assist those who have fewer means. Yet in cities such as London it is expedient for centralised locations that can provide for those with and without means. Can you guess how many dispensaries there are in London?"

"Three," said Kitty with a smile.

"Good guess, but try higher."

"Fifteen?" asked Kitty, excited for this guessing game.

"Higher still."

"Thirty?"

"Higher."

"Forty?"

"Forty-two," said Dr. Robertson, his smile for Kitty. He looked at each of them in turn before continuing. "This dispensary was begun in 1798 and is supported entirely by private philanthropy. The goal, first and foremost, is to relieve suffering. Now come, let me show you the rest of the dispensary."

Mary tried not to be impatient as Dr. Robertson led them through the facilities, showing them rooms where people with various conditions were treated. Some people came to the dispensary for an hour or a day, but there were beds holding people who had been there for weeks. While some of the people were hidden behind doors and curtains, many others were not, and Mary felt self-conscious as a spectator of other people's pain. She wondered if they often gave tours to those they saw as potential donors.

"This facility blurs the lines between a dispensary and a hospital," observed Mr. Darcy. "I was not aware that dispensaries provided this sort of treatment to patients."

"If hospitals refuse to care for the poor, then someone must."

Mary thought of the arrow Mr. Rice had drawn between "Sharp Place" and "dispensary records" and the words he had written, "repeated injuries."

"I have read that factory injuries are a major problem," said Mary. "Do you treat anyone for these sorts of injuries at this dispensary?"

"Yes, there are several factories nearby, and sometimes the injuries are severe. One of our factory patients, little Georgie, could use visitors. He broke his leg and we set the bone, but now it is infected, and we may need to amputate."

He led them into a room where a little boy lay in a bed, staring listlessly at a wall while a woman pressed cold rags on his head. Another woman, likely his mother, sat in the corner sobbing.

None of them quite seemed to know what to do, but then Georgiana stepped forward. "Georgie, may I sing to you?"

The boy gave an almost imperceptible nod.

Georgiana sang quietly at first, but as she progressed, her voice became more confident and almost angelic.

The mother stopped crying, and the boy turned to look at them. He glanced at the door, and Mary turned to see what had drawn his attention. Fanny was walking down the hall. She had arrived.

Georgiana finished the song and received the thanks of Georgie's mother.

Dr. Robertson led them out of the room and into the hall. Mary wanted to follow after Fanny, but she was in the middle of the group and unable to leave.

"Was Georgie visiting a factory?" asked Kitty. "How did he become injured?"

"Many factories employ young children," said Dr. Robertson. "Children can climb into or around the machinery and fix small parts. Unfortunately, it leads to many injuries."

"Are there not protections for factory workers? Especially children?" asked Kitty.

"There are, but they are limited. In 1802 the Health and Morals of Apprentices Act was passed to provide better working conditions for children and limit them to working twelve hours a day. Unfortunately, it is not often enforced, and it does nothing to protect the many 'free children' who work at factories but are not apprentices."

"That is dreadful," said Kitty.

Georgiana looked a little pale, and she leaned on her brother's arm.

Suddenly, Dr. Robertson's attention was drawn away. "Mr. Sharp," he said, and gave a little bow. "Is there anything I can assist you with?"

Mary felt as if something were stuck in her throat. Mr. Sharp, here, now. This could not be a coincidence.

"Not today, Doctor," said Mr. Sharp hurriedly, "but I appreciate your concern." He strode down the hallway and walked purposely up the next flight of stairs, and Mary had a sudden, awful realisation. Mr. Sharp was following Fanny.

He must have observed her at the factory, and now he had followed her here, with enough time and distance between them that Fanny would not realise she was being followed.

Mary took a step to follow him, but Kitty hooked her arm in Mary's, fixing her in position.

"This has been very enlightening," said Mr. Darcy, "and it seems that you are doing a great work. Unfortunately, we now have other matters to attend to, but I will contact you soon about making a donation."

Mary's chest felt as if it were tightening. How would she possibly stay if Darcy had decided that they would leave? It would not be easy to convince the others to stay, especially not with Georgiana looking pale. Yet Mr. Sharp had strangled a man with his bare hands. Fanny could be in grave danger.

"It has been a pleasure to meet you," said Dr. Robertson, "and any assistance you give to the dispensary will be much appreciated."

Kitty let out a long, disappointed sigh. "I was very much hoping I could stay longer. I would like to meet a few more of the patients, perhaps hear their stories, or tell them a tale to lift their spirits." She turned to Elizabeth and Darcy. "Please, can I stay longer? Mary could stay with me, and I am sure Dr. Robertson could arrange for a reputable carriage to take us home."

"That would be well within my power," said Dr. Robertson.

"I would be willing to stay with Kitty," said Mary.

Elizabeth and Darcy looked at each other and seemed to come to an agreement.

"Very well," said Elizabeth. "But make sure you are home by seven at the very latest. We do not want to keep our guests waiting."

Kitty and Mary both nodded. Mary could hardly believe her luck, yet she also wondered at Kitty's behaviour, for her younger sister had never shown a strong propensity for charitable activity before.

As they said their farewells, Mr. Darcy, Elizabeth, and Georgiana paused to ask Dr. Robertson about the specific charitable needs of the dispensary.

Kitty spoke quietly to Mary. "I know that Mrs. Hunnicutt is not actually Mrs. Hunnicutt, and that you have been engaged in some very peculiar activities this past month." Mary's eyes darted to the door, and then back to Kitty. "Do not worry. I am an excellent secret keeper. Of course, I would appreciate if you gave me a few more detailed explanations of events sometime soon. But for now, I am prepared to distract Dr. Robertson, and you can go and do whatever you need to do, or if there is anything more I can do to assist you, simply say the word and I will do it."

"Thank you," said Mary, and strangely, she felt the beginnings of tears in her eyes. She blinked them away. Kitty stood poised and serious, willing to help her in her work without even knowing what it was. Kitty was a much better sister than she deserved, and Mary regretted all the years of not knowing her well.

"Allowing me to do my work is help enough," said Mary, then paused. She had spent too much time trying to do everything on her own, as if that would prove herself. "Actually, if you could find out from Dr. Robertson how many of the patients were specifically injured at the Sharp factory, if this number has increased over time, and particularly, how many patients there were in January and where they are now."

"That is a lot to ask discreetly." Kitty raised her eyebrows. "But I am cunning. Have no fear: I will find the information you require."

The family left and Dr. Robertson turned to them. Before he could speak, Kitty said, "My sister wishes to speak with little Georgie again, and I have a few additional questions about factory injuries."

"Of course, Miss Bennet." Dr. Robertson seemed willing to do anything Kitty requested. Kitty led him down the hall, and he did not even spare a glance for Mary. As they descended the stairs, Kitty looked back at Mary and winked. Mary gave her a grateful smile. Once they were out of sight, Mary rushed up the stairs to the third floor.

Mary peered into room after room, occasionally parting fabric dividers, but she saw no sign of Mr. Sharp or Fanny. Then she noticed an open door to a small yet comfortable parlour—perhaps for donors, or dispensary officials. Mr. Sharp stood in the parlour, next to a wall that held another door which was cracked open. His ear was inclined towards the cracked door, and he listened in to the conversation happening on the other side.

Mary crept into the room, willing Mr. Sharp not to turn

and notice her. She positioned herself on the floor behind a sofa, where, in theory, Mr. Sharp could not see her.

From this position, she could just make out the voices on the other side of the door.

"None of them were factory injuries. No, it was stomach complaints. Food poisoning, we thought." The woman paused. "Ah, but there is a note. Yes, I remember speaking to them. They were each employed at Sharp Factory."

"I assume that these men all recovered," came Fanny's voice.

There was a shuffling of papers. "No," said the woman. "They all perished, between a few days and a week later."

"From food poisoning?" said Fanny. Mary could imagine the scepticism on Fanny's face. "Do you have a visitor log?"

"Yes," said the woman with a bit of hesitation.

"Did Mr. Sharp visit these patients?"

"He always visits the patients who come from his factory. He is a charitable, benevolent man, and has provided great assistance to the dispensary."

"But did he visit these men…within a few hours of their deaths?" asked Fanny.

Silence from the room, but Mr. Sharp took in a deep breath.

"I can check that, Miss Cramer."

The door to the room scraped open, and Mary peered out from behind the sofa to see Mr. Sharp step inside.

"That will not be necessary, Mrs. Sancho," said Mr. Sharp.

Mary walked quickly across the parlour so she stood next to the door, taking up the position Mr. Sharp had previously occupied. She looked into the room—a records room of sorts. With the exception of a fireplace, which was close to the door, it was filled, wall to wall, with files and papers and books.

Mr. Sharp now stood in front of a desk. Fanny, who was inches from him, rose from her chair, but a woman in an official-looking brown dress remained seated on the other side. A pile of papers was spread out across the desk.

"In fact, Mrs. Sancho," said Mr. Sharp, "I need all of the records you have been examining, as well as the visitor log. And then I will need you to leave for a few minutes."

Mrs. Sancho pulled the records closer to her side of the desk. "I am afraid that I cannot give these to you, Mr. Sharp."

He lunged for the records, snatching a number of them with his left hand, and then seized Mrs. Sancho's collar with his right hand. "You are going to give me all records related to my factory."

"I will not," said Mrs. Sancho, and he began to shake her.

Fanny grabbed at Mr. Sharp's left arm, trying to pull him away from Mrs. Sancho, and Mary stepped into the room, then stopped. Mary did not know what she should do—what could *she* possibly do?

Papers flew off the desk and into the air. Mr. Sharp's grip seemed to grow stronger on Mrs. Sancho. She scratched at his face, and he pushed her backwards where she landed on the ground.

Mary needed to move, to do something, but she did not know what.

Mr. Sharp reached for more of the papers. Fanny still held onto his arm, trying to stop him, and Mrs. Sancho scrambled to her feet.

Mr. Sharp elbowed Fanny off him, and then seemed to change his mind. He grabbed her shoulder, and his hand seemed to be shifting, closer, closer to her neck as she struggled against him.

If he tried to strangle Fanny, in ten to fifteen seconds she could be knocked out, and then she might die, in the same manner as Mr. Rice.

To Mary's left was the fireplace, and hanging on her side of it, a large porcelain teapot. She lifted the pot as if by instinct, rushed at Mr. Sharp's back, and smashed the pot on the back of his head.

The pot broke into a dozen pieces and scalding hot water poured over Mr. Sharp's head.

He let go of Fanny, let go of the papers, and toppled to the ground.

Mary looked at the ceramic pot handle, which was still in her hand. Had she really just attacked a man with a teapot? And done so successfully?

Fanny crouched on the ground next to Mr. Sharp. "We must restrain him before he comes to." She pulled Mr. Sharp's hands to his back and held them together. "Mrs. Sancho, do you have any rope? Or a cord, or a length of fabric?"

Mrs. Sancho pulled a pile of heavy fabric bandages from her desk, and Fanny held Mr. Sharp's hands as Mary tied them together.

"Tighter, tighter," said Fanny. "Good."

Suddenly, Mr. Sharp began to struggle. He forced himself to his feet but could do little with his hands tied. Fanny, Mary, and Mrs. Sancho were trying to compel him into a chair when Dr. Robertson and Kitty entered the room and stopped.

"Dr. Robertson," said Mrs. Sancho. "Your assistance, please."

He stood there, unmoving.

"Kitty, go get a constable," said Mary. "And if possible, an officer named Detective Donalds, who is working on a case involving Mr. Sharp."

Without pause, Kitty rushed out of the room.

"Dr. Robertson, some help, please," said Mrs. Sancho.

Dr. Robertson finally moved and helped them seat Mr. Sharp in the chair and tie him to it. "Why are we doing this?"

"Mr. Sharp attacked me," said Mrs. Sancho, and her voice trembled. "And I think he has been murdering our patients."

"I will bring criminal charges against you for this," said Mr. Sharp. "I will shut down this entire organisation."

"I am sure that there will be a thorough investigation and that this will all be sorted out," said Dr. Robertson. "For now, we will wait for the authorities to arrive."

Mrs. Sancho and Dr. Robertson set to work picking up all the scattered papers. "The detective will need to see this one," said Mrs. Sancho. "And this one. And this one as well." A few had been dampened by the hot water, so they spread them out to dry.

Fanny kept watch on Mr. Sharp while Mary looked through the papers that Mrs. Sancho chose not to include in the pile to give the authorities. All of them were irrelevant, except for one, which mentioned a Fred Zeeger. Minerva Randall had called her attacker Fredzie, but maybe she had meant Fred Z. He had been treated for something in the same room as one of Mr. Sharp's victims, and perhaps Mr. Sharp had met him at the dispensary, and that had eventually led, somehow, to the explosion at the Custom House.

A few minutes later, a constable arrived, and a few minutes after that, Kitty with Detective Donalds.

Kitty took Dr. Robertson and Mrs. Sancho aside while Mary and Fanny told Detective Donalds all that had happened and all that they had learned.

Once they had finished their story, Kitty stepped over to them.

Mary did not know what to say. It was one thing for Kitty to know that Mrs. Hunnicutt was not Mrs. Hunnicutt, and quite another for her to have been witness to such a torrid affair. Would Kitty's knowledge prevent Mary from future work as a spy?

Kitty spoke first. "I convinced Dr. Robertson and Mrs. Sancho to not tell Mr. Darcy a single word about what occurred—I extracted all manner of promises from them. I explained that you both were random witnesses to a previous crime, and so knew what the good detective was looking for, and then happened to be here at the right moment. I did allow Dr. Robertson to order us a carriage. If we leave soon, we will arrive before dinner, and no one need know that anything unusual occurred."

"Thank you," said Mary, amazed by her sister's perceptiveness and ability to quickly deal with problems as they arose. Perhaps Kitty's knowledge would not cause any difficulties after all.

Once inside the carriage, Kitty said, "You both look like you have been in a street fight."

Mary looked down at her hands, which had ink residue on them, and her dress, which was damp. A few scraps of paper clung to it.

"I have some cream I can use to cover my scratches, and Mary will need a new dress," said Fanny. "Perhaps, Miss Catherine, you could provide some sort of distraction as we enter the house, so we can make our way unseen up to Mary's room."

"I can certainly provide a distraction," said Kitty, a glint in her eye. She turned to Mary. "Ever since you sent me that letter last year, asking me to look through father's letters, I have amused myself by thinking of you as if you were a character in one of my books, having grand adventures, with none of us even noticing. It turns out I was right."

"Your sister and I simply help out…when there are problems," said Fanny. "I hope we can trust you to keep this a secret."

"You can trust me," said Kitty. "I will not say a word to a single soul. I swear it." She seemed desperate to prove herself, desperate to be believed.

Mary set her hand on top of Kitty's. "I would trust you with my life."

"If Mary trusts you, then you have my trust as well," said Fanny.

Kitty beamed.

Mary turned to Fanny. "How was your visit to the factory?"

"Folks were scared, but I convinced them to talk to me. I did not even see Mr. Sharp there, and did not know that he had followed me to the dispensary." She shook her head. "Mrs. Sancho could have been seriously injured."

"Or you could have been," said Mary.

"I shall never forget the sight of you smashing a teapot on his head. You were there when I needed you. Thank you for being my partner, and for being my friend."

Mary smiled.

"And thank you, Miss Catherine, for being so sensible and getting the constable and detective so quickly."

"My pleasure," said Kitty.

The carriage arrived at the Darcys'.

"Are you ready with a distraction?" Mary asked.

"Yes, I am." Kitty rubbed her hands together, as if she had

hatched some nefarious plot, and preceded them into the house.

From outside, they could hear Kitty's coughing fit, and then she was screaming, "Spider! Get it off me! Get it off me!" Mary and Fanny slipped into the house unnoticed, for all its occupants were running through the rooms chasing Kitty as they attempted to assist her. As they made it up the stairs, they could hear Kitty collapsing dramatically on a sofa, Elizabeth offering smelling salts, and then Kitty wailing, "My nerves! My poor nerves!" in a manner that would have made their mother, Mrs. Bennet, proud.

# CHAPTER TWENTY-THREE

*"Much has been speculated on the death of Mr. Oliver Rice, but police believe they have finally found the murderer, a Mr. George Sharp, who they apprehended on Tuesday. Mr. Sharp was an esteemed member of Parliament, yet he was negligent in his duties to his inferiors, and when Mr. Rice confronted him for his travesties, Mr. Sharp strangled him to death. When pressed for details on how Mr. Sharp's culpability was ascertained, the detective on the case said that he was given tips by several anonymous parties, who, out of proper concern for themselves and their families, do not desire that their identities be made known."*

—*The Times*, London, February 25, 1814

S OMEONE KNOCKED ON Mary's door, and both Mary and Fanny started. It had been two days since Mr. Sharp's arrest, and they were preparing their final notes that they would deliver to Mr. Booth during their meeting with him that afternoon. Fanny hid the papers under her skirt and resumed repairs on one of Mary's older dresses, and Mary pretended that she had been reading a book.

The knock came again.

"Come in," said Mary.

Hannah pushed open the door. Mary had not seen her

since the explosion of the Custom House, and she still felt guilty for tricking Hannah.

"You have a visitor, Miss Bennet," said Hannah with a curtsy. She kept her eyes on the floor. "A Miss Forster, who would like to make your acquaintance."

"Thank you," said Mary. "I will be down momentarily."

Hannah shut the door.

"I take it you know Miss Forster." Fanny was quite skilled at reading Mary's thoughts from her face.

"Miss Levena Kendall knows her, from the ball." Mary crossed her arms and looked out the window. "I cannot see why she would want to meet me, unless she realises that *I* am Miss Kendall."

"Quick, switch gowns," said Fanny, pulling out Mary's oldest, most worn dress.

Mary dressed in it, and then Fanny used a cream on Mary's face to make it look a bit more pale. "I will also make it look like you have not slept well," said Fanny, adding bags under Mary's eyes.

"You should teach me how to do this someday," said Mary. "I do not necessarily need to be as expert as you, but some basic skills would be useful."

"Agreed," said Fanny. "Now go, be Mary, and remember that you have never met this woman before."

Fanny shooed her out of the room. Mary walked slowly down the hall and the stairs, disturbed by Miss Forster's presence. It was one thing for Georgiana and Kitty to have a limited knowledge of Mary's outside activities, but it would be quite another for that knowledge to be possessed by a stranger.

Mary entered the sitting room and Miss Forster and Georgiana stood.

"This is one of my acquaintances, Miss Forster," said Georgiana, "and this is my sister-in-law, Miss Mary Bennet."

"It is a pleasure to meet you," said Mary, and she performed her most awkward curtsy.

"The pleasure is mine," said Miss Forster. "Come, let us sit."

Mary sat at the end of one of the chairs and hid her hands in the fabric of her skirt.

"You must be surprised that I came here today specifically to meet you, and indeed, my purpose is rather unusual. I believe that you employ a maid named Fanny Cramer?"

"Yes."

"I do not know if you are aware of her skills as a seamstress, but I saw a dress that she had made at a ball I attended—your family was there, but you were not—and it was the most beautiful dress that I have seen!"

"I saw that dress as well," said Georgiana with a knowing smile, that risked drawing attention to the fact that she knew more than she could tell. "It was worn by a Miss Levena Kendall, was it not? It was exquisite workmanship. I have a dress that was made by a very popular dressmaker, but unfortunately it was not fit properly, and did not fall correctly on me, and Miss Cramer both fixed the fit and made modifications to it, and now it is my favourite dress."

"I admit," said Mary, "that I have not employed Fanny's full skills at dressmaking, yet I understand that she has done a large amount of work in the past."

"I was hoping that you would give me your permission to speak with her, about future possibilities for her dressmaking career."

It seemed rather terrible that someone's servant—or in this case, pretend servant—was beholden to whether or not their employer wanted them to have future employment opportunities. "She is her own person. Of course that is all right. I will go ask her if she is able to speak with you."

"That is much appreciated, Miss Bennet."

Mary returned to her room and told Fanny of the true purpose of Miss Forster's visit.

"I am not sure how she found out that you live here, but I think she may want to hire you to make her several dresses."

"Well then, I shall not keep her waiting," said Fanny, who then proceeded to spend ten minutes fixing her hair, applying a dark brown cream to a few spots on her face, and critically considering her dress in front of the mirror.

"You should wear the new evening gown you made, to demonstrate your skills."

Fanny smiled. "You are right."

Mary helped Fanny into the dress, and then Fanny stood, peering at herself in the mirror. While the coral-coloured dress had an empire cut, the tops of the sleeves had slits, in a Renaissance style, revealing a slightly contrasting colour of silk beneath. A few inches above the hem of the dress, Fanny had twisted tulle and satin together, and these traversed the outside of the dress, in a rising and falling pattern.

"She is already predisposed to like you, so you have nothing to worry about," said Mary.

"I know, I know," said Fanny, nodding at herself in the mirror.

Mary handed her some papers on which she had sketched her designs. "Take these, too."

"Could you come with me downstairs?"

"Of course," said Mary. This was the first time she had ever seen Fanny act nervous.

By the time they reached the drawing room, she practically had to pull Fanny inside.

"Miss Cramer, what a pleasure to meet you!" said Miss Forster. "It took a great effort to track you down. I had to pry your name out of a mysterious debutante who has since disappeared, and then I went to every single dressmaking shop in London looking for anyone who might know you, and then I returned to one because I realised she was lying, and I found out your parents worked for her, and I met them—they were quite charming, excellent storytellers—and then they gave me this address."

"I apologise for being so difficult to find," said Fanny. "That was never my intent."

"I am certain it was not, Miss Cramer." She turned to Georgiana and Mary. "Miss Darcy, Miss Bennet, would it be possible for me to have a private conversation with Miss Cramer?"

"Of course," said Mary. "Georgiana, would you like to take a turn about the house?"

"Naturally," said Georgiana, beaming broadly.

They left the room, and Mary had to banish the temptation to eavesdrop through the door.

A few minutes later, Fanny emerged, and the sparkle in her eyes made Mary think that the conversation had gone well.

The moment they entered Mary's room, Fanny said, "She wants to enter into a partnership with me! For a dressmaking shop. At first she only planned to commission a few dresses, but partway through our conversation, she realised we can do so much more if we work together. It will be an upscale establishment where my employees earn proper wages. She thinks she knows an available location, near St. James's Palace. I would be part owner, with the possibility of buying her out in several years, though if I do, she will reserve the right to several new dresses for herself every year. She is preparing the contract now. She will also pay for a lawyer of my choice, who will read through the contract to make sure it protects me."

"That is incredible. This is everything you could have hoped for."

"It is a dream come true," said Fanny. "I did ask for twenty-four hours to decide. I need to speak to Mr. Booth, and see if I would be able to continue my work as a spy."

"I think it would be ideal," said Mary, setting aside her sudden sadness at the possibility of Fanny leaving. "Your clientele will be wealthy and well-connected, and I am sure you will be able to gather much useful information."

"That is an excellent argument. I will use it on Mr. Booth."

A few hours later, Mrs. Granger came to the house in the persona of Mrs. Hunnicutt. She fawned over Elizabeth, grasping her hands in her own. "I appreciate so much you allowing me to borrow your sister for a few more hours. I am going on a trip, you see, a long trip, and this will be my last visit with Miss Bennet for a long time, and I am so very happy to see her once more."

After another ten minutes of Mrs. Hunnicutt's commentary on Elizabeth's dress, the hall, the servants, the weather, and the pork that she had eaten the previous evening, Mary finally followed her out the door.

"If it becomes too dreadful, I recommend you flee from her presence," said Elizabeth quietly in Mary's ear.

"At least it is the last time for a while," said Mary, to which Elizabeth smiled.

Fanny was already in the carriage—she had left the house

through the kitchen door—and the horses hurried them on their way. "Every few months we switch locations for our base of operations," said Mrs. Granger. "As the new location is not quite ready, we will be meeting at a park."

It was a grand park, with tall trees, a large amount of shrubbery, and a number of meandering paths. "This way," said Mrs. Granger, leading them along to a remote section with a grouping of trees in the middle of the clearing. This partially shielded them from view of others, but because it was in a clearing, they could see if anyone approached.

To Mary's surprise, Mr. Withrow was there.

"I did not know you were in London," she said. "Again."

"I have had reason to come much more often than I had planned," he said. "You seem to be in better spirits."

"Very much so," said Mary.

"Good," said Mr. Withrow. "My aunt will be pleased to hear it."

"*I* am pleased to hear it as well," said Mr. Stanley, bowing gallantly to Mary, "and I see no need to pretend that it is only someone else that feels these emotions."

"A discussion of my own personal sentiments is irrelevant," said Mr. Withrow. "Yet because of their friendship, Lady Trafford *will* be pleased." He shot a pointed look at Mr. Stanley. "Please do not attempt to assign me sentiments that are not my own."

Mr. Booth cleared his throat. "This is all quite amusing, but we should begin."

They all stepped a little closer to him. It felt a little like Mary's first day in London, with many of the same people: herself, Fanny, Mr. Stanley, Mr. Withrow, and Mr. Booth, with the addition of Mrs. Granger. Yet so much had happened in that time.

"Thank you, Miss Cramer and Miss Bennet, for discovering Mr. Rice's murderer."

"Do we have enough evidence for a trial?" asked Fanny.

"I was able to obtain a warrant to search Mr. Sharp's home, and we discovered a number of Mr. Rice's letters, purloined from Mr. Rice's home. Several of the letters to Mr. Rice were from Mr. Sharp's factory workers, detailing the abuses Mr. Sharp inflicted on his employees, which went much beyond the normal travesties suffered in factories. Mr. Rice seems to have encouraged the workers to organise and bring these abuses to the public, and it was after this that these very employees were poisoned."

Mary resolved to write a letter to Sir Francis Burdett, detailing some of the abuses endured by factory workers and outlining legislation that she thought the Radicals should propose.

Mr. Booth continued, "In addition to the letters, we have pressured Mr. Corbyn, who has agreed to testify against Sharp in exchange for not being prosecuted himself. Add to that the evidence from the dispensary in connection to the deaths of Mr. Sharp's workers, and his attack on Mrs. Sancho, and it should be sufficient."

"What about the explosion of the Custom House?" asked Mary.

"There is nothing to tie any of them definitively to the Custom House. Detective Donalds found papers that showed that Sharp lost a lot of money because of decisions made by Colonel Kelly; that is motivation, but not evidence. Mr. Corbyn being seen near Fred Zeeger who was seen near the Custom House is no evidence at all, and Corbyn is certainly not going to testify against himself in that matter." He paused. "It is my personal opinion that Corbyn and Sharp never intended for Zeeger to set fire to the Custom House. They simply wanted him to apply extra pressure to Colonel Kelly."

No one had ever meant for Minerva Randall to die. That did not make her death any easier for Mary to bear; she would prefer if someone was punished for the act. In her work as a spy, she wanted to fix everything, understand every detail and mystery, yet she needed to accept that absolute resolution of a problem was not always a possibility.

They discussed final details of the case and answered all of Mr. Booth's questions so he could send out the final reports. He also gave out final assignments: he would speak to Mrs. Knowles himself, Mary would write to Mrs. König, as she had promised, Mr. Withrow was asked to provide a comprehensive report to Lady Trafford, and Fanny and Mr. Stanley were assigned a few other minor tasks.

"Do you think Mrs. Knowles might have an extra mourning ring, or other memento she would be willing to give to Mrs. König?" said Fanny. "I think it would ease her suffering."

"I will ask," said Mr. Booth. "Anything else?"

"I need some basic combat or weapons training," said Mary. "I found myself woefully unprepared."

"Your skills with a tea pot are actually quite commendable," said Fanny.

"True," said Mr. Booth. "Yet more training can likely be arranged."

"Also, if you need more spies, may I make a recommendation. I think my sister, Catherine, would do quite well."

"She did make positive contributions, and seems to have a way with people," said Mr. Booth. "While we do not need any additional spies at the moment—we have no budget for anyone else—I will keep her in consideration for future opportunities."

"Thank you," said Mary.

There were no further questions, so Mr. Booth adjourned the meeting. Fanny asked if she could speak to him privately, and Mary hoped that their conversation went well.

Fanny and Mr. Booth walked down one of the lanes, and Mr. Stanley approached Mary. "Miss Bennet, may I speak to you?"

"I believe you already are."

"No, I mean, may I *speak* to you? Privately."

Mary pressed her lips together. She did not understand his meaning.

"Please, will you sit?" He gestured to a bench. It was not very private—Mr. Withrow and Mrs. Granger were well within hearing. Nevertheless, Mary joined him on the bench. From here she could look down the lawn and see the Thames in the distance. The ships frozen in place and the fair on the ice already seemed like a distant memory.

Mr. Stanley took her hand, and Mary was so shocked that she did not immediately pull it away.

"I wish to make you an offer of marriage. You are charming, full of wit, beautiful, intelligent, a woman that any man would be proud to introduce to his family. And with your family, I am certain that my parents could have no objection."

The only one of those adjectives that was typically used to describe her was "intelligent." The rest, to her, seemed misplaced.

He must have seen the look on her face, for he rushed to add, "My income is 1500 pounds a year. It may not be what you are accustomed to, but we have no extensive property to maintain. I employ a cook and several other servants, and when we have children, I will hire a governess. I can make sure that you live comfortably, and you would no longer need to work as a spy."

Mary swallowed. Fanny had likely predicted Mr. Stanley's proposal. His continuous compliments, the gift of the Irish music—it had all led to this moment. In fact, he had probably planned to propose to her on the day when Mr. Booth had thought to close the case unsolved, but Fanny had prevented him.

"Of course, you could continue to work, if you desired. Though I will not recommend this facade of the drab clothing you wear to hide your beauty—with me, you will be able to be publicly who you really are."

Mary's throat was suddenly so dry that she could not protest. Did he not know her at all? Did he really think that her normal attire was a facade?

"What I mean to say, Miss Bennet, is that I want you by my side for the rest of my life. Will you join your life with mine?"

Mary was no romantic. Unlike her sisters, she had never planned or pined for a marriage of love, so her lack of warmth of emotion towards his proposal should not in itself be a deciding factor. Yet his assumption that she might want to both leave behind her work as a spy and constantly play a part of a more refined, more fashionable woman, could certainly not be a good foundation for a favourable marriage.

With a little tug, she managed to withdraw her hand from Mr. Stanley's. "I am sorry," she said, "but I cannot marry you."

"Please, if you cannot marry me, at least explain why." He reached again for her hand, but Mary managed to keep it away.

"I do not believe we would be suitable for each other," said Mary. "I do not think you truly know me, or…" She could not find the right words. "I do not think you understand me."

"But Miss Bennet, I know that we suit each other."

She stood abruptly, and her eyes darted around the park, looking for some sort of excuse to end the conversation. "I am sorry, but I must go. I have something I must ask Mr. Withrow."

"Very well, Miss Bennet." Mr. Stanley's shoulders slumped, and he looked like a puppy who had been thrown out on the street.

She determined to hold to her resolve—she could not marry someone simply to alleviate his suffering. She turned quickly and marched up to Mr. Withrow.

"Will you walk with me?"

"Of course." Mr. Withrow held out his arm. She took it, and they walked down, closer to the Thames.

"What did you need to ask me?" asked Withrow.

"Nothing in particular. I take it you heard Mr. Stanley's proposal, and I hope you do not mind being used as an excuse."

"I thought you would have leapt at the opportunity for a comfortable life. Does Stanley not have enough of a fortune for you? Are you waiting for your own Mr. Bingley or Mr. Darcy?"

"1500 pounds would be more than enough for me. It is extravagant compared to my current income, though of course, I am benefiting from the Darcys' income."

"Are you not…inclined towards marriage?"

She looked at him quizzically.

"Some women are not inclined to spending their life with

a man."

"I understand. I know several women for whom that seems to be the case, but for me, I have always assumed that I will marry. I once fancied my cousin, Mr. Collins. If he had given me an offer, we would not have lost Longbourn to him. But now that I have been gone from home and seen more of the world, I can no longer picture myself as mistress of his house."

"Are you one of those women who will settle for nothing less than a marriage of love?"

Mary shook her head. "My sisters have all felt that way to a varying degree. I have never harboured those illusions. I am a much more practical sort of person." It was strange, but although she did not feel comfortable attempting to explain herself to Mr. Stanley, she felt quite able to do so with Mr. Withrow. "Why all the questions?"

"You keep surprising me, Miss Bennet. I am attempting to figure you out."

He did not ask again why she had turned down Mr. Stanley's offer, but she decided to tell him anyway. "The reason I turned down Mr. Stanley is he does not actually want to marry *me*. He wants to marry the woman he met on the road to Castle Durrington. He wants to marry a woman who is refined, flirtatious, likes fine clothing. A woman who walks with poise and who will restrain herself from saying what she really thinks. What he wants is very far from the real Mary Bennet."

They walked a little farther. Mr. Withrow paused as they approached the water. "I have found that the pretence becomes a part of me. That it reflects a facet of my identity."

"That is true," said Mary, surprised at him sharing his own personal thoughts. "I like fine dresses more than I would

327

ever care to admit. But that does not mean I want to wear them all the time."

Her mother would probably threaten to disown her if she discovered that Mary had declined an offer of marriage. She could picture herself as a spinster, never having received another offer of marriage, and there was something refreshing about the thought. There was a freedom to belonging only to oneself.

"Do you need me as an excuse any longer?" he said abruptly.

Her eyes swept over the park. "He appears to be gone. I had best find Fanny."

He removed his arm, and suddenly she felt cold.

He gave her a brief bow. "It was a pleasure chatting with you, Miss Bennet. I will give my aunt your regards, and I am sure she will send you a letter in short order."

As he walked away, she realised that Kitty was correct: she did find Mr. Withrow to be a handsome man. She did not know what to do with that realisation, so she decided to save the thought and analyse it another time.

Fanny was waiting for her at the trees, an overly serious—perhaps suspiciously serious—expression on her face. "I told Mr. Booth and Mrs. Granger that we would hire our own carriage home."

"Perfect," said Mary. "Now, will you tell me or will you not?"

Fanny's face broke into a grin. "Mr. Booth thinks it an excellent plan! I did not want to have to choose between my work as a spy and my dream of having my own shop, and now I do not need to."

"I hope you will still make me the occasional dress."

"Of course," said Fanny. "Now I saw you having private

conversations with both Mr. Stanley and Mr. Withrow. You must tell me everything."

And Mary did.

For the first time in her life, Mary had a friend, a true friend, and not just one—she could count Kitty and Georgiana among that number, and maybe even Elizabeth, though that might take more time. She had uncovered a financial conspiracy, learned confidence in herself, and done her part to solve a man's murder, which was truly the best one could hope for from a London Season. She smiled with satisfaction as she and Fanny walked and talked and then talked some more. Eventually they hired a carriage and made their way home.

# EPILOGUE

*Excerpts from the journal of Miss Mary Bennet*

April 11, 1814: The French surrendered—they surrendered! Napoleon Bonaparte has abdicated. It took me hours to believe that the news was real, despite a series of credible sources. There are fantastic light illuminations on buildings all around London.

April 18, 1814: Fanny's shop is progressing quickly, and now I am relying on Hannah as a maid.

May 27, 1814: I am now in Derbyshire for the foreseeable future, in part to see Jane's new baby. Elizabeth cannot keep secrets from Jane and has announced that she is with child.

June 10, 1814: The stock exchange trial is over, and all parties were found guilty. Mr. Johnstone fled England weeks ago, and his whereabouts are unknown. Lord Cochrane did not attend the trial, because he was so certain that his innocence would declare itself, and now he will be thrown into prison and likely stripped of his title. I wish Mr. Booth had allowed me to attend the trial and testify, but he was certain Lord Cochrane would be able to prove his innocence. If Lord Cochrane had attended, his presence and his powerful manner of speech would surely have convinced the jury.

Georgiana expressed her happiness that things did not progress between her and Mr. Johnstone.

June 23, 1814: Mr. Sharp was convicted of murder. He has been sentenced to hanging, followed by public anatomisation (they will cut open his body in front of a crowd), and then private dissection by those training to be surgeons. Fanny plans to attend the anatomisation, but I am glad I do not have to witness it.

June 30, 1814: Lady Trafford and Mr. Withrow came to visit me in Derbyshire. Mr. Withrow said only four sentences to me the entire time. Yes, I counted, but I am not ashamed of doing so, though Kitty teased me for it.

The Allies have great regrets that Bonaparte has been exiled to the Island of Elba, because of its proximity to France. The British government cannot decide whether they want to protect Bonaparte from assassination, or whether they want to assassinate Bonaparte themselves. To me, this seems like a rather vital distinction. Lady Trafford has given me a small assignment—to discover the roots of some unrest in Derbyshire. She feels confident that she will have a larger assignment for me soon. I feel quite ready to be back to work.

Want more? Check out Mary's first adventure in
*The Secret Life of Miss Mary Bennet*!

Join Tule Publishing's newsletter for more great reads and
weekly deals!

# Historical Note

Throughout his life, Lord Cochrane proclaimed his innocence, and in 1832 he was pardoned by the Crown. Whether or not he was guilty is still a matter of debate. His many exploits are detailed in a number of biographies, including David Cordingly's *Cochrane the Dauntless*, and he is the main inspiration for the novel (and the film) *Master and Commander*.

The Baron de Berenger, also known as Charles Random de Berenger, later went on to start a gymnasium—a 24-acre academy called "Baron's Stadium" where he taught combat skills. He published a book titled *Defensive Gymnastics*.

Mr. Johnstone actually went by his full hyphenated name, Mr. Cochrane-Johnstone, but early readers of this novel found it difficult to follow passages which included him, his daughter Eliza, and Lord Cochrane together. For ease of reading, I shortened Cochrane-Johnstone's name to Mr. Johnstone throughout.

By falsely inflating the market on February 21, 1814, Cochrane-Johnstone himself profited by what, in today's money, would be close to half a million pounds. Cochrane-Johnstone fled to France and then to the West Indies, though he was not able to regain most of his property in Dominica. He never returned to England; ultimately, he died in poverty in Paris in 1833. Eliza Cochrane-Johnstone's inheritance was independent of her father, and it does not seem that her prospects were too terribly injured by her father's deeds. In

1816 she married Lord William Napier.

Sir Francis Burdett finally got his parliamentary reform in the Great Reform Act of 1832. Universal male suffrage in the United Kingdom was not achieved until long after his death, in 1918.

With only two exceptions, the chapter epigraphs are real excerpts from newspapers.

Mr. Rice, Mrs. Knowles, Mr. Sharp, Mr. Eastlake, Mrs. König, and Fred are all products of my imagination.

February 1814 was the last time that the Thames River froze over enough to hold an ice fair.

The Customs House did burn down in February 1814, though the fire may or may not have been started by arson— no firm conclusions have been reached. Two orphan girls were killed in the Customs House explosion, but Minerva Randall's name and the details around her life are fictitious.

I consulted dozens and dozens of sources, but the ones I relied on most heavily include the aforementioned Cochrane biography; Edward Vallance's *A Radical History of Britain: Visionaries, Rebels, and Revolutionaries*; Norma Myers' *Reconstructing the Black Past: Blacks in Britain 1780-1830*; Jenny Uglow's *In These Times: Living in Britain Through Napoleon's Wars, 1793-1815*; Sir Francis Burdett's *Magna Charta and the Bill of Rights*; the 1814 text *Frostiana: or a History of the River Thames, in a Frozen State*; Katie Rawson and Elliott Shore's *Dining Out: A Global History of Restaurants*; and the full text of the trial concerning the Great Stock Exchange Fraud (the trial text is more than double the length of this novel, and I take very Mary Bennet-esque pride in having read every single word of it).

I did make some intentional changes to history for the sake of narrative; despite my research, I am sure I have also made other unintentional errors.

# Acknowledgements

First, I would like to thank London itself and the amazing people I interacted with during my 2019 visit. That trip had a huge influence on this novel, especially my walks along the River Thames, as well as visits to the Tower of London, the Monument to the Great Fire, Westminster Abbey, and the Museum of London.

The second draft of this book was the most difficult draft I have ever written, and I feel that the year 2020 should be acknowledged as being at least partially responsible.

Thanks to my Kalamazoo writing group, who read early versions of the chapters: Anna Lunt, Michelle Preston, Erin Brady, Lynn Johnson, and Meghan Decker. This book would not have been possible without my amazing critique partners: Sarah Johnson, Jeanna Mason Stay, Brooke Lamoreaux, Pam Eaton, Emily Goldthwaite, and Whitney Woodard. Thank you to Kerry Cowley for amazing, last-minute editing assistance. Also, thanks to the love and care of countless other friends, writers, librarians, bloggers, and community members who have supported me and my writing in numerous ways. Thanks also goes to Chris Nagle, who let me into his WMU graduate class about Jane Austen adaptations even though I was not a WMU student. Many of the conversations we had in class influenced the choices I made in this novel.

Thanks again to Rebecca Davis for assisting me with the French in this novel. Richard Johnson helped me choreograph the final confrontation in a manner that was realistic and intense yet would not cause any serious injuries to my main characters.

Special thanks to my agent, Stephany Evans, who always sees the heart of my stories and helps me make them the best they be. Thank you for saving the tone of this book and encouraging me to find the humor. Also, a huge thanks to my incredibly supportive editor at Tule, Sinclair Sawhney, whose excitement for this project motivates me to keep writing. Thanks also to the rest of the Tule team, including copyeditors, proofreaders, covers designers, and Nikki Babri, who patiently answers my many questions.

Thanks to my husband, Scott Cowley, who goes above and beyond as he supports me in my writing and in my other goals. Thanks to my three daughters, who love watching Jane Austen adaptations with me and like to come up with their own creative riffs.

Finally, I would like to express my gratitude to Jane Austen for bringing me light, joy, and meaning in times of darkness.

If you enjoyed *The True Confessions of a London Spy*, you'll love the next book in…

## The Secret Life of Mary Bennet series

Book 1: *The Secret Life of Miss Mary Bennet*

Book 2: *The True Confessions of a London Spy*

Book 3: *The Lady's Guide to Death and Deception*
Coming in September 2022!

*Available now at your favorite online retailer!*

## About the Author

Katherine Cowley read *Pride and Prejudice* for the first time when she was ten years old, which started a lifelong obsession with Jane Austen. She loves history, chocolate, traveling, and playing the piano, and she teaches writing classes at Western Michigan University. She lives in Kalamazoo, Michigan with her husband and three daughters. *The Secret Life of Miss Mary Bennet* is her debut novel.

Thank you for reading

# The True Confessions of a London Spy

If you enjoyed this book, you can find more from all our great
authors at TulePublishing.com, or from your favorite
online retailer.

TULE
PUBLISHING

Made in the USA
Thornton, CO
06/05/23 11:14:24

079e78ee-b969-4101-8c17-a9d6667b57c9R01